About the

A.C. Arthur was born and raised in Baltimore, Maryland where she currently resides with her husband and three children. Determined to bring a new edge to romance, she continues to develop intriguing plots, sensual love scenes, racy characters and fresh dialogue – thus keeping the readers on their toes! Arthur loves to hear from her readers and can be reached through her contact form or via email at acarthur22@yahoo.com

Stefanie London is a *USA Today* bestselling author of contemporary romance. Her books have been called 'genuinely entertaining and memorable' by *Booklist*, and her writing praised as 'elegant, descriptive and delectable' by *RT Magazine*. Originally from Australia, she now lives in Toronto with her very own hero and is doing her best to travel the world. She frequently indulges her passions for lipstick, good coffee, books and anything zombie related.

Jessica Lemmon is a former job-hopper who resides in Ohio with her husband and rescue dogs. She holds a degree in graphic design currently gathering dust in an impressive frame. When she's not writing emotionally charged stories, she spends her time drawing, drinking coffee, and laughing with friends. Her motto is 'read for fun', and she believes we should all do more of what makes us happy. Learn more about her books at jessicalemmon.com

Fake Dating

Fake Dating:
I Dare You

A.C. ARTHUR

STEFANIE LONDON

JESSICA LEMMON

MILLS & BOON

First Published in Great Britain 2024
by Mills & Boon, an imprint of HarperCollins*Publishers* Ltd,
1 London Bridge Street, London, SE1 9GF

www.harpercollins.co.uk

HarperCollins*Publishers*
Macken House, 39/40 Mayor Street Upper,
Dublin 1, D01 C9W8, Ireland

Fake Dating: I Dare You © 2024 Harlequin Enterprises ULC.

At Your Service © 2020 Artist C. Arthur
Faking It © 2019 Stefanie Little
Temporary to Tempted © 2019 Jessica Lemmon

ISBN: 978-0-263-32326-9

MIX
Paper | Supporting
responsible forestry
FSC™ C007454

This book contains FSC™ certified paper and other controlled sources to ensure responsible forest management.

For more information visit: www.harpercollins.co.uk/green

Printed and Bound in the UK using 100% Renewable Electricity at CPI Group (UK) Ltd, Croydon, CR0 4YY

AT YOUR SERVICE

A.C. ARTHUR

To my law clerks: Vanessa, Manti, Gita, Beatrice and Ashley.

Thanks so much for your endless support.

CHAPTER ONE

LET'S DO THIS.

Whispering the mantra as she stepped out of the ladies' room, Nina smoothed her palms down the front of her navy-blue pencil skirt. With her portfolio tucked under one arm and her black leather purse hanging on the opposite shoulder, she walked easily in four-inch black pumps. Until she turned the corner and collided with something hard and delicious-smelling.

Her portfolio hit the ground as she threw her hands up and felt a strong grip on her upper arms.

"Whoa, there."

His voice was deep but smooth and made her feel like warm water was streaming down her body, easing to her core.

"Sorry," she mumbled with a shake of her head.

Nina pulled out of his grasp and went down on her knees to snap up the pages that had escaped from her folder. As if in rebellion, or just because they wanted her to look like a complete idiot, the papers had scattered across the dark-carpeted floor a distance away from where she was standing.

"Here, let me help," he was saying, but Nina didn't reply.

And she didn't look up, just continued to gather the wayward sheets, cursing herself and what had been a horrific start to this very important day. Clutching a handful of pages, she started to stand when her purse decided to slip from her shoulder. *Oh no, I'm not dropping anything else today.* She lifted her hands and caught the bag as Mr. Helpful came closer.

Anxious to just get this uncomfortable encounter over with and to make it to the meeting she was already in danger of being late for, Nina glanced up to meet his gaze. Warm root beer–brown eyes stared back at her while lips of medium thickness parted slightly as if he were ready to speak again. His words were halted when her hands took that moment to continue moving upward, brushing over this gorgeous guy's pants on the way.

No, not just his pants but his…

Nina's jaw dropped, heat immediately fusing her cheeks as her eyes widened and she yanked her hands back against her chest so hard she almost lost her breath.

"Are you all right?"

Hell no!

Nina was on her way to a meeting that would make or break her business and she was standing here touching a man she didn't know. A man who was the epitome of tall, bronzed, handsome and apparently very aroused.

"I'm fine," she managed to croak and then cleared her throat. Stuffing the papers under her arm, she reached for the black case he held. "Thank you."

"You're welcome. Can I help you get your belongings together?"

"No. Really. I have it. It's no problem," she said because the problem was obviously her. Or it could have been the train from York to Manhattan that was late because something had spilled on the tracks, or the gigantic rip in her stockings from when she'd slid across the torn seat of the taxi upon finally arriving at the Ronald Gold Fashions headquarters. Either way, this day was not getting better.

Nina stepped around the man, hoping he wouldn't say anything else to her. She walked as quickly as she could without running and appearing more like a crazy person. Not knowing exactly where she was going, she continued down the long hallway, turning the moment she saw an opening on the right and then moving just as fast in that direction.

Her phone buzzed and she stopped to dig into her purse to retrieve it.

"Hey, Angie," she answered after seeing her sister's name on the screen.

"Hey. I won't be able to run past Dad's tonight to check on him and Daisy's got a photo shoot so she doesn't think she'll get there until after eight."

Nina closed her eyes as her fingers tightened on the phone. She didn't scream the way she wanted to because everything that could go wrong today had already gone wrong. She inhaled deeply once more and let the breath out slowly before replying. "I'm in New York for a meeting, as I told everyone at dinner last night. I won't be back until tomorrow morning. So somebody's gonna have to go over there and make sure Dad takes his medications as directed and doesn't end up passed out on the floor."

It was, to Nina, as simple as that. But to her sisters what she'd just said wouldn't make any sense. Younger than her by four and six years, Angie and Daisy were so used to Nina taking care of everything—from their father to them when they were young girls—that the idea of doing some of the grown-up heavy lifting was too much for them to fathom. They'd much rather continue to dump it all on Nina's shoulders. Well, not today.

"I thought you were coming back tonight," Angie argued.

"No. I changed my mind. I don't get away from home often so I'm going to spend the evening in New York. I told you that also, in the reminder text I sent earlier when I was on my way to the train station." Nina lifted a hand to touch her hair, double-checking to make sure it was smooth and neat after her run-in with the hot guy.

"Well, that's not fair, Nina. Daisy and I are busy tonight and you're gonna be in New York living it up. You know Dad needs to be checked on daily."

Yes, she did know that, mainly because it was something she said on a routine basis to her sisters.

"It's one night, Angie. You and Daisy can figure something out for just one night." Her temples started that slow, persistent thumping that signaled a migraine, which wasn't good.

"Look, it is what it is. And I have to hang up because I need to get into this meeting. I'll call Dad to check on him as soon as the meeting is done, but you and Daisy are responsible for him tonight."

"But—"

"But nothing. Goodbye, Angie."

Nina pushed the button to disconnect the call. Technically she hadn't hung up on her, even though sometimes Angie and Daisy deserved just that. They were beyond old enough to handle a night without Nina giving detailed outlines of what they needed to do. And having just celebrated her thirtieth birthday last month, Nina deserved one night in New York, the fashion capital of the United States.

First, she needed to get to this meeting, make her presentation and grab this account. Everything was riding on this—having the money to get her father into an assisted-living facility and giving her app the boost it needed to compete in the big leagues of the fashion industry.

You can do this. It's what you've been working so hard for these last two years. You're going to get this account and everything else will fall into place. You've got this!

Nodding to herself, Nina dropped her phone back into her purse.

It took her another five minutes to walk all the way to the other side of the floor where there was a set of glass doors with the gold letters RGF on the front. Once she pulled the door open and stepped inside, the rapid beat of her heart ceased. The heat that had still burned her cheeks subsided and she walked toward the reception desk, her shoulders squared, chin held high.

After introducing herself to the receptionist—a pretty woman with coal-black hair that fell down her back—Nina was directed down another hallway to the last door on the right. Nina entered the room with her ready-to-take-on-the-world attitude and superstar smile, only to have it falter the minute she locked gazes with the man sitting at the far end of the table.

The same man she'd bumped into only moments ago. The man whose hard dick she'd felt...inadvertently, of course.

Damn.

Major sat back in the leather conference room chair with one hand on his thigh, the other rubbing the shaved skin of his jaw. He couldn't take his eyes off her throughout her presentation. Nor could he stop the erection that had sprung so quickly when they'd first met in the hallway and he'd watched her bend over in that tight skirt. Of course, that hadn't been their official meeting. No, that awkward moment had come the second she'd walked into the conference room where he was seated with his brothers and two of his tech department staffers.

Nina Fuller, owner and operator of the At Your Service fashion accessorizing app, was beautiful with toffee-brown-colored hair hanging past her shoulders and cinnamon-hued skin. Not only did her skirt fit the round curve of her ass and the stretch of her thighs just right, but the pale blue blouse she wore with it was tucked neatly into a high-waist skirt, the blouse's sheer material hanging alluringly over her breasts. Major's palms itched with the thought of cupping them and watching as they spilled over his fingers.

His dick jumped again and he eased his hand up higher on his thigh to give the pulsating shaft a gentle push. *Get it together!*

"What's the traffic like on this app?" RJ asked. "Is there so much that it could possibly become inundated and freeze? Customer complaints spread like wildfire online and an app crashing could be a PR catastrophe."

As the director of sales for the family business, Major's older brother RJ—Ronald Gold III—was always concerned about the customers and how much merchandise they were buying. RJ's comment solicited a nod from Maurice, Major's younger twin brother. But since this presentation was for a tech product, Major—the company's technical developer—was front and center on the decision making. That meant he should stop gawking at this woman like he was a horny teenager and get his head in the game.

His fingers involuntarily moved closer to cup his hardened dick. *Not that head!*

"What he means is…how are your configurations designed?" he asked. "Will the overflow in use cause the app's algorithms to go haywire?"

Technical speak was Major's thing and apparently so was getting turned on by a woman he barely knew.

Her gaze found his, and her tongue slipped out to lick her lips for just a second. Long enough for him to swallow. Hard.

She clicked the button on the small control device cushioned in the palm of her hand. The images on the screen across the room flipped back to one of the previous presentation slides where she'd outlined the beginning sketches of her app.

"Two years ago, when the first thoughts of At Your Service entered my mind, I planned exactly what I wanted it to do. Match accessories to outfits. Nothing more, nothing less. By staying focused on what the app absolutely needed to do to succeed, I was able to avoid many common pitfalls in new app development—overreaching ideas. With that said, during the first two years of the app's startup, I've fine-tuned and streamlined its function so that even with high volume it still functions as seamlessly as if there were only ten to twelve users."

Confident. Knowledgeable. Intriguing.

All things that were required for a good sales pitch. And things that aroused Major on a level he hadn't quite explored before.

Sure, he'd been dubbed the Fashion House Playboy three months ago by the press, but as the last thing on his busy schedule was to deal with the lies that oftentimes floated through the tabloids and on-line gossip sites, Major hadn't given the title or its implications the time of day. The executives in RGF's marketing department, on the other hand, had. It was now an actual agenda item to be dealt with when this meeting was over.

At the moment, however, he was staring into the lovely topaz-brown eyes of a woman who wanted RGF to integrate her app on its website. In essence, this was business. Not pleasure. He took another second to try to send that message to his aching dick.

"Your plans look detailed and well thought out. And you say this has been up and running for two years. How many clients do you currently have?"

"The first year was for planning, developing and trial runs," she said. "The second year was for getting all the licenses required and finding vendors to facilitate the app's main function. Three independent fashion designers have been satisfied with the application in the last five months. Letters of recommendation are included in the information packets I passed out. But my goal is expansion. This app in its current state is primarily designed to be a corporate plug-in. Eventually, as my brand gains visibility, I'll be expanding to target individual customers." She stood a few inches away from the projector screen, hands clasped in front of her, shoulders back.

A light layer of makeup covered a very pretty face, and hair that looked silky and shiny made his fingers itch to touch the long tresses.

"Amelia Jewelers is one of the vendors we work with for showings along the East Coast," RJ said, looking down at the papers Nina had referred to.

"Yes, they're reputable and reliable. I trust Amelia Cane's words implicitly." That came from Jenner Carlson, the lead tech developer in Major's department. "And the layout you've created is simple, yet efficient. All a customer has to do is upload the clothes they've purchased and accessory ideas are immediately assembled."

"Correct." Nina continued, "This is after they've set up their user profile, which collects pertinent information like body type, style preferences and budget. The customer will have a seventy-two-hour period to consider their selections before either being directed to purchase via third-party sites or to re-accessorize. A schedule of gentle reminders in that time frame keeps the app and the clothes just purchased prevalent in the customer's mind."

"But this app doesn't drive customers to the RGF site. We would essentially have to bring the customers to you, which makes this a winning opportunity for you and just an added benefit for us," RJ noted, leaning back in his chair, hands clasped in his lap. This was the not-so-impressed stance his brother took just before he was about to shoot down an idea.

"But what if there was a widget for the app on the RGF site telling the customer that we care about their overall look and not just the garment they purchase from us," Major said. "Then everyone benefits from the sale we've secured because we were savvy and compassionate enough to consider our customers' overall needs, bringing us even more customers who will like the idea of a sort of one-stop shop."

His comment was rewarded with a slow smile and

nod from Nina. An action that sealed the deal—his hard-on wasn't ceasing anytime soon.

The part of his brain that was determined to focus on work tried to press through. After all, he'd originally intended to shoot this idea down. He could admit it was partially a selfish act since some of the things Nina's app offered were in direct competition with what he wanted to feature through his own company—the company he'd be launching soon, which his family still didn't know about.

Discussion continued for a few moments more, ending when RJ mentioned he had another meeting to get to. "You're in that meeting, also, Major. So, Ms. Fuller, we'll be in touch."

Nina didn't falter even though Major recognized the dismal tone of rejection in RJ's voice.

"Thank you so much for your time, gentlemen," she said, clicking the button on the remote to clear the screen.

Major took his time tucking the packet she'd provided into his padfolio before closing and zipping it shut. He slipped his phone out of his pocket and quickly checked it for text messages.

"Ten minutes," RJ said. "Don't be late, we've got a tight schedule. Major? Are you listening?"

Lifting his gaze from his phone, Major found both his brothers staring at him. "Yes. I'll be there in ten minutes. Just have to rearrange my schedule a bit."

Landra, his assistant, had had to postpone the meeting with the agent and actresses Major was scheduled to meet with this afternoon so that he could attend yet another meeting with the marketing department to talk about the very reason he needed to hire an actress in the first place.

His brothers headed out of the conference room along with Jenner and Ken, leaving Major alone with Nina Fuller and that very tight skirt, which continued to make his mouth water.

CHAPTER TWO

HE WAS STARING at her and she liked it.

The warmth that had thankfully moved from her cheeks had spread down her neck and pooled in her breasts so that they now felt full. With every move she'd made during the presentation she'd felt his gaze on her and had reveled in it. Feeling attractive and wanted wasn't the norm for Nina and she'd forgotten how much she enjoyed it.

Now, she would enjoy him offering her a contract much more, but since she'd likely have to wait a couple days or possibly weeks for that answer, she was content with just feeling sexy beneath his intent gaze.

"Your bio says you're from York, Pennsylvania. Did you move to New York when you started this business?"

He'd shaved his beard, that's why she hadn't immediately recognized him in the hallway before the meeting. But she was certain she was never going to forget his voice. Not the way the rich, deep timbre eased over her skin like a massage, or the spurt of awareness it brought to every part of her body each time she heard it.

"No. I still live in York," she replied as she gathered the last of her documents and slid them into her portfolio.

Out of the corner of her eye she could see that he'd moved from the end of the table to stand closer to her, but she kept her gaze averted. Instead she zipped the case and picked her purse up from the chair then placed it on the table beside her portfolio. At that point there was nothing stopping her from looking at him and she sucked in a breath before turning to face him.

"But I can commute when necessary. However, one of the great things about this app is that it's a mobile function. Once my system has been integrated with RGF's, we'll be all set and I won't have to request any more meetings that will clog up your busy schedule."

He held his phone in one hand and the black-leather padfolio under his arm. She hadn't seen either of those things when she'd collided with him in the hallway. Then again, she hadn't been looking for them. Nor had she been planning to feel the guy up. Considering who he was in the company, she wondered if she should apologize for that now.

"I would gladly make time in my schedule for you," he said.

The easy tilt of his mouth into a smile came with a punch of desire that Nina was certain she'd never felt before. Not that she was a prude or inexperienced where men were concerned, it was just that none had ever affected her the way this one did.

But she wasn't going to let that distract her. "That's nice to hear. Do you have any other questions about the app?"

"I do, but unfortunately I have another meeting to get to. Are you heading back to York right away?"

"No. I'm actually going to stay and enjoy the city tonight. My train leaves tomorrow morning at eleven." She gave the specific time just in case he wanted to schedule a follow-up meeting sooner rather than later.

He was nodding slowly as he kept staring at her with those warm disrupting eyes. But she wasn't supposed to be looking at this man's eyes and thinking that way. She could, however, admire the fit of the black suit he wore and the purple tie that added a splash of color and highlighted his tawny-hued skin.

"That's great. I've gotta head out, but I definitely want to speak with you again. Do you have a business card with your contact information?"

That request came with him taking a step closer to her. Instinct told her to step back, to keep a safe, professional distance between them. But hell, she'd already somewhat fondled him earlier, what harm could it do to have him up close and personal again? Besides, she loved the way he smelled. That cologne had to be an expensive designer fragrance. Possibly even European. It was a heady, spicy scent mixed with something rugged and yet unique. It made her think of cold winter nights cuddled in front of a roaring fire.

But back to business. "Yes. All of my contact information is on the packet I passed out, but I do have cards."

She pulled her purse open and reached inside for the sky blue card case her father had given her last Christmas. She removed one embossed ivory-colored card, handed it to him and wasn't at all surprised when he touched more of her hand than was necessary to retrieve it. There was definitely some flirtation going on here in what should have been a simple business meeting. Maybe he thought she was easy considering what had happened in the hallway. But that had been an accident—surely he recognized that. And the question still remained: Why had he been aroused while walking down a hallway? Who had he been thinking of?

"I'll call you," he said in that delicious tone that this time had her thighs trembling.

How bad would it be if he tossed her on this table and she opened her legs to him in invitation?

Very, very bad.

"I'll answer," she replied before snapping her lips closed because maybe that sounded a bit too coy.

But there was no lie in the two words. If Major Gold called her phone, Nina was definitely going to answer on the first ring and there was absolutely no shame in that. After all, this was her career she was talking about.

"Good," he said with another nod.

His hand was still on hers. Nina knew the connection was lasting too long and she thought about letting it linger until it wore itself out or led to them climbing up on that conference table. But she had to be professional. If she were misreading his signals—even though she was certain she wasn't—she still needed to play this like the only thing either of them was considering was this business deal.

She eased her hand from his grasp. "I hope you make it to your meeting on time," she said, turning to pick up her things.

She was heading toward the door when he fell into step beside her. "I'll walk you to the elevator."

"Thanks, but I think I can find it." *This time.* She left that part out and continued walking, knowing that once again, he was staring at her ass.

This really was a totally different feeling for Nina. Back in York there'd been no suave and debonair businessman who could make her feel desired and wanted—on a business and a personal front. Not that she'd craved this type of attention; relationships weren't on her radar because they could abruptly leave a trail of pain that lingered. No, she was just fine focusing on work and her family. But, as strange as these new physical reactions were, they were exhilarating, too.

"How do you plan to enjoy the city?" he asked when they stood in front of a bank of elevators. "Catch a Broadway play? Visit the museums? Go shopping?"

"I actually don't have a plan, but all of your suggestions sound fun. It's almost five now, so I don't have much time, but once I get to the hotel I'll figure it out."

"Which hotel are you staying at?"

"The Hilton Midtown." She was giving him a ton of information that at any other time may have been considered unsafe. There was no explanation for why she didn't think that was the case now.

"Not too far from here," he said with another nod.

What was he thinking?

He'd tucked her business card into his inside jacket pocket and still stood abnormally close to her for someone she'd just met.

The elevator dinged and the door opened. Nina stepped into the car and leaned to the side to push the lobby button. She gave him another smile before saying, "Thanks again for your time. I hope to hear from you soon about the project."

His response was a broader smile. "Oh, you'll definitely be hearing from me very soon."

"You want to do what?"

Major ignored the shock lacing RJ's tone and stared directly at Desta Henner, the marketing director who was working closely with Maurice, the company's public relations manager, and his team. Desta stared back at Major with expressive dark brown eyes, arms crossed and resting on her desk.

"Let me get this straight. You're suggesting we bring this woman, whom we haven't decided to do other business with, into a meeting regarding a secret marketing strategy and use her as your fake fiancée?" Desta raised a perfectly arched brow in what was known as her signature questioning glare.

Major had seen that look many times before in the five years Desta had worked for RGF. He pushed on regardless.

"She's perfect," he said, feeling those words take on a very different meaning inside his head than what he'd meant to convey to everyone seated in the room. He cleared his throat. "A fresh face. She's not a model, which was your idea. And neither is she an actress, my first idea. Instead, she's a woman from York, Pennsylvania, that no one in the fashion industry has ever seen before. That makes her just like every other woman in the world, precisely who the Golden Bride Collection was created for. A career-focused woman earning a paycheck she hopes can cover the amount of her dream wedding gown."

"And she's never been seen with Major before," Maurice chimed in.

Major shot a quick look in his brother's direction but held back the "Thanks for your support."

Desta immediately glanced in Maurice's direction, as well. "Pot calling the kettle…" she quipped with a half grin. "But I think I see where you're going with this. If we're going to have Major plan a fake wedding so we can generate buzz and promote the Golden Bride Collection, using a fresh face as his fake fiancée does make sense."

"What he's not saying is that she's created an app she wants us to sign a contract to work with," RJ said.

Major had thought about that on the elevator ride up to Desta's office. The immediate physical draw he'd felt toward Nina still puzzled him. As a thirty-three-year-old man with a sizable bank account and high visibility in the fashion industry, Major had been on his share of dates and had had a number of lovers. None of them had ever hit him like a bull-dozer the second they'd bent over in a tight skirt. But what had really impressed him about the woman was the way she'd confidently stood in that conference room and made a slam dunk presentation just minutes after touching his hard dick.

Desta sat back in her chair, rubbing a finger over her chin. "You want to make a bargain with her that concerns her app and this marketing plan, don't you?"

Major slipped both hands into the front pockets of his slacks and smiled. "If she pretends to be my fiancée for six weeks, we'll use her app, exclusively, for six weeks."

RJ shook his head. "You're crazy. That woman's looking for a much longer connection to RGF than six weeks and she didn't look at all interested in anything else, let alone hanging around you for the next month and a half."

"I don't know, RJ," Desta said. She kept her gaze on Major, that smile she'd given Maurice just a few minutes ago now aimed at him. "He is the Fashion House Playboy."

"A completely bogus title that I wish we'd all stop referring to around here," he added, exasperation clear in his tone. The press had given him that name when they took the three dates he'd had in succession with three different models in the span of three nights as a sign that he was actually sleeping with each of those women.

If ever a label were unwarranted, it was that one.

"We took the Fashion House Playboy course the press has been on into consideration when talks about a campaign to heighten sales for Golden Bride began. Right now, a lot of fashion media is focused on you and who you'll date next, so we'll build on that momentum with the announcement of your engagement," Desta said.

Major folded his arms across his chest as he stood there staring at the people in the room. He spent more time with them than any woman, but nobody reported that to the tabloids.

"I wasn't the only option," he countered.

Desta shook her head. "To be fair, no, we considered RJ, but you know—" she nodded in RJ's direction "—he's RJ. He only talks about the company to the press and nobody's ever seen him on a date. I think he must sneak women into the basement of his brownstone."

"It's called being discreet. Nobody's entitled to the details of my private life but me. A very simple concept that people should learn to accept," RJ said in his very cordial but no-nonsense tone.

Desta shrugged his comment off. "And Maurice is with so many women all the time that making it believable that he's settling down was going to be an uphill battle."

"But it's more believable that ten seconds after I'm given the silly name of Fashion House Playboy, I'd mysteriously pop up married?" He'd entertained all these questions before and the outcome hadn't changed.

"Look," Desta said, lifting that brow. "You guys flat-out told me not to approach Riley with this plan even though she's dating a guy from RGF's rival fashion house. But I definitely understand you're her big brothers and you wanted to protect Riley from any more tabloid assaults. She's definitely had more than her share. But that just put the three of you on the hot seat, and Major, honey, as I said, your current media attention will work so well with this fake fiancée plan."

Actually, he'd acquiesced without putting up too much of a fight because now was not the time to ruffle feathers in his family. He already had a bombshell he was waiting to drop when he announced he was leaving the company. If agreeing to this marketing plan was going to keep things chill until he was ready to go public with his solo business venture, Brand Integrated Technologies, then so be it. He could endure for six weeks.

He nodded. "I'm fine with that. But this is the woman I want for the job of my fake fiancée." Each time he said those words he felt ridiculous.

"I just don't know about that," RJ said.

Desta stared at Major, considering everything he'd

said. Plans were already rolling around in her head. That's how she worked. Silent thinking and then, *poof!* great marketing idea, which is why she'd risen to the top of the department in such a short time.

"I say go for it," Maurice added. "If she says no, there's nobody better to convince her than Major with his brash good looks and unexpected heart."

The last was their family secret. Major was nothing like the press portrayed; his twin was the flamboyant lover of the Gold men. Major was the quiet computer geek.

"Do it," Desta said. "Get her to say yes by noon tomorrow and we can add your engagement announcement to the lineup at our annual Summer Sip 'n' Chat tomorrow evening," she told him. "Let me know when the agreement is made and I'll take care of everything else."

He resisted the urge to do a fist pump as he immediately turned and headed for the door. The sobering voice that resembled their father's stopped him.

"Get the agreement in writing. And this app better work to our advantage," RJ said.

Major looked over his shoulder at his older brother. "No worries, bro. I've got this."

CHAPTER THREE

MAJOR GOLD LOOKED worried that Nina's answer
would be a resounding no. As he damn well should
have been. What an arrogant thought to assume she'd
fall over herself in a hurry to be his fake fiancée for
six weeks in exchange for the biggest career break
she'd ever imagined. Just who the hell did he think
he was?

"Have a seat. I need to hear more details about
this proposed arrangement," she said.

He'd showed up at her hotel room half an hour
after she'd returned from seeing *Ain't Too Proud* on
Broadway. She'd invited him in, anxious to hear what
he had to say and if it involved a contract with RGF.
She'd changed into black skinny jeans and a red cam-
isole. The ballet flats she'd worn to the theater were
still on her feet and the high ponytail she'd pulled
her hair into was still intact. Now he was standing—
well, he'd just hiked his slacks up a bit before taking a seat on the couch—looking even sexier than
he had when she'd bumped into him at his building.

"I'm offering you a six-week contract to work exclusively with RGF. Think of it as sort of a test run for a possibly longer contract. Our marketing team will get started on a formal announcement to let our current customers know we're adding a new feature to their shopping experience. You'll be in touch with members of my tech team on linking At Your Service to our online store. After customers make a purchase, they'll be immediately routed to your app to open an account and get started with accessorizing their outfit. Win-win for both of us."

She didn't have to force herself to keep her gaze trained on him. Major Gold was a lovely man to look at. Six feet two and a half inches of lean muscle and gorgeous man. The light mustache accentuated the medium thickness of his lips. Dark low-cropped hair gave his tawny skin a bronze glow, while the Italian suit he wore fit every inch of his well-toned body to perfection. And he still smelled good at almost ten-thirty at night.

Nina cleared her throat. "First, regarding exclusivity. I already have contracts with two designers. They're small and in no way competition to RGF."

His hands looked strong, thick veins roped across the backs as they rested on his thighs. "We can probably work with that as long as you don't sign any other clients for the six-week term."

"Second. You also said something along the lines of me pretending to be your fiancée for six weeks. That's the part I'm not sold on, Mr. Gold—"

Actually, that was the part that confused the hell out of her.

"Major," he interrupted.

Fine. She could call him by his first name. He was sitting just a few inches away from her, in a hotel room. This was a pretty familiar setting, so first names made sense. Or at least she wanted all of this to make sense.

"Why do you need a fake fiancée, Major? And why do you think I'd fit that role?"

Because she didn't. Before her meeting, she'd done preliminary research on the family executives at Ronald Gold Fashions. She knew the father, Ron Gold, Jr., in addition to being CEO, was also the chief designer at RGF. She knew what his three sons did for the company, and that the youngest, and only girl in the family, was Riley, chief executive of market research and product development. She'd read about the matriarch, Marva Gold, who held a master's degree in education, served on RGF's board of directors and was currently developing several scholarship programs for underprivileged students across the US.

Nina's focus on the family had been solely on where they'd gone to college, what job they did, and how much the company made in just clothing sales last year. She hadn't bothered with any of the tabloid stories that had come up in the search; they didn't matter to RGF's bottom line. And she'd paid even less attention to the many pictures of each of the Gold children that filled the internet. It didn't matter how they looked—all Nina needed was for them to agree to work with her. It was that simple.

Yet now, Major was sitting too close and the task

of focusing on business was becoming much more difficult than it had ever been before.

"Look, I'll be totally honest with you. The reason I want you to do this is because of how you look."

Okay, he was going to be candid. Well, that was refreshing.

"And how do I look?"

"Great." He said the word as if she should have already known.

"I'm not the only great-looking woman in the world. Not even in New York. And you of all people surely know that. You can have any woman you want."

"I want you," he said. "I want someone who doesn't want me and isn't trying to fool me into getting what she really wants."

"I would like to work with RGF on a long-term basis, but if I can work with your company, for even six weeks, other larger fashion houses will take that as a gleaming recommendation. My business will take off. That's all I've ever wanted." Because she could be candid, too.

"Then say you'll be my fake fiancée for six weeks. Agree to take this assignment and I'll have contracts ready for you to sign first thing tomorrow morning."

He was serious. She'd been sitting there waiting for him to tell her this was all a joke and just go back to talking about her app, but that's not what was happening. This was real. His offer—every part of it was real.

"What do I have to do? As your fake fiancée, I mean?"

She sat back against the couch and crossed one leg over the other.

"Attend some functions with me, act as if you're planning a real wedding. Try on lots of gowns from the Golden Bride line, select bridesmaids gowns, and a host of other wedding stuff that our marketing department has planned."

"That's all. No kissing. No touching. No...nothing?" She needed to know all the terms, especially since she'd decided earlier that he had very kissable lips. Now, with him talking about fake engagements, kissing him had quickly popped into her mind again.

He paused and chuckled. Then he rubbed a hand over his mustache, down to his clean-shaved jaw, as he shook his head slowly.

"Ah, no, I don't think any of that's on the agenda."

"Then how will people believe we're really engaged? I'm guessing you want this to be believable. I mean, if not, then what's the point?"

A few seconds of him giving her a very heated glare only increased Nina's awareness of the sexual attraction buzzing between them since the first moment they'd met.

"The point of this arrangement is to boost sales for the new line. Our marketing department is convinced that seeing a Gold actually planning their wedding and selecting items from the bridal collection will encourage others to check it out for themselves," he said.

"And what happens at the end of the six-week period? After this wedding has been planned?"

He shrugged. "I'm told we'll have a huge and very public argument, followed by a press release the next morning announcing the unfortunate demise of the relationship. In this industry, negative publicity can sometimes work just as well as positive, as I'm sure you saw a few months ago when that ridiculous story about RGF stealing a design from King Designs surfaced. Marketing and sales are convinced that story, even after it was debunked, was partially responsible for the Golden Bride's phenomenal debut."

She was the one nodding now as the concept of "any publicity is good publicity" came to mind. "How very dramatic. Suits the Gold brand perfectly. So, like I said, you're banking on people buying this act, without kissing or touching. Do you not like to kiss and touch, Major?"

His gaze immediately moved to her lips. As if they were suddenly under pressure, she licked them slowly before clearing her throat. She should think of something else to say, to ease this awkward moment… Too late, he'd found her eyes again and now they were staring at each other, speaking that silent but knowing language of physical attraction.

"To the contrary, Nina. I like kissing and touching very much. I especially enjoyed the way you touched me earlier today."

She swallowed as the combination of his proximity, the silky tone of his voice and the blatant memory of her hand brushing over his magnificent erection shot to mind.

"Is that the type of touching you're referring to?"

"I'm not convinced we have to go that far," she said, because that was definitely going too far with a man she'd be entering into a business deal with. "But something along the lines of holding hands in public, perhaps a few chaste kisses...those might go a long way to creating the façade your company is banking on."

His hands had been resting on his thighs, but she could now see them moving to his knees, his fingers clenching slowly and releasing. If she dared to trace her gaze back just a little more she was certain that erection she'd felt earlier was making another appearance. Her breasts had begun to feel full and she barely resisted the urge to clamp her thighs together to keep the throbbing that had increased in her center at bay.

"I think—" he cleared his throat "—we'd just play it by ear in that regard. See what's needed and when. Go with the flow."

"Is that what the contract is going to say?" She prayed disappointment wasn't apparent in her tone.

"What would you like the contract to say? That we'll kiss five times in six weeks, hold hands ten times, hug twice?"

"If you think five kisses will be enough." Nina wasn't so sure anything would be enough where this man was concerned.

This time he licked his lips at her words. She did the same.

"Maybe we leave out a number. I wouldn't want us to be committed before we've considered how much we may like it."

"You think I'll like kissing you?" There was absolutely no doubt in her mind that she would.

"No," he replied. "I *know* I'm gonna like kissing you."

Nina couldn't stop thinking about kissing him and she had no idea why she'd even brought up holding hands or kissing in public. Especially since she wasn't a fan of PDA. Holding hands, touching, ogling, and yes, kissing, were reserved for behind closed doors. That's the way she'd been brought up and it was a rule she'd stuck to.

Your personal business is your personal business. Nobody else's.

Jacoby Fuller had said that more times than Nina or her sisters could count. But not for the same reasons that Nina had decided to adopt them. Her father didn't like public displays of affection because it reminded him of how much he still loved and missed his wife. Nina didn't like them because it reminded her of how quickly a happy couple could become a lonely man raising three daughters on his own.

Which was precisely why she didn't do relationships. The thought of investing her time, emotions and trust into one person who could potentially walk away without a care in the world, wasn't something she liked to entertain. But that wasn't what this was.

Major Gold had come to her with a business pro-

posal, one she'd spent the bulk of last night con-
templating. If this fake wedding was going to bring
publicity—good and bad—to RGF, then what was
she going to get out of it? Besides the six weeks to
work with the company and the possibility of a longer contract, there was a measure of exposure here
that Nina couldn't ignore. For every public appearance she made with Major, she was adding a face to
her brand. The Nina Fuller behind At Your Service
would be up close and personal with the industry
she'd dreamed of working in all her life. And while
she totally understood that any publicity was good
publicity, she wanted as much of her exposure to
this industry to be as positive as she could manage.
Creating the most believable fake relationship possible was a must.

Her traveling outfit was jeans and a T-shirt with
her school mascot—a mustang—on the front. She
couldn't wear that to what technically was her second interview at RGF, where she knew she would
be receiving and accepting a job offer. After a quick
run to Macy's and the purchase of a gray pantsuit
and white blouse, at exactly nine forty-five in the
morning, she walked through the glass doors of RGF
again.

Major was already seated at the same end of the
conference room table as yesterday. Across from him
was Maurice. Twins, not identical, but who favored
each other enough that she hadn't needed Google to
tell her they'd been born together. But the internet
had informed her that Major was older and, while

he wasn't as brash and indiscriminate as his younger brother, he was still quite popular with women. A fact that made no difference to her—this was a temporary assignment. One she'd spent some time plotting out.

She'd used RGF's online sales figures—retrieved from an article in a top financial magazine that had compared the fashion industry's growth from five years ago to the present—to approximate how many new accounts At Your Service would obtain and the percentage she would earn from each of her vendors once the app had successfully accessorized each customer. It would bring her more than enough to pay for her father to move into an assisted-living facility and remain there for at least two years. In that time, she would land more clients. King Designs, RGF's biggest rival, was next on her list to approach, and there were others. All of which would be impressed by her work with RGF and would pay her even more for the use of her app.

"Good morning, Ms. Fuller," Maurice was the first to speak when she entered the boardroom.

"Good morning. Please call me Nina," she said and watched as he stood and walked to her. When he extended his hand, Nina accepted it for a quick shake.

"Thank you for agreeing to meet with us again on such short notice," he said.

"It was no problem," she lied. She was going to miss her train and the ticket was nonrefundable.

"Yes. Thank you very much for coming back.

Now, let's get down to business. We don't have a lot
of time before our first event."

The woman who talked while entering the room
hadn't been in the meeting yesterday. She wasn't
as tall as Nina's five-foot-eight height, but she was
dressed just as sharply. Probably sharper since Nina
was certain the woman's skirt and jacket were RGF
originals from their Make the Woman professional-
wear line. The outfit was a bold royal blue and she
wore a pale yellow blouse beneath the fitted jacket
and patent leather slingback pumps. The blond-
frosted tips of her black hair fell in big curls to her
shoulders as she gave Nina a quick look and then
closed the door behind her.

"This is Desta Henner, our marketing director,"
Major said.

Nina looked from the focused woman to Major.
He wore another black suit today—this one with a
more casual jacket that zipped—and in place of a
dress shirt and tie he was wearing a butter-colored
pullover that molded against his muscled chest.

"Our legal department worked double-time to get
these two contracts drawn up," Desta announced.
"Have a seat, please, and we'll go over everything."

Maurice had returned to his seat and this time
Major was the one to stand, pulling out the chair
next to him.

Nina took the seat, dropping her purse into the
empty chair to the other side. "Yes," she said in a
voice she knew sounded as levelheaded and professional as Desta's. "Let's go over everything."

* * *

She'd signed both contracts.

A part of Major hadn't thought she would.

Nina Fuller was an entrepreneur. She'd graduated top of her class from the Harrisburg Area Community College in York, and had taken additional online classes to obtain her master's in computer technology and engineering. She'd used those degrees to build a sophisticated app that could be groundbreaking in the fashion industry. That is, if it didn't almost mimic some of Brand Integrated Technologies' functions, a fact that could potentially become a conflict of interest between them. Initially, he'd felt the urge to be honest with her about the possible overlap of their companies, but then he considered that by the time this fake engagement and her trial period at RGF were over, they could go their separate ways and their companies could exist as a form of healthy competition. At least, that's what he was telling himself.

Major had spent most of last night going through her app as a user, easily figuring out every step she'd taken from coding to debugging and creating the user interface. It was intricate, but Major had a master's degree in computer technology and engineering, as well. A degree he'd also used to help keep RGF three steps ahead of their competitors where technology was concerned.

"Well, that's done," he said when they were the only two remaining in the conference room.

"Yes, it is." She'd stored her copies of the contracts in her case and now stood a few feet away from him. "So, are we heading to the tech department to get started on the integration now?"

He couldn't help but notice that the suit she wore fit her nicely. The pants flawlessly molded the natural curve of her hips, accentuating thighs that were thicker than the models he was used to seeing. The jacket was an acceptable fit, the wrap blouse beneath hugging her full breasts tightly. But it wasn't an RGF ensemble.

"Ah, no, not just yet. My assistant, Landra, will be emailing you a copy of our itinerary for the upcoming weeks. There's a cocktail party scheduled for tonight at the Midtown Loft & Terrace. I believe you'll be assigned a stylist, but I'm not sure who that will be. Landra or possibly Desta will take care of that."

She nodded slowly.

Her hair was pulled back from her face again, this time held at the nape of her neck with a black band so that she looked almost demure. A look that was perfect for this campaign but didn't begin to touch the fiery passion he'd seen brimming in her eyes last night. Heat instantly began to stir through his veins as he thought about sitting on that couch with her in the hotel talking casually about how she'd felt him up only hours before. If he was half the Fashion House Playboy he was dubbed to be, there was no doubt Major would have spent the night in her bed, bringing them both the pleasure he knew they'd been thinking about.

"An itinerary. A stylist," she said and exhaled slowly. "I guess that's part of the agreement. Should

I just wait here or return to my hotel? How do we play this?"

Major stepped closer to her.

"I think we start by getting this out of the way."

His hands, which had itched to touch her all night and throughout this morning's meeting, rested on the tops of her arms as he pulled her against him. The motion was quick and her hands came up to slap against his biceps as she tilted her chin to meet his gaze.

"You asked about kissing last night?" His voice sounded unfamiliarly gruff.

She blinked, long, natural lashes brushing her skin before he was afforded the sight of her gold-flecked eyes once more. "You said it wasn't required."

"Not required," he whispered. "Desired. At least on my part. If you're not interested, say so now." Before he combusted from the desire that had boiled inside him all through the night.

"I'm interested."

The words were barely out of her mouth before his lips crashed down over hers, heat soaring through their connection, a force unlike anything Major could have ever imagined taking over every part of his body.

CHAPTER FOUR

NEVER BEEN KISSED.

The three words floated around in her mind as his tongue moved salaciously over hers. *Not like this, anyway.*

Major's hands had slipped from the tops of her arms to her waist until he was holding her tightly against him. It was a stern and commanding hold. A you're-not-going-anywhere type of hold that she actually enjoyed. So much so, that Nina laced her arms around his neck, pulling his head down farther so that she could sink deeper into the kiss. A kiss they probably shouldn't be sharing since there was no one to see them and hence wasn't moving their fake relationship forward.

But hell, she wasn't complaining.

When they finally broke contact, both breathing as if they'd just run a race, he rested his forehead against hers and Nina let her eyes remain closed for a few seconds more.

What the hell is going on? Twenty-four hours ago, she'd been preparing for a meeting she'd known could change her life. Never in her wildest dreams had she thought of how drastically things would change in such a short amount of time.

"Okay, that was…" He paused, searching for the words.

They popped into her mind effortlessly. *Explosive. Delicious. Addictive!*

"It was the kiss that sealed the deal" was what she actually said before pushing away from him and smoothing her hands down the front of her clothes.

He ran his hand across the back of his head while nodding. "Yeah, I guess we could say that."

As if on cue, her phone chimed and she moved much too quickly to retrieve it from her purse. "Itinerary!" she said, her pitch higher than normal as she held up her phone as if to explain what she meant.

Major cleared his throat. "Right. I'm going to head downstairs because I have a couple of things to take care of before tonight. There's a car waiting out front for you. The driver's name is Claude. He's great and he'll get you wherever you need to go in the city. He's at your disposal for the next six weeks. Landra will be sending you all of his contact information."

She'd been reading the first of a five-page document attached to the email sent by his assistant. Today was already jam-packed with things to do.

"Oh, okay. Um, I guess I'll be invoiced for all of this."

"All of this" meaning drivers, tips, clothes—their seemed to be a ton of fittings and makeup sessions scheduled and she'd only bought this one suit just a couple of hours ago. The only other thing in her hotel closet was the skirt suit she'd worn yesterday and her train-ride outfit. None of which would be acceptable for the events listed in the itinerary document.

"Everything you need will be taken care of and, if we miss something, just let me know."

She looked up at him, her gaze automatically going to his lips before she scolded herself and forced her eyes up to meet his.

"You're going to take care of all of my expenses?"

"Yes, for the next six weeks. That's part of the deal."

It made sense. The only reason she was staying in New York longer was this fake fiancée assignment. So why shouldn't he completely accommodate her? Making sense was totally different from being comfortable, and Nina wasn't comfortable with the thought of this guy she'd only met yesterday paying her way. Thinking back now, she recalled the contract vaguely mentioning expenses, but she'd been so focused on the language pertaining to her business functioning with RGF's that she hadn't considered the implications. No worries, it was all good, she'd get used to it, because again she had no other choice. There was no way she could afford to stay here and buy all the things she'd need before she began seeing any profit from doing business with RGF.

She took a deep breath and released it slowly, telling herself to let go of the trepidation and take this situation for what it was at the moment.

"Then I'll head out now. It seems I have a spa appointment and a fitting this afternoon."

For what seemed like endless moments, they both stood still, staring at each other.

"Thank you," he said when the silence stretched between them. "For doing this, I mean. I know it seems like an unusual arrangement."

"If the rhythm of the drumbeat changes, the dance step must adjust."

He frowned. "What?"

She shook her head as she grabbed her purse. "Sorry, it's just an old African proverb my father used to say."

"Your father is African?"

"Yes. His mother came to America when he was five years old. When she remarried, her husband adopted my father and so his last name was changed, but he was born in Sierra Leone."

"Interesting," he said, still staring at her.

"Yes. It's always interesting to know where you come from and it helps in determining where you're going."

And she had no idea why they were talking about this. He had work to do and she had a spa appointment to get to.

"Anyway, we'd better get started with this. Today's going to be a busy day."

He walked with her to the door. "You're right. I'll speak with my team this afternoon and arrange for you to meet with them tomorrow morning. If there's time on your schedule, Landra will coordinate everything. But I'd like to get you set up quickly. If this fake wedding works out, we should see an immediate bump in sales, especially since we're at the peak of wedding season."

"Then maybe we should have gotten engaged earlier this year," she said as they walked to the elevators in what felt like a moment of déjà vu. "We're already in the first week of May. If a woman's getting married this season, she likely already has her gown."

"Until she sees a Golden Bride original being tried on by a real-life bride who's also going to be a member of the Gold family," he said before leaning in to push the button to summon the elevator.

Except there was nothing "real" about this arrangement.

"So we're hoping for the impromptu bride. Or the indecisive one." She nodded as she thought about her vendors who specialized in bridal items.

"Or the one who's just been swept off her feet with a wildly romantic proposal and can't wait to be married. She plans a quick wedding but wants all the bells and whistles, starting with a couture gown." He talked while she stepped into the elevator car. Following her inside, he pushed the buttons for his floor and the lobby.

"Not couture, RGF already has their wealthy customers on lock," she said. "Think about the average woman who's looking for something fancy, unique, but economical. I'll do some research on the bridal line, see what budget-friendly gowns you have."

"But you don't need to select budget friendly. I told you I'll take care of everything for you," he insisted.

Was that a look of pity she saw flash quickly in his eyes? Lord, she hoped not.

"The rich won't care about the Fashion House Playboy being engaged," she pointed out. "It won't seem romantic and dazzling to them because they're already living their own dazzling lives. But the woman who picks up the fashion magazines in the supermarket and runs her fingers over the glossy pages full of designer gowns? She's the one who'll appreciate this whole charade and she's the one you should be targeting."

"You're a techie like me, how do you know all this stuff about marketing bridal gowns?"

"I'm that 'regular' woman. Wasn't that what Desta said in the meeting earlier? That's why you chose me and that's how I know what I'm talking about."

The elevator door opened on his floor, but Major didn't immediately move to get out.

"You should go, you have a lot of work to do today," she told him even though she sensed he wanted to stay.

She, on the other hand, needed some space. That kiss, her mentioning her father to him, and then the talk of weddings had her feeling a bit unsteady. Considering the old proverb, she'd just experienced a giant misstep in her dance routine and she needed to regroup.

"I'll see you later," he said finally as the door began to close and he extended his arm to stop it.

Nina nodded. "I'll be ready."

Every muscle in her body felt limp. In fact, when Nina flopped down onto her stomach on her hotel room couch, she felt as if she might melt into the upholstery. That guy at the spa had massaged every muscle in her body until they were like jelly. And she'd never felt better!

She'd need to hold on to this feeling when she made the call to her family to tell them she'd be here much longer than anticipated. Her text earlier today saying that she'd missed her train wasn't going to be enough. But she'd been putting that off, instead deciding to enjoy the luxurious offerings of the Tranquil Mornings Day Spa. From champagne to sparkling water, fruit to decadent chocolates, and a menu to order lunch or dinner, the place had accommodated all her needs—even the ones she hadn't realized she'd had.

Claude was waiting to take her to her dress fittings, but she'd wanted to stop and grab her laptop before heading out again. She was just about to push herself up from the couch, grab it and head back downstairs when someone knocked at the door. She moved across the room much faster than her very relaxed body wanted to.

"Hello," she said when she pulled the door open to see a woman standing there.

"Hello," the woman replied before stepping inside unannounced. "Bring the racks in and put them over there. Have makeup set up near the window so Natalia will have the best light. We have a couple hours until it's time to head to the venue, but I want to make sure everything is perfect, and we may have to go through a couple outfits first."

The woman—dressed in gray pants tapered at the bottom, bright yellow pumps and a white high-low blouse with the sleeves rolled up to her elbows—breezed into the room.

"Excuse me?" Nina asked, taking a step behind the three racks of clothes that had been wheeled into her hotel room. "I think there might be some mistake."

"There's no mistake."

Another woman spoke and Nina turned around to see her closing the door.

"Hi, I'm Riley Gold and you're Nina Fuller. It's a pleasure to meet you."

Yes, this was Riley Gold, the Ice Princess of RGF as the press had called her for years, until she'd started dating Chaz—Chadwick Warren. Her beauty far surpassed any of the pictures Nina had seen of her online.

As realization immediately set in, Nina accepted the outstretched hand and calmed down just a bit. "Hi. It's nice to meet you, Riley. I thought I was being driven to the fittings."

Riley nodded, her dark brown hair falling in deep waves over her shoulders. She wore a black, round-necked shift dress with gold stripes at the end of the three-quarter sleeves and across the hem, and cute strappy black sandals.

"I thought you'd be more comfortable here," Riley said. "As comfortable as you can get in this situation."

She was right about that. Nina's fingers clenched the strap of her laptop bag as she stood amid so much action not really knowing what to do. There were now seven people in her not-so-big hotel room. The stylist, whom she presumed was the woman giving all the instructions, four people moving clothing racks, shoe boxes, bags and hat boxes, a woman with super-long eyelashes, and a man wearing dark shades and dime-size diamond earrings in both ears. He was on his phone and carrying a huge clear bag with flat irons, combs, brushes and other hair paraphernalia inside. Nina and Riley made nine—enough for a softball team.

"Thanks for that," Nina said and set her laptop bag on the floor next to the nearest chair. "As much as I've always loved fashion, computers are my first love. Besides, the last twenty-four hours has been a bit of a whirlwind. I mean I haven't thought of what clothes I'd wear beyond the initial meeting."

Riley nodded again. "I can imagine. You look great in this suit, by the way, but I'm here to dress you up. I work with numbers and charts primarily, but clothes are my business and Lila over there, she *knows* clothes. She's one of the best stylists in New York and works with many of our high-end customers."

Looks by Lila, owned by Lila Cantone. Nina had heard of her, but she'd never imagined the woman was probably no more than five foot two without her heels and moved like an Energizer Bunny.

"Tonight, we want chic but grab-you-by-the-throat elegant. The annual Sip 'n' Chat is one of RGF's most notable functions where fashion critics, photographers, reps from modeling agencies and specially selected members of the press are going to get the surprise of the year with this engagement announcement." That was Lila giving her crew a pep talk. "She's being presented to the fashion world tonight. Let's make her dazzle so that every single woman that's still breathing will wish she were her."

Riley wrapped an arm around Nina's shoulders. "I know she seems scary, but I promise you this is the way to go. Major wanted the best and I assured him I would get it for you."

So he'd sent his sister to work with her. Nina didn't know how she felt about that. Did he not think she could pick out a suitable outfit on her own? So many questions whirled through her mind but she had no time to entertain any of them because Lila was heading straight for her.

"Okay, I was told size twelve or fourteen, so I brought both." Riley's arm had slipped from around Nina, leaving space for Lila to step in and touch her shoulders. "Turn," Lila directed Nina.

"I'm Nina, by the way. It's nice to be working with you, Lila," Nina said before moving because no matter how important this agreement was, there was absolutely no excuse for rudeness.

Lila blinked, wide gray eyes flanked by long lashes that looked natural. Her hair was shaved on one side and layered in perfectly glossy auburn strands with pink tips on the other.

"Hello, Nina. We'll see how nice you think this is when it's all over. I can be a real bitch."

Well then, honesty was going to be the name of all her dealings with RGF and the Golds. Nina smiled, because in her mind that was a good thing. Dishonesty, secrets and lies had played a big part in the demise of her parents' relationship and Nina had promised herself she'd steer clear of those things in business and in pleasure.

"Now, let's get started. You have nice curves, let's show them off, make some men as envious as all the women will be."

The comment was followed by Nina being whisked off into the bedroom to try on dresses.

The first was a black-and-blue, A-line, round-necked dress with a beaded waist.

"Hmm," Riley said. "Major's wearing a navy-blue suit, Excellence in Men line. Single button and a pale gray shirt. She should complement him, but they shouldn't be too matchy."

Nina glanced in the full-length mirror that had been brought in and propped against the wall in the living room. She looked like she was going to the prom and shook her head to express her dislike.

"I agree," Lila said, waving a hand to signal she needed to go and change into another dress.

Seven dresses and forty-five minutes later, Nina stepped in front of that mirror once more.

This one was an asymmetric panel of overlays with a one-shoulder fitted bodice and straight skirt of dark blue sequins. Her breasts looked amazing thanks to the strapless shaper Lila's assistant had brought into the room while Nina was changing. Thankfully, no undergarment lines showed and when she turned to glimpse the dress from the back, she smiled at the admirable, definitive curve of her ass.

The dress was gorgeous and more expensive than anything she'd ever worn before. She knew because there was no price attached. The only tag on these clothes was RGF Style or RGold Original, which equated to expensive because those were the signature lines at the fashion house. RGolden Label was their couture line and all other lines simply had the RGF logo attached somewhere on the inside of the garment.

The material of the dress was impossibly soft and hung decadently over her usually too-curvy butt and hips. Her body looked great in this dress, even with the slight pouch of a belly that on bloated days could push her into the next pant size.

Garen, the hair stylist came over and pulled Nina's hair up, leaving out a few tendrils.

Lila stood behind her to one side and Riley was on the other.

"I think this is it," Nina said as she continued to look at the shimmering material.

"With these shoes and the pounded-metal cuff. Cheree!" Lila yelled to one of her assistants and set a pair of silver, five-inch-heel slingbacks next to Nina's feet.

One by one, Nina slipped her feet into the shoes and waited while Anya, another assistant, buckled the straps.

Cheree placed the pounded-metal bracelet on her right wrist.

"Classy and retro. Not only will folk in the industry not have a clue who you are, they're gonna fall over themselves trying to label your style. We're gonna use this moment to set the stage for a whirlwind of different looks that will put you at the top of the fashion game." Lila was obviously excited as she nodded her head, hair swaying over one shoulder.

For a moment Nina didn't know who she was. This wasn't why she'd come to New York. But it was beginning to be a hell of a lot of fun!

CHAPTER FIVE

"WHAT ARE YOU laughing at?"

Major frowned as Maurice chuckled.

"You and this crazy situation you've gotten yourself into," his brother responded.

"First, I didn't get myself into this situation, it just happened."

Maurice frowned now, his full brows tilting downward, which added a more ominous look to the thick beard he sported.

"You're the one who suggested this tech woman become your fake fiancée."

"Yeah, but I'm not the one who came up with the whole fake fiancée idea in the first place. Oh no, that was Desta's brilliance, which you happily cosigned." Major walked around the king-size fourposter in his room, trying his best to ignore the suit, shirt and tie that had been laid out neatly on one side of the mattress.

Maurice had left the office and followed him to his penthouse. For what reason, Major didn't know. But considering what his brother was doing at this moment—lounging with one leg draped over the arm of a leather recliner across the room, staring at him and making irritating comments—he would assume his presence was meant to antagonize him to no end. If that were the case, he was doing a damn good job.

"We needed a plan, something that would grab the customer's attention and keep it riveted on the Golden Bride line."

Major shook his head as he yanked his shirt out of his pants before pulling it over his head and off. "And I look like the one to do that?"

"Your reputation—" Maurice started, but Major quickly cut him off.

"I'm not the one with a reputation, man. You know that's all you. You're the one who flaunts every affair you have. Hell, you pose for pictures for all those photographers and tabloid workers. You give them so much ammunition."

"I wasn't named the Fashion House Playboy. A snub, I might add, I'm still considering being salty about." Maurice gave a fake pout.

Major tossed his shirt into the hamper a few feet away and sat heavily on the bed—his back to the clothes. "Those dates were a coincidence. And, actually, one was a favor to Mom and Dad. I couldn't say anything about it because it would have embarrassed poor Hannah Lincoln, whose parents didn't want her to go out in public alone because her jet-setting, race-car-driving boyfriend had just dumped her."

Major's head fell back and he groaned. He loved his mother above all else in this world, but if she ever called his cell phone and started the conversation with, "Hi, my favorite son," again, he was hanging up on her. She'd made that sugary-sweet request for him to take Hannah out so she wouldn't appear depressed and lonely over the breakup and he'd agreed.

Hannah had spent the entire evening talking about her ex and how she was being super strong and not crying over her ex, and how her ex was the love of her life, but how glad she was to be rid of her ex. It was a long and insufferable evening that had capped off the three-day stint earning him the ever so wonderful title in the fashion industry. The tabloids loved to take any snippet of information and run with it. That was their job, and while Major could totally respect someone being dedicated to a job, he didn't have to like being caught up in it.

"But you still selected the woman to be your fake fiancée," his twin pointed out.

"That, right there—" Major turned to see that his brother had grabbed a beer out of his refrigerator on his way to the room and was now twisting the top off so he could take a long swallow. After a shake of his head, he continued. "That's the best part of this stupid stunt. At least she's someone I have something in common with and won't die of boredom or irritation from when I'm alone with her."

"So you like her?"

Major blinked and then shook his head. "That's not what I said. But yeah, I like that we're both IT techies and that she's smart and courageous enough to start her own business." Thoughts of how their companies overlapped popped into his mind and Major instantly pushed them back.

"Like you did," Maurice said.

Major leaned over and untied his Tom Ford leather sneakers, but he sat up before taking them off. "Yeah, like I did."

Maurice was the only person in his family who knew about Brand Integrated. Being fraternal twins came with a certain amount of closeness that didn't resonate with his other two siblings. And while he and Maurice weren't constantly on the phone or, notwithstanding this present moment, sitting in each other's bedroom talking the night away, he and Maurice told each other pretty much everything.

So when Major had started to feel a little itchy working solely for RGF, Maurice was the first to notice. And when Major confided in his brother about the idea for his new business venture, Maurice had stood firmly in his corner. As a matter of fact, Maurice hadn't agreed with Major keeping his business a secret from the family. He believed that Major should be proud of himself and bold enough to step away from the Gold fashion house, especially considering none of the other siblings had been able to do that.

"You've signed the lease in the building, started hiring staff, and have your first marketing plan ready to roll out on day one. I'd say you're set to do this," Maurice said before taking another drink.

"Yeah, I am," Major said. "But first, I've gotta get this fake wedding on a roll. After that, I'm out."

"Not out," Maurice said. "You'll always be a Gold,

no matter what building you walk into for work each day."

"Dad's probably not going to feel that way. You know how he is about loyalty. That was the crux of the whole family feud that almost threatened Riley's happiness." He sighed heavily, reliving how his sister's plunge into love a couple months ago had only made his decision to move on to other things in his career another sticky family issue to cope with. "But I'm through thinking about that. It's what I'm doing, so they can either accept it or disown me."

"You know Mom's never gonna let him disown you. She didn't let him disown Riley."

Major stood and took the sneakers into his closet. "That was never going to happen, I don't care who she slept with. Dad would have seriously considered shooting Chaz and Tobias before he'd ever thought about firing Riley."

Even though the news of his sister's affair with Chaz, whose uncle Tobias King was head of King Designs, had spread like wildfire through the industry, bringing old assumptions about the Gold/King feud back to the surface. While Major secretly hoped his engagement façade would help take the residual bad press from Riley's saga away, part of him knew that the subsequent announcement of his leaving RGF to run Brand Integrated Technologies would fuel its own fire.

"And look at them now," Maurice said. "Riley and Chaz are inseparable. When he's not at her place, she's at his. He's at Sunday dinner with the family and she's seen out at parties with him and Tobias. They're really in love, whatever the hell that is."

Oh yeah, in addition to being the twin who actually loved going on dates with different women and getting attention for it, Maurice was the one who hated, loathed and despised the word *love*. Major didn't let the word get that deep under his skin, although he didn't imagine himself feeling it any time soon. His new company, as well as continuing to help with RGF's technology development, were his priorities right now. The one time he'd ventured to believe he might be feeling something like love, Stacia Hudgins had given him a hard-and-fast lesson—love wasn't worth a damn.

"I gotta get home. If we don't get ready, Riley, Chaz and the rest of the family are going to be at the cocktail party before us," Maurice said.

Major stood and was about to walk toward the bathroom when he looked back at the clothes on the bed. "I still can't believe Riley picked out clothes for me."

Maurice eased his tall frame from the chair, tilted his head back to swallow the remaining dregs of beer from the bottle and then shook his head. "You know Riley's in control of everything that concerns the Golden Bride line. Whether or not you gave her permission to be involved with your fake fiancée, she was going to do it. And she's damn sure gonna make certain she controls everything you do and say regarding this engagement."

Major groaned. "That's what I'm afraid of."

* * *

No, what Major Gold was actually afraid of, an hour and a half later when he stood near the bar at the Midtown Loft & Terrace and glanced toward the door, was swallowing his tongue or otherwise making a fool of himself as Nina Fuller walked in.

She smiled when she met his gaze and began walking toward him. Major stuffed his hands into the front pockets of his pants, forcing them to remain still and not move toward the center to soothe the growing ache that was happening there.

Nina looked stunning in blue, the dark hue playing expertly against the lightness of her complexion. Her hair was pulled up, loose pieces hanging at each ear just brushing the skin of her neck. He'd bet every dollar in all four of his bank accounts the skin right there was soft to the touch and sweet to the taste. Silver earrings sparkled at her ears and matched the chunky bracelet on her wrist. His gaze lifted from that wrist up her arm to where her bare shoulder was showcased. A shoulder he wanted to rub his fingers over and drop featherlight kisses against. Her shoes were silver but her legs were really the clincher, grabbing his full attention. They looked long and luscious, coated with some type of glistening oil.

She walked like a temptress across the mahogany floor, her hips swaying from side to side, healthy breasts held high to tempt him and most likely every other guy with good vision in this room. He swallowed hard and tried not to think of the word *hard*. Not that it was going to help; his dick was well on its way to another stunning erection at just seeing this woman. He wished for a drink but didn't want to turn away from her to request one from the bartender.

"You look fantastic," he said the moment she was close enough to hear because he had to get those words out of his head.

"Thanks. I tried on so many dresses today, I'm glad to be standing in just one at this moment."

"This is definitely the best dress. Ever," he confessed and swallowed again.

She tilted her head, her smile wavering slightly. "Are you okay?"

For a few seconds he clamped his lips shut. He wasn't totally sure he could resist asking her to find some private place for them to hang out tonight.

"I'm good," he said and gave himself a good mental kick. It'd been a long time since he'd been a horny teenager chasing after models at fashion shows. Most of them had been around his age, even though they'd hit the runways in outfits that made them appear much older.

"Well, I'm not. I mean I'm a little nervous. I've never been to a Sip 'n' Chat before."

She was looking around as she spoke and Major finally managed to pull his gaze from her long enough to do the same.

"We rely on the media, but we can't always control what goes into print. The Sip 'n' Chat is our way of having an informal press conference where we release only the information we want the media to have, at the exact moment we want them to have it."

She nodded. "Smart."

"Yeah, just like me." He winked.

"You? I thought we were talking about your team who came up with this very smart idea." She smiled and he enjoyed the light that came into her eyes. A jolt of awareness hit him as he realized she really was different from the other women he'd met.

"I'm talking about how smart I was to have finally agreed to meeting with you when I did. Otherwise, I wouldn't be standing here with you." He'd stepped closer to her as he said those words. Another step or two and he would be on top of her, which wasn't a bad idea—except he wasn't down for an audience.

"Hi! You made it! That dress looks fabulous on you. Doesn't it, Major?" Riley asked when she approached, Chaz right beside her.

Why she was asking him the obvious, Major had no idea, but he gladly answered. "It does."

"Thanks," Nina said, holding a silver clutch in front of her as she nodded at Riley and Chaz. "I hope it photos well. I came up on the elevator with three reporters and two photographers."

"Nina, this is Chaz Warren, my boyfriend." Riley smiled as she glanced at Chaz and he returned the look before extending his hand to Nina.

"Hello, Nina. It's nice to meet you. Riley's told me all about you, your company and, ah, this marketing plan."

Major wasn't sure how he felt about that. While his first instinct was to be happy for Riley—who seemed more relaxed and content with Chaz than he'd ever recalled—there was still a small part of him that was on guard. Telling Chaz about their marketing strategies when he was still working—even if only on a part-time basis—with his uncle, didn't seem like the best idea. But tonight, Major had other things to worry about.

"King Designs is doing great this season. I've been keeping up with your shows and sales," Nina said.

"Ah, yeah. Wow, you're keeping tabs on us," Chaz replied. "Not sure if I should be worried or impressed by that. But, um, our line is doing really well after the relaunch and we're hoping for the same success with a couple other lines."

"That's good to know. And yes, in my line of business, I try to keep my eye on the top companies in the industry," she told him.

Okay, add another thing to the list of things for Major to ponder. Was Nina really going to stand there and pitch her company to their biggest competitor?

"It's almost time for the announcement," Desta said when she joined them.

Thankful for the interruption, Major slipped his arm around Nina's waist and gently led her in the direction Desta was now speed-walking.

"We're going to begin with pictures. The family has already started, but you two are up next. Reporters are chomping at the bit trying to figure out what's going on." Desta talked as she walked and

Major followed, enjoying the feel of his hand resting at the small of Nina's back.

The venue was crowded with people, most of whom he knew from the industry, some of whom he'd never seen before in his life. He supposed he should feel some measure of nervousness or possibly anxiety, but all he felt was anticipation.

"There are so many people here," Nina said when they made their way to the other side of the terrace.

It was a gorgeous night for a terrace party, not too humid and the sky full of stars.

Major came around behind her, his hand still at her waist as they moved through a group of people, one of whom did a double take when she saw him. It wasn't someone he knew, but he could tell the buzz around tonight's announcement was growing because the woman's gaze had immediately shifted from him to Nina with an inquisitive quirk of her brow.

"Are they normally like this?" Nina asked.

"Like what?"

"So hungry for whatever is going to happen next. Surely they've been to this event before, so they know what you're going to be talking about—your fashion house. But their anticipation is almost palpable."

That question came when they were just a few steps from an arch covered in white flowers made to look purple by the up-lighting positioned on the floor.

"Everyone here was sent a private invitation that

spoke of a big announcement," he said. "Are you all right? Is it too much for you?"

He wanted to say he'd take her out of here if it was, but he knew Desta would probably have a cardiac episode if he even thought about doing that. Even though RGF still held its title as the US's top fashion house, keeping a comfortable lead over their competitors was their marketing director's priority.

"No. I'm fine," she said. "Just wondering how this is all going to play out."

Major stood beside Nina, waiting for Desta's signal to step forward for pictures. He'd reluctantly moved his hand from her waist when his fingers had begun to tingle with the desire to either slide to the generous curve of her ass or up to the bare skin of her shoulder. Both, he was certain, were inappropriate movements on so many levels.

"As soon as the announcement is made, we can leave. Maurice and his team can field all the questions. All we have to do is stand here and smile for the cameras," he said.

She looked surprised at that comment. "You're not making the announcement?"

"No. My father's going to handle that. Is that a problem?"

There was a slight hesitation then a small shrug of her shoulders. "If this were real, I'd think you'd be so excited about getting married to the woman you love that you'd be bursting with the need to announce it to the world," she said, but then held up a hand and shook her head. "Don't get me wrong, I'm no expert. It just seems like the sort of thing they'd do in one of those romance movies."

Romance movies that she was obviously watching and paying close attention to.

"I don't know that this was planned for romance," he said. "It's just a hoax, remember."

He really needed her to remember that. Nothing personal or real was going to come of this six-week plan. That's not what he was in the market for and he was banking on them being so focused on their business goals that there'd be no risk of losing sight of the goal.

She nodded her agreement and in the next moment they were being moved to stand under the arch and positioned for one pose after another.

The photographer hired specifically to commemorate the event had been given a list of names and pictures Desta wanted. The guy, who was dressed in all black, directed Major to stand behind Nina and put his hands around her waist. It was the dreaded prom picture pose. He was inclined to frown once he realized it, but as her body settled back against his, Major felt something else entirely.

In addition to the warmth spreading throughout his body at her proximity to him, there was a rush of something akin to joy, excitement or—no, it was more intense, possibly ownership. As he looked toward the photographer, ready for the guy to snap the picture, Major was acutely aware of the men in the room staring his way. Surely they weren't looking at him, so they had to be staring at Nina, whom he already knew looked phenomenal in the blue dress.

He tried valiantly to keep from frowning as he realized he was the one forgetting this was all a hoax and that Nina wasn't his to feel jealous, protective or anything else about.

"Now, you stand still and, Ms. Fuller, you turn around." The photographer had moved on to another instruction that Nina dutifully followed.

She turned until she was facing him.

"Put your hands on his shoulders and turn your head to me," the guy said.

Again, she obeyed.

Now her front was pressed into his and Major's hands immediately went around her waist once more. Without instruction.

He could smell the floral scent of her shampoo and felt the curve of her breasts even through the material of his jacket and shirt. His fingers tightened at her waist before sliding down slightly until he could feel the curve of her ass. This time when the flash of the camera erupted, Major was clenching his teeth. He was holding so still he thought his bones might crack from inactivity. But that was preferable to giving in to the heat spreading through his veins like wildfire and pressing her closer to him.

Several pictures were taken in that pose and he was about to complain or pull away—anything to stop the assault his arousal had taken on his body when she looked up at him.

"You don't like holding poses for pictures, do you?" she asked with a smile.

"Not really," he replied while staring down into eyes that appeared to have more yellow highlights than he'd noticed before. "But I enjoy holding you."

She blinked as if trying to figure out if she should smile at his words or feel something deeper, something more potent than he'd assumed either of them would feel. When she remained silent, he lifted a hand to brush the backs of his fingers lightly over the line of her jaw. She continued to smile and surprised him by leaning her head into his touch. It was a quick and impromptu movement, one that had his breath catching seconds before more pictures were snapped.

With the warm air around them and the sound of violins, harps—or whatever instruments the quartet at the other end of the room was playing—echoing toward the sky, he was locked in her gaze, wrapped in this blissful attraction. She must have felt it, too, because she suddenly looked puzzled. He wanted to say something reassuring, to convince them both that they were simply beginning their series of acting assignments for the next six weeks, but Riley's voice interrupted the music and stopped his thoughts.

"Ladies and gentlemen, thank you so much for joining us tonight. While we have a few upcoming things happening within the fashion house that we'll also be talking about tonight, we don't want to keep you in suspense any longer about the big reveal. As always, the patriarch of our family, my father, Mr. Ron Gold, will start the announcements."

Major had taken Nina's hand without thought, moving them until they stood to the side with Riley. The white podium where his sister had introduced their father was alight with the same purple accent as the flowered arch, lounge chairs and high-boy tables throughout the space. On the other side of the podium stood Maurice and RJ, watching as his father stepped up to the microphone.

A tall, distinguished-looking man with a bald head and stern facial features, Ron Gold was the epitome of fashion dressed in an original RGF chocolate-brown suit, crisp white shirt and canary yellow silk tie.

"I'll echo my daughter's gratitude for your attendance tonight. We know you're normally ready for a few industry announcements at this event, but this year we have something a little more special," he began. "As you know, we've had a very successful launch into this year's Fashion Weeks with the unveiling of our Golden Bride Collection in February. Well, tonight the Gold family is pleased to announce that not only are we celebrating a phenomenal episode in bridal fashion, we're also overjoyed with the engagement of our son Major to the lovely Ms. Nina Fuller."

At first there were gasps followed by the low buzz of murmurs before multiple camera flashes lit up the room. Applause began with a quick burst and Nina's fingers trembled in his. Major gave her hand a little squeeze and then lifted it to his lips to kiss. Another impromptu action that sent the crowd into more clapping and more picture-snapping.

Normally, this would be the point where Major would turn away, leaving the beast of pictures and questions behind. If it wasn't after an RGF show, where Ron liked for each of his children to make comments to demonstrate they were all personally and professionally vested in the presentations, then Major didn't deal with the tabloids or the press. Yet tonight, he stood a little straighter and squared his shoulders. For the first time, he didn't mind having pictures taken with this woman beside him. Perhaps because this time he—meaning the marketing team—was orchestrating the response of every reporter and photographer in this space.

It was a surreal moment, one he'd never thought he'd experience. The announcement of his wedding. He reminded himself it was fake and shook off the feeling of excitement that had started to blossom in the pit of his stomach. Instead, he turned to look at Nina, who was smiling—no, she was beaming as she looked from one camera to another, the tilt of her head and easy movement of her body as if she'd practiced for this moment all her life. She appeared so natural, her hand so comfortable in his. That odd stirring he'd had when they first stood under the arch moved through him again and this time he knew it wasn't solely arousal. Desire was a definite between them and very easy to acknowledge and understand. This other thing, not so much.

When she returned her gaze to Major's, he immediately felt at ease. So, when the first question came directly to him from a reporter, he didn't think twice before responding.

"This is all so exciting and fast, Major. Where and when did you and Ms. Fuller meet?"

"We met earlier this year and I wasn't aware there was a time clock ticking on love." He had no idea where that response had come from, but it seemed like a good answer. And, if he wasn't mistaken, it made Nina's smile a little brighter.

Another reporter took advantage of the fact that Major was actually answering questions, even though it hadn't been announced that he would.

"So how did he sweep you off your feet, Ms. Fuller?"

She didn't look at him to gauge his response, she simply continued to smile and began a story that sounded very real.

"It was Valentine's Day and neither of us had a date. We ended up at the same bar, *not* crying in our drinks." Nina chuckled and so did the reporter. "Next thing I know, we're having dinner on a rooftop like this one, talking about all the people who put too much emphasis on Valentine's Day. After that we were together every weekend, either here in the city or in Pennsylvania where I'm from. So if you count quiet walks in Central Park and sitting in rocking chairs on my dad's back porch as being swept off my feet, then yeah, that's just what he did."

"Aww, that's so sweet," the woman reporter said.

"So you're the Fashion House Romantic instead

of the Fashion House Playboy. That's not as good a headline," the guy said, chuckling when the woman elbowed him.

"These lovebirds have lots of planning to do," Ron interrupted. "And we're going to keep you up to date with those plans. But for now, we have more announcements."

Thankful for the reprieve, Major offered the press another smile, before leaning in to whisper in Nina's ear, "Our part's done. Let's get out of here."

Her quick nod and the instant look of relief that washed over her face also reminded him the smile and natural movements he'd just glimpsed were part of the sham. She didn't want to be there any more than he did.

If Cinderella hadn't run away from the ball at the stroke of midnight, she may have walked into a room with Prince Charming following closely behind, feeling the quick jolt of excitement, anticipation and lust.

Nina was feeling every one of those things and then some as she slid the card over the panel on the door and walked into her hotel room. Just twenty-four hours ago she'd entered this same room, but she hadn't been wearing a designer dress that sparkled with what she'd now identified as success, nor had there been a great-looking guy standing just a few feet behind her.

"Would you like a drink?" It sounded cliché but polite nonetheless.

"Sure. I'll pour," he said as they moved into the

living area of the suite. Just a few feet away stood a large round table with two chairs on either side. It sat in front of the only window with a view of one of the New York streets. Buildings, people and lots of cars were below even at almost eleven at night.

"I'll be back in a sec." She made her way into the bedroom when she heard her phone ringing inside her purse.

"Hey," she answered as she sat on the bed.

"Where are you? I've been texting and calling you all night," Angie said. "Dad's worried sick and ready to call the police to file a missing person report, and Daisy wants to get in the car to drive up there to bring you home."

Nina sighed. She hadn't called them back after telling them this morning that she'd missed her train. So much had happened in those twelve hours that she hadn't completely forgotten about her family, but she had put them on the back burner for a change.

"Sorry. I meant to call you sooner to explain what's going on."

"Okay. Well, explain now."

Right. Explain how the deal she'd finally been able to land had somehow morphed into a six-week assignment that could either make or break her experience in the fashion industry. She glanced over at the window, to the night sky in the big city, still in awe of where she was and how she'd come to be there.

"They offered me a project for six weeks. It's kind of like a trial run for the business with a few other duties." There, that didn't sound so crazy.

"What do you mean 'other duties'? Are they going to use your app or not? And why'd you have to stay longer just to get the job? Dad's been asking for you and I can't spend another night here. I've got the night shift for the next five days at the hotel."

Angie worked at a casino hotel and often had the night shift, which meant Nina had the night shift with their father because Daisy was the most unreliable of the Fuller sisters.

"You and Daisy will have to work out a schedule. I'm going to be here for the next six weeks as part of this deal I've accepted."

"What are you talking about? It's just an app. Either they're using it or they're not—and if they are, it's not necessary for you to stay there during some trial period."

"It's necessary if I'm also pretending to be the guy's fiancée to help their company boost sales," she blurted.

After only a couple seconds' hesitation, Angie all but yelled through the phone, "What? Are you serious? You're like some escort?"

"I am not an escort," she snapped. She wasn't aware of escorts wearing designer gowns and getting a personal driver. Although she could be mistaken, considering she'd never made it her business to know what escorts did or didn't do, or have or didn't have.

"Look, this is the biggest opportunity of my life and I'm taking it. So for the next six weeks, I'll be Major Gold's fake fiancée and his company will be featuring my app on all of its web sites."

Angie was silent for a moment. "And what happens after that? He offers to put you up in an apartment and you continue to be at his beck and call?"

Nina rolled her eyes even though Angie wasn't there to see how exasperating her comments were. "This isn't *Pretty Woman*," she said, referring to one of the Fuller sisters' favorite movies. "It's a job that I plan to do to put my business in a better position in this industry."

"This is insane and Dad's not gonna like it."

"He'll like it when it provides a way for me to take care of him on a long-term basis," she quipped. "Look, I gotta go. Just figure out a new schedule with you and Daisy and keep me posted. I'll be home as soon as this is over."

Angie wasn't happy when she hung up and Nina wasn't nearly as giddy as she'd been when she'd first walked into the room. In fact, as she disconnected the call and let her hands drop into her lap, she wondered briefly if Cinderella's coach had just turned into a pumpkin.

Ten minutes later, she walked back into the living area. Major had removed his jacket and tie, and was sitting on the couch, surfing TV channels.

"Everything okay?" he asked when she took a seat beside him.

She nodded. "It's fine. My sister called, so I had to give her an update on the change in plans."

"Do you live with your sister?"

"Ah, no. I have two sisters and we each have our own apartments, but we take care of my dad, so we're in constant contact with each other about schedules and such."

"Is your father sick?"

The immediate hint of concern in his tone initially surprised her, but that was because Angie's comments about escorts were still rambling in her mind.

"COPD. He was diagnosed years ago, but it's getting worse." To the point where he was almost debilitated, although Jacoby would never admit that.

Major's expression turned thoughtful, his brow furrowing a bit. "I'm sorry to hear that."

She shook her head, wanting to think of something else and feeling slightly guilty for admitting that fact.

"Thanks. Actually, that brings up something I was thinking on the ride over here."

He muted the television and dropped the remote on the cushion between them. "What's that?"

"If we want this charade to be believable, we should get to know each other better. We managed to do pretty good tonight, but what if I'm asked some personal questions about you? How will I know what to say?"

He frowned, thick brows slanted over brown eyes. The top button of his shirt was undone and Nina could see not only the tawny hue of his skin but also the slight ridge of his Adam's apple. She licked her lips quickly as a flash of thought—her tongue gliding over that ridge—soared through her mind.

"I don't give interviews unless it's right after a show. You aren't required to give interviews, either.

Take pictures, attend parties or whatever events are on the itinerary, and that's it."

Like arm candy. She'd often looked through fashion magazines or watched shows where dashing industry big shots had gorgeous women on their arms. Those women never spoke, just smiled for the camera and looked beautiful.

"That's not going to work," she said. Late last night and well into the early morning hours, she'd decided that if this was going to be her first big introduction to the industry, she wanted it to look good. Playing the part of his fiancée as convincingly as possible would lessen the chance that someone might find out it was fake, and thus damage her credibility. "We need to be convincing."

For a few quiet seconds Major just stared at her. In those moments, she breathed in the scent of his cologne, loving the spicy edge to the fragrance. She let her gaze linger over the breadth of his shoulders and the way his pale gray dress shirt molded his biceps and chest. His hands were resting on his thighs, a gold watch on his wrist, a chunky gold ring on his third right-hand finger.

"Are you saying you want to kiss me again?"

Noooo, that wasn't what she was saying, but now that he'd mentioned it...

"I'm saying that we should take this time to get our story straight. We improvised how we met and the whirlwind love affair, but I'm betting word will spread fast that you actually talked to the press without being at a show and that's going to give every other reporter even more guts to ask both of us questions."

"Questions like when was our first kiss?" he asked with a lift of a brow.

"You're obsessed with kissing."

"I didn't used to be," he said with a shake of his head. "But I can admit that I've been thinking a lot about kissing you again."

She swallowed and wondered if Prince Charming had thought about kissing Cinderella. *Most definitely!* Hadn't he gone through an entire village using a shoe to try to find her? That wasn't just so he could ask her name and make sure she was wearing both shoes...

"The kiss was very nice, but I'm referring more to how we'll make our appearances seem believable."

He sat straighter, seeming to shake off whatever was preoccupying him. "You may have a point. So let me ask you this, how did you like feeling my hands on you tonight?"

Oh, she hadn't thought of that. He had kept an arm around her for most of the time they'd been at the cocktail party and it had felt...good. Before the announcement, it had also drawn lots of attention from the women in the room. For a few moments, her mind had wondered if Major had been romantically linked to any of them before. She'd told herself then that it was a silly thought and reminded herself again at this moment. Worrying about Major running off and leaving her for whatever reason or doing something else to break their trust wasn't something she had to worry about, because none of this was real.

"I liked it," she admitted.

"Good, because there were lots of pictures being taken. I fully expect to see us on the front page of one or two tabloids in the morning."

Even after her personal admonishment, she couldn't help thinking back to how his hand had stayed fixed at the small of her back, her side flush against his. There were also the tight embraces while they'd posed for pictures, the embraces that had left her feeling warm all over. The physical attraction between them was off the charts and there was no use trying to deny that.

"That's, uh, good, right?" She sounded hopeful, even though she prayed he couldn't hear that.

"In this instance, yes. You want to know what else was good?"

"What?"

"Feeling your body against mine. Do you think we should practice more of that to be more convincing to the public?"

CHAPTER SIX

"Yes."

It was a simple word. She could have begged off and talked more, sticking to them rattling off facts about each other, but she didn't want to. Tonight she'd worn a gorgeous dress and attended a lavish rooftop party in New York City, something she'd dreamed of happening once her position in the industry was solidified.

Well, if this were really her dream then Nina was going to make it the best damn dream ever!

"What I mean is, if we were really engaged, what would we be doing right now?"

He eased closer to her, his eyes going just a bit darker as he kept them focused on her. "Do you really want the answer to that question?"

"I do." Because she suspected his answer was similar to hers.

Nina couldn't even remember the last date she'd been on, which meant that the last time she'd had sex was even further back than she'd first imagined. It had been too long and here was Major, looking handsome and smelling like a slice of heaven. They were pretending they were involved in a relationship, why not pretend a little more?

"Well, if we were really engaged, I'd probably be ready to get you out of that dress."

She'd crossed one leg over the other when she'd sat a few minutes ago and now she was thankful because she could press her thighs together tighter this way. The timbre of his voice combined with the idea of his hands moving over her body to remove the dress was deliciously enticing.

"Then, once you were naked, I'd bend you over this couch so that I could taste you."

She didn't reply, thinking if she remained silent, he'd keep talking and the warmth of desire spreading through her veins like wildfire would continue. Her tongue wasn't as obedient and it snaked out to move over her bottom lip. His gaze immediately dropped, following the action.

"Do you know how you taste, Nina? You're licking your lips like you recall. Tell me, are you as sweet as I believe you are?"

He was inside her mind. It was an eerie feeling to believe that he could see into her deepest thoughts. Share her memories of when she was alone in the bedroom of her small apartment in York, using her favorite vibrator to find her pleasure. And afterward, when a deep urging inside had her lifting that vibrator to her lips so that she could taste herself.

"Sweet and spicy, like a delicious drink that leaves you feeling just a little light-headed and a lot addicted," she said with the same confidence she'd felt when she'd presented her app to him.

Now he was licking his lips. She recalled those lips pressing into hers and wanted to feel them again.

"I'll bet you're slick and warm right now."

"And I'll bet you're growing just as hard as you were the first time I met you."

He'd been very hard, like her hand was brushing over steel, warm and enticing steel. The memory had her clenching her thighs together again, but this time the pulsating continued to the point of throbbing.

"If we were really engaged, I'd fuck you on this couch. In that bed. Over that table. Against that wall."

His voice was gruff as he moved close enough that the side of his body touched hers. Initial contact sent sparks soaring through her, to the point she thought she might just combust with the friction.

"If we were really engaged, we'd have been unable to keep our hands off each other while we were riding in the car." Because, yeah, she'd wanted to reach out and touch him then, but she'd refrained. Now, she wasn't so sure they were going to keep playing by those same rules.

Seconds later she had her answer when Major reached out a hand to cup her jaw. He leaned in closer, his gaze once again on her mouth.

"This is the beginning," he whispered, his breath warm as it fanned over her face. "If you don't tell me right now that this is not what you want, that you're only down for the façade we put on in public, I'm going to continue."

Her hand came up from her lap to press against his toned chest where his heart thumped persistently beneath.

"I won't object if you continue." In fact, she might be at the point of begging.

He closed the distance between them, taking her mouth in what she knew was going to be a heated and hungry kiss.

It was delicious, the way her tongue instantly moved to meet his, the way his tangled with hers in a hot duel that felt at once familiar and decadent. He tilted her face as he leaned in closer, deepening the kiss. She moaned and wrapped an arm around his neck. The hand on his chest flattened against his taut pectoral.

"As beautiful as it is, I want this dress off." The words were a ragged whisper as he briefly pulled his lips from hers. His teeth scraped along her jawline as she tilted her head back to give him better access.

In seconds his tongue was stroking up and down the line of her neck while his words tumbled through her mind. Was he asking permission to take her dress off? Had she already answered him?

She couldn't think beyond the heated path of moisture moving along her neck and the feel of his hands on her shoulders, going down her arms until they brushed the sides of her breasts. She sucked in a breath and released it on a ragged moan.

The zipper to the dress was on her right side. She

could reach it, but she'd have to move her hands from where they'd flattened on his chest and the back of his head. She didn't want to, but the urge to be naked beneath him was quickly taking charge.

"Now..." he grumbled, lifting her right arm to join the other one locked around his neck.

Whatever he'd said before that one word led to his fingers nimbly easing her zipper down, until the dress felt loose against her chest. He eased away from her and stood, his breath coming in heavy pants that matched hers. Taking her hands, he pulled her to her feet and removed the dress.

For what seemed like much longer than a few seconds, he simply stared at her body. She'd decided against wearing the uncomfortable shaper Lila and her crew had provided earlier. Now she wore only the black strapless bra and matching thin wisp of lace that constituted panties, which had come from the small suitcase the crew had also left in her room. In those seconds, a quick spurt of insecurity shot through her. Did he like what he saw? Was her stomach too round? Were any stretch marks visible?

Swallowing and squaring her shoulders, she said, "Your turn," and reached for the buttons on his shirt.

He kept his gaze locked on her fingers as she worked along his torso and then to each wrist until she could push his shirt off. She wasted no time lifting the undershirt up and over his head, wanting to touch his warm skin as quickly as possible. Just a shade darker than his complexion, her fingers looked as if they belonged splayed over his muscled chest.

She slid her hands across smooth skin, letting the tip of her pointer finger linger on the tight nub of his nipple before moving down to the cut of his abs. When her hands went lower and brushed his belt buckle, he grabbed each wrist.

"Turn around." The words were gruff and a bit more forceful than anything else he'd ever said to her, sending a rush of pleasure through her body.

She stepped out of the dress and turned until she was facing the couch, her backside vulnerable to his perusal.

"What is this?"

His fingers touched her waist, raising one of six rows of waist beads she wore.

She'd almost forgotten she was wearing them. It was something she'd worn since she was a teenager, changing the colors to match whatever mood she was in at the time. She always wore them as a sign of femininity and also as a way of keeping an eye on her weight.

"African waist beads," she told him and left off the complete history and function of the beads because his hands were moving around her waist, lifting the beads and caressing the skin beneath.

"I've never seen anything so sexy before in my life," he whispered.

Sensuality was another effect of the beads, so while she'd had a moment of insecurity over the appearance of her body to him, it had quickly been replaced by her own assurance that she was a sensual and desirable woman. Hearing his confirmation that he was feeling the same way was only a boost to the confidence she already possessed.

When his exploration of the beads was over, his hands moved down farther, until his fingers were slipping beneath the lace panties. He pushed them past her hips and down her legs, keeping an arm around her waist to steady her as she stepped free of them. His hand cupped her juncture and he pulled her hard against his body.

"Soft, wet, hot." He leaned his face down and whispered into the crook of her neck. "Just how I knew you'd feel."

His fingers separated her folds, easing between to feel the moisture of her arousal.

"So good." He groaned. "So damn good."

He wasn't lying. His fingers, moving so intimately between her legs, felt better than anything she could have ever imagined. When he thrust a finger inside her, she hissed, coming up on the tips of her toes as pleasure shot through her like fireworks.

Her head fell back against his shoulder and she cupped her breasts.

"Let me see 'em," he mumbled as his teeth nipped her neck.

She pushed the bra down and her breasts were bared. Squeezing them in her hands, she kept her eyes closed while knowing that he was looking down at her ministrations. This position felt wickedly erotic, with him behind her, his finger thrusting inside her, his mouth at her neck and his gaze zeroing in on her breasts. She kneaded them harder, being sure to play with her nipples. He groaned, his dick getting harder as it pressed against the slit of her ass.

"I can't do this," he said, stepping back from her.

For a second Nina felt confused and incomplete, thinking this interlude might be over before it had really begun.

He pulled his hands from her and, just when she was going to turn and ask what was going on, she heard his belt buckle as he undid it and then dragged down the zipper of his pants. Okay, well, that answered her question. He wasn't done with her yet, and she was glad. Twisting her arms around her back, she unhooked her bra. She had no idea where he'd gotten it from, but the next thing she heard was the tear of the condom packet. Barely a minute later, he bent her over the couch, her hands planted on the soft cushions as he spread her legs.

"It's not going to be slow, but it'll be good. Damn, I can't wait, it's gonna be so good."

"I'm ready for good," she said and nodded her agreement before sinking her teeth into her bottom lip as desire and anticipation gripped her throat.

He didn't lie. He thrust into her in one fast, deep stroke that almost sent her soaring over the couch. But she'd planted her feet on the floor and clenched the cushion in her fingers. She did gasp as her body stretched and acclimated to his presence.

"My fiancée," he said as he pulled out slightly and thrust back in. "You're my fiancée."

He pumped fast, in and out, until she was breathless, full and so wet her essence dripped down to her inner thighs.

"Fiancé," she whispered. "You're my fiancé."

They were trying to convince each other and themselves. Taking the charade they'd agreed upon to a level neither of them had anticipated.

"Mine," he groaned.

"Mine!" she screamed when his hand came around to toy with her clit as he continued to pump into her.

Hard and fast and damn delicious, that's what this was. Fake engagements, contracts for app usage, bumping into him in the hallway, showing him her waist beads—none of it mattered. Not in these seconds, because there was only this. Only the pleasure that was soaring through her.

When her legs were through shaking, he eased out of her, maneuvering them until this time he sat and she straddled his lap. He ran his fingers over the beads again as she settled onto his length.

"These are driving me crazy. Do you wear them all the time?"

She sighed at the sensation of him filling her once more and circled her hips until his balls pressed against her wet lips. "Mmm-hmm," she replied.

"All day. Every day." He talked while he pumped and she gripped her breasts, kneading them as pleasure built inside her once more.

"Let them go," he told her. "I want to see them bounce."

She did as he requested and clamped her hands

onto his shoulders, bracing herself as his thrusts increased. She matched his movements, riding him until the sound of their joining echoed in the air. He leaned in until the movement of her breasts could slap against his cheeks.

"So good," he mumbled. "So damn good."

"Yes!" she yelled when she knew another release was imminent. "Yes!"

"Yes, so…damn…good." He held her close, his face buried so thoroughly between her breasts she wondered if he could breathe. She came at the exact moment her thighs trembled around him once more.

She wasn't his.

This was an arrangement; one designed for their mutual benefit. And since it was a business agreement, there should have been boundaries. Lines that they would not cross. Things they would not do that could interfere with the goals they'd each set.

An hour after leaving her hotel, Major rested his elbows on the desk in his home office and dropped his head with a heavy sigh. He'd messed up big-time.

But he could fix it before his slip endangered the arrangement. The last thing he wanted was for Nina to think he was taking advantage of their business deal, using it as an opportunity to have sex with her. So, he sat straighter in the chair and put his fingers on the keyboard. Nina's email address was already typed and now he added the subject line: GUIDELINES.

He shook his head and pressed the backspace button. Then he typed again: RULES.

No, that wasn't going to work, so he deleted that, too.

In all his years, he'd never had to type an email like this. He'd also never left a woman almost immediately after having sex with her.

"I'll see you in the office at ten," he'd said after coming out of the bathroom.

She'd been sitting on the couch. While he'd been in the bathroom, she must have gone into the bedroom to grab her robe because it was belted tightly at her waist as she sat with her hands in her lap.

"Right," she'd replied. "I received the email adding that to the itinerary."

"Good. Okay. Well then, good night." The words had come in a clipped tone and he'd walked out of her hotel room, closing the door soundly behind him.

Now he was at his desk, preparing to tell her that what had happened would never happen again. Via email. It struck him then that this might be a tad immature, or perhaps even unnecessary. What if she was having the same never-again conversation with herself right at this moment? What if…he'd really messed up. It never occurred to him that sex with her would be so…so fantastic and intense and, damn, he'd messed up bad. Yeah, he was definitely sending her an email because in person this might turn into a discussion and the boundaries he needed to set for his own sanity weren't up for negotiation.

FOLLOW-UP.

He stared at the letters for a moment before deleting them, too.

This was ridiculous. Was he really going to tell this grown and exceptionally attractive woman that they couldn't touch each other again? Because that's what it was going to take. He'd decided on the ride back to his penthouse that touching her—in any capacity—was only going to make him want her more. There were plenty of couples who didn't engage in PDA, so that wasn't out of the ordinary.

But he and Nina weren't a real couple. They never would be after Stacia's conniving ways. Major had learned his lesson about being a Gold and trying to have a real relationship.

With that thought, Riley and Chaz immediately sprang to mind. His sister and her boyfriend were always touching—holding hands, Chaz touching her arm, Riley leaning in to him as he said something. All acts that, as Riley's big brother, made Major uncomfortable to see. But his parents were no different. How many times had he seen his father squeeze his mother's ass while growing up? He closed his eyes tightly and groaned. The answer was too many for his comfort. But Ron Gold loved his wife Marva without reservation. They were a partnership in love and in business and still going strong after thirty-seven years of marriage.

ADDENDUM.

Major typed the letters and this time didn't stop typing until a five-item list and two paragraphs were complete.

He hit Send and closed his computer before he could think better of the action. Sex with Nina had been great—if he were inclined to be specific, it was jolting, surprising, tantalizing—but it wasn't part of the plan. The plan that Major had worked on for far too long to be curtailed by a beautiful woman wearing colorful and sexy-as-hell waist beads that he knew would forever stay on his mind.

CHAPTER SEVEN

"I RECEIVED YOUR EMAIL" was the first thing Nina said when she walked into Major's office the next morning.

He was sitting behind his desk and had looked up the moment he heard her voice.

"Landra told me to come right in since you were expecting me." She set her bag on the floor next to one of the guest chairs across from his desk but didn't take a seat.

Before getting started with business, she had to say what she'd rehearsed since reading his message at two this morning.

"What happened last night was consensual, just in case you may be thinking you used your Fashion House Playboy vibes to seduce me. You didn't. I do what I want when I want."

That came out much better than the dozen or so times she'd said it to the bathroom mirror.

"I'm aware of that," he replied as he put down the pen he was holding and stared at her. "I just thought it would be a good idea to outline some rules."

"Rules to outline a charade." She nodded. "Okay,

I can get with that." She didn't really have a choice. She wasn't walking away from this deal and she'd had him once, that would suffice. "I've noted each of the rules you've set—from the 'no kissing' all the way down to the 'no standing too close to each other in private'—and replied to the questions about my basic likes and dislikes."

"I saw them."

But he hadn't responded. So they were going for the cordial coolness. She could do that, too.

"Good. Now if we're questioned on the basics of our family, where we came from, schools we went to and future goals, we've got that covered." By habit, she smoothed the gunmetal-gray pencil skirt down before sitting, even though it was so tight it wasn't moving anywhere without some assistance on her part. This was definitely one of her size-fourteen days.

"They won't ask us questions like that. All they're really concerned about is the wedding date and who'll be designing your gown."

And yet his email had asked questions like "What's your favorite movie?" and "Do you read while sitting on your father's back porch?"

"Well, I'd think that would be obvious," she said and tried her best not to think of how handsome he looked sitting behind his cherrywood desk in that mammoth burgundy office chair.

He was just a guy and there was no need for her to act any differently because she'd thought about this guy all night long.

"The others on my team will be here in a few moments. After I make the introductions, they'll take you to an office we had set up for you and get you started on the integration."

"But you're going to stay here," she said slowly. "You have other work to do. More important work."

He ran a hand over his chin and sat back in his chair. For endless moments he didn't speak, only stared at her as if he were memorizing everything about her. It made her wonder if he was possibly reconsidering this distance he'd decided to put between them, but then he cleared his throat and shook his head.

"I run an entire department as well as a few outside projects. I can't be at every meeting."

Nor did she need him at every meeting with her. She was being silly when she was supposed to be presenting a strong and unshakable front. That had to stop now.

"Great. I'm ready to get started. There's nothing on our agenda for tonight, so I'll make some plans to take in another play or possibly do some shopping to pick up something nice for my dad." And he didn't need to know all of that.

"Sounds good," he told her and went back to staring at whatever papers were on his desk.

Well, that hadn't been awkward at all. Except, yeah, it had.

Obviously, Major wasn't as good as she was about being calm, cool and collected. When Ken and Jenner, who'd been in her first meeting, came into the room, she stood and shook their hands. Major made more formal introductions and they ushered her out of his office. He didn't say another word to her and she didn't bother to look back at him or say anything else to him, either. If this was how they were to conduct their working relationship, so be it. She hadn't signed up for anything more, anyway.

Three days later, Nina sat in the backseat of the town car looking out the window while Claude drove through traffic. This afternoon her style was sexy bohemian. At least, that's what Lila had told her three hours ago when she'd entered Nina's hotel room as if she were a runway model.

"You're going to look subtly sexy in this, honey!"

Nina had smiled at the woman's exaggeration as she spoke. She was getting used to how the woman talked and worked. And since this was the first runway show she'd ever attended in person, Nina figured she'd trust the stylist's directive. Riley had also told Nina she could decline to wear anything Lila suggested if she truly didn't like it or felt uncomfortable, but Nina was finding it pretty easy to trust the woman's judgment.

And true to form, Lila had been correct. The light material fell over her body like a soft breath, the muted-color stripes complementing her complexion. The plunging halter neckline was super sexy. She wondered how Major would react to seeing her in the dress.

Number three on his list of things they weren't going to do anymore was "touch each other sexually." And he hadn't, not since the night they'd had the hard, fast and totally titillating sex in her hotel room.

Of course, not touching had been much easier since they'd only been together one other time following the meeting in his office the day after their sexcapade.

Yesterday's lunch had been at Sarabeth's Central Park South, a restaurant where Desta knew they would retain maximum visibility. And she'd been right; they'd been stared at the entire time they were eating by other guests at the restaurant and even some of the staff. Nina was certain that a few people snuck pictures on their cell phones. But there'd been no touching. In fact, Major seemed to have gone out of his way to be as reserved as he possibly could—a fact that was slowly starting to bug her.

Not for the obvious reasons. She wasn't falling for him and didn't need him to reciprocate feelings that weren't there. But they did need to appear comfortable with each other for their charade to be believable.

Nina brushed those ideas from her mind as the car came to a stop in front of what looked like an industrial building. The itinerary stated she would be attending an intimate showing of RGF's couture gowns with Major.

"I'll walk you inside," Claude said when he opened the door for her.

Nina stepped out onto a quiet sidewalk in the Financial District, which was in stark contrast to the streets around her hotel or the RGF building. Claude closed the car door and walked with her a few feet until he could open a huge steel door for her to enter.

Inside, the place looked very different. Golden lights hung in large circles from an exposed-beam ceiling, creating soft light that mingled with the natural light pouring in from a wall of paned windows. Bleached hardwood floors stretched throughout and up the wide staircase.

"I'll call when I'm ready," she told Claude after she'd looked around, but he was already shaking his head.

"No need. Mr. Gold informed me that he would take care of your transportation for the remainder of the evening."

Oh he did, did he? Well she wondered what that meant.

But it was too late to think too hard on that because Maurice came up to her, devilishly handsome smile already in place.

"Hey, Nina. How are you?"

"I'm great. How's everything going here? Is there anything I can do to help?"

His thick brows furrowed, an action she'd seen Major do on a few occasions. It was amazing how much alike the two of them were without being identical. There was, of course, a resemblance—but there were differences, as well. While Major seemed to always be in control of his thoughts and actions, Maurice gave off a more relaxed demeanor. His ready smile, and that twinkle in his eyes she knew women were most likely dying for, identified him as the more extroverted twin.

"Not at all. We've got a great event staff and they're

taking care of everything. How've your first few days been at the fashion house?"

"So far, so good," she replied. "The integration went better than expected and we've already started to see sales."

"Cool. That sounds like a good sign."

"It is. And this place is great, so I know the show will be terrific. I'm really excited to be here." And that wasn't a part of the charade.

"The production team has put a lot of planning into it, so I'm sure you're right and it'll be terrific. But we're about to start and I was told to escort you to your seat."

He extended his arm to her and she accepted it, telling herself there was no need to ask who'd sent him. It was Major, who was obviously still trying to keep his distance.

The room they entered was full of photographers standing with cameras in hand, and she was willing to bet there were several reporters, bloggers and fashion journalist seated in the chairs positioned in rows around a glossy white runway.

The show started seconds after she sat, and she crossed her legs, trying to ignore the empty seat beside her. Maurice had walked behind a black curtain and, when Nina looked around, she didn't notice anyone else. But there were many eyes on her, so instead of looking the way she felt—confused and teetering on angry—she smiled and pushed one heavy curl of hair behind her ear. Anything was better than the obvious—that Major wasn't with her.

The music was hip-hop, the models were amazing and the gowns exquisite. When the show was over, Nina stood, clapping just as loudly as anyone else in the room. Until Major stepped up beside her.

"Glad you're enjoying yourself," he said when he leaned in to whisper in her ear.

"Glad you could finally join me," she replied without turning to look at him.

Maurice and two other men stepped through the black curtain with smiles and partial bows as the crowd continued to applaud in appreciation of the twelve gowns they'd just been treated to. Cameras were busy clicking throughout the space.

"We're going to go out this side door before the crowd begins to disperse. The room is set up for a press conference, but Maurice and the designers from today's collection are prepared to deal with it. We're just here to be seen."

He spoke to her like he would to any other employee and Nina tried her best to accept his cool demeanor as the new norm.

"Fine. Shall we go now?"

This time she did look at him, but she ignored the way the beige jacket hung enticingly on his broad shoulders. The white shirt that molded to his chest and the matching beige slacks completed what should have been a bland outfit choice but instead, on him, was just another symbol of how attractive this man really was. He nodded at her and she stepped in front of him, walking toward the only exit she saw and praying he was following closely behind her. Otherwise it might appear that she was angry and walking away from him, something that would most likely set tongues to wagging.

"It should only take twenty minutes, then we have reservations for dinner. After that we'll be done for the night."

"I read the itinerary, Major. I know what we have to do tonight."

He snapped his lips shut tightly and when she thought he might give a different retort, the first of the reporters filed into the room. Maurice came up behind them and Major clapped one hand on his brother's shoulder while shaking the other.

"Another slam dunk," he said.

"You bet your ass!" Maurice replied. "Cordell and Expo are phenomenal designers. This limited Spring in the City line is going to do great, especially once it hits the overseas market."

As if to magnify his words, Cordell Spriggs and Expo—one name only—the designers who had walked the runway and taken their bows with Maurice, came up to join them.

"Congratulations," Nina said, looking at each of them. "The dresses were fabulous."

"Thanks," Cordell said. "You should wear one to something. Maybe as your second outfit at the reception. We can make some changes, cater it specifically to you and your theme. Have you selected a theme for the wedding yet?"

Her mouth opened then shut, and then she simply

shrugged. "Not just yet. But your gowns have definitely given me some ideas."

"It's time to get the press conference started," Major interjected. "We don't want to mess up our timeline."

"He's right," Maurice added after a questioning look between Major and Nina.

Maurice stepped up to the podium, an act that quieted the crowd already assembled in the room.

"Thank you for coming this afternoon. Now, as promised, for the next fifteen minutes, we're going to take a few questions."

A woman in the front row raised her hand and immediately stood.

"I have a question for the new addition to the Gold family, Nina Fuller," she said pointedly. "What's it like working with your fiancé? You've joined the Gold family on two levels—business and pleasure. How did you and Major manage to keep not only your engagement but also your new business partnership a secret for so long?"

Silence filled the room as all eyes rested on her. For a few seconds, Nina wondered if she should speak and, if so, what she would say. Maurice came to the rescue.

"Let me clarify, Cordell, Expo and myself will accept questions about today's show."

"Then why are they here?" the reporter persisted with a nod of her head at Nina and Major. "Are they just showpieces for the company?"

She was brash and persistent, wearing a black

jumpsuit and red mules on her feet. The way she was staring at Nina said she knew something that nobody else knew. Or that she was making an assumption that maybe others were too afraid to make.

"If the Fashion House Playboy is actually getting married, why can't we talk to him or his fiancée about it? Why wasn't the business collaboration announced the other night at the Sip 'n' Chat? Oh, and the most important question, where's her engagement ring?"

It took every ounce of control Nina possessed to not look down at her left hand or the finger she knew was missing an engagement ring. Dammit! Why hadn't she thought of that in her quest to make this fake plan seem as real as possible?

A better question: Why should they have to talk about anything they didn't want to, or that wasn't directly related to this show? But then, that's how this marketing plan was supposed to work—to spark interest and keep the buzz going around the Golds and their new bridal collection. It was her debut in the industry and its very public lifestyle, so if she didn't like invasive questions about an engagement ring she probably should've been wearing, well then, she'd just have to get over it.

"I'm not in the habit of answering questions about my personal life," Nina said to the shock of everyone in the room, except maybe the reporter.

Nina moved until she was behind the podium, multiple microphones banked on the edge to point directly at her.

"But I recognize your need to intrude, especially since we made such a bold and exciting announcement just a few days ago."

"Exactly," the reporter replied with a look of measured satisfaction. "Shall I repeat my question?"

Nina held her gaze and smiled. "That's not necessary. Major and I believe in keeping our personal relationship to ourselves. So while we've announced our engagement, and you'll probably be hearing a lot more about the upcoming wedding plans, everything else between us, including the ring, will stay that way. Regardless of how many surprise questions are tossed at us. And on the business front, the At Your Service app is designed to work alongside fashion houses to offer customers a complete experience. There was an announcement on the home pages of RGF's domestic and international websites a few days ago, which is how I presume you found out, so that hardly qualifies as a secret."

The woman's smirk faltered a bit at Nina's words and, out of the corner of her eye, Nina could see Maurice grinning. She didn't bother to try to see Major's reaction. He probably wasn't having any.

"So you've been dating for four months and now you're getting married. How nice. When's the big day? Have you picked out a dress? Will Riley be one of your bridesmaids? I must admit I thought if there were going to be a wedding in the Gold family, it would be Riley. But then again, she is dating the company's biggest competitor, so making that union legal would probably be a stretch."

This woman is a piece of work. Correction, she's an ass.

"So glad you mentioned Riley. She's been such a great sister-in-law-to-be these past few days. You're correct in assuming she'll be in the wedding, along with my sisters, and we'll all be wearing dresses from the Golden Bride Collection. I'm very excited about selecting the perfect gowns. Are there any more questions about the wedding plans, or should I turn this over to the talented men who made today's show possible?"

Another reporter thankfully spoke up, directing a question to Expo and the phenomenal—his word, not hers—turquoise gown they'd just seen in the show's finale.

As Nina stepped away from the podium, Major reached for her hand. She hesitated just a second, looking up at him in question. His facial expression was still grim and he didn't offer any explanation, but she placed her hand in his and stood beside him for the remainder of the press conference. If he'd thought them not touching for the past few days was in any way going to dull their attraction to each other, he was wrong.

Warmth instantly spread through her body at his touch and her fingers clung to his as they walked. He didn't say a word until they were in the backseat of the car, and that was when he pulled her so close her lips parted on instinct in preparation for his kiss.

CHAPTER EIGHT

"I'M NOT GOING to kiss you, not again." The words hurt his throat as they came out in a scratchy growl.

His chest was heaving as anger poured through him. How dare that annoying Morgana McCloud question Nina the way she did? Major should have known this would happen. There were some reporters and bloggers who hated that he never gave them the comments or interviews they requested. Morgana hated that he'd never accommodated her and that he'd never accepted any of the advances she'd made toward him. If he were the loneliest man on earth, he wouldn't have sought the company of such a woman. He'd known a woman like her before and had sworn to never again get sucked into their clutches.

Now the news about At Your Service was out and that had him wondering once again about the division of Brand Integrated that involved accessorizing for fashion house designs that was very similar to Nina's. When Brand Integrated made its appearance in the fashion world, there was no doubt that very fact would be mentioned. But their charade would be over by then.

"I...um, I didn't ask you to kiss me," she said and then licked her lips.

But she didn't pull away from him. They were in the backseat of the limo he'd reserved for tonight. He released the grasp on her arm and extended one hand to press the button that would close the privacy barrier between them and the front seat.

"It's what got me in trouble the first time. The kiss." He shook his head because he knew he sounded irrational, but that was exactly how he was feeling. It was how he'd been feeling for the past few days, the longer he'd stayed away from her. "Kissing is too intimate. I'm not going to do it again," he stated, trying to calm his tone because her eyes had grown a little wider.

"I'm not going to ask you to kiss me, or to do anything with me, Major." She looked down to where his other hand still gripped her arm and then back up to him in question.

He pulled back as if he'd been burned, cursing at the mere sight of his fingers pressing into her arm. "I'm sorry," he said and sat back against the seat. "I don't know what's going on."

And that was the truth. He didn't know what was happening to him because whatever it was had never happened before. So he'd slept with her, big deal. He'd slept with other women before, and he and Nina were pretending to be a couple, so it should've been fair game. Everything that had happened between them up to this point had been consensual, so why had he needed to write that list creating rules to separate them? And if he'd thought that list was the best plan for them to move forward without any threat of entanglements later, then why had he spent these past few days feeling like crap and needing desperately to be alone with her, to see her, to touch her?

Nina cleared her throat. She sat back and smoothed the skirt of her dress, letting her hands rest in her lap. "Look, maybe you don't have to take this seriously, but I do. Everything we do from the night of the Sip 'n' Chat to the day we have our fake argument is part of my first impression to the fashion industry.

"My work so far has been on a much smaller scale, but this is my opportunity to show the industry who I am and what my business can do for them. We're supposed to be an engaged couple. But I've gotta tell you, we need to do better. That reporter in there was intentional in her questions. There's doubt about this relationship. For whatever reason, she doesn't believe us and if one person doesn't, then others may be wondering, as well."

She was right. Appearances were everything, especially in this industry. Wasn't that why Desta and Riley had come up with this idea in the first place? It's why they knew including a Gold in the campaign would ensure its success. And now, this woman who had no stake in his family company was essentially telling him he wasn't pulling his weight.

"What do you think we should do?" If she said get naked in the back of this limo right now, he'd do it. Damn him, he would.

"First, you've gotta relax and you've gotta act like a man in love."

His head snapped to hers and he saw that she was staring at him. She looked spectacular today. He'd noticed the moment he'd peeked through the curtain and seen her walking in on Maurice's arm. A spurt of jealousy had pierced his chest before he'd cursed and pushed it away. But he hadn't been able to look away from her, not for minutes after she'd taken her seat.

The dress wasn't formfitting but flowing breezily down past her ankles. The halter top cupped her breasts the same way his hands had before. And the muted colors complemented everything from her skin tone to her eye color, to the soft, barrel curls that fell past her shoulders.

"I'm not going to give the press the innermost details of my life, they're not entitled to that." No one was.

"But you'll agree to a stunt that has the prime purpose of playing to the public? Look, whatever we say to them is a lie. It's all a lie." She shrugged as if it were that simple. "We're not engaged. We're not a happily-in-love couple and we never will be. This is a means to an end for both of us."

He wouldn't kiss her. Major had sworn he wouldn't kiss her again. But the touching rule? That was out the window. So he closed the slight distance between them on the seat and he reached for her. She came willingly, sitting across his lap.

"This..." he said quietly. "The tug you feel between us? The one that starts deep in your gut and reaches out, wanting to cling to something, some-one… We cannot deny this. You can't deny it."

She shook her head. "No. I can't. I'm not. But I'm also not going to play this game with you. I'm okay with taking our façade into the bedroom. I can sepa-rate work from personal. But I'm not going to be at your call. Either we stick by your rules implicitly for the duration of this agreement or we don't. There's no in between and there's no up and down."

Basically, she was telling him to get it together. As she had every right to since he was being a jerk with this hands-off, hands-on situation.

He was impressed. He'd thought watching her masterfully handle Morgana in that press conference was awe-inspiring, but holding her on his lap while she fundamentally just ripped him a new one was damn commendable. He cupped her face in his hands and leaned in. Her lips parted and he almost… Major tilted his head and kissed her neck, suckling slightly, creating a path to the skin between her breasts, which was the softest he'd ever touched.

When her arms came around his shoulders and she arched into him, he sighed with relief and with resolution. He was going to play this game by her rules, but first, he was going to have her again.

He continued running his tongue and lips over her skin, moving his hands so that one was at the nape of her neck, pulling her hair gently to tilt her head back. The line of her neck was bare to him and Major stared down as if he were a vampire, hungry for the taste of her. He licked a straight path from between her breasts up to her chin and back down again. She hissed and arched further in his arms. He loved kissing her. It was a fact he could not deny.

To push that thought out of his mind, he eased a hand beneath the halter top of her dress, cupping her bare breasts and sucking in a breath at how good it felt.

"Why do I want you so much?"

Had he said that aloud? He'd been thinking it so much, he no longer knew whether or not it was in his head or if he finally was ready to hear an answer.

"Take what you want," she whispered, bringing her hand up to cover his, moving it so they were both squeezing her breast. "Take what we both want."

Permission. She'd given it before and she was giving it again. Another woman may have walked away from him and this arrangement because of the ridiculous way he'd been acting these past few days. Stacia had walked away from him for less. Any other woman certainly wouldn't have come to his rescue at the press conference, after he'd asked for answers to his questions in that juvenile email he'd sent her. And she damn sure wouldn't be in his arms right now, asking him to give her what she needed.

What he *desperately* needed.

He pulled his hand away, running it down her torso and to her legs where he could pull the material of the dress up. Her legs were bare, and she opened them the moment he touched her skin.

"I'm gonna give you what you need, baby."

"Please," she whispered. "Please give it to me."

It took almost no effort to push the thin silk material of her panties to the side and slip his fingers along the warm folds of her pussy.

She moaned, the arm wrapped around his shoulders tightening against him.

"Yes, baby. You're so hot and ready for me. Ready for this pleasure."

He was, too. His jaw clenched with the need to sink himself so deep inside her that he could no longer think of his past mistakes with women, the present situation he found himself in, or the future that seemed to rest on this beautiful woman in his arms.

She gyrated against his fingers even before he could press them inside her.

"You're ready and you're hot."

"You're talking too much and not doing enough," she said, grabbing his hand with her free one and pressing it into her juncture.

He needed no further encouragement but eased two fingers deep into her, loving the feel of her inner muscles tightening against his intrusion. It was like a cave, a hot cavern of deliciousness that only he could taste, only he could have at this moment. It took him seconds to twist her around until she was lying flat on the seat. He dragged the panties down her legs, dropped them to the floor and propped her legs up onto his shoulders before dipping his head low. His mouth was on her in seconds, tongue stroking over the plump folds of her pussy, lapping up the thick nectar that tasted sweet sliding down the back of his throat.

She yelled out at the contact and he continued, reveling in the sound of her taking the pleasure he offered and the feel of her soft inner thighs rubbing against his face. He suckled her clit, taking the tight bud into his mouth and holding it there until she squirmed beneath him. When her hands went to the back of his head, pushing him further, he groaned and whispered, "Greedy little goddess."

But he gave her what she wanted, thrusting his tongue inside her and moving it with the same urgency he would have moved his dick if he were pounding into her.

"Yessssss."

He would never get tired of that hissing sound in her voice. Never get tired of the scent or taste of her. The taste that was melting all over his mouth at this moment. She moved with his motions, undulating her hips as she held him to her, giving as good as she was getting.

He worked his mouth over her until he thought his chest would explode with desire. Pulling back slightly, he sank his fingers into her again before dragging them out and letting one slide back to her rear. This time she sucked in a breath and held completely still. He rubbed his finger over the tight sphincter, using her juices to ease only the tip of his finger into her.

"Major, I don't... I can't," she whimpered.

He knew the feeling. He couldn't think, either, not past the need and the hunger. His mouth was on her again, tongue easing deep into her just as his finger moved slowly into her other opening. She shivered beneath him, and yelled out until he was certain anyone on the street would hear her. And with that cry came her release, pouring like liquid heaven into his mouth. Major swallowed and he held on tight to the sensation moving through his body along with her essence.

He'd never felt anything like this before and he knew he never would again.

If somebody had told Nina that she'd have a backseat sexcapade in a black limousine, she would have called them a bald-faced liar. Yet, here she sat, closer to the window this time than she had before, staring out at the New York skyline while they drove to her hotel. They'd decided to skip the restaurant and Major was on his phone arranging for dinner to be brought to them there.

She had an elbow propped up on the door, her cheek leaning against a closed fist while thoughts of what they'd done in the back of this limo ran through her mind. Her inner thighs still tingled, and thoughts about whether or not she was doing the right thing ran rampant while her hormones continued to take charge.

There simply was no more right thing to do other than what she was doing. For too long she'd sacrificed everything for someone else, namely her family. Her father hadn't been the same after her mother had left seventeen years ago. And while only twelve at the time, Nina had known that it would be up to her to help Jacoby in any way she could. And so she had. It had never occurred to her to do anything else. It had also never occurred to her that at almost thirty years old, she'd still be dedicating so much of her time to her father and her sisters. But not for the next five weeks. This time was for her, while all that she was doing would ultimately help her family, these days in this city, with this man, doing this job, were for her. And she planned to make the best of every minute.

Even if that meant spending every minute irrevocably aroused by a man she'd never imagined being with.

"The food will be there shortly after we arrive."

His voice jolted her out of her thoughts, and she sighed before looking over at him with a wan smile. "Thanks. I didn't really feel like being out in public again."

"That makes two of us," he said with a nod. "It's been a pretty long day."

"I bet. How long does it normally take to get ready for a show?" She'd been learning more about the inner workings of the industry while working with RGF. The business aspect of the design house seemed to be a smooth-running machine, but it definitely took the skill and expertise of every one of its three-hundred-plus employees. Before this week, it had been easy to believe her app's target was just the Gold family because they called all the shots and had made what was one of the world's most influential and successful Black-owned-and-operated fashion houses what it was today. But this past week she'd definitely learned differently.

"I don't personally do much with the planning of the shows. I make sure all the technology they need to facilitate them is up to par."

"A man of my heart," she said and then clapped her lips shut. It was probably best not to talk about her heart where he was concerned. This wasn't that type of party and she didn't want it to be. Watching her father nurse a broken heart was enough to swear her off any type of emotional connection with a man.

"The programs you've put in place at the fashion house are innovative and seem to be helping to keep things running smoothly," she continued, trying to stay focused.

He stuffed his phone into his pocket and looked over at her. "Technology is the way of the future. And nobody else in my family has the patience for it, so that became my contribution to the company."

Nina felt the same way.

Her sisters worked and sometimes—when berated and guilted to no end—contributed to the expenses associated with taking care of their father when his savings and insurance didn't meet the need. Her love of computers and desire to create had landed her a few contractual jobs that pulled them out of a financial bind a time or two, but she wanted something more stable, something that would allow them to live more comfortably without having to go through the guilt and arguments with her sisters.

"Everyone in your family seems to have found their niche," she said.

"Yeah. I think so."

"Did your parents always expect you'd go into the family business?" She figured if she talked more about his family, she'd feel less depressed about her own.

"Ah, yeah, I think so. I mean we didn't grow up with sketch pads in our hands or fashion magazines instead of literature for reading time. But we learned how much the company meant to our father and my grandfather at a very early age. We all went to college and selected a major with the notion that we'd bring that knowledge back to RGF. It was like an unspoken expectation."

"And none of you strayed. That's amazing and commendable. There's something to be said about family loyalty." Jacoby had taught her and her sisters that when they were young. While Nina knew it was her father's not-so-subtle jab at her mother's leaving, she could also see the overall value in the lesson.

Major didn't reply, but it didn't matter, they were already pulling up in front of her hotel.

Minutes later they were walking into her room.

"I'm just gonna go freshen up a bit. I'll be right back." She headed to the bedroom, did a quick washup and changed into leggings and a bright yellow shirt that hung past her hips, its black-sequined letters spelling "QUEEN" across her chest.

An hour later Major had removed his jacket and

they'd finished the most delicious stuffed cheese-burgers, fresh-cut fries and chocolate milkshakes she'd ever tasted. When he'd suggested they order from the burger place instead of some fancy restaurant, she'd almost hugged him. Now, full from the good food and amiable conversation, she sat back against the cushions and sighed.

"I'm sorry for being such a jerk these past few days." He was sitting with his head resting on the back of the couch, just like her, both with hands folded over now full stomachs.

"It wasn't how I intended to start this agreement between us," he continued.

"Me, either," she admitted. "I mean I really hadn't thought our pretending would lead to actual sex, but I wasn't totally bothered by it."

"I wasn't, either." He paused for a second. "At least, not while it was happening."

"What bothered you about it afterward?" Why she wanted to know, she had no clue. If Major Gold, the reputed Fashion House Playboy had some hang-ups about sex in real life, that was none of her concern.

"I didn't want to seem like I was taking advantage of the situation or mislead you in any way."

"Oh." She hadn't expected that answer. Truthfully, she didn't know what to expect from Major from one minute to the next, but this solemn, compassionate admission definitely wasn't it.

"Despite what the press says, I never want any woman I'm with to have misconceptions about what our relationship is or what it isn't. Even though our connection is more rooted in business, I feel obligated by the same standard."

"That's understandable. But so is being physically attracted to someone."

"I agree."

"So how did you manage to get this reputation that follows you around like a lost puppy, if you're so careful about how the women you date perceive your relationship?"

"When people don't have enough information, they make things up."

"And you don't care to give them more information," she said, thinking back to the way he'd refused to speak at the press conference.

"They're not entitled to know every aspect of my life. Nobody is unless I want it to be so. Just because my family is notable and our business is in the spotlight, doesn't mean I have to personally be there, as well."

She was quiet while she digested those words. Being in the spotlight had never been a problem for her, but she wondered if there was something to the thought that her family wasn't entitled to every aspect of her life, either.

"But you did date three different women in three days. That's gotta mean something." She chuckled lightly after the statement because the pang in her chest as she'd thought about her relationship with her family was far more uncomfortable than ever before.

"One was a distribution rep that was in town from London and was having problems with her laptop. Another was a family friend and a favor to my mother. The other was a real date that I'd scheduled weeks before and didn't feel comfortable backing out of at the last minute. Does that sound like the life of a playboy?"

It didn't. It actually sounded kind of lonely, because at no point had he said he "wanted" to be on a date with any of those women. At least Nina made the choice when and who she dated and, for the most part, she was active in that date. Major sounded as if he were just along for the ride.

"Well, you've got yourself a fiancée now, Major Gold." She reached out and grabbed his hand, lifting their arms up over their heads in a combined fist pump.

He laughed. It was the first time she'd heard the sound and she immediately liked it. She liked it a lot.

"Yeah, I guess I do. And she's a pretty terrific fiancée if I must say so."

"Oh, yes," she said when she'd lowered their hands. "Definitely say so. Frequently."

They both laughed then, and in that moment Nina realized she'd never felt as at ease with another man before. They weren't thinking about having sex—or at least she wasn't—and they weren't discussing work. They were just talking, just being, and she just liked it. A lot.

CHAPTER NINE

THE DUPLEX ON the Upper East Side was bigger than two of her apartments back in York. The stripped-wood flooring and private rooftop terrace were amazing. Nina loved it and she'd told Major so when he'd brought her yesterday to stay here for the remaining month of their agreement.

Today was the first bridal dress fitting. Last week, she and Riley had gone to lunch and afterward sat in Riley's office for the duration of the afternoon going through sketches of wedding gowns, fabric swatches and color wheels. By the time they were finished, six sketches had been selected for Nina, there were three color-scheme finalists and she'd discovered that when it was her turn, Riley didn't want a big wedding.

"Something small, maybe on an island, with just our family and closest friends. That's the perfect wedding for me," Riley had said.

Nina had noted the light in her eyes when she'd spoken about her wedding ideas. A spark that Nina presumed was from being in love and actually believing that a wedding was on the horizon at some point. Nina didn't have that type of imagination.

But she was ready for today. Sitting at the table next to the biggest set of windows with the best northern view of the city, she monitored the activity on her app in correlation to the sales directly from RGF. All the numbers were up. This trial run was going well so far. She clapped her hands together and reached for her mug, frowning when she sipped very cold coffee.

Minutes later she walked out of the gorgeous gray-and-white kitchen with a bottled water and a banana when she heard the doorbell ring.

Somebody was early.

Nina went to the door and smiled when she saw Riley looking fashionably chic in dark jeans, a tan blouse and heels that were way too high for a Saturday afternoon. After greeting Riley and stepping to the side so she could come in, Nina looked down at her weekend attire: gray sweatpants with a matching sweatshirt that was a couple sizes too big, so she looked like a sack of potatoes.

"Sorry I'm so early. I was just eager to get this started and Chaz is out of town until Wednesday. This place is great," she said as she walked straight through the living room/dining room and into the kitchen.

Nina followed.

"Yes, it is. I know Major wanted to make sure we were in a nice place for the fitting and photo shoot, but this might be a little above and beyond." She'd been thinking that ever since last night when Claude had carried her bags from the hotel to the car and driven her over here.

Riley leaned on the island. The eight-foot-long, gray-and-white-marble waterfall island had a stainless steel sink in its center and five clear-backed stools along one side. Nina slid onto one and set her water bottle on the marble top before peeling back the layers of her banana.

"You think he rented this apartment just for the photo shoot?" Riley asked.

"Of course he did. Why else would he rent it?" She took a bite of the fruit and chewed it slowly.

Riley watched her and slipped a grape from the fruit bowl into her mouth.

"I suggested we do the fitting at the office, where we normally have our sample showings. There's a runway there and space to do anything else we wanted."

"That would've been a good option, too," Nina said and seconds later realized the point Riley was trying to make.

"The office is only ten minutes from here and, just like the rest of us, Major spends most of his time there. So this apartment was kinda extra effort."

Nina chewed on another piece of her banana, knowing the woman watched and waited for her next comment to refute the assumption that there was a personal reason Major had gotten this place specifically for her.

"Well, your brother is smart, I can tell you that.

The light in this place is amazing. Pictures are going to come out great. How soon do you think they'll show up in a newspaper or tabloid?" Nina took her last bite of the banana before throwing the peel in the garbage.

Riley was still moving with deliberate slowness, putting one grape at a time into her mouth while watching Nina as if she thought some different words were about to spout out of her mouth. If Major's sister thought she was about to tell her that they were lovers, she was mistaken. While Nina enjoyed Riley's company and had secretly wished her own sisters were as mature and business-minded, there was no way she was telling Riley that there were aspects of this fake engagement that she and Major had decided to make come true.

"We only hire the most reputable photographers in the industry and they've each signed a privacy agreement. We'll get first look and final approval of any pictures to be published and have already sold them to *Infinity* magazine. It's not a fashion-only magazine, but it's Black-owned and respectable. My father is good friends with the owners, Reginald and Bruce Donovan. They're doing a complete spread on the engagement."

It made sense that they would contact a reputable magazine for a story about this engagement. Calling that magazine respectable, however, flew rudely in the face of the fact that the Golds knew this engagement was a sham. So they were asking this great Black-owned magazine to lie. Nina twisted the top

off her water and took a gulp to get the bad taste of
that idea out of her mouth.

"I know what you're thinking," Riley said. "And
remember the argument and breakup that's planned
for the end of this campaign. Nobody will know that
it wasn't ever real to start with."

"Morgana McCloud doesn't think it's real." Nina
couldn't believe she was still thinking about that reporter after Major had explained the woman's fixa-
tion with him.

Morgana had written two stories since the one
after that show that featured her, Major, the engagement and the mention of the At Your Service/RGF
business venture. In each she'd placed a lot of emphasis on where Nina had come from and how she
was apparently "marrying up." The words stung because Nina knew she wasn't getting married at all.
The only consolation was that other tabloids had run
with Morgana's lead but were actually highlighting
the innovative idea that the two businesses connect.
Still, Nina couldn't shake the feeling that Morgana
was specifically feeling some type of way about her.

"She's fishing and has no source that will tell her
any different," Riley stated.

It had been suggested that Nina bring her sisters
to the fitting since Morgana had mentioned her quote
about who was going to be in the bridal party, but
Nina had been vehemently against that. She wished
she'd thought about what she was saying when she'd
said it, but there was no way she would bring Daisy
and Angie into this farce. As much as she wanted

this to seem believable, she hadn't considered that it would put her family in the spotlight. Now, with Morgana hot on her trail, she wasn't sure how long she'd be able to stop that from happening.

The doorbell rang again and Nina quickly slid off the stool to go answer it. She usually liked talking to Riley but she couldn't shake the feeling that their conversation was about to shift in a direction Nina didn't want to go. When she opened the door this time she fully expected to see Lila and her crew, but instead Marva Gold smiled at her.

"Mrs. Gold. Ah, hello. I wasn't expecting you to attend the fitting." And now she was a little more uncomfortable, not just because of the conversation with Riley, but because there were two Gold women in the room with her.

"Hello, Nina. When Riley told me about today's events, I thought it only right that I be here. Do you mind?"

The woman was Black royalty with her tawny-brown complexion and thick silver-streaked hair that was curled and pulled back from her face with a thin black band. She wore a white pantsuit with a pale pink blouse beneath it. Diamond studs dotted her ears and a thin bracelet cuffed her left arm. On her left ring finger was a massive diamond. Nina instantly balled her hands into fists, hoping nobody would see that she still wasn't wearing an engagement ring. Major hadn't mentioned it since Morgana's comment about it—or the lack of it—at the fashion show, and there was no way Nina was asking him to get her a ring. Her pride just wouldn't allow it, not even to make this fake engagement look good.

"No, of course not, I don't mind at all. Come on in," she said and stepped out of the way to let the woman in. She was about to close the door but heard someone clearing their throat.

Nina pulled the door open again and Lila came in with the crew, clothing racks, bags, boxes and her normal flair. By the time Nina closed the door this time she was breathing a sigh of relief that a buffer— or rather a whole group of buffers—had arrived. This should definitely take the pressure off.

It didn't.

Two hours later and the fitting was in full swing. Three photographers from *Infinity* had arrived. Anya and Cheree were pulling the gowns and matching them with shoes and veils while Riley and her mother sat on the couch giving their opinions as Nina walked out into the living room. Garen would quickly give her hair a new look each time she tried on a gown, talking her to death while he worked. And Lila was announcing each gown as if she were the emcee of her own fashion show.

"Now this long-sleeved nude gown includes a pleated tulle overlay and a dusting of shimmering gold Chantilly lace," Lila stated the moment Nina entered the living room.

The photographers immediately moved in, each capturing a picture from a different angle.

"I'm not sure about this one," Nina said as she

moved closer. "It might be a little too nude. My father would have a conniption if he saw this."

Growing up, her father had been extremely strict about his daughters' clothes—how much showed through sheer or tight-fitted items. Although Nina believed she possessed her own style and appreciated clothes that made her feel sexy, some of Jacoby's teachings had stayed with her into adulthood.

"I can understand that," Marva added. She'd risen from the couch and was now standing next to Nina, lifting the tulle out so that it flared even more from her waist down.

"But this is a classic look. It's formfitting but gives the illusion of being natural," Riley added when she joined her mother, standing on the opposite side of Nina.

"And it's so sexy. There's just a hint of innocence in that it covers her completely, but that punch of desire as it hugs her natural curves," Lila added.

"I agree," Marva said. "I love how each of the gowns complements a diverse body type. That's one thing this line does very well."

Riley, who wasn't nearly as curvy as Nina, stood back, one arm across her chest, a hand to her chin while she continued to survey Nina. "Definitely something we were aiming for," she said. "But I can see what she's saying. If I wore this, Dad would have solid opinions about the almost sheerness."

Marva chuckled. "You're right about that. Fathers can be very particular about their girls."

"Too particular," Riley quipped.

"You can say that again," Nina added.

"Okay, let's try another one," Lila prompted.

The photographers had snapped photos of the two Gold women standing with her, adjusting and commenting on the gown. In her mind, Nina could visualize how it would look in print. Normal. Sentimental. A slice of time a woman and her family would remember for the rest of their lives. A pang of unexpected sadness hit her.

They went to the next dress and the next, repeating the process until deciding on a gown that evening. While Nina's personal favorite had been a wine-colored tulle over an ivory fitted bodice and A-line skirt, they'd collectively chosen the classic white trumpet dress with bias-cut organza tiers and rosettes that Garen called romantic.

"I'm exhausted," Nina said when she returned to the living room once again, this time back in her comfortable sweats as she dropped down onto the cushioned chair across from the couch.

"We should grab some dinner," Riley suggested.

"Oh no, I have to get back home," Marva said. "Your father and I have an engagement this evening."

Riley nodded. "That's right, the Rutherford Gala is tonight."

"Yes. You and your brothers should be there, as well. You know your father likes to present a united front at these gatherings," Marva said as she reached for her purse.

"The Rutherfords are old friends of yours and

Dad's. They have nothing to do with us or the company, so we figured we could skip."

"Yes." Marva nodded. "The four of you like to team up whenever possible."

The words weren't spoken with any sting, just a mother's love for her children.

Riley stood with her mother and hugged her. "But we still love you lots," she said with a huge smile just before kissing Marva's cheek.

The sadness that had punched Nina in the gut earlier this afternoon now draped her body like a horrific plague. Lynn Fuller had left her family seventeen years ago, so why did it feel like it was only yesterday?

Nina was just standing when Marva came over and pulled her in for a hug.

"You look tired and we've monopolized your entire day. We'll get out of your hair now so you can get some rest."

Nina had been thinking of doing that and probably squeezing some work in while she ate something quick, like a chicken salad sandwich, in bed. Now, however, a hot bath and burying herself beneath the covers for the next few hours seemed like a better plan.

"Thank you," Nina said without mentioning how good that brief hug felt.

"We're going to have a girls' night soon before we get too crazy with planning and appearances." This time it was Riley who stepped up to pull Nina into a hug.

How did these women know exactly what she needed right now?

"But you'll join us tomorrow for Sunday dinner," Marva said and turned to walk toward the door.

"Oh yes. That's a good idea, Mom." Riley had picked up her purse and was now walking behind her mother.

Nina followed them, not sure what was happening. She'd been here for two weeks and hadn't attended any private family gatherings. "Ah, tomorrow? Dinner?"

"Yes," Riley said, looking over her shoulder at her. "Sunday dinner is a Gold family tradition. It takes place at six every Sunday evening, unless we're all out of town. Then it's usually a phone call from wherever we are in the world."

"Because, above all else, family is first," Marva said.

Nina looked at her and could almost hear her father quoting another African proverb. Jacoby did that often, especially after Lynn had left them. It was as if he'd thought by pouring the teachings of the importance of family from his ancestors into their heads, they would never make the same mistakes.

"Nina, are you okay? You seem so different now. Would you like me to order you something to eat before I go?" Riley asked after her mother had opened the door and they'd walked through.

Nina stayed in the apartment, placing her hand on the doorknob to steady herself. "No. Thanks, really, for being so kind to me, but I'm okay. I have some stuff in the refrigerator and I'm going to have a bath and just chill for the evening." Or wallow in how much she'd missed by not having a mother-daughter relationship to lean on, or even a sister relationship that didn't feel like everyone was leaning on *her* all the time.

Marva stepped close, cupping Nina's cheek. "All will seem better in the morning," she said before kissing Nina's forehead. "I'll see you tomorrow."

Riley smiled at Nina. "Yes, tomorrow. But call me tonight if you just want to chat."

"I will," she said with a nod, really believing that she would reach out to Riley if she could no longer bear the silence or her thoughts tonight.

Nina was lying in bed two hours later, watching some old movie on the television, when her cell phone rang. She glanced over at the phone and saw her father's name on the screen. It was as if Jacoby had somehow known she needed her family tonight.

Nina smiled as she answered. "Hi, Dad. How are you?" She sat up, the pillows behind her back.

"Not too good since I found out my daughter's been lying to me."

Oh no, what had Daisy or Angie done now?

"Who's been lying to you and about what?"

"You and you know what."

Okay, she had to refrain from replying with a "what" because her father wouldn't like that. Instead she rephrased her question.

"I don't understand what you're saying, Dad. What's going on?"

"How's it possible that my oldest child is getting married and I didn't know about it? Just who is giving you away and to what type of man? I don't understand these young folks that don't respect any kind of tradition. He couldn't come ask me for your hand in marriage? Or maybe you didn't want him to."

CHAPTER TEN

"IT'S NOT WHAT you think, Dad," she replied after the silence had stretched too long and she knew her father was getting antsy for a response.

"Well now, I think I can still read pretty well. Daisy brought me my papers when she went to the market for me the other day. And I sat out on the back porch like I always do and read them. Damn near choked on my coffee when I saw those pictures of you and some guy named Major Gold announcing your engagement. What kind of name is that for a man, anyway? And now you're in that big city planning some fancy wedding when you know I've always told you girls that you should have a traditional African wedding. It's what your grandparents always wanted."

Damn, he was bringing up the African wedding.

After going on permanent disability leave from the hospital where he'd worked in the maintenance department seven years ago, Jacoby had developed a routine of fixing a pot of fresh-ground coffee every morning. He'd pour that coffee into the old, stained, white carafe with the faded flowers on the front and take it to the back porch with him. There he'd sit from eight to ten, listening to the birds and smelling the fresh morning air—at least that's how he explained it.

She should be pissed at Daisy for taking him the paper with her picture on it, but then again, at least her sister was doing her part to help take care of him.

"It's my job," she said and then wanted to snatch the words back.

"You're working as some man's fiancée?"

That sounded awful.

"His family's company is the one I came here to meet with. They've agreed to give me a six-week trial period." She paused and took a deep breath. "In exchange for this opportunity, I agreed to be the guy's fake fiancée. It's to help with a sales campaign they're running. That's all, Dad. It's not real."

And that somehow didn't make it sound better. She was sure her father would feel the same way, which was precisely why she hadn't told him these details.

"Why would you agree to such foolishness? Running around with some man you're not in love with, trying to fool the world into believing you're something that you're not."

"I need this deal to work, Dad." It was as simple as she could explain her reason for being there.

"Why? You were doing just fine here starting your business. You can't always put the cart before the horse, Nina. Growing a business takes time. I don't know why my girls always want everything with such urgency. Never want to take the time to see how things will turn out, just like…" His words trailed off and Nina tried not to feel the bite of the comparison he'd almost made between her and her mother.

"I'm not doing this just for me. I want you to be able to move into that facility we looked at a few months ago."

He was quiet for too long and she braced herself for an explosion of temper. Although it didn't happen frequently, Jacoby could yell and argue just like his daughters.

"If I wanted to go into that facility, I could. I've got some money saved up. You don't need to worry about me. I want you to be happy. That's all I've ever wanted was for all of my girls to be happy."

And by "all" of his girls, Nina knew he was including her mother. Lynn hadn't been happy with the man she'd married and the three children she'd given birth to. But that wasn't their fault. Nina only wished her father would finally come to that conclusion. She also wished that everything her mother had done didn't affect everything she was doing now. Nina needed to believe that if she wanted a relationship for herself it could flourish. But the demise of her parents' marriage had a much bigger impact on her than she'd ever believed before she'd met Major.

"Your savings isn't enough, Dad. There are ongoing expenses and we have the portions of your medical bills that the insurance doesn't cover. I'm just trying to do what's necessary for my family. If relatives help each other, what evil can hurt them? You taught me that." Tossing old proverbs back at her father might not be the best idea, but it was all she had. She wasn't going to let him talk her out of what she'd started.

"I don't want to be a burden," he said quietly. "And I definitely don't want you degrading yourself in any way to help me."

"I'm not. I promise. Major is a good guy and this is a wonderful opportunity for my business to get the exposure it needs."

"If he's such a good guy, why can't he find himself a real wife?"

Nina didn't have an answer for that. In fact, hours after the conversation with her father while she lay in the dark bedroom, she let herself think about Major finding his real wife and how she would ultimately feel knowing it wasn't her.

Maybe if she were a different type of woman, one who hadn't been showed so early in life the devastation that failed love could bring. Perhaps then she could allow herself the dream of falling in love with a man like Major and him falling in love with her. But that barrier she'd had no choice but to build around her heart just wouldn't allow her to trust those types of thoughts. It wouldn't allow her to hope for something that just couldn't be.

"I wasn't expecting to see you here," Major said when Nina was escorted into the den at his parents' house on Sunday evening.

He hadn't been avoiding her this time. Something had come up at Brand Integrated that had taken him all weekend to deal with. But he'd wanted to see her.

Major had also been dealing with the engagement ring. Among all the other plans, that detail had somehow fallen to the wayside. It had taken six days for the ring Major wanted for Nina to be ready and it had been delivered to his apartment yesterday morning. He'd refused to address why he felt a jewelry designer was required for a fake engagement, but he wanted the ring on Nina's finger before their next public appearance.

Now, she was here, in the house he'd grown up in, looking around the room, one hand to her chest before she settled her gaze on him. "Sorry, still trying to catch my breath from that magnificent foyer I just walked through. That staircase is breathtaking, and I've never seen anything like the brown-and-gold marble floor." She gave her head a little shake and then cleared her throat, dropping her arm to her side. "But yeah, your mother invited me to dinner while we were at the fitting yesterday," she said, waving to Maurice and RJ who were sitting in chairs behind him.

"She was at the fitting?" Was that on the itinerary?

"Yes, Mom was at the fitting. Everything doesn't have to be on the itinerary, Major. It's all right to be impulsive sometimes," Riley said as she entered the room. The smile on his sister's face solidified the feeling of dread in the pit of Major's stomach. "We had a wonderful afternoon. The gowns were all so beautiful on Nina. We had a terrible time deciding on the final one."

RJ stood and went to the bar in the far corner of the room to fix himself a drink. "Why? It's not like there's really going to be a wedding."

The room went silent for a few seconds and Riley chimed in again.

"The name of the game is to get customers to buy into the whole process, which is why we have *Infinity* doing the six-page spread for June. The dress is the center of any wedding, so it made sense that we start there. Next week there will be coverage of our venue hunt and talking to artists about the reception." Riley, wearing a long, pleated green skirt and casual T-shirt, sat on the coal-colored couch, leaning back on its huge fluffy pillows.

RJ shook his head as he dropped ice cubes into his glass. "For all this effort, I sure hope this fake wedding campaign works to our advantage."

"Oh come on, RJ. Man, you were just talking about the bump in orders in the casual wear sections," Maurice said.

"I saw that, too," Nina added, excitement clear in her voice. "Since the media has decided that, in addition to the wedding, they want to do stories on who I am and our business partnership, I took a chance and ran a digital ad on some of the fashion blogs and did numerous posts on my Instagram page, tagging fashion groups and other influencers."

Major noted how lovely she looked in a long

animal-print skirt. He wondered if she and Riley had conferred on their attire for tonight. Her plain tan T-shirt was also on the casual side, as well as the three-quarter dark denim jacket she wore over it. For a few seconds he wondered about the beads riding low on her hips beneath the clothes she wore.

"That was a great idea," Maurice continued. "Customer service reported some mentions in their feedback box when we met with them Friday morning."

"That's in the area of the app. I'm talking about this engagement sham," RJ continued before taking a swallow of the vodka he'd just poured.

Marva wouldn't like that he was drinking before dinner, but Ron would defend his oldest son, claiming if a man worked hard he had every right to drink hard whenever he wanted to. As long as the work was done and above reproach—that was always the unspoken part of anything their father said to defend them. He could condone just about anything if RGF came first. A fact that had Major's jaw tightening.

Nina moved around him to take a seat in one of three brightly colored and mildly disgusting salon chairs his mother had added to this space a couple years ago. He realized he hadn't offered her a seat and had basically left her hanging in a room full of siblings. To compensate, he moved over to the chair as soon as she sat. "Can I get you something to drink while we wait for dinner?"

"That would be great. I'll have a—"

"Cranberry juice with lime," he said before she

could get the words out, and the room went silent once more.

She smiled up at him and, in that moment, it didn't matter what his siblings were doing or saying behind him. Major smiled in return and went to the bar thinking of the ring in a black-velvet bag in his pocket. Before learning she'd been invited tonight, his plan had been to take it to her after dinner. Now he was thinking there didn't need to be any special moment or perfect words said; he should just give it to her. That idea was tabled when RJ moved to the side while Major reached for a glass.

"Ain't that cute, you know what she likes to drink," RJ jokingly whispered until Major elbowed him and continued.

He did know what she liked to drink and that she only liked extra cheese and onions on her pizza. When he kissed her neck and palmed her breasts, she melted in his arms. And on the two occasions he'd spent the night at her hotel over these past two weeks, he noticed she liked to sleep on the right side of the bed. But none of that meant anything—it couldn't.

"It's a drink, don't get it twisted," he replied, keeping his voice low, as well.

"I think I should be saying the same to you."

Major frowned. "What's that supposed to mean?"

"Where've you been spending the bulk of your evenings? At your place or at her hotel? And before you answer, think about why you really got that apartment for her. After that, think about how this is going to end when the six weeks are up."

"Dinner is served," Kemp, the Golds' longtime butler, announced just in time for Major to slip away from his brother and the assumptions he was making.

"You were very quiet during dinner," Nina said later as they walked along one of the many stone pathways outside the main house.

He'd needed some air after sitting at the table listening to the talk about work and wedding plans. Major wasn't usually the quiet one of the family— laid-back, but not quiet. Riley had taken that torch and held it for years. Now that she was in love, that seemed to have changed.

"I know, sorry. I've got a lot on my mind."

"About the fake engagement? Because, really, I think that's going well."

She was right. The charade was going well. Desta's last email to him asking that they keep up whatever they were doing had confirmed that. What had they been doing? In the last few weeks they'd been dating. That was the simplest way of putting it. Dinner out, even more dinners in, watching movies, laughing, touching, sleeping together—all the things a dating couple would do. All things that had tabloids abuzz with wedding speculation, which always included comments about Nina's wedding gown. He was pretty sure they were doing a great job as far as the campaign was considered.

"It's not that," he said, stuffing his hands into his pockets as he walked.

It was a warm evening, not humid as it had been

earlier. A summer thunderstorm had rolled through while they'd been inside having dinner, cooling the air down slightly.

"But whatever it is, you don't want to talk about it." She didn't pose that as a question, just a simple statement she let hang in the air like bait.

After another few steps, Major gave up the pretense. He didn't know what it was about her, but whenever they were together he was always changing his mind about something, doing more than he'd anticipated, adjusting. It wasn't something he did often, there wasn't usually a need. He knew what he wanted and he did whatever it took to get it. Simple. But not this time—at least not when she was around.

"It's business, but not RGF business," he said, feeling a bit uneasy about what was on his mind.

"Okay."

That one word didn't seem like enough and, after a few seconds, he realized he wanted Nina to ask the question so that it wouldn't seem like he was giving her the information. To the contrary, she seemed content to give him space to decide when and if he wanted to tell her more.

"I'm starting my own company. It's called Brand Integrated Technologies." And it might be your biggest competitor. For some reason, he couldn't bring himself to say that part.

"Good for you," she said when they took the curve that would lead to the garage or down farther to his mother's gardens. "Starting a business can be a mixed bag—exciting and daunting."

"You're right about that." He managed a light chuckle. "Launch day is a few weeks away, so we're just ironing out some final things. But the last couple days, there've been some wrinkles."

She nodded, her hair, which she'd left alone so that it lay straight down her back, swished a little with the movement.

"That's always the case. And it probably won't get better after launch. I know I was troubleshooting almost 24/7 in my first couple of weeks. But what got me through was knowing that it was all mine—my concept, my execution, everything. That motivated me to keep going and to get it right."

Looking over at her, he saw the light in her eyes as she talked about her business. He'd seen it before and realized it was always there when they talked about work.

"My dream," he said and only briefly wondered why he'd found it so easy to admit that to her. "I've wanted to do something like this for a long time and now that it's happening, I just want it to be perfect."

"Perfection is a myth." There was an edge to her tone, but when she glanced over at him and caught him watching her, she smiled. "It's designed to pull every bit of action and reaction from you until you're either spinning in circles in search of more, or falling flat on your face from exhaustion. Completion is a more attainable goal."

He thought about that for a second and eventually decided there might be some truth to her words. "Brand Integrated is a consulting and design firm.

We'll assess the technological needs of a fashion house and design unique software to facilitate their growth. Kind of what I've been doing at RGF, but on a larger scale."

"That sounds amazing, Major. And there's definitely a need. The shield program you've developed to seamlessly combine all aspects of RGF is phenomenal."

So far so good. He gave her a tentative smile.

"Thanks. At Brand Integrated, all of that would be expanded. We have plans for more personalized technological development such as fabric generators, accessory hubs, data extrapolators and more. The idea is to get into a company and create a skeleton that will support the entire body of its work."

"Yes! I can see that. There's certainly a demand for that type of technological support, especially in the fashion industry. This way it lets designers focus on just the clothes. Are you targeting smaller houses? Because I feel like they're the ones who could really benefit from programs like this. It would position them to be competitors."

"Exactly," he admitted. How was it that she got him so completely and so quickly?

A light drizzle of rain started to fall and Major led them toward the garage.

"So, anyway, the past couple days have been filled with little problems. I feel like it's some type of conspiracy designed to make me think of turning back."

"You getting cold feet, Major?" She chuckled. "I wouldn't have expected that of you."

Her tone was light but the fact that she had any type of expectations of him on a level outside of their fake engagement was a little surprising. And a lot intriguing.

They approached the garage. There was an automated keypad on the wall beside the door and he pressed the code. When the locks disengaged, he pulled the door open and held it so that she could walk past, giving off a hint of her perfume as she did—warm, floral, charming.

"So wait—you said accessory hubs. You have plans for programs that will accessorize? Sort of like my app?"

Major had just pulled the door closed behind him and was about to reach for the light switch when she asked that question.

"Ah, yeah, that's in the portfolio. I mean, we wouldn't contract with any vendors, we're solely technology focused. But a simulator that takes the designer from sketch to prototype to runway, complete with suggested accessories, is on the menu."

He found the switch for the lights and the fluorescent bulbs across the large, open ceiling came on, bringing thirty vintage cars and motorcycles into view.

"Oh," she said and looked around. "Well, I guess a little healthy competition is good."

Of course he'd known about this similarity since the day she'd pitched At Your Service; what he hadn't wanted to consider was whether or not it would mean anything at the end of these six weeks.

Logically, she could go her own way with her company and continue doing business. He could do the same and they'd just be two people working in the industry, same as RGF's competition with any other fashion house. But this was different—the deal he'd made with her, having Sunday dinner with her at his parents' house, a seventy-five-thousand-dollar ring in his pocket, talking and walking with her on a quiet summer's night... He couldn't help but admit things were totally different now.

She walked farther into the space. "These are amazing. Whose are they?"

The place was set up almost like a runway with vehicles parked along the two sides of the structure, leaving a wide walkway in the center to be used for perusal.

"My Dad and RJ have always been into vintage cars. Another thing they have in common."

"But you don't like them?"

"I didn't say that. They're nice, but just not my thing. I'm more impressed by the room of control boards and digital infrastructure at my place."

"I'm sure that's impressive, but since I haven't been invited to your place yet, I'll just have to enjoy these cars." She walked toward a sage-green Jaguar, running her hand over the shining hood. "My dad would get such a kick out of this. He loves cars."

"I do, too. They get you from place to place."

She looked over her shoulder at him. "Ha."

He chuckled.

It was so easy being with her, much easier than

he'd ever thought it would be with another woman. Stacia was the only other woman he'd ever brought to his parents' home and the whole time she'd been there that night, all she'd wanted to do was talk about the fashion house. Major's technology ideas or anything about their future together had seemed to be off-limits.

"This one reminds me of *Grease.* You know, the movie with Danny Zuko and the T-Birds? Every time I see an old Thunderbird, I think about it."

He was grateful for her question, disliking the turn his thoughts had taken. "No, I don't know the movie, but I do know this car. It's probably from the fifties or sixties as my Dad is fixated with that time frame. This one used to be my grandfather's, I believe."

They'd stopped by the red convertible and she walked down to the driver's side, leaning over to look at the steering wheel and the white-leather interior.

"Ever made out in one of these?"

The question was so off topic from what they'd been discussing. It was also more than a little arousing.

"If you mean any car, uh, yeah. A couple weeks ago with this really hot chick who came to one of our shows and took over the press conference." The memory of that day would forever be etched in his mind. How beautiful and amazing she'd looked while taking Morgana down a notch and then how sweet she'd tasted as he'd feasted on her in the back of the limo.

She blushed, heat fussing her high cheekbones to add a sexy flash of color to her face. A more enticing sight he'd never seen.

"I meant a T-Bird," she told him as she shook her head and looked away. "In the movie they go to this drive-in and all these cars are lined up. Only a handful of people are watching the screen, the rest are necking in the back of the car."

Her hand caressed the soft leather of the seat and then moved to the side of the door. Major watched that hand, growing hard at the thought of it running over him that way.

"Let's do it," he said.

Her head popped up from where she'd been looking at the sideview mirror. "Do what?"

"Do *it*." He nodded toward the backseat of the T-Bird. "In here."

She followed his gaze, a smile spreading across her face. "*It?* Now? Here?"

His dick was hard and the hint of intrigue in her tone was encouraging.

"Hell yeah. Right now. Right here."

He stood at the passenger side of the car and, for a few seconds, their gazes held, his heart beating just a little faster as he waited for her response.

She pursed her lips—sweet, suckable lips—and shrugged. "Let's do it!"

CHAPTER ELEVEN

"So ARE WE going for seduction here, or just hard-core reach-for-the-orgasm as quickly as possible?"

Her question only made him harder—if that was even possible. Major already felt as if he were going to explode from the force of the arousal or go into some type of coma from the most painful erection ever. They'd both opened the doors of the car and climbed inside. He dug out his wallet and found a condom, dropping it onto the seat between them as she watched. Then he reached for her, clasping his hand at the back of her head and pulling her close. She licked her lips and he parted his, moving in closer, prepared to answer her question.

"I need to be inside you right now," he whispered, the words rough.

"Say no more." She pushed him back on the seat and undid his belt and the snap of his jeans.

He reached for the jacket, pushing it off her shoulders and down her arms. She paused so that he could pull it off and it fell to the floor. The zipper to his jeans made a loud sound as she eased it down, her fingers brushing over his thick erection just like the first day they'd met. Without wasting a second, she reached through the slit of his boxers and wrapped her hands around his dick, pulling his full length out.

The groan that rumbled in his chest and ripped through his throat was savage. Her hands were too warm around him, rubbing along his skin and sending rivulets of pleasure throughout his body.

"You said you want to be inside me." Her voice was a throaty whisper as she lowered her body to fit between his spread legs.

She wasn't going to... He would never make it if she did. When her head was bent over his groin, Major let his head fall back, his eyes closing slowly. She was going to and he was definitely going to explode.

The moment her mouth closed over the head of his dick, his hips jutted forward, his hands falling first to the seat where his fingers dug into the upholstery. As her tongue circled his tip, he moved his hands, burying them in her hair.

"I'm gonna take you all the way inside," she whispered, her breath warm and teasing over him.

He simply nodded in agreement, rubbing his fingers along her scalp before wrapping her hair around his hand in preparation. There was an explosion—not the one he'd been predicting—but another one, as sparks burst behind his closed lids. She had one hand on his balls, massaging them until they tingled. The other hand was wrapped around the base of his dick as she held him upright and lowered her mouth down his length.

Gasping for air—that's the sensation he first felt. It was immediately followed by an insatiable thirst for more. He applied light pressure to the back of her head, his body aching to be fully ensconced in her. The tip of his dick touched the back of her throat and air burst from his lungs, coming through his mouth in a ragged moan.

He cursed and his fingers tightened in her hair, somewhere in the back of his mind, cautioning against hurting her. She lifted her head, dragging her tongue along the underside of his erection, causing it to jerk and release pre-cum that she immediately licked away.

"I didn't imagine." The words were rough and tumbled free of his thoughts. He hadn't imagined being inside her this way. Thrusting in and out of her pussy was one level; it was erotic and good as hell. But this, being drenched in the heat of her mouth, touched by the stroke of her tongue, it was more and it was intense, pulling him in a direction he'd never thought he'd go.

She eased her head down again, until she was actively sucking him, applying pressure so that he felt as if she might actually drain his release from him the second he came. But before she could do that, she pulled her mouth away.

"I need more," she said through panting breaths. "Now."

Without wasting another second, Major reached

for the condom. She took it from him, ripped the packet open and sheathed him. Major pushed her skirt up around her waist, feeling those colorful beads moments before he ripped the flimsy strings of the thong she wore straight from her hips.

"You keep destroying my underwear," she said as she climbed on top to straddle him.

He cupped her ass cheeks, kneading them as she positioned herself over him and then, when she'd aimed his tip at her center, he pressed her down until she was completely impaled. "I'll buy you more," he groaned, and she moaned as she settled over him.

The only other sound throughout the garage was that of their skin slapping together. He groaned as he dropped his face into her cleavage and she screamed as she cupped the back of his head and bounced on top of him. Minutes later her thighs tightened around his waist and his fingers gripped her ass harder.

"Yessssss," she moaned.

"Yes!" He followed her lead, gasping as his release pulsated and poured into the condom.

For endless moments they just sat there, both struggling to catch a breath. She leaned forward with her hands on his chest, her head resting on his shoulder. Major turned his face to hers, letting his chin rest against her forehead as thoughts flailed around in his mind.

What was he doing? Why was this happening? And when had it happened—when had this arrangement started to feel like so much more?

He'd opened up to her about his business, something he hadn't done with anyone else besides his twin, and he wanted her to feel free to do the same with him. To tell her his secrets and know that they were safe with him, to come to him when she was feeling conflicted, worried, even happy. This was a new feeling, an eerie and confusing one, and he didn't know what to do with it.

His hand slid from where he'd been rubbing it up and down her back, until he could reach his pants and fumble to get his hand into the front pocket. The black-velvet bag almost slipped from his fingers to fall on the leather-covered seat, but he held on to it, bringing it up to his other hand. Her eyes were still closed, lips slightly parted as her panting began to slow.

With the fingers of one hand, Major pulled the strings of the pouch apart and reached inside to pull out the ring. He dropped the bag to the seat and grasped for her left hand.

"What...not yet—" she started to say and then stopped as she pulled back to look at what he was doing.

Major slid the ring slowly onto her third finger and frowned as he watched her hand shake. When the ring was on and she didn't speak, just stared down at it, he did the same, watching the sparkle of the four-carat, emerald-cut diamond set in platinum with tapered baguette side stones. That was the complete description the jeweler had given him, but all Major saw as he looked down at her slender fingers and manicured nails was a memory.

His gaze moved up to her face. When he saw that she was still staring down at the ring, he lifted a hand to touch his finger to her chin and tilted her head up. There was a bit of confusion in her eyes, but a lot of light, like a shield had been raised. Warmth spread in the center of his chest and one side of his mouth lifted in a smile.

"You can't be engaged without a ring," he said while his throat felt tight and his hand still shook a little while holding hers.

She smiled, a slow and dazzling smile that reached into his chest and squeezed so tight he struggled to breathe.

"And this is one beautiful ring," she said, her voice hitching on the last words.

"I would say for a beautiful woman, but that seems so cliché and there's nothing cliché about you, Nina. Not one single thing." This was the part where he should kiss her. And damn he wanted to. He wanted to wrap his arms around her and drown in her kiss, feel the warmth of her surrounding him until all his cares and worries disappeared and there was just her.

She looked like she wanted to say something or to do something. Their gazes held but hesitancy hung between them like a blockade.

"I think I like doing it in the backseat of a T-Bird," she said playfully, then eased her left hand away from his and lifted it into the air to wiggle her fingers. "You get great gifts!"

Major chuckled, part of him appreciating the way

she'd broken that uncomfortable tension between them, another part wishing the moment would have ended differently.

"I like doing it in the backseat of a T-Bird with you."

Two hours later Nina was at Major's penthouse, stepping out of his shower. If her legs weren't so sore from their second backseat sexcapade and her mind wasn't filled with new questions about the huge diamond on her finger and the foreign emotions sifting through her soul, she might have been overwhelmed by being here in Major's private space.

"Here, let me help," he said when he stepped out behind her.

She'd already grabbed a towel from the shelf near the dual vanity but had been holding it in her hands while she struggled to get a hold on what was happening. And letting the water drip from her naked body pool onto the heated gray-slate floor.

Major reached for another towel and wrapped it around her, turning her to face him when he was done.

"I suppose you'll want me to dry you off in return." It was easier to joke than to put words to what she was really feeling.

"Of course. That's how this works," he said and proceeded to move the towel over her body. He eased the soft, fluffy material along her arms, over and under her breasts and down her stomach.

"These beads are going to be the death of me,"

he said while rubbing the towel past her hips, down and between her thighs.

"I've got some aunts back in Sierra Leone who could probably use their skills to add death as a result of looking at the beads. Or, most likely, loss of a limb, impotence or something along those lines."

He hissed and pulled back, looking up at her from where he'd knelt down with a horrified expression. "That's not funny."

She chuckled. She couldn't help it. He was adorable when he was scared. "Yeah, it is."

He shook his head and eased the towel between her legs, lifting one off the floor to rub down to her feet, then up again. He did the same with the other and before he stood, eased the towel between her legs taking special care to dry her there.

"Your turn," she said when those stirrings of desire started to buzz.

How could she be so turned on by him, so frequently and so soon? The tryst in his father's vintage car was different from the limo on so many levels she didn't know where to begin. Perhaps at the part where she was certain his family would despise her if they knew she'd just disrespected their dinner invitation in such a way.

The moment he stood to his full six-two-and-a-half inches stark naked in front of her, she knew that what she was feeling had nothing to do with what his family thought of her and everything to do with him. Drops of water still rolled over his tawny-hued skin and he stared down at her with dark brown eyes that held more warmth than any she'd ever seen.

She raised the towel and rubbed his chest then moved down each of his arms before returning to his torso, all while that diamond on her left hand sparkled like a bright reminder of what this could never be.

"I don't think this was in either of our job descriptions," she said, her voice hollow to her own ears. They weren't supposed to be doing any of this and yet they were doing it, and she suspected they were doing it as well as any real couple.

He caught her hands just as she was about to drag the towel past his waist. "That's because there's really no accurate way to describe you."

And what exactly was that supposed to mean?

Maybe he was just as confused as she was about what was happening between them, or what she thought might be happening. She'd never felt this way before and wasn't sure if she was ready to take it from lust to love, but knew for certain it was more than what their fake scenario called for.

"Yes, that's me." She dabbed the towel over his hips. "The indescribable fake fiancée." Reminding herself that keeping things light between them was for the best, she bent down to dry his thighs—strong and fit—then his calves and his feet, which were a lot prettier than she'd imagined. Coming up again, she rubbed the towel over what could arguably be one of the best parts of him. To say this part of Major felt the same way about her might have been an understatement if it hadn't begun to stiffen at her ministrations.

He took her by the shoulders and pulled her up to stand in front of him. "Come on, Fake Fiancée. Let's get ready for bed."

She hadn't realized she'd frowned until he asked, "Whoa, what's that look for? You don't want to sleep with me in my bed? Should we have gone back to your apartment instead?"

"Oh no, that's not it." In fact, she'd been flattered when he'd announced during the drive from his parents' house that they would be coming to his place. She'd refused to ask why he hadn't brought her here before, chalking it up to their little charade instead of any other personal reason he might not want her there.

He looked at her strangely, a brow lifting in question. "Then what is it?"

"I'm hungry," she said, because it was true and because she wasn't sure what she was feeling for him at this moment. Or what he was really feeling for her.

"I mean no offense to your mother's dinner. It was a wonderful spread, but I'm used to a little more than soup, salad and the smallest portions of beef rib tips and asparagus that I've ever seen."

That's right, insult his mother instead of telling him she was afraid she was really falling for him.

When he threw back his head and laughed, Nina relaxed. Laughter was definitely better than his ordering her to get dressed and get out.

"I planned to wait until you were asleep before

sneaking into the kitchen to grab something else to eat."

It was her turn to laugh. "Why didn't you say something? I thought that's the way your family was used to eating, so I didn't want to comment."

"My mother doesn't cook, so dinners are always catered. The only time we get loads of food is on Thanksgiving and Christmas. My father says that's the best time of the year."

He continued to laugh while they finished with the towels and dropped them into the hamper by the door.

"You go on into the bedroom and find something to sleep in. I mean, I'm good with you staying just the way you are, but I'm guessing you'd like to be dressed to eat."

They were still naked. Yet they'd been standing there talking as if they showered and talked in the nude every day.

"Oh, are you going to order something?"

"No. I'm going to cook us something."

"You cook?"

She knew she was frowning this time because she couldn't believe that Major was good in the kitchen.

As it turned out, twenty minutes later, when they were sitting on stools in his kitchen, he could bake a homemade pizza that tasted just as good as any pizzeria she'd ever been to, if not better.

"What's on this?" she asked as she took another bite.

"Alfredo sauce, ricotta and mozzarella cheeses, plenty of black pepper and oregano."

"It's delicious," she said over the mouthful, and wasn't lying. "Where'd you learn how to cook if your mother hires caterers?"

"In college. I didn't like going out much, so I figured it was best to not starve for four years."

"Why didn't you like to go out?"

He hesitated, took another bite of his pizza, chewed and then used a napkin to wipe his mouth.

Nina hadn't realized she was waiting for his response until he looked at her and shook his head.

"It's not such a big deal now since I've learned how to deal with it. But it was because of a girl."

Never in a million years would she have guessed he'd say that. "What? A girl had you holed up in your dorm for four years?"

"Not exactly. It was during my sophomore year. I thought it was love. Stacia Hudgins poured it on real thick, was talking marriage, kids, the whole package. Come to find out she and her parents had it all set up. They knew who I was, who my family was, and they wanted in. A fake pregnancy scare, lots of tears and then a threat of scandal, and it was over by the time I came home for the summer. That's when I knew relationships weren't for me."

Nina chewed another bite all the while thinking she'd like to have been at school with Stacia Hudgins so she could serve the girl a good dose of "get a life." Or, as Nina and her sisters would have called it, "whoop ass."

"Yeah, I'm not into the 'happy-ever-after' thing, either." She was almost positive that was still true.

"But not because of any guy in particular. My culprit was my mother. She left when I was twelve. Had enough of the family life and decided there was something better away from the home she'd built. Left my dad with three girls and a broken heart that he's still nursing. Probably why he's gotten so sick, but I guess that's not medically possible."

"Broken heart" had likely never been listed on anybody's death certificate.

"Your father has COPD, right?"

She nodded. "Yes. It wasn't so bad at first, but seven years ago he had to stop working and go on disability because it had gotten to the severe point. He's weak most of the time, has intermittent swelling in his legs and ankles, and gets confused easily. The confusion isn't a symptom of COPD, I think it's more from loneliness. Anyway, my sisters and I have been taking care of him up to this point, but the doctor suggested he might need more assistance to make sure he's taking his medications and to help him do some of the daily getting around."

It had been a hard conversation to have as a family, but they'd had it. Her father didn't want to be a burden to his children, insisting he could take care of his own arrangements when the time came.

"That's a tough situation," Major said. "Do you have a facility in mind?"

"We've visited a few and there's one that he favors." She drank from the glass of wine he'd poured for her. "This boost in business from partnering with

RGF will be just what I need to get him into the care home."

She took another bite of pizza because she'd had enough of talking about herself.

"Maybe I could help. I can make some calls, maybe find a place for your father here in New York." When she only stared at him, he cleared his throat and continued, "I mean, that way you'll be close to two of the biggest fashion houses in the States, stylists, models and plenty of other industry people that could talk up your app and provide endorsements."

"But I live in York. That's where my family and everything I know is." That was the truth, but there was suddenly something sad about the way it sounded.

"Right," he said with a curt nod and a quick smile. "If you're done, we should clean this up and get to bed."

"Right. I can take care of the mess since you cooked."

"Nonsense, we'll do it together."

Like a couple did things together. Nina didn't say that but went along with his suggestion until the kitchen was clean and they headed off to bed...to Major's bed where she would lie all night wondering if he was the man to make her think twice about happy-ever-after.

CHAPTER TWELVE

THE WINE-COLORED tulle was even more beautiful as it swayed around them on the dance floor. With Major's arms wrapped securely around her waist, Nina's arms remained locked at his neck as they danced. The screens positioned around the banquet room, having earlier displayed a lovely video of their childhood years all the way up to their engagement party, now showed them dancing. Even the people at the back of the four-hundred-seat room could see them close-up.

A slow song played, one that was a favorite of theirs. But she couldn't hear the lyrics. She just swayed to the rhythm and stared up into his face, remembering the exact moment that she'd agreed to become Mrs. Major Gold.

They danced until the scene changed and she was once again walking through the doors of the RGF building, with a determined smile on her face as she approached the now familiar pretty receptionist with the coal-black hair.

"Good morning, Mrs. Gold. Are you here to see your husband?"

The question startled her and Nina looked down to see the huge emerald-cut diamond on her ring finger.

"Uh, no. I'm actually here to work. I need to check in with a few vendors and make sure that products are being shipped on time." She continued to talk even though the woman was frowning at her. "There were a couple complaints on the website and I need to get things ironed out."

"I don't understand. Maybe you want to report some issues with the company site to your husband?"

"No. I want to take care of the issues—they're with my company, At Your Service."

The woman was shaking her head, her silky hair moving from side to side. "You're welcome to go see your husband. But I've never heard of At Your Service..."

Nina's eyes opened wide into a room filled with slashes of moonlight coming through the partially closed blinds. She pressed a hand to her chest, her heart beating wildly. A few blinks later and she swallowed hard, her gaze falling on the nightstand beside the bed where a clock flashed bright white numbers: 3:54. Beside the clock was her phone, plugged into its charger. She'd put it there just before joining Major in the shower.

She was at Major's penthouse... He'd fixed her pizza...

A sigh of relief rushed from her as she realized it had only been a dream. The wedding, going to RGF...it was all a dream. A strange and alarming dream that now had her sitting up in the bed.

The sheet slid to her waist and she rubbed her hands over her face. That dream was strange and it left her feeling even stranger. Full of emotion and empty at the same time. But it wasn't real, nothing about being with Major was real, even this moment.

She glanced over her shoulder to see him sleeping. One arm was thrown above his head while the other lay across his bare stomach. The sheet was riding dangerously close to revealing what she already knew was a delicious part of him.

He seemed real.

Leaning back and propping herself up on one elbow, she stared down at him. He had thick eyebrows that she wished she had. Hers were thin and most times she penciled them in. His nose was straight, wide and proportional with his face, his squared jaw and average ears. Her gaze fell on his lips and her own parted. They were usually warm when they met hers. And soft. Did men like being told they had soft lips?

She was leaning over before she thought better of the action. But when her lips hovered just seconds away from his, Major's eyes opened, and she froze.

His response was to move the arm that had been resting over his abs, snake it around her waist and pull her on top of him. She licked his bottom lip as his hands splayed over her ass. Then her tongue stroked his top lip. Their gazes held.

He parted his lips slightly, just enough so that his tongue inched out, and she pounced, sucking it deep into her mouth. He groaned and pressed her bare mound into his thickening erection. Only the thin sheet separated them, but she sucked on his tongue like it was his dick, and desire pierced through her, falling with clever accuracy in her center. She spread her legs so that she was now straddling him, rubbing her pussy over the sheet. He thrust his hips up to meet hers, his hands moving upward to bury themselves in her hair.

He pulled her back then, her mouth reluctantly releasing him. For endless moments, they just stared at each other.

She didn't know what he was thinking. The only thing running through her mind right now was that this felt real. From the throbbing in her center to the tightening in her chest, as she continued to stare down at him, it felt very real.

"I don't know what this is," he said, his voice cracking slightly.

"Neither do I," she admitted. "But I don't want it to stop."

It was an admission she hadn't planned to make. That made sense because she hadn't planned for him.

In response, he pulled her head down and took her mouth in a kiss that was as achingly slow and sweet as it was deliciously tempting and erotic.

He rolled her over and kicked the sheets aside before reaching over her to the nightstand and pulling open the top drawer. He tossed the condom to her and she caught it, ripping the paper and retrieving the latex. Coming up on his knees, he whispered in a hungry voice, "Put it on."

She sat up, rubbing her hand along his thick length as her mouth watered. She couldn't resist dipping her head and taking him in deep.

"Dammit," he cursed loudly. "You're killing me."

And he had awakened an insatiable need in her.

With deep suction, she slid her mouth from his base to his tip before easing down once more. This had never been a favorite of hers during sex. It was more intimate than she'd ever wanted to be with any-one else, but she loved the taste of him. Loved the feel of him in her mouth, pressing at the back of her throat, sliding over her tongue and easing past her lips.

"Put it on. Now!"

She let him slip from her mouth with a popping sound and inched the condom on until he was cov-ered. He pushed her back onto the pillows before leaning his head down to drag his tongue along the first row of beads at her waist.

"Yesssss." She let her hands fall to his head. He captured the beads between his teeth and lifted his head slightly to watch her as she looked down at him.

With a quick yank he ripped the beads free. At any other time, with someone different, this may have upset her. Tonight, coupled with the roller coaster of emotions she'd been feeling about him, the touch of the beads that empowered her sensu-ality rolling over her skin mixed with the passion swirling between them and the anticipation of more, caused her to come with a fierceness that left her breathless and trembling. Before she could recuperate, he'd moved up the length of her and was inside her, thrusting wildly.

The rush of sensations swirled through Nina like a tornado, twisting and hitting every part of her, even the part she'd never wanted to be touched. When he leaned forward, flattening his hands on either side of her to brace himself, her hands pressed against his chest. Her mouth opened as if she were going to say something. Tell him to stop because she felt overwhelmed with sensation and emotion? Or beg him to continue because it all felt so damn good?

It felt real. Too real.

She raised her legs and wrapped them around him, locking them in place.

"You," he whispered before dropping his head to take her mouth. She slid her arms from his chest to cup his face and hold him to her, dragging her tongue over his, tilting her head to take the kiss deeper.

You. The one word echoed in her mind. *You.* Him. It was him. This warm feeling spreading throughout her chest was all because of *him*.

On a ragged moan, he pulled his mouth from hers as he moved in and out of her at a slower pace. The change was fast and intense, pleasure now building with his strokes in a slow, methodical rhythm that had her biting her bottom lip and dropping her arms to the bed and gripping the sheets. He eased over her again, this time scooping his arms beneath her to hold her firmly to him. His lips were right next to her ear as he thrust into her repeatedly. She wrapped her arms around him, holding him just as tightly as he was holding her, as if they were each afraid to let go.

"I want you, Nina." He whispered those words over and over again.

She closed her eyes tight, savoring every syllable. "I want you, too." It was a quiet admission, but an admission nonetheless. And it was real—his comment, her response, it was all real.

They came together in a storm of moans and sighs, bodies trembling and pressing together as if being any other way was not an option.

By Wednesday afternoon the following week Major was in a pretty foul mood.

In a month, Brand Integrated would go public and he still hadn't told the rest of his family that he was significantly cutting his time at RGF and branching out on his own. The fake fiancée proposal would also be over. Desta had just sent an updated itinerary for the last activities he and Nina would complete together.

He sat back in his desk chair, moving his feet so the chair would spin slowly while he stared out the wall of windows in his office. With his hands clasped and resting on his lap, his mind whirled with the most pressing issues in his life at the moment. The fact that there should only be one pressing issue didn't escape his notice.

But Nina Fuller was intertwined in his every thought in a way that he hadn't anticipated. She'd been at his place, in his bed, since attending her first Gold family dinner. At night they fell asleep, cuddled in his bed, and in the morning, they awoke and moved around his bedroom and bathroom like a couple getting ready for work.

Each day had become a repeat of wake up, sex somewhere between the bedroom and bathroom, traveling to work together, then home again in the evening.

Home.

That's what it'd felt like for the past week and a half, until now, it seemed permanent.

He spun the chair until he was once again facing his desk and could see the dual monitors with the business plan for Brand Integrated on one and the services offered by At Your Service on the other. Nina had pointed out what he'd already known and what had been floating in the back of his mind since before their first meeting.

The accessory hub Brand Integrated would offer was very similar to what her app provided. The only difference—and the one thing Major had repeatedly reminded himself of—was that his company did not retain vendors, nor did it plan to sell anything directly to the consumer. Their product—software and consultation services—was exclusively designed to benefit fashion houses.

But the similarity was still there, and it had been nagging at him for days. Their businesses were poised to clash big-time. His brow furrowed with the thought and he let out a little huff as he once again searched for a viable solution. There had to be one. There had to be a way for his business to coexist with hers without compromise or confusion, and he needed to find it before their planned breakup.

Or it could be the reason for the breakup. That thought came with a sharp sting to the center of his chest as he stopped moving in the chair and his frown deepened. Desta still hadn't outlined what the final argument would be. The end of their engagement was coming quickly and he had no idea what it would be like. So what if it was the realization that their businesses would clash? Did that make sense? Was it believable? He sighed at the irony. It was the one thing that had come of their time together that was actually the truth.

A knock at the door jolted him out of his thoughts just as that pain in his chest started to spread.

"Hey, what's up? Got a minute?" RJ opened the door without consent and walked in talking. He hiked up his slacks and took a seat in one of the chairs across from Major's desk. "I need you to do something for me. You and Nina."

His brother had his full attention the moment he mentioned her name.

"What?"

"Riley wants to meet with Dad and me in an hour at a proposed location for this expansion idea she's got," RJ said.

Deciding it was probably best for the moment to wrap his mind around something else, Major sat forward, resting his elbows on his desk. "Yeah, she copied me and Maurice on an email she sent earlier this week outlining her proposal. Her research and data pan out. An RGF-exclusive storefront in the city is a good idea. Lots of other fashion houses have one, especially overseas."

"Look, I'm not totally opposed to the idea. So, Riley doesn't need you to be her cheerleader," RJ said with a sigh.

"That may be the one thing our sister has never needed. She's always been capable of being her own biggest supporter, which is probably why she was able to fall in love with the family enemy and not bat an eye when we approached her about it." Why his thoughts always returned to Riley and her relationship with Chaz, Major didn't know. Perhaps he admired the fact that she'd found love, even though he didn't believe in the concept himself.

"Ugh, that's the last thing I want to talk about."

Major chuckled, more so to keep his mind from drifting from the word *love* to the woman who would soon be meeting him in his office to go home. Or, rather, to his apartment.

"Fine, then what do you want, man? You come barging into my office at the end of the day like it's some big emergency."

"It is." RJ leaned forward, resting his elbows on his knees. "I was supposed to go to this trade show tonight to check out some new vendors for the Paris and Milan Fashion Weeks coming up, but now I can't go, so I'd like you and Nina to go instead."

"Isn't that the production department's responsibility? And did you say you want Nina to go?"

"Riley's not the only one thinking about taking RGF to the next level. I've had some thoughts about expanding in the area of accessories. We already have purses and luggage. Why not create a full line, accessorize our customers from head to toe? So, yeah, I've been looking into Nina's business a little more and watching the numbers from our temporary collaboration closely. If anybody should be checking out new vendors and giving her thoughts on specific items for the company, I think it should be her."

"Wait, you weren't even certain making this temporary arrangement with Nina was a good idea. What changed your mind?"

"You're right. I wasn't sure about her in the beginning because she was some woman from Pennsylvania who we'd never heard of until you agreed to meet with her and she presented this new app that would tap into our existing and new customer base. She had no experience with large fashion houses. So, yes, I was skeptical." RJ took a breath and shook his head. "And I definitely didn't think she was a good pick for this marketing plan. Hell, I wasn't even certain this marketing plan was a good idea on its own."

That was something Major could agree with. The moment Desta and Riley had come to him with the idea, he'd been doubtful and had wanted to beg off, to push it onto Maurice who would have loved spending a few weeks in the company of some random woman. But then he'd thought about the fact that he was planning to jump ship on RGF and figured the least he could do was submit to his family, and this company, one more time. His father would appreciate that in the end.

"But I've seen her at the office every day, working diligently, and I've heard of how she's been handling the press," RJ continued. "Then, after seeing the two of you together at Mom and Dad's house, I changed my mind."

RJ Gold never changed his mind. Ever. He was a decisive man with a proven track record in everything from commanding the sales force at RGF to building his own unique brand as the next head of the company. He was a debonair young businessman and unapologetic bachelor.

"It's her job, and that was just dinner." Major didn't believe these words so he only half expected his brother to believe them.

RJ laughed. "Yeah, keep telling yourself that. Look, here's the info and your passes. You, Nina and I will grab some lunch tomorrow and we can talk about her thoughts."

Major accepted the envelope RJ had stood to hand him. "She doesn't work here. I mean, she has her own company, and her own goals. Do you really think we should have her making decisions on behalf of the company?"

"You're going to be with her," RJ said. "And something tells me she's gonna be around long after this fake scheme you've got going. So get yourself together, stop brooding, put your game face on. Do all that, grab your woman and get to that show."

RJ walked out the same way he'd come in: quick, unannounced, without taking any questions, comments or concerns.

"She's not my woman," Major mumbled into the quiet office as he sat back in his chair once more.

Was she?

CHAPTER THIRTEEN

"LOOK AT THIS PICTURE! He's with another woman and this was just last week," Daisy said, her lips pursed, head tilted as she stared at Nina through the computer screen.

Nina had been on this Skype call with her sisters for approximately six minutes and already her temples throbbed with an incoming migraine.

"This woman looks like a model. There was a fashion show that day and I was there," Nina said as she glanced at the tabloid Angie so helpfully held close to the camera for her to see.

She remembered the beige outfit Major had worn that day and the model. Of course, the girl, wearing a very short skirt and a gold-lamé blouse that barely covered her tits with its plunging neckline, had draped her slim body over Major's shoulder as if she were somehow physically attached to him.

"You were there but he was taking pictures with her? I thought you were supposed to be his arm candy for six weeks." Angie, the matter-of-fact sister, dropped the paper and stared pointedly through the screen.

How rude would it be if she slammed the laptop closed and went on about her business?

"That's pretty rude of him. But then again, he is the Fashion House Playboy," Daisy quipped.

"Is there a point to this conversation?" Nina asked because she did have other things to do. And none of those things included thinking about Major leaving her for another woman. Even though he'd have to actually be with her to leave her. And he wasn't… Or, rather, they weren't really together.

"Aren't you bothered by this?" Angie asked.

"Why should I be? This was a business arrangement and it's almost over." In seventeen days.

"What were you doing while he was feeling up on this model?" Daisy asked.

"I was probably with his brother, Maurice, or seated in the audience where the reporters could see me—or rather, Major's fiancée. Look, if you two don't have anything better to do, I do have work to take care of."

"Work? That looks like a new dress you're wearing. And by the looks of the pictures you're showing up in with him, it seems like you're living one big shopping spree," Angie said.

"And going to lavish restaurants and Broadway shows. I read somewhere that you even met Michelle Obama at one of her appearances in the city. You're having the best time there and it's not fair!" Daisy whined.

"First, I got both of you a signed book from Michelle Obama when I met her. And I am working.

The app is doing great numbers for me and for RGF. I'm certain they're going to extend a formal contract for me to keep working with them at the end of the six weeks." She huffed. "Besides all of that, the press I'm getting personally as a result of this business deal will have my name firmly set within the industry. And from there I'll be able to move on to other companies. But I'll be home soon and then we can get Dad moved into the assisted-living facility and all of our lives will get a little easier."

That had been the plan from the start. So why did saying it aloud now make her feel unsettled?

"Are you really coming back here after the six weeks are up?" Angie asked.

"Of course I am. Why would you ask me that?"

Daisy rolled her eyes. "Because you look like you're having the time of your life."

Angie elbowed her sister. "Because you look like you might be taking this business a little more personally than you planned."

"Knock, knock." Nina looked up from the screen to see Major standing in the doorway. "Hey, we've got a change of plans for this evening. You ready to go?"

"Yeah. I'm done here, so we can go now," she replied and then looked back to the screen. "I'll call you tomorrow." She hurriedly disconnected the chat and closed her laptop.

"You okay? Did I interrupt something?" he asked as he entered the office.

She shook her head, trying to clear it of her sisters' accusations and the picture of him and that model that still floated there.

"No. Nothing. Just my sisters calling with an update."

"Oh yeah, how's your dad doing?"

"He's good." She stood and grabbed her purse, adding, "He has a doctor's appointment in the morning and Angie's going to take him, so I'll check in with her tomorrow afternoon to see how that goes."

"I had my assistant get a list of all the facilities in York and two of them are owned by people my dad's done business with at some point. I wanted to run it by you first, but if you approve, I could reach out to them and see if we can get your dad in sooner and without any big payments on your behalf."

She put her purse strap on her shoulder, slipped her laptop into her bag and stepped around the desk. Coming to a stop in front of him, she looked up in surprise. "What? You would get my dad into a facility for me?"

"Yeah, I want to help you in any way I can. You want your father to be well taken care of and you said you didn't plan to move to New York, so I found some places in York."

He was talking as if he'd just told her he'd selected something off the menu for them to eat. His tone was nonchalant as he stood with one hand in his pocket. He reached out the other hand to tuck some strands of hair that had escaped her messy bun back behind her ear.

"Thanks," she managed to finally say. "I mean… really. You didn't have to do that, but thank you."

"Don't thank me," he said. "I wanted to do it."

"But why? You didn't have to take time out of your busy schedule or ask Landra to do that. It's not your responsibility. But, again, I really appreciate you doing it." She smiled at him then because she wasn't sure what else to do. Part of her wanted to throw her arms around him and hug him tight, but she wasn't going to do that. Since her admission that night after the family dinner that she wanted him, and the subsequent nights she'd spent in his arms, she'd been trying to rein in her emotions where he was concerned.

"This is why," he said, tracing a finger along her cheek and down below her lips. "Because I like seeing you smile. And when you talk about taking care of your dad, you always frown with the stress of it."

And now she thought she might break with the force of her growing feelings for this man.

"What's the change in plans?" she asked when the silence stretched between them.

He dropped his hand and pulled an envelope from the inside pocket of his suit jacket. "Accessory trade show at the Javits Center. RJ needs us to go and check it out. He specifically wants your input on new vendors."

RJ. The one who hadn't been sure of her after their first meeting in the conference room.

"Sure. I'd love to provide input. Let's go." Now this, she could do. Work. Focus on her company and her most prominent client so far. The rest—her sisters, the way that picture had made her feel and the subsequent reaction of Major's soft touch and sweet words—she could deal with later.

The convention center was full of booths with vendors displaying everything from earrings to nose piercings, belts to custom-designed hats and patterned socks.

"This is going to be great," Nina said, pulling her phone out of her purse. "I want to take some pictures. You said Major wanted to get my thoughts on items for the upcoming shows overseas? Do you know if he's looking for anything specific?"

From the moment he'd mentioned this show, her spirits seemed to have lifted. When Major had walked into her office earlier, he'd been afraid something had happened to her father because she'd looked so distressed. He'd been glad to share his news about assisting in her facility search, even though it was in York and not here in the city...with him.

"He's actually looking for two things—items for the upcoming shows and your thoughts on specific pieces."

"Why specific pieces? Does he need a gift for someone? Does RJ have a girlfriend?"

He chuckled as they moved further into the exhibit hall. "Not hardly. The very last thing RJ's interested in is a girlfriend or any other type of commitment other than the company."

"Is that true of all the Gold men? Because Maurice makes it known he loves his player status and isn't looking to stop anytime soon. And you…"

Her words drifted off, but he filled in the blanks.

"I've been focused on Brand Integrated and making my personal mark on the fashion industry."

"Everyone has a reason," she said with a shrug. "I have mine."

She didn't want to be abandoned again. A completely understandable reason, but one that made him much sadder than he thought anything ever could.

"Anyway, no, RJ's other reason for this outing is based on this preliminary idea he has about adding a full accessory line to RGF."

"Oh." She took a few steps farther before stopping at an earring vendor. She picked up a set of gold hoops that were almost as big as her hand. There were flecks of sapphire around each hoop and she held them up, staring, he presumed, at the color in the light.

"A full accessory line will eliminate the need for an app like mine." She put the earrings down and continued walking.

"It's not my idea," he said because he felt the need to defend himself against the suddenly bland tone of her voice.

She waved a hand and crossed in front of him to get to another table. This one had more earrings, but these were made with feathers. He watched, entranced by her fingers as they moved lightly over a deep burgundy feather earring.

"It's a smart idea," she said, moving to investigate another pair of earrings. These were of peacock feathers and she picked them up, holding them to her ear while she stepped over to a large oval mirror sitting on a glass case. "If RGF is making their own accessories, they'd be cutting out the middleman and making a bigger profit, all while catering to their customers in a one-stop fashion shop."

"Which was exactly what your app offered," he said. He was standing behind her, so she could see him staring at her through the mirror. When he shook his head, she nodded her agreement and put the earrings back on the table.

"Everybody wants the complete effect. RJ's thinking of gaining a competitive edge. There are plenty of other designers that have already ventured into accessories. And there are some accessory designers who're trying to dip their feet into the high fashion arena." She shrugged. "That's business."

"Are we business?" He had no idea where that question had come from.

No, that was wrong and he knew it. The idea came from the myriad emotions playing throughout his mind since the night at his parents' house.

She turned to him and smiled. That genuine one he looked forward to seeing every second of the day.

"We—" She corrected herself. "What we're doing is probably one of the most innovative ideas I've ever come across. Riley says the uptick in searches on the Golden Bride website is in direct correlation to our engagement announcement and each time a picture of us is printed in a tabloid, they get even more hits.

Orders are trickling in." She paused when a woman bumped into her and then continued, "There's even one from an R&B singer. She already had a dress but when two of the designers appeared on one of those stylist reality shows and mentioned they were working on my gown, she had to have an original design for her wedding that's coming up in four weeks."

"And you said people who already had their gowns wouldn't buy another one," he replied with a smirk.

"Yeah, I did say that. I was wrong."

And so was he. This was no longer just business between them. Thinking back to their first meeting, he wondered if there ever had been.

They walked for a few more minutes, passing other stalls. She stayed a bit ahead of him and he took that time to watch her walk, not in a way that aroused him, but more in a way that amazed him. She'd come all the way to this city just to meet with him and pitch her business, and had ended up staying as part of a business deal and to begin an affair that neither of them had been prepared for.

"Do you design and manufacture these?"

He snapped out of his reverie when he saw Nina had stopped and was holding up a leather handbag. She was talking to a tall man with gold, wire-framed glasses perched on his nose, his hair styled in locks.

The man walked over to the end of the table. "Yes," he replied in a heavily accented voice. "The bags, necklaces and earrings. I design and make them all. Do you like this tote?"

Nina continued to glide her hand over the dark purple bag.

"This is great craftsmanship," she said.

"It is called the Mawu, named after the African goddess of creativity," he told her.

Major stood at the other end of the table, watching the exchange, curious as to what she was thinking.

"Yes, I'm aware of who she is. The leather is supple, sustainable."

He nodded. "From the Karoo region of South Africa."

She seemed pleased to hear that and left the bag to pick up a necklace from another section of the table.

"And this is an African talisman," she said.

"Yes, you are familiar. It is the Springbok Horn and it is believed to bring good luck to those who wear it."

"It's simple and beautiful, whimsical and magical," she whispered.

"We'll take it," Major said, reaching into his back pocket for his wallet as he stepped up to the display table.

"Oh no," she said, shaking her head. "I didn't mean for you to buy it. I was just admiring it."

Major passed his credit card to the man and waited while it was being swiped. "It's pretty. You like it. You should have it." He ended with a shrug because he wanted everything with her to be that simple.

She didn't argue. Instead she handed it to him and turned around, lifting her hair from her neck. Major stepped closer to her, reaching around so that he could fit the necklace at her neck and clasp it. His fingers lingered at her nape, gliding along the soft skin as he inhaled the fresh floral scent she always carried. He stepped back, prepared to leave the table.

"Do you have a business card?" she asked and thanked the man when he handed her one.

"What are you thinking?" Major asked when they stepped away.

"How do you know I'm thinking something?"

"You get all crinkly right here when you've got an idea or something on your mind." He pressed a finger to the center of her forehead and she immediately relaxed until the crinkle was gone.

She smiled. "I do not."

He laughed. "Liar."

It wasn't until two hours later, when they were in the backseat of the car, that she decided to tell him what she was thinking. Even though she wore a seatbelt, she turned sideways, lifting one leg to rest on the seat.

"What would be really great to see is a complete line of African-inspired accessories from an African American fashion house. Let's uplift and display our heritage. RGF did a collection a few years back where they worked with a Nigerian designer. Maybe it's time for a new collection, find some new, talented African designers, and this time stretch it beyond the clothes to include accessories. This could be the kickoff to the accessory division and you could probably create an entire show based around these collections."

Major didn't miss the excitement in her voice as she talked. He could see where she was going with this.

"It has appeal," he said. "A lot of appeal."

"Right! Unique pieces like this one could be included," she said, reaching up to feel the necklace he'd bought her. "Maybe something inspired by your mother's grace and beauty and your father's strength and leadership."

"And your tenacity," he said before unhooking his seatbelt and sliding across the seat until he was touching her. One hand went to her leg that was on the seat while the other reached around to cup her face. "Your beauty and your independence. Your intelligence and compassion."

"No," she said softly, blinking quickly. "This would be about your family, the Golds, and everything they've built. It would be a direct reflection of all that your family has come to mean in the fashion industry."

"A reflection of love, loyalty, family—all things that are important to you."

She was shaking her head again and he didn't want to hear her denial because he knew better now. He could see it so clearly. Everything she really wanted in this world and all she would deny herself so that her family could have it instead. Before she could speak, Major leaned in to touch his lips to hers. The kiss was soft, slow, lingering, and before long she was moaning and leaning in to him.

"It's my turn to thank you," he said when he was finally able to pull his mouth from hers.

She looked as dazed and off balance as he felt at this moment. "Thank me for what?"

"For coming into my life and opening a door I thought I'd bolted shut."

She was about to say something else but the car came to a stop. Minutes later they were climbing out and walking through the lobby to the elevators that would take them to his penthouse.

They walked in silence and, for the second time tonight, he wondered what she was thinking. Had what he just said been too much? Were they never going to talk about how this arrangement had changed both their lives?

It wasn't until after they'd prepared dinner together, eaten and then moved to the couch in his living room, that he broached the subject again.

"We have a little over two weeks before the public breakup is scheduled." He'd thought about this during the meal and wanted to see how she was feeling about it first. Then he'd drift into the muddy waters of feelings.

She tucked her legs under her and draped an arm over the back of the couch, tilting her head as she looked at him. "I was thinking about that earlier today. We could always say I caught you cheating. I saw a picture of you with another woman in a tabloid and decided this is not the life for me."

"Wow, that's all it would take? A picture and you'd walk out on me?"

He'd exaggerated his reaction on purpose but the insinuation that he'd cheat on her prickled.

She shrugged. "I mean, it plays right into your title, so at the end of the engagement you'd just go back to being the Fashion House Playboy again. We both walk away unscathed."

That wasn't likely. He was already feeling the effects of being with her and doubted that would get better when she was no longer in this city with him.

"What if it's just a picture? And you're overreacting?"

"But what if it's not? What if settling down with one woman isn't going to work for you?" She seemed so adamant about this, a little more than he liked. "I mean... Look, you've been scorned before, so I wouldn't blame you. We've already gone over my trust issues, so if anybody understands, you know I do."

But he didn't want her to understand and, for the life of him, Major didn't know how to best get that point across to her without possibly scaring both of them to death with some mushy declaration of love.

Was he in love with her?

"Look, it's been a really long day. Can we talk about this tomorrow?" She uncurled her legs and stood. The nightshirt she wore was like a football jersey but it was hot-pink with double zeroes on the front and "Sexy" written on the back.

"Yeah, sure. We've got time."

She nodded. "Right, seventeen days."

So she was counting, too. Major stood and pulled

her to him, wrapping his arms around her. She hesitated but eventually gave in to the hug. He didn't know how long they stood there like that, his face buried in her neck, hers buried in his, their arms holding on tight because the time to let go was getting close.

Too close and he had to do something about it.

After she'd gone to bed, he went into his office to think about how he could keep Nina in his life. Because suddenly the thought of her not being there was more important than anything else, including his new business.

CHAPTER FOURTEEN

"COME IN!" MAJOR called and straightened his tie seconds before the door to his office at RGF opened.

"Hey, what's up man?" Maurice said as he walked in.

Major frowned.

"What'd I do? I just got here."

"I was expecting someone else," Major said, shaking his head.

The huge grin that immediately spread across Maurice's face was annoying.

"Oh. Let me guess. Nina?" he asked because Maurice obviously couldn't resist being in a position to pick on the older twin for a change.

"Yes, Nina. I sent her a text asking her to come down, so she should be on her way. What do you want?"

"Just checking on you. Is everything ready for the big launch? I'm ready to start passing out Brand Integrated cards."

"Not quite," he said. "And before you start, it has nothing to do with Dad. In fact, I'm going to talk to him tonight. I should have done this a long time ago, but better late than never."

Major had been thinking along those lines all night long. By the time he'd gone to bed, Nina had been asleep, and he'd eased into the bed so he wouldn't disturb her. But she'd awakened anyway and had rolled over to where he'd been waiting with open arms. They slept cuddled together all night. Or rather, she'd slept and he'd rested his chin on top of her head, going over the plan he'd made and praying it would work.

"Good. And, yeah, you should have done it a long time ago. Anyway, I also wanted to give you a heads-up that Mom wants to talk to you."

"About what?" Major asked, not looking at his brother but reading the latest email Ruben, his lawyer, had sent him. They'd been going back and forth all day.

"Don't know. She wasn't specific when she questioned me about why you weren't answering your phone and sent me to find you."

Major had asked Landra to hold his calls today and he hadn't paid much attention to his cell if he glanced at the screen and it wasn't Nina or Ruben. "I've been working on something important and time sensitive," he replied.

"Okay, well you can tell Mom that when she finally catches up with you. But I'll get out of your hair right now and let you handle whatever it is that's got you so focused."

He looked up to see that Maurice was standing but

wasn't walking out of the office. Instead his brother was looking at him closely, as if he could see through the words Major wasn't offering. It was moments like these that he hated being a twin.

Major sat back in his chair and rubbed a hand over his chin.

"I did something I swore I'd never do."

Maurice crossed his arms over his chest. "And that is?"

"I want her to stay so I needed to figure out a way to make that happen," he told him.

There was no clear reaction from Maurice, which was usually the case. Only those who knew him very well could tell what he was thinking or feeling; that's how good he was at keeping his poker face. To let Maurice tell it, that's the way it had to be in the world they lived in. After his college years, Major agreed with the characterization to an extent.

"So is she staying?" Maurice asked after a few seconds of silence.

"Not sure yet," Major admitted with a shake of his head. He swiped his hands down his pant legs because he was worried about the answer to that question. "Gonna tell her when she gets here."

"What if she doesn't want to stay? Or if she doesn't want to stay to be with you? How're you gonna handle that?"

"Like we handle everything else—we move on to the next thing," he said, praying that wouldn't be the outcome.

"I got a feeling she isn't like anything else you've ever dealt with before."

"How do you know?"

Maurice shook his head then turned to start for the door. "I know you better than you know yourself, bro. And that probably goes the same for you with me. I knew you'd fallen for her that first day in Desta's office."

And that's exactly when it had happened—that day she'd bumped into him. That had been the start of it all.

"If you were her, would you stay here and continue to build your business?" he asked when Maurice was at the door. "If it was a great business opportunity and helped you achieve all your goals, but you'd be leaving your hometown and your family... would you stay?"

"If it were just about business, yeah, I'd stay."

That was cryptic even for Maurice and Major was left staring at the empty doorway because his twin was gone before Major could ask him to explain.

She still wasn't here yet and he'd texted her fifteen minutes ago. Major stood and paced his office second-guessing himself and hating that feeling. He never second-guessed, always knew the right thing to do for himself. But now there was someone else. And what if she didn't want to stay?

There wasn't time to explore the issue for the billionth time because his cell phone rang. He leaned over to grab the phone and saw that it was Ruben.

"Yeah?"

"Okay, I'm working on these new contracts and there are a few places that have to remain blank until you get me more information," Ruben said.

"Fine. Can you just email them over to me now? I need them like ten minutes ago." His tone was testy, and he didn't want to admit it was because he was so nervous.

"Are you sure this is what you want to do? I mean, it seems sort of sudden and Brand Integrated has been your project for a while."

Major pinched the bridge of his nose and let his head fall back. He'd thought about this all last night and had decided it was the best solution.

Next to her family, Nina's business was everything to her. So, if he could make it that she had access to the best technology and equipment while continuing to build on the platform she'd created, she'd definitely think twice before turning down the opportunity. She was too good a businessperson to not at least give it sincere consideration. For Major, the decision was about making it easier for them to be together as a real couple. And because he didn't know if she'd readily accept that, this business plan was his best option.

"Yeah, I'm sure," he said to Ruben. "Bringing Nina into Brand Integrated takes care of the problem of our businesses overlapping each other. She can just oversee the accessory hub division, combining that with her app, and we'll still be able to offer fashion houses the same benefits. In fact, bringing At Your Service under the Brand Integrated umbrella will benefit her, too, because she'll get immediate recognition instead of having to build her name."

"What are you doing?"

Major spun around at the sound of her voice. She was standing in the doorway, looking every bit as good as she had when she'd walked out of his penthouse an hour before him this morning.

"Hey," he said to her and then, "Ruben, I'll call you back. Send the papers over now."

He disconnected the call, slipping the phone into his pocket just as Nina stepped all the way into the office.

"If the papers you're referring to involve At Your Service coming under the Brand Integrated umbrella, you won't need them because I'm not selling my company to you," she said, her voice even, cool and very angry.

"Just hear me out," Major started after he circled around her to close the door to his office.

But Nina was already shaking her head. "I know what I heard, Major. And I'm telling you now it's not going to happen."

"It can be a great thing," he said.

She whirled around and he was right there just inches away from her.

"For who? And how long have you been thinking about this?" Her heart was thumping in her chest, her fingers clenching and releasing at her sides.

"Not long—but just let me explain. There's so much more I want to say." He ran a hand across the back of his neck and sighed heavily. "This isn't how I wanted to start off. Let's take a seat."

"No," she said, yanking her arm away when he reached for her hand. "I don't want to sit."

She'd rather be standing when he tried to stab her in her back. Just as her mother had done to her husband and children. The comparison came quick, slicing through her with white-hot pain.

"How could you even suggest something like this?" Because, dammit, she'd started trusting him. She'd started to feel things for him even when she knew she shouldn't. But she wasn't going to fall apart in front of him. She wasn't going to let the ridiculous fantasy she'd begun to weave in her head make her look like a fool in front of him. Not the way her father had cried over her mother's leaving.

Instead she squared her shoulders and lifted her chin before asking, "What gave you the impression that I'd ever want to come under the umbrella of your business to gain recognition?"

"Nina, that's not what I said. You only heard part of the conversation. What I'm proposing is much bigger. It means so much more than just you gaining recognition for your little app."

"My 'little app'?" She backed away because on top of the pain freely flowing now, fury bubbled in her stomach and her entire body began to shake. "Is that how you see my company? Haven't you seen the bump in sales RGF has gotten since we linked my 'little app' to your website?"

Sales in three of their key casual clothing lines

had jumped forty-three percent since the partnership began. RJ had even sent her an email this morning requesting they get together to discuss how they could make the arrangement permanent. She'd spent the bulk of the afternoon preparing a report on drafting terms for a formal permanent agreement. On top of that, RJ had asked her to be prepared to share her thoughts about the trade show with him. She'd outlined her complete idea for the African-inspired accessory line for RGF and how they could link its launch to At Your Service.

But Major wanted to take her company and make it part of his. He wanted to take every ounce of trust and genuine rapport they'd built in these past weeks and treat it as if it were nothing, as if they were nothing.

"I didn't mean to say it that way. I know your app is doing well. That's part of the reason I thought of this. Could you just calm down for a second and let me explain everything?" He'd dropped his arms to his sides, giving up on trying to touch her.

That was a good thing because she wasn't sure how well that was going to go if he tried again.

"How dare you?" she began, trying like hell to keep her anger under control. She needed to move or she was certain she would explode. She'd trusted him. Dammit, she'd promised herself to never trust anyone, not on this level. People broke your heart, always.

"Was this your plan all along? Was the whole trial period and fake engagement all a part of some diabolical takeover of the company I've worked so hard to build because it was similar to your own?" The words stung her throat, hurt and some other emotion swirling to form a sour mix deep in her chest.

"Nina," he said, his tone stronger than he'd ever used on her before. So strong it stopped her in her tracks where she now stood close to the window. "I'm in love with you."

Her hands began to shake. A sign of weakness. She was breaking, just like her mother's departure had broken her father. Jacoby's drinking and smoking had increased in the months after Lynn left. Twelve-year-old Nina recalled the extra packs of cigarettes she saw in his bedroom trash can and the bottles of vodka that appeared throughout the house.

"Don't." She whispered the word as if it were her last breath. "Don't say that to me."

"I need to say it." He took a step toward her and she shook her head to warn him away. He stopped, sighed and then started again. "I don't want you to go. Last night we were talking about the fake breakup and you had a plan for how it would go, but I was hastily thinking of a plan to make you stay."

"You can't make me do anything, Major."

He closed his eyes, the eyes she'd been staring into every night for the past few weeks. Eyes she thought she'd come to know and to lo— Now, she was shaking her head.

"I know I can't. But I was hoping, I thought we were feeling the same thing."

"When did I ever give you the impression that

I'd be willing to sell my business to be part of your world?" She wasn't part of his world. Angie and Daisy had tried to tell her that yesterday. All these weeks she'd not only been part of a fake engagement, she'd been living a fake life. A life she'd never imagined for herself because it wasn't who she was or who she wanted to be.

"This isn't just about business, Nina. It's so much more than that, and I dare you to stand there and truthfully tell me it's different."

She couldn't and he knew it. Damn him, he knew how she felt about him. Just as Lynn had known how much Jacoby had loved her and yet she'd still walked out.

"My business is not for sale. *I* am not for sale!"

"Is that what you think this is?" he asked her quietly. "You think I'm so desperate for a fiancée that I'd try to buy your love in a mutually beneficial business deal?"

"You obtained a fake fiancée in a mutually beneficial business deal," she snapped back.

His brow furrowed and, for the first time, she thought he looked as angry as she felt. Good, he could be angry. She didn't care. He wasn't going to run over her and take what he wanted just because he was one of the fabulous Golds! His money and prestige in the fashion industry wasn't enough to take the life she'd worked so hard for away from her without a fight.

She was just about to say that and tell him exactly what he could do with his business deal and any other collaboration between her and RGF, when her phone rang. It was tucked into the back pocket of the pants she wore because she'd left her purse in her office.

"Please," Major said solemnly. "Can we just sit down and talk about this like levelheaded adults? I could be wrong—this may not work. We should just talk it over and see how we can fix this."

Her cell rang again and she yanked it out of her pocket, staring down at the screen. It was Angie. Nina turned her back to him and answered the phone.

"What is it?"

"It's Dad," Angie replied. "He fell. It's bad, Nina. You've gotta come now."

Her heart dropped and the room seemed to spin around her. Nina held tight to the phone as if that could ground her and keep her from falling. She took a deep breath and released it as slowly and as evenly as she could. "Okay. I'll be right there."

Disconnecting the call, she turned back to see Major staring at her. He looked so good in his gray suit pants and white dress shirt. The tie was a deep purple; she'd seen it hanging in his closet on the tie rack full of over one hundred others in different colors and patterns. He looked stricken, but maybe that was just because she was feeling that way. Maybe he'd looked so good and appealed to her so quickly because a part of her had wanted to see him that way. Perhaps everything she'd wanted to see and believe about this man and the situation he'd offered her was just a fantasy, a dream she hadn't known she wanted to live, even if temporarily.

None of that mattered now.

"I have to go."

"Nina—" he started to say.

"No!" Now it was time for her tone to be strong, for her to take the control her father had lost the day her mother walked out on them. "I'm leaving now, Major, and you need to let me go."

"Please, just… Okay, let me take you wherever you need to go. If it's back to your apartment, I'm okay with that, just don't walk out of here without… I don't know, Nina, just don't."

He couldn't get his words out and she thought that was strange. Major always knew what to say. Well, that was fine. She knew what needed to be said.

"I have to go and Claude will drive me." She didn't wait for another response as she started for the door. This time when he reached for her, Nina didn't pull away, she couldn't find the strength to do so.

He touched her elbow lightly at first and then let his fingers trail to her wrist and finally lace with hers. "I messed this up," he said quietly. "Let me fix it."

She looked over her shoulder at him.

"There's nothing for you to fix because I never planned to let you break me." She let her hand slip from his grasp and walked out of the office.

CHAPTER FIFTEEN

MAJOR HAD NO idea what time it was or how long he'd sat in the dark on the couch in his living room glaring at the city skyline. He'd stood in his office for endless minutes staring at the open door that Nina had walked through before cursing fluently and grabbing his jacket and phone and leaving, too. He'd thought he'd find her at his place, gathering her clothes, but she'd been there and gone. The engagement ring he'd given her left in the center of the coffee table. So he'd just dropped down onto the couch where, coincidentally, twelve hours before they'd sat talking about their impending breakup.

He leaned forward, letting his elbows rest on his knees and feeling his head drop down. Where was she? How was she feeling? What could he say or do to make this better? Or, at the very least, to make the burning pain that had spread throughout his chest and settled there like an impending storm go away.

The doorbell rang and he ignored it. Whoever was on the other side wasn't going to make this better.

Because no matter who it was, it wouldn't be Nina. He was certain of that.

She wasn't coming back, not to him, and definitely not to RGF. RJ was going to be pissed about the latter but Major didn't care. Once upon a time, business—his family's and the one he'd built for himself—had been all he'd cared about. But that was before the marketing plan. Before Nina.

The bell rang again and this time it was followed by a familiar voice.

"Major Frederick Gold, if you don't open this door, I'm going to take it off its hinges."

He lifted his head at the sound of his mother's voice.

When he was seven years old, he and Maurice had spread peanut butter over the floors in one of Riley's dollhouses. When Riley had seen it, she'd been hysterical for hours. Maurice had laughed it off and taken his punishment in the nonchalant way he always did. But Major had been devastated by the pain in Riley's cries as well as the fury and disappointment in his mother's voice. He'd locked himself in his bedroom to get away from it all and Marva had stood outside the door, knocking for a few moments before repeating the same threat she'd just stated.

Major stood and walked to the door. Moments later he found not just his mother but Riley, too, standing on the other side.

"Silly boy," Marva said as she entered, stroking him on the cheek.

Riley shook her head as she walked past him.

He closed the door and prepared himself for the barrage from the only two women he'd ever thought he'd love.

Riley sat in one of the side chairs, placing her purse on the end table. Marva sat, too, and patted the cushion beside her as a signal for Major to take a seat.

"Are you done sulking?" she asked once he settled beside her.

"I'm a grown man, Mom. I don't sulk," he said.

"Ha!"

That came from Riley and Major chose to ignore it.

"What did you do to mess things up with her?" Marva asked.

He didn't even bother to question how she knew. Somehow his mother always knew everything, and he suspected Landra may have overheard the last portion of his argument with Nina. His assistant didn't miss much that went on in the office.

"She overheard me talking to Ruben about combining our businesses so that she wouldn't have to work to get recognition in the industry."

"Dumb ass," Riley quipped.

Major glared at his sister.

"Well, you have to admit that wasn't very smart," Marva said.

He sighed. "In retrospect, I can see that. But at the time—"

"You thought you were doing her a favor," Marva finished for him.

"You thought you were saving her," Riley added. "Men are so dense sometimes."

He should have left them in the hallway.

"If you wanted her to stay with you, Major, why didn't you just ask her?"

"I didn't know how."

"Oh, it's simple. 'Nina, I love you. Please don't go.' Seven measly little words," Riley said.

Times like these Major hated having a sister, especially one as smart as Riley.

"Again, at the time, I didn't think to start it off that way. But I did tell her I loved her. She didn't seem to care," he admitted, feeling a renewed wave of pain soar through his chest.

"It's hard to believe someone loves you when they try to take what you've worked hard for. Isn't that what you thought your father would do if he found out about you wanting to leave RGF to start your own business?"

Major straightened and stared at his mother.

"Your father and I've known for some time that you were itching to move beyond RGF," she replied in answer to his unspoken question. "You and Maurice always thought you were keeping your little twin secrets, but you forget Ruben's mother and office manager is a longtime friend of mine."

He sighed again because he hadn't forgotten that, but he *had* instead relied on confidentiality from his attorney's office. While that professional courtesy should've stretched to Ruben's staff, Marva didn't play when it came to her children and if Ruben's mother had let anything slip about Brand Integrated, Marva would've pried the full story out of her.

"Look, I'm not here to talk about your business. You know I love and believe in you, whatever you do and wherever you do it," Riley said. "But Nina's a good woman and I'm really pissed off that you pushed her out of your life. Out of our lives."

It was hard for any of them to have real friends, unless they'd been there since childhood like Ruben had been for Major. But for Riley, with all that she'd been through with her past scandals involving idiotic men, it was doubly hard for her to form bonds with people other than family. She'd obviously bonded with Nina.

"I didn't want her to go, Riley. I tried to get her to stay."

"Well, now it's time to try to get her back," Marva said as if that were as simple as making a phone call.

"I don't know how," he said, dragging his hands down his face. "She's got so much on her plate right now. I don't want to be another issue in her life. If this isn't what she wants, I have no right trying to force it on her."

"Did she say it wasn't what she wanted?" Riley asked. "I don't think having you in her life is adding a responsibility. To the contrary, I think the time she was here may have been the most relaxed she's been in years."

Just last night she'd been in her element at the trade show. The moment she'd found those African pieces, she'd lit up like a Christmas tree, all bright and giddy with her idea. And it was a brilliant idea, one that had sparked the plan he'd eventually come up with.

Major stood and walked over to the window. He folded his arms across his chest and stared into the night, wishing it were as simple as reaching out into the big city and touching her.

"There are probably trains leaving for York as early as seven tomorrow morning," he said more to himself than to his mom and sister. "Or I could just drive. Be there first thing in the morning, ready to grovel if need be. Anything, just so long as I get the chance to apologize to her and to tell her how much I love her."

He didn't wait for a response from anyone, just went into his bedroom and started to pack.

Jacoby yelled out in agony as he sat up in his bed.

"I told you to wait and let me help you," Nina said, coming around to the side of the bed and slipping her arm under his to help bear his weight so he could stand. "And you need to use the crutches, like the doctor told you."

"Well, I want to go sit out on the back porch. That pain pill had me sleeping so long this morning, I missed my normal coffee time."

That was true, but Nina had appreciated those three hours of solitude. It had been the first time she'd been able to sit with her thoughts since she'd raced home yesterday morning.

"I got some iced tea in the refrigerator. I want a glass and some cookies while I sit outside," Jacoby said.

"Okay, I'll get you settled outside and then I'll get your tea and cookies," she told him.

"Where're your sisters? Did they run out the moment you got here? Those two stay busy."

Nina sighed and concentrated on easing her father to the crutches so that she could get his weight properly distributed and keep them both upright. His fall down the last four stairs in the basement had left him with a broken left ankle and a gash on his head that had to be sutured. He was now sporting a white patch of gauze over his right eye to match the white cast on his ankle.

She settled him on her right side and worked her way around him with the other crutch, tucking it under his left arm.

"There, now take it slow. I'll get your snack and sit on the porch with you and go through my emails."

Since she was certain her deal with RGF was over.

Jacoby huffed and mumbled some more as she stayed a few steps behind him to offer support should he need it. Her father was a proud man; a stubborn and opinionated man who loved his girls more than he loved life at this moment.

"I want the Oreo cookies, not those dry butter ones Daisy keeps buying," he said when they finally made it into the kitchen.

The master bedroom of the ranch-style house was closer to the kitchen than the other two rooms, so their trek had been short. Nina immediately went to the cabinet to grab a glass and filled it with the crushed ice her father preferred from the ice machine on the refrigerator.

"The butter cookies have less sugar," she told him even though she knew he couldn't care less.

"Yeah, well all the baked goods and snacks could cause elevated cholesterol or diabetes. Everything does something bad and something good. So with the time I have left, I'm doing whatever makes me feel good. I want eight cookies. Count 'em and put them in a napkin for me."

He was already heading for the back door, which Nina had left open when she'd gone out onto the porch to sit while he slept. After this morning, she now knew why her father liked to sit on that porch so much. It was quiet, peaceful, revealing. She'd come to terms with a few things about herself and her life while sitting in one of the twin rocking chairs just staring out toward the sky.

With the glass in one hand, his eight cookies folded into a napkin in the other, and her laptop tucked under her arm, she walked out onto the porch just as her dad was trying to settle himself into a chair. She hurried over to him, placing the glass, cookies and laptop on the small wooden table between the rocking chairs that looked as if they were on their last legs.

"Here, let me help you," she said and eased the crutches from one arm and then the next.

Standing in front of him, she put both her arms under his and then bent her knees as he reclined into the chair.

Jacoby huffed when he was finally seated. "Your sisters should have stayed here to help," he grumbled.

She ignored him because she was glad Angie and Daisy had left. They'd been a nagging, arguing pain in her ass from the time she'd arrived yesterday, until the moment she'd told them to go late last night. They weren't being helpful, just judgmental and annoying, traits they'd spent most of their lives perfecting.

"It's okay, Dad. We're fine," she told him, sitting in the chair next to him before grabbing her laptop from the table.

"Not okay," he said when he reached for his cookies.

She could hear him crunching on the first one as she booted up her laptop and waited to log in to her inbox.

"You should be in New York working," Jacoby said after a few moments.

"You weren't happy that I'd stayed in New York, remember?"

"No, I wasn't happy if you were in New York pimping yourself out to some rich dude," he snapped. "But you said that's not what you were doing."

"It's not," she replied, clicking on an email from RJ Gold, wondering if this was his message telling her she'd breached her contract with them by leaving town.

"And that guy you were in New York with? He was helping you with your business?"

She was only half listening to her father now, but

she replied, "Yeah, his family's company was taking a chance on my app."

If you're reading this right now, I'm on my way to you and it's too late for you to stop me.

That's what the first line of the email read and her heartbeat had immediately picked up its pace.

I hope you'll hear me out this time and once you do, whatever you want, whatever you tell me to do, I will.

RJ hadn't written this email. Her eyes shot up to the subject line of the message again as she read the oldest Gold brother's name and email address.

"He sounds like a good guy. You should hear him out."

Her head snapped up at her father's words and she looked over at him and then past him.

Major walked around from the side of the house and her laptop almost slipped off her lap. He wore dark blue jeans and a crisp, white polo shirt. His hair looked freshly cut and his shape-up was sharp, his thin mustache trimmed. Her pulse rate quickened as her mind whirled with questions.

"Hello, Mr. Fuller. It's nice to meet you in person, sir."

She watched as Major walked up onto the porch and immediately went to her father, extending a hand for Jacoby to shake. Her father, the surly old grouch that he'd become, accepted that hand and looked up at Major.

"You mess this up again and I'll beat you with my crutches."

Major nodded. "I understand, sir."

"What's going on? You two know each other?" She put her laptop on the table because she couldn't afford to pay for another one and if one more surprise popped off, she was sure to drop this one.

Her father answered. "Got a call from this gentleman early this morning while you were sitting out here rocking in my chair like you thought you could find the answers to your problems."

"I thought you were asleep," she said.

"Not with my chair squeaking the way it does when it's being rocked too fast. And then that cell phone you and your sisters insist I keep close to me started ringing."

She looked to Major then. "You called my father?"

Before he could answer, Jacoby spoke. "You got something for me, young man?"

"Ah, yeah. I have it right here." Major reached around to his back pocket and pulled out some folded papers. "All you need to do is read over the lease and sign it. I can take it back to the facility today and you can move in as early as tomorrow."

Nina stood. "Move? What facility? Will somebody please tell me what's going on?" Her hands were trembling and her heart was about to pump right out of her chest.

Jacoby took the papers Major handed him and

then waved his free hand. "Go on, take her in the house and say your piece before she flips out. She never did like not knowing or controlling everything. Gets that from me, I suppose."

Major stepped closer to her. "Can we go inside and talk for a minute?"

She didn't know what to say and still couldn't believe he was there. "I guess that's what we're supposed to do at this point."

Before Major or her father could say another word, Nina walked into the house. She passed through the kitchen and stopped in the center of the living room, turning to see Major as he followed her inside.

"What are you doing? You got my father into that facility you were talking about, without consulting me?"

"I consulted your father," he said with a nod. "And before you go off telling me I had no right to do that, I wasn't going to. When I called your father this morning, it was strictly to ask him if he would mind me coming by to see you. He brought up the facility, asking if I knew of any places in New York that he could afford on his budget."

"No," she said, her voice cracking slightly. "That's impossible. His budget isn't enough to hardly cover the expenses in this house. And his home…our home…is here in York."

"I wish it could be in New York with me," he said quietly.

"Major—"

"Wait," he said, holding up a hand. "Just give me

five minutes. Let me just get this out the right way this time and then you can react. You can tell me to kick rocks and leave you alone forever, if that's what you want. But please, just listen."

She folded her arms over her chest because the warmth that was now swelling there alarmed her. This wasn't supposed to be happening. Early this morning she'd sat on that porch resigning herself to having fallen in love when that hadn't been her plan and to making the best of the help she'd gleaned working with his family's company for the short time she'd been blessed to do so. She hadn't thought of contacting Major again or going back to New York to see him. She would deal with whatever legal repercussions were brought on by her breaching the contract, but her new plan was to move on.

"I love you," he said when she nodded for him to continue.

"I didn't plan on falling in love and neither did you. We planned to do what was best for our businesses. And to be totally honest with you, Nina, I believe in my heart that you and I partnering together in a consulting and development firm that will cater to a full scale of technological needs to the fashion industry is the best career move for us."

She opened her mouth to speak and Major stepped closer, touching a finger softly to her lips.

"I'm not here to save you, your father or your business. Because you don't need to be saved. You're a brilliant, beautiful woman with a bright future ahead of you whether or not you take me up on this offer.

But I don't know how to move forward without you, Nina. You walked into that building all those weeks ago and the moment you bumped into me, *you* saved *me*."

He slid his finger away.

"You saved me from the lonely life I'd resigned myself to because I refused to trust again. You agreed to do what was a crazy job from the start and, every step of the way, all you were concerned with was doing your very best to make that crazy job work, for my family's company as well as for your own. I can't thank you enough for your help and I couldn't let you go without admitting to you that I need you. I want you, for real this time."

Tears welled in her eyes but she refused to let them fall.

"You knew all I wanted was to take care of my father." Her voice was shaky and she wanted to stop. She wanted to turn away from him and go somewhere alone to break down under the pressure of emotions that had steadily built with each word he'd spoken.

"You've taken care of your family for so long. You thought it was your job, but it wasn't. Your father asked me to find him a place in New York because he feels that's the only way you'll follow your dreams. I did it because I love you and I want your dreams to be my dreams. I want us to do this business thing and the family thing together."

The first tear rolled down her cheek and she cursed the warm, wet feel of it.

Major used his thumb to brush that tear away.

"You weren't planning to buy my business," she said slowly. "You wanted us to be partners all along?"

He nodded. "I would never take anything away from you. I believe what you've built can enhance what I've started. And my father and RJ loved your ideas about the accessory line for RGF. I told them about it when I was hijacking RJ's email account to schedule that message you received."

She chuckled and shook her head. "I knew RJ hadn't written that."

"No, but he had a good time saying he told me so while I typed it. My dad appreciated my groveling to you a bit more than I expected, as well."

He used both hands to cup her face now, tilting her head up to his. "I'm dying to kiss you."

"Kisses aren't part of the negotiations this time, Major."

He froze at her words.

"I want more," she said, coming up on the tips of her toes to touch her lips to his briefly. "I want a real engagement party where you'll officially slip my ring back onto my finger, and a huge wedding and when we launch *our* business, I want it to be called the Gold Service."

His smile spread slowly and warm tendrils wrapped around her heart. "I think that can be arranged," he replied.

* * * * *

FAKING IT

STEFANIE LONDON

To all the readers who emailed me asking why
Owen never got his happy every after…this book
is for you. xx

CHAPTER ONE

Owen

I KNOW IT'S going to make me seem like a cruel bastard, but there isn't much in this world that pleases me more than getting the drop on someone. The element of surprise is my catnip. I love the moment my target realises they've been duped. Maybe it's because nobody ever expected a thing from me.

Who actually thinks the class clown will amount to something? No one.

So yeah, I like it when the tables are turned. Especially when my target comes in a five-foot-two-inch package filled to the brim with bristling indignation.

"No." Miss Indignation shakes her head, a frizzy brown ponytail slapping her ears like she's a puppy shaking off the water from an unwanted bath. "Can't we pretend to be brother and sister?"

"I'm not sure which part of this meeting you misinterpreted as a negotiation, Anderson." My old boss, Gary Smythe, raises a bushy silver eyebrow. "This is your first assignment as a detective. I thought you'd be champing at the bit."

Hannah Anderson, now known as Detective Senior Constable Anderson, straightens her shoulders. "Yes, sir, and I'm very grateful for the opportunity—"

"Then I suggest you quit shaking your head like you're trying to dislodge something."

I snort and stifle the noise with a cough. Neither one of them buys it. We're sitting in a meeting room at the Victoria Police headquarters. It feels strange to be back. I'd never planned on returning to Australia, let alone to my old job. But that's life, right? The second you think you've got your shit together, fate punches you in the nuts.

"Yes, sir." Hannah looks like she's about to erupt. She clutches her coffee cup in a way that tells me she's trying to mentally crush my skull.

Nice try, Anderson.

"Not exactly the warm welcome I was hoping for," I chime in, returning her fiery glare with a cocky grin. If there's one thing that makes Anderson blow her stack, it's people who take life less seriously than she does.

Spoiler alert: that's literally everyone.

"Shut up, Fletcher." Gary takes a sip of his cappuccino. He's drinking out of a mug that says "I like big busts and I cannot lie" with a picture of a pair of handcuffs beneath it. A white line of milk foam caps his Ned Flanders–style moustache. "If you want someone to fawn over you, then pay your grandmother a visit."

"Will do, sir."

Anderson rolls her eyes. If it's not completely obvious at this point, she kind of hates me. Well, *hate* might be a strong word although she *has* said it before. It's a weird kind of hate. The kind that feels prickly and cold but is really a front for a gooey centre of white-hot attraction. Yeah, she has the hots for me and she hates herself for it.

So I'm scoring another point in the bastard category, but that pleases me very much.

"We're going undercover," I say, leaning forward against the table and not even trying to hide my glee. "As man and wife."

I swear she somehow manages to tell me to go fuck myself with her eyes. "Right."

"We thought we'd put this to bed before you left." Gary frowns.

He told me the pertinent details before I submitted my leave at Cobalt & Dane, the security company I work for in New York City. A folder with everything required for this undercover gig—ID for my new identity, keys and an access card for the apartment I'm going to call home for the next month, and surveillance info that's been collected to date—is already in my backpack.

This is an evidence-gathering mission, in the hopes of convincing the higher-ups to put together a task force. And I'm going to enjoy the heck out of being cooped up with Anderson.

"So did I, Boss." The name comes out of habit. Gary Smythe will always be "Boss" to me.

We'd cracked the old case before I left for New York. But organised crime is a tricky beast. You think you've cut off the snake's head and suddenly it grows back. If there's one thing I've learned over the years, it's that greed is unrelenting.

"It looks like one of the relatives took over the family business," Gary continues. "We suspect they're running the operation out of an apartment complex in South Melbourne. We've secured an apartment for you. You'll move in on Monday morning and make friends with the neighbours."

Easy as pie. I love making friends.

But I suspect Anderson might have trouble with that. Friendliness isn't her strong suit.

"I want you two to get reacquainted. Finish your coffees and figure your shit out." Gary pushes up from his seat, his belly straining against his navy uniform shirt. Today he's in office dress—proper trousers instead of the tactical ones, and a black tie at his neck. Probably had a meeting with the big boss. "See if you can keep from killing each other."

"Our reputation precedes us," I say as Gary exits the meeting room, leaving me alone with my soon-to-be fake-wife.

"*Your* reputation precedes *you*," Anderson corrects me. "Mine is nice and quiet. The way I prefer it."

"Always so argumentative." I lean back in my chair and fold my arms over my chest. Unlike her, I'm not dressed in uniform since I'm here as a consultant.

They might be able to drag me back for a case, but I'm not signing any long-term contracts. I'll do this job as a favour for my old boss. I like the guy. I *don't* like the life I left behind. Too many demons. The second this job is over I'm getting my ass back to New York.

"Look, this is my first assignment as a detective," she says, nailing me with her wide brown eyes. "And I know you have a penchant for wreaking havoc, but I will not let you screw this up. You might have left this life behind, but this job is important to me."

Anderson is all spit and polish, just as I remember. Perfectly pressed shirt and slacks, neat ponytail. She's clearly catching up on paperwork before her big move into a detective's role. I bet she stayed up late last night shining her shoes.

"Message received, Anderson. No tomfoolery."

"You should start calling me Hannah. Get into the habit so my surname doesn't slip out in front of anyone while we're on the job." She sticks her thumb into her mouth to chew on a nail, but then thinks better of it and folds her hands in front of her. Outside the meeting room, people wander back and forth—some in uniform and others in civilian dress. "I wanted to keep our first names the same. Make it easier to remember. Although I still don't see why we can't be brother and sister. It seems ludicrous that *anyone* would think I'd marry you."

"Oh yeah, speaking of which…" I dig my hand into my pocket and pull out a worn velvet box. Anderson's eyes widen as I flip it open, showing her the old, ornate ring nestled inside.

The ring is legit. It belonged to my mother and since I'm never, *ever* getting married I'm pleased to use it for something. It wasn't her engagement ring— that one lives with my grandmother. But my mother loved jewellery enough to have a personal jeweller on retainer when she was alive, so I wasn't short on options for this fake proposal.

Fun fact: I don't need to work. My parents were rich. Like, travel around the world on a private jet rich. Like fly in a bunch of diamonds straight from Antwerp rich.

Not that I want anything to do with the money. It's been sitting in a bank account for the last fifteen years while my financial adviser plays with cryptocurrency like he's got a great big pile of Monopoly money in front of him. I told him to pick the riskiest ones and not even think twice if he lost the lot. He didn't, not by a long shot.

And for this job, I'm going to have to embrace the upper-crust lifestyle.

"You've got to start wearing this," I say.

Anderson blinks. "This is *not* how the fairy tales led me to believe a proposal would happen."

The gold band cradles an interesting stone in a smoky shade that's somewhere between brown and grey, which is nicer than it sounds. It's surrounded by tiny white diamonds that glimmer under the artificial lighting.

The ring is unusual and pretty, like Anderson.

"I guess I'm not doing it right." Clearing my throat, I slide off my chair and drop down to one knee. "Detective Senior Constable Hannah Anderson, will you—"

"Fletcher!" she squeaks, and several people outside the meeting room snap their heads in our direction. She gives me a shove and I fall to one side, laughing and landing on my palm. She snatches the ring box out of my other hand and shoves it into her pocket. "Are you trying to give me a heart attack?"

"What? I thought I was being nice."

She shakes her head as though I'm the biggest idiot this side of the Yarra. Which, to be fair, might be true. "Couldn't you find one of those gumball machines and get me some crappy little trinket? I'm going to freak out wearing this." She pats her hand over the pocket containing my mother's ring. "This is...real."

"Yeah, it is. Topaz or some shit. And we're going to be tracking a band of jewellery thieves. Ever think of that? Might be good to have a sparkly conversation starter."

Her expression tells me it was a good call but there's no way in hell she'll say it aloud. Anderson—sorry, *Hannah*—doesn't like to admit when other people are right.

"We should meet early on Monday morning. I've arranged for Ridgeway to drive a van with some boxes to the apartment building."

"What's in the boxes?"

"Nothing much. Files and stuff. But we have to look like we're moving in."

I grin. "It's a new adventure for us. Newlyweds getting their first place together. You'll have to practice looking excited."

"I don't know if I have it in me," she drawls. Then she stands. Even with me sitting and her standing, she doesn't have much height on me. What did I call her back then? Pocket Rocket. "Monday morning. Seven a.m."

"Seven?" I groan. "Who moves into a house that early?"

"People who are excited to be living together." She picks up her coffee cup. I'm already imagining how strange it's going to be to see my mother's ring on her finger. For some reason, it doesn't repulse me as much as it should. "Don't be late."

"Seven a.m. it is, my darling wife."

She rolls her eyes again and I contemplate warning her that the wind might change. But this time I hold my tongue. I'll have many hours ahead of me to drive her nuts. Gotta take the perks of the job wherever they come. I pull the file out of my backpack and scan the summary page containing the key details of our assignment. Seven a.m. at 21 Love Street, South Melbourne.

Love Street? Sounds like the perfect place for a fake marriage.

CHAPTER TWO

Hannah

OWEN'S LATE. I'm shocked…not.

I bounce on the balls of my feet, trying to ignore the strange feeling of the ring on my left hand. The big stone chafes me, reminding me constantly that it's there. It's irritating. Like the man who gave it to me.

It's also insanely beautiful and makes me feel like a princess, but I'm not telling a soul *that* little piece of information.

"Have you got a coping strategy in place?" Max Ridgeway leans against the small van parked in the loading dock of the place that will be my home until this assignment is over.

21 Love Street is the kind of place I would never actually live. It's one of those "boutique" apartment complexes—only six stories in height, with a grand foyer and all the trimmings. It's not meant for people like me, people who grew up with a family crammed into a house without enough bathrooms to go around.

Sure, this place isn't the most expensive building in the city…but it's *well* beyond my means. And we're going to be living in one of the penthouse suites.

So yeah, you could say I was feeling a little out of my element. And that was *before* my "husband" arrived.

"A coping strategy?" I ask.

"To avoid homicide."

I laugh in spite of the strange churning in my stomach. "No. I need one, though. Any tips?"

Max adjusts the dark cap covering his thick brown hair. He's dressed in plain clothes, like me. Civilian-wear. Old jeans and a hoodie. Blundstones. He skipped his morning shave, too. Now he looks like a furniture removalist instead of a cop.

"Don't take things too seriously." He winks. "That'll only give him fuel."

Max gets along with both of us. He's good at his job and I respect him a lot. His wife, Rose, gave birth to their daughter, Ruby, about six months ago. Now he spends most of his free time at home with his adorable family, so I don't see him as much as I used to.

He was in Manhattan for a while, when he met Rose, working with Owen in the private security field. They're pretty tight. Have been since we were all in the academy together in our early twenties. But I don't hold that against Max. *He* didn't have anything to do with "the diary incident."

I check my watch. "Owen is going to be late to his own funeral one day."

"You've got the wife act down pat." Max's eyes sparkle. "Although I hope you're not planning to accelerate his funeral."

"Ha," I say drily. "That's entirely up to him."

A cool wind whips past me, ruffling my hair. Today I left it down and it feels like the first time in forever that I've ditched my standard scraped-back style. But it's all part of the act. Anything to help me get into character. For the foreseeable future, I am not Hannah Anderson. I am not the only girl in a family of rough-and-tumble boys. I am not awkward and shy and trying so hard not to let other people see it.

Last night, I sat down with all my files and a cup of tea to work on my story, so that when I arrived at 21 Love Street, I would be Hannah Essex. Lady of leisure, newlywed, a woman obsessed with shiny, material things. A pretty magpie.

My polar opposite.

I wonder if my boss is screwing with me, pushing me into the deep end to see if I sink or swim. I could think of a dozen other female officers who would be *way* more convincing than me. Who are prettier and look like they *could* belong in this world.

Meanwhile I burned my thumb while straightening my hair this morning so I'd look like Owen's wife, instead of his poodle.

"Party people." Owen announces himself with a *whoop*, sans apology for his tardiness—as expected—and slaps a hand down on Max's back. When he leans in as if to kiss me, I place a hand on his chest to stop him getting too close. "That's a chilly greeting."

I chide myself. He's right, of course. We have to be in character now, even if I want to strangle him with my scarf. "The concierge manager is due to meet us in ten minutes."

"Ten minutes?" Owen looks at his watch. "I thought you said seven a.m."

"I did. And I booked the move-in for eight, knowing your lazy ass wouldn't be here on time." I shoot him a smug grin. "So you're early."

"She got you there." Max chuckles and heads to the back of the van. "I'll start getting these boxes out now and we can load them straight onto the flatbed."

"I'll help."

I resist the urge to join in and speed up the process. Hannah Anderson is a hands-on person who can lift a box with the best of them. However, Hannah Essex is worried about her manicure. I glare at the pearly pink polish I applied last night. I'd toyed with the idea of fake nails to compensate for my terrible nail-biting habit, but I have to draw the line somewhere. The last thing I need is a nail flying off while I'm chasing a perp.

"Mrs. Essex?"

For a second the name doesn't register, but then my brain kicks into gear and I smile at the man and woman approaching me. "Yes, that's me."

"Welcome to 21 Love Street." The woman is older—late sixties, maybe seventies—with a genuine smile and a neatly pressed uniform of white shirt and grey slacks. "I'm Irma and this is my colleague Dante. Looks like you're all ready to move in. I understand you've already picked up your keys and access cards."

"Yes." I stick my hand out to shake Irma's and then turn my smile to Dante, who's about my age. "Nice to meet you both."

"Dante will set the elevator to freight mode and make sure you get up to your level okay," Irma says. "Let us know if you have any questions at all."

I give my thanks and wait while Owen and Max finish unloading our boxes onto the flatbed trolley. Owen is wearing a pair of fitted jeans and a simple V-neck grey jumper that sits close to his body. A heavy silver watch decorates one wrist. The neat, casual outfit is at odds with Owen's overlong dirty-blond hair, which seems to be permanently two weeks overdue for a haircut. The thick strands kink and curl at the back of his neck. At one point in my much younger, much *stupider* years I'd fantasised about running my hands through it, about kissing his full-lipped, smart-ass mouth.

"She can hardly keep her eyes off me." Owen looks smug as hell and I realise I've been caught staring.

"Newlyweds?" Dante asks with a knowing smile. I want to punch them both.

"We're so very in love." Owen walks toward me with that careless rolling-hip gait that makes women adore him. I can't walk away. Can't break character. "Isn't that right?"

"It sure is." I tip my face up to his, aiming for a loving look while hoping he can hear the obscenities I'm screaming at him in my mind. As he lowers his lips, I turn my face so the kiss catches my cheek. Nice try, Fletcher. "And I'm also madly in love with this apartment. Are we ready to go up?"

Owen chuckles. "My wife, the drill sergeant."

"Tell me about it," Dante says as he leads us through the loading bay into the building via a room where recycled waste is kept. I make note of my surroundings, mentally jotting down details about building access points. "I've been married for two years now. My wife is about to have our first baby."

"That's sweet." I try to sound like I mean it. But my mind is on the job...well, it should be. And it should definitely *not* be occupied with the enticing way Owen's butt looks in those fitted jeans.

Dante leads us to a bay of elevators, one of which is open and protected with heavy-duty fabric. "You're good to go. Shouldn't take more than three or four trips, by the looks of it. I have to stay in the loading bay to make sure we don't end up with any traffic jams, so I'll see you when you come back down for the next load."

Max, Owen and I squeeze into the elevator with the trolley and boxes. The door slides shut.

"The whole team is taking bets on who strangles who first," Max says as we rise up to the top floor. "Money's on Anderson, ten to one."

"Ten to one?" Owen's lip curls in disgust. "Traitors."

"It's better odds than you deserve," I mutter, my

thumb rubbing over the ring on my left hand. I can't stop touching the damn thing. It's driving me nuts.

The other thing driving me nuts is the smell of soap on Owen's skin—creamy and warm, like sandalwood with a hint of vanilla. I don't remember him smelling that good in our academy days. Though, to be fair, I don't know if many guys in their early twenties shower as often as they should.

I should *not* be thinking about what Owen looks like in the shower.

The glowing green numbers count up to level six. I really need to get a hold on my imagination—because this assignment is going to be difficult enough without giving him *any* indication that I still harbour an attraction to him. And I don't. He's awful and childish and irreverent and not the kind of guy I would ever marry because I like serious men who do…serious things.

Ugh. I'm no good at lying, even in my head. I train my eyes on the glowing numbers. Maybe if I don't look at Owen, I won't get affected by whatever hot guy voodoo he's using to mess with my head.

When we reach our destination, the elevator opens with a cheerful *ping*.

"Apartment 601." I exit with more speed than is necessary. As I march toward the front door, I dig the key out of my bag. "Home sweet home."

The apartment is bigger than anywhere I've ever lived, including my family home that housed five of us. Even though we're only six floors up, we have a lovely view of South Melbourne made even prettier

by the buttery morning light. The apartment itself
has been staged by someone who knows the fine
line between style and comfort, and there's a mix
of textures—light, warm woods and soft grey fabric
and faded gold metals—that make me feel instantly
at ease. The neutral tones are brought to life with a
few pops of colour, including a vibrant sunflower
yellow chair and a canvas splashed with shades of
teal and lavender.

"This'll do," Owen says as he walks in. Max follows with the trolley. "Not really my style, but it
looks like we have money."

No kidding. I spot a Herman Miller Eames chair
in the corner of the room, and it looks like the real
deal. Those things cost more than what I paid for
my first car. I dated a guy once—*very* briefly—who
owned one of those chairs. Talked about it like the
damn thing was his child.

"I'll get the next load of boxes," Max says. "And
I'll make conversation with the concierge guy, see
if I pick up anything interesting."

Owen nods. "Good idea."

The second the door swings shut behind Max, my
body is alight with awareness. The tingling sensation of being watched is an itch beneath my skin. At
one point, I'd craved this with all my being—a moment alone with Owen.

"We'll have to make sure we don't damage any of
this furniture," I say in a desperate attempt to keep
my mind where it belongs—on work. "Budget won't
accommodate eight grand for a chair."

"And how do you think we're going to damage the furniture, huh?" Owen walks up beside me, and I feel his presence right down to my toes.

"Not like *that*." I don't need to spell out that sex isn't part of playing man and wife for this job. Owen might be a larrikin, but he's not an asshole. In fact, the one time he had the chance to take advantage of our situation—the time I *asked* him to—he declined due to "personal ethics" and I never quite got over the humiliation. Even thinking about it now makes my stomach churn. "But I do remember one young recruit who managed to break both a dining chair *and* a bed frame in one evening."

"Harmless fun." He slings an arm around my shoulders and I force myself not to lean into him. "It's been a long time, Anderson. I missed you while I was in New York."

I snort. "I didn't think about you once."

"Liar." He laughs and his delicious scent fills my nostrils again. Damn it. How does he smell so freaking good? "You ready to take the bad guys down?"

"Absolutely." This time my response is genuine. I love my job and I'm damn good at it. "They won't even know what hit them."

CHAPTER THREE

Owen

IT TAKES LESS than a day for us to argue about every little thing—our approach for gaining the trust of the people in the building, where to set up discreet surveillance…what flavour pizza we should get for dinner. She wanted Hawaiian. Gross. Pineapple does *not* belong on pizza.

We compromise and get Thai food instead.

"We should be talking to people already," Hannah argues. Her dark hair started the day floating around her face, brushing the tops of her shoulders, but now it's pulled back into a messy little knot. "You think they want to pay us for sitting around? That might be how things work in your cushy world, but we're wasting taxpayers' dollars right now."

"Sorry, I was under the impression you were a detective senior constable, not the chief commissioner." I spear a piece of duck and make sure I get some coconut rice on my fork, as well. Damn, it's good. "And cushy, my ass. My job keeps me fit as a fiddle, and don't think I didn't notice you staring earlier."

When some women blush, it's like a delicate pink flush over their cheeks. Hannah's blush goes *everywhere*—over her cheeks and nose, down her neck and under the edge of her simple black T-shirt. But my favourite bit is how it colours the tips of her ears.

"I have to stare. It's not often I see a class-A idiot in the flesh," she snaps.

The defensive comeback bounces right off me—I've been called worse. No-hoper. Slacker. Troublemaker. I saw my eleventh-grade science teacher in my first month of being a constable and her eyes almost popped out of her head. To say most people didn't expect me to do much with my life is an understatement.

Have you done much with your life? Really?

I promptly ignore that inconvenient thought and file it away where it belongs: in the corner of my mind marked "shit not to think about."

"You've got such a way with words, Anderson."

"It's Hannah, remember? You can't mess that up." Her cheeks return to their usual colour as she tucks into her Pad Thai. "Now, back to work. We've got to get out and talk to people."

"Have you ever met a newlywed couple who wanted to become BFFs with their new neighbours the second they got married? No, they want to fuck like animals and not leave their apartment."

She rolls her eyes. "You *would* think that. How many times have you been married?"

"Zero. But if I *did* get married, I wouldn't make hanging out with the neighbours my first priority." I reach for my Coke. "However, I do agree we can't sit in here all night."

"Then what?"

"We go for a romantic evening walk in the garden."

She looks at me like I've sprouted a second head. "A romantic walk?"

"It will give us a chance to scope out the property, look for anything out of the ordinary and find some surveillance points."

"And then we can talk to anyone we come across?"

I sigh. "We don't need to talk to them yet. It's not a good idea to come across too eager."

"Is this some weird guy logic?" She narrows her eyes. "Like needing to wait three weeks before you call a girl after a date?"

I raise a brow. "If he's waiting three weeks, he's not interested."

She stabs at her dinner like she's trying to make sure it's dead. Either that, or she's imagining it's me. "I'm talking hypothetically."

I would usually take the opportunity to stir her up some more, but for some reason I don't want to talk about Anderson's dating life. It makes me feel a little stabby myself, so I move the conversation on. "If we come on too strong, we might tip them off. We need to seem interesting, so they come to us."

"And by 'seem interesting' what you really mean is 'seem rich,' right? We need to make ourselves a target."

"Exactly. And it needs to be subtle. We can't *look* like we're trying to get anyone's attention."

She makes a sound of frustration that's music to my ears. Winding her up is way too easy. "So we have to attract attention without looking like we want it, and we have to avoid talking to people so they want to talk to us? Doesn't that seem a little counterintuitive?"

"No, it seems like the right way to do things. Trust me, I know how these guys work. Last time—"

"Yes, last time you brought down a crime ring almost single-handedly. I remember the bragging." She shakes her head and scoops up a pile of noodles with her fork. "Why *did* you move to New York, anyway? It seemed like you were on the rise, and then suddenly I hear you've taken off."

Speaking of things to file under "shit not to think about…"

"I'm a free spirit, baby." I use the smile that comes naturally to me—the one that's been convincing people for years that I don't give a crap about anything. "I go wherever the whim takes me."

She shakes her head and concentrates on her meal. In the silence, I watch her. I liked Anderson the second we crossed paths in our first week at the academy. She's smart—if a little traditional in her approach to things—and she's calm in a crisis. I've seen her outrun some of the fittest men I know to take down a bad guy. I've seen her talk herself out of dangerous situations and I've seen her stick up for some of the most vulnerable people in the communities we serve. Despite my teasing, I respect her a hell of a lot. She deserves to be a detective.

And I can't take my eyes off her.

"Who's staring now?" She smirks at me with a self-satisfied expression that's a flashing cape to a bull.

"You have a little something…" I lean forward to point at an imaginary spot on her cheek and when she moves I flick her nose with my finger.

"You're such a child," she says, rolling her eyes. But that doesn't stop her dabbing at the imaginary spot with a napkin. "Fine, let's try it your way tonight. Romantic walk in the garden…but we might want to bring a bucket in case I need to puke from the pressure of pretending to be attracted to you."

"Who's the child now?" I mutter, stacking the empty containers and stifling the grin that wants to burst forth. If I'm going to be back in Australia, then at least I have some fun to distract me from the growing list of things I don't want to think about.

CHAPTER FOUR

Hannah

THERE'S A SURPRISING amount of garden space out the back of 21 Love Street, considering we're in South Melbourne. From what I've read on the building, this used to be a big warehouse lot that was rezoned to accommodate residential construction. The original building was torn down, but instead of filling the space with a huge apartment tower, they went for quality over quantity. It makes for a nice change from the other massive towers popping up all over the city, which are slowly blotting out the light in increasingly cluttered streets.

There's a shared barbeque area with tables and chairs adorned with striped cushions. A curved path leads to a communal vegetable garden already budding with zucchini and thick bushes of thyme and mint. I take a moment to crouch down and breathe in the enticing scent. A lemon tree fills one corner, bursting with yellow fruit. Several lemons lie on the ground, half-consumed by some creature who must have stumbled across the bounty.

That's when I notice a small single-door gate next to the tree. Between the darkness of the evening sky and the fullness of the lemon tree, it's somewhat concealed.

"See that?" I turn to Owen. "It would be pretty easy to slip in and out here at night without being seen."

The sky isn't too dark yet—but soon it will be. There aren't many lights in the garden, beyond the barbeque area and the entrance to the building that houses the indoor swimming pool. This part of the yard is shadowy and private.

"I'm assuming it's locked," Owen says, taking a closer inspection. "There's a latch and a padlock, so it's not accessible with the key cards."

"That means it's not for resident use. What's behind it?"

Owen jumps up and wraps his hands over the edge of the fence, hoisting himself up. I suck in a breath at the sight of his muscles bulging beneath the sleeves of his jumper. He's always been fit, but the last few years have filled his body out in a way that sets off a warm burn in my stomach. He's broader in the shoulders, fuller in the arms, rounder in the butt. But his waist is still sharply defined in that delightful V shape that tells me he hits the gym regularly.

"An alleyway," he confirms and I nod, hoping he hasn't caught me looking again. "We'll take a look down there tomorrow, see if there's any evidence of people hanging around."

"So there's four ways into the property that I've seen—front entrance, car park, loading bay and this door." I tick the options off my fingers. "I doubt they're hauling bags of jewels and cash in and out via the front door. If we're talking about the kind of money that Ridgeway mentioned...they're not sneaking that through in a gym bag."

"And the car park has as much surveillance as the front entrance. There's cameras all over," Owen adds. "In the loading dock, too. This might be a hand-off point."

We know jewels are coming into this building thanks to a diamond cuff that had been fitted with a tracker. Unfortunately, the person who'd stolen the cuff from the small exhibit where it was being shown as "bait" had done a good job skirting the surveillance cameras. After that, the trail went cold.

The current estimation is that the thieves lift the items and bring them to 21 Love Street where a jeweller strips the gems out. Then the gems are sold either individually or in lots and residual metal from the settings and chains is sold to a gold buyer who melts it down.

By that method, there are no pieces of evidence floating around which might provide a trail back to the operation. It's smart. And while it might not provide the same kind of cash as other criminal activities—such as drug production or trafficking—it's a good place for would-be criminals to cut their teeth. The larger worry was that the Romano crime family had a new figurehead. This case wasn't simply about stopping theft. It was about gathering information so we could go after the bigger problem. But there wouldn't be budget for a task force unless we could prove that the Romano crime family was back in action.

"Someone's watching us," Owen says quietly.

The words cause goose bumps to ripple over my skin as my brain switches to high-alert. It's like the air has dropped a few degrees, and suddenly I'm conscious of every little detail around me—the whisper-quiet sound of footsteps on grass, the scent of cigarette smoke coiling into the air, the shifting shadows of the lemon tree as a breeze causes the leaves to shudder in the wind.

"Kiss me," he says.

"What?" I resist the urge to turn and look at whatever he can see behind me.

Owen's fingers encircle my wrist and he pulls me closer, further into the dark shadow of the lemon tree. "We're a newlywed couple out for a romantic stroll...so let's look romantic."

Shit. I have no idea what he can see and I hate being the one in a vulnerable position. But protecting the cover *always* comes first—before my comfort zone, before my own desires. Only now, the cover and my desires converge, and I wind my arms around Owen's neck. He takes a step back and hits the fence, allowing me to pin him there.

We don't have to kiss, not really. Holding my head

close to his would have been enough to maintain our position as horny newlyweds, but my lips part before I can logic my way out of doing what I've dreamed of since I was a fresh-faced academy trainee. I press my mouth to his and his fingers tighten at my waist, pulling me closer. His lips are firm and his grip is confident and his tongue slides along mine in a way that makes my knees buckle. God, he tastes even better than he smells—like earth and man and a hint of spice. Delicious.

My fingers drive through his hair, fisting the lengths so I can hold myself upright. I don't protest as his hands slide down my back and cup my ass, because there's not a single cell in my body that *doesn't* want this. I've kissed a few guys before—some of them weren't bad. One or two were good kissers.

But Owen is a master. He kneads me in a rhythmic way that makes my sex throb, like he's simulating the tempo of fucking. But it's the moment he yanks me up an inch and jams me firmly against him that takes my breath away. He's hard as a rock and his jeans do nothing to conceal the thick, curved length of his cock as it digs into my belly. *That* isn't part of our undercover script.

Because kisses can be faked and affections can be feigned, but a hard-on tells me that maybe I'm not the only one who's super into this right now. And that's a terrifying thought, because it's easy for me to hate Owen for rejecting me all those years ago. For teasing me about my crush on him. It's easy for me to write him off as someone who's totally wrong for me.

But unfortunately, I've never stopped lusting over Owen Fletcher. Now the floodgates have been opened and I have to live with him as man and wife. Screwing your co-worker isn't exactly a great career move.

But something tells me that I'll be going to bed with this kiss on my mind every damn night until we either crack this case, or until I give in to the feelings that have been haunting me for the past decade. Right now, as I writhe against him, I'm not sure which option I prefer.

CHAPTER FIVE

Owen

HANNAH FEELS LIKE heaven in my hands, but she kisses like the devil. Dark and sinful and so tempting my mere mortal brain has no hope of withstanding her. When I pulled her toward me, I hadn't expected her to respond with such enthusiasm. The kiss was a legitimate action to maintain cover and within the boundaries of our work.

The wood in my jeans was *not*.

I'd been prepared to keep my hands at ten and two—high school dance style—until the second she'd rubbed against me, purring like a kitten and taking a lit match to my decency. The sound coming from her mouth scrambles my brain, making me think of long sweaty nights and the feeling of thighs clamping down on my head. My fantasy woman always has dark hair and dark eyes, and it didn't occur to me until right now that Anderson could be that woman. She *has* been that woman…more times than I will ever admit.

But Anderson is a family woman. A heart-and-soul kind of woman. A forever woman. And that means we'll never be anything more than friends.

Her lips work against mine, her tongue sliding into my mouth as she presses herself against me. Grinding. I'm pinned to the fence, my body temperature skyrocketing. I want nothing more than to spin her around so I can use the fence to brace her back while I drag her legs up and encourage her to lock her heels behind my back.

But this is work. And this kiss is veering into the space where one of us is taking advantage of the situation—only I don't know *who*.

"He's gone." I whisper against her lips. It's dark outside and I can't see the details of her expression, but I feel the effects of the kiss in the puffiness of her lips. In the quickness of her breath.

"Well," she says shakily. "*That's* a relief."

"Yeah, I got the impression you thoroughly hated that." The teasing comes easily, naturally. It's like breathing for me. Like walking.

But what I really want is to tell her that she's got me hot and bothered. That I'll have to scrub this memory from my mind if I have any hope of keeping my focus on the case. But my focus is no better than a crystal glass thrown against a brick wall. It's thousands of irreparable glittering shards. I want to punish that sweet mouth of hers and haul her over my shoulder so I can take her straight to my bed.

"What now?" she asks.

I want to stay in this bubble forever—me and her.

That kiss. The feel of her subtle curves against me. "We take the show back to the apartment."

"What?" she squeaks, stepping back suddenly. No longer covered in the shadows of the tree, the moonlight bounces off her face—off her wide eyes and lush mouth. I bet the tips of her ears are bright red.

"We're newlyweds who've gotten distracted by a kiss and now we're heading back home to finish what we started." I grin and step forward, causing her to back up. "Do you have a problem with that, darling wife?"

She rolls her eyes and turns, heading back across the garden. In a few strides, I catch up to her and sling an arm around her shoulders. I'm surprised to find a smirk on her lips. "I think if anyone thoroughly enjoyed that kiss, it was *you*, by the way," she says.

Our footsteps fall in time. "What powers of deduction did you use to figure that out?"

"You're going to make me say it?" She shakes her head. There's more light overhead now as we approach the barbeque area and her ears are definitely pink. "It was pretty bloody obvious."

"I have no idea what you're talking about."

She opens her mouth to respond, but we're interrupted by a group spilling out of the building and into the shared barbeque area. There are three men dressed in casual attire, laughing and carrying food. Two of the men look to be brothers and all appear to be in their early thirties.

"You're new." One of the brothers points a pair of

tongs in our direction. The others wave and set themselves up around the barbeque. "Level six, right?"

"Word travels fast." I stick my hand out. "Owen. This is my wife, Hannah."

The W-word rolls off my tongue *far* too easily and it stirs something uncomfortable in my gut.

"Dom." The guy is built like a bear and has a grip to match. "That's my brother, Rowan, and our mate Matt."

"We moved in today," Hannah says, her smile a little too wide. I reach for her hand and squeeze—hoping it looks more loving and less like the warning it is. Rule number one of being undercover, never offer more information than you need to. "This morning, actually. We've been unpacking all day."

She's nervous. Hannah is like a fountain when she's nervous, which normally I am *all* about. But now is not the time for verbal diarrhea. I squeeze her hand again.

"It's a great building." Dom nods. "Ro and I moved in about two years ago."

If it's true, it doesn't really seem to fit the timeline, since the activity only started up within the last six months…but that's a *big* if. Could be part of their cover story. I'll get my hands on the building management documents and corroborate that information.

My eyes drift to the two men firing up the barbeque. They're laughing and joking. Matt is dressed in all black and he could very well have been the shadowy figure who interrupted us in the garden.

"How did you all meet?" I ask.

"Matt went to high school with us. He's a chef."

Rowan looks up from the barbeque and grins. He has a cavalier air about him, like he's a bit of a joker. "You wouldn't know it with the way he butchered this meat. Looks like it was done with a hacksaw."

"I can't work magic with shitty tools," Matt grumbles. Unlike Rowan and Dom, he's fair-haired and has sharp grey eyes.

"What do you do?" Hannah asks, looking up at Dom.

"Ro and I run the family business, an art gallery."

I have to actively conceal my surprise. Dom looks more like a bricklayer than the owner of a gallery—though admittedly, I know as much about art as I do about bricklaying. Zip.

"I run all the events," Rowan says, wandering over and handing his brother a beer. "Deal with the temperamental artists and mingle with the buyers."

In other words, he's a professional party boy. Could be a good cover, getting to mix and mingle with all the big players in Melbourne and making connections. Maybe he scopes out the targets.

"And I make sure my brother doesn't blow all our profit on champagne and canapés." Dom grins. "You should come and visit us sometime. I'm sure we have something perfect for your new apartment."

"That would be lovely." Hannah brings her hand to her chest, so the stones on her engagement ring wink in the light. The gesture is subtle—authentic—which is why it's perfect. I watch Rowan and Dom carefully, noting the way their eyes drift down to Hannah's hand. "We were saying today that we'd like something special for the bedroom. Our old pieces don't feel quite right anymore."

That's my girl. She's finding her feet in the role now, which I know to be far from her real "true blue Aussie" life. I've met her family—her dad was a sergeant before he retired. Nice bloke. For some reason, watching Hannah in action brings back the surge of attraction I've been trying so hard to keep under wraps. What can I say? Capability gets me hot.

"Isn't that right, Owen?" She looks up at me with those luminous brown eyes and I wonder how in the fuck I am going to get to sleep tonight.

"Yes, dear." I say it with just enough of a patronising tone that I get a chuckle from Rowan. It makes me feel like a class-A dick, but it's part of the act. Still, I can practically hear my grandmother scolding me. "Whatever you'd like."

"We've got an opening for a new artist later this week. Why don't you join us?" Rowan looks back to where Matt is throwing the steaks onto the grill. The sound of searing meat hisses into the night air. "I'll put an invite into your mailbox."

"We're number six-oh-one," Hannah clarifies, looping her arm through mine. "It's nice to meet you. Enjoy your barbeque."

The men turn their attention to their dinner and Hannah leads me inside the building.

"What do you think?" she asks as we're in the elevator.

"Not much to go on, but the gallery thing is unexpected. They don't seem the type."

"Agreed." She bobs her head. "And I know what I'm doing, okay? You don't have to freak out every time I open my mouth."

"You seemed a little nervous."

"I wasn't."

I would call bullshit, but I cut her some slack. Hannah's nerves only ever come from wanting to do a good job. This position means everything to her. She told me week one of our academy training that she was going to make detective by thirty-five and she's a couple years ahead of schedule.

It's a tough job and competitive to even get the opportunity. She's probably thinking about all the things that could go wrong.

"If I seemed nervous it was more likely revulsion," she adds. But her clipped tone is all bark and no bite. "From kissing you, I mean."

"Whatever helps you sleep at night, Anderson," I reply. "So long as you look the part when we have an audience, that's all that matters."

The way she kissed me is playing on my mind, however. It wasn't the kind of kiss I expected, and she could easily have kept it low-key. Faked it.

But that *wasn't* faking it, for either one of us.

I'll have to do my best to ignore the burning chemistry and hope she'll do the same. Because I have a feeling if Hannah asked me to fuck her senseless tonight, I'd have a *really* hard time remembering why it's a bad idea.

CHAPTER SIX

Hannah

DAY TWO OF my fake marriage and I'm already questioning why I didn't put up more of a fight when Max suggested bringing Owen back for this operation. I should have nipped it in the bud. But oh no, I had to go and think the golden boy's shine might have worn off with absence. Mistake number one.

Mistake number two was not pushing the brother-and-sister undercover plan harder. But like any good public servant, I fell into line.

Mistake number three was kissing him. Well, kissing is kind of a soft description. I basically dry humped him against the fence.

Cringing, I shake my head. Last night I acted out of line—unprofessional. Owen made it clear *years* ago that he wasn't interested and yet I threw myself at him the first chance I got. Pathetic. He's probably having a good laugh about it.

But what about the fact that he was hard enough to drill holes?

Natural physical response. Endorphins. Adrenaline. Pick a reason.

It's like the universe has designed the perfect situation to test me. This morning I burned my toast while getting lost in my imagination. Getting lost in a fantasy starring him. How am I supposed to do my job when I can't even make a bloody piece of toast without screwing it up?

Ugh, don't think about screwing. Don't think about screwing. Don't think about screwing...

"Whatcha thinking about?" Owen walks into the kitchen, a pair of tracksuit pants riding low on his hips and a white T-shirt clinging to every muscle in his chest. His blond hair is damp, which makes his blue eyes even brighter.

It's borderline disgusting how attractive he is.

"I'm thinking about the case." I busy myself by putting the dishes away from our dinner last night. "Obviously."

"Obviously." Amusement dances in his voice. "By the way, this arrived. I noticed it when I came back from my run this morning."

He's holding a crisp white envelope in the kind of paper that usually signifies something fancy—weddings, galas, charity balls.

He grabs a knife and slips it under the seal at the back, slicing the envelope open. Inside is a single piece of paper. It's grey and industrial-looking, with rough edges and an asymmetrical shape but the fancy gold-and-white font screams money.

"A personal invitation from Galleria D'Arte to

join Dominic and Rowan Lively in presentation of artist Celina Yang." Owen looks up. "It's a cocktail party tomorrow night."

A cocktail party. Great. Unfortunately, the work budget doesn't extend to fancy wardrobe purchases, and I'm pretty sure Owen doesn't own a tux. Or is a tux more black tie than cocktail? I have no earthly idea.

"What should I wear?" I bring my thumb up to my lips, ready to bite down until I remember that I need to look the part. No more biting my nails.

"Cocktail dress?" Owen supplies less-than-helpfully.

"I don't own any." I have one dress that *might* pass at a nice restaurant since it's black and simple. The last time I wore it was to a funeral. And if it passed muster at a funeral, does that mean it's no good for a cocktail party?

Damn it. When it comes to outrunning the bad guys and clipping on handcuffs or diffusing a tense situation, I'm at the top of my game. But I don't do parties and dresses and high heels. How am I going to convince *anyone* that I'm a trophy wife?

"You go. I'll pretend to be sick," I mutter.

"Do we need to go shopping?" Owen places the invitation on the kitchen counter and leans his forearms against the sleek marble. "We can get you something to wear."

"That's not an appropriate use of the budget and you know it." Maybe I can slap on some fake leaves and pretend to be a potted plant, Scooby-Doo style.

"Don't worry about the budget."

I sigh. "Of *course* I worry about the budget. There are more important things to spend that money on and I can't be seen taking advantage of the situation to fill out my wardrobe."

"I'll cover you." When I raise a brow, Owen shrugs in that careless way of his. "I'm a consultant and I have expenses. No big deal."

"I'll pay you back," I say. The thought of him footing the bill for a dress feels totally and utterly wrong, but if I'm being honest my five-year-old Target dress isn't going to cut it for an upper-crust gallery event.

"Stop worrying about the money." He turns and heads toward the spare room, which he's graciously taken so I can have the master suite with the more private bathroom. "Go grab your things."

We catch the tram to Collins Street, where the designer shops sit like glittering beacons of unattainable style. The only time I come to the "Paris End"—aka the section with all the fancy stores—is to have the odd drink with friends. But Owen whisks me into the Gucci store like he's done it a thousand times before.

We bypass the shoes and bags and head into the quieter part with the clothing. "This is excessive," I say under my breath. "Can't we go to Myer?"

Department stores are a little more my speed. And I'm already wondering what kind of payment plan I'll need to buy a dress here. I love my job, but it isn't for the thickly padded pay cheque.

"You need to grab everybody's attention. We're drawing them to us, remember?"

We walk into a room with huge screens playing footage from a runway show. The models are wearing strange, avant-garde creations and they all look terribly unhappy. Biting down on my lip, I glance around the store.

I walk over to a simple dress in emerald green with a ruffle draping from one shoulder all the way to the hem. It's not my style, but it looks like something my undercover alter ego might wear. But when I glance at the price tag, I almost faint.

"We need to leave," I say under my breath as a well-heeled sales assistant approaches us. "Please."

"Hannah, it's fine." Owen touches my arm like we really *are* a married couple and that only makes my stomach swish harder. I'm going to send myself into life-long debt for a cocktail dress.

"Can I help you?" The woman has a cool confidence that I immediately envy. But maybe I could learn a few things from her to help bolster my persona.

"My wife is looking for a cocktail dress," Owen says when I remain stubbornly quiet. "We've got an important event to attend."

The woman's gaze sweeps over me, assessing my size and shape. Her fingers drift over a rack of clothing, and she pushes the hangers to one side to reveal a hot pink monstrosity that looks like some cruel fashion joke. When she notes my expression, she immediately moves to another rack.

"What kind of an event?"

"A gallery exhibition." I can barely find my voice. I *hate* feeling so out of my depth, and over such a stupid thing, too. I've had a gun pointed directly at my face and yet I'm scared of a few metres of silk?

"Ah, so you might want something artistic." She taps a well-manicured finger to her chin. "How daring are you?"

Not very. Not even a little bit. "Uh, I'm probably more classic than daring."

"She's very daring," Owen says, his gaze scorching me from the inside out. "My wife doesn't see it in herself, but I do. She's got a spark like nobody else."

Does he really see that in me? Or is it part of the doting husband act?

My head and heart have been a jumbled mess ever since Owen set foot back in Australia. I thought I'd gotten over it all—over the desperate desire and humiliation. Over the way he'd looked at me, with clear eyes while mine were glassy with champagne, as he'd told me that he wouldn't sleep with me because he valued our friendship. The humiliation had burned me to ash, and it made his act now all the more painful to swallow.

Because despite the time that had passed, I still wanted it to be real.

The woman's face lights up as she pulls another garment from the rack. It appears to be a blazer made of reflective black material. "Is there a pair of pants to go with that?" I ask.

She ushers me to a changing room. "It's a dress

made to look like a blazer. It's classic *and* daring, to suit both what you see and what your husband sees."

When she closes the door behind me, I stare at myself in the mirror. Even with the flattering gold tones of the change room and the specially engineered lighting, I don't love what I see. I'd never call myself ugly, but I wouldn't say I'm anything special to look at, either. Brown hair, brown eyes, eyebrows that could do with some TLC. I've always viewed my body for what it can do—for speed and strength and agility—rather than looks. And I've told myself over and over when relationships fizzled, that it was because men are intimidated by strong women.

But now I wonder if I'm a bit…boring. Unsophisticated.

"How's it going in there?" Owen's honey-smooth voice jolts me out of my negative thought spiral and I shuck my jeans.

"This is my worst nightmare," I admit. Somehow, without having to face him, it's a little easier to be honest. "I can't afford anything in here and I feel like a little girl playing dress-up."

The silence stretches on for a beat more than is comfortable.

"Firstly, the dress is my treat. And secondly…" The lock rattles lightly and I can tell he's leaned against the door. "You need to stop being so hard on yourself."

I raise a brow at my reflection. It's the most un-Owen-like thing he could have said. I'm down to my bra and undies now, and pulling the blazer/dress thing off the hanger. It's surprisingly heavy, and I notice it's covered entirely in glimmering beads.

"You deserve to be where you are because you work harder than anyone else. Because you're smarter than anyone else. Maybe more people should be like you, rather than you trying to be like someone else."

The statement warms my heart, kindling an old fire. I can't help the goofy grin that stretches my lips as I slip into the dress. The sales assistant was right—it *is* the perfect mix of classic and daring. The long sleeves and padded shoulders give a structured, powerful vibe and the short hemline and plunging neck are sexy as all get-out. But the fact is I *am* a girl playing dress-up. Because I would never wear this dress, and I would never be with a guy like Owen who flits from one thing to the next, always chasing a new whim.

I like him. I always have. But I need to remember what I told myself all those years ago—it's a good thing he rejected me. Because a guy like him would chew me up and spit me out. I need to find a relationship where I'm an equal partner, where the other person is invested as much as I am. And unfortunately, I'm *always* more invested than the other person.

When I open the change room door, Owen's eyes widen. "Wow."

He's looking at me like it's the first time he's seen me. But I don't want to have my *She's All That* moment right now. Because this transformation is a lie—like the ring on my finger and the apartment

we're sharing. I'm never going to be the "after" picture in some "ugly duckling to swan" advertisement.

I'm not sure I want to be, either.

"Thanks." I swallow my awkwardness. "Don't get
used to it. I'll be back in leggings tonight."

I refuse to let his reaction affect me. If there's any
attraction here, it's not because of who I *really* am. I
can't afford the delusion that there will ever be anything between us…no matter how much I can't stop
thinking about that kiss.

CHAPTER SEVEN

Owen

By the third day of living at 21 Love Street, we've met a number of our neighbours in passing. Hannah ignored my suggestion to let them come to us, and I have to admit she's playing the role of social butterfly well.

We've met a communications manager and her investment banker fiancé from level one. A quiet schoolteacher named Ava and her friend Emery, who live in the apartments next to Rowan and Dominic on level five. I'm thinking they could be a good source of information on the brothers' activities. And Matt the chef lives on level three. We haven't seen anyone on level six—I suspect the other penthouse might be owned by someone who travels a lot. There are also two young families on the first floor, and an older woman on level three who seems to keep to herself but gave a friendly wave in the mailroom as I pretended to inspect our mailbox.

Nothing suspicious yet. Based on what we have,

I feel Dom, Rowan and Matt are worth looking into further. Which is why Hannah and I are waiting outside L'Arte Galleria in a line to have our tickets checked by a beefy guy in a black suit.

"This place is fancy," Hannah whispers. She's hanging on to my arm and has a black trench coat covering her new dress. That dress has been on my mind *all* day. "I bet they have Swarovski-encrusted toilets."

I snort and make a poor attempt of covering it with a cough. We step forward in the line and she's careful to keep her balance on a pair of pencil-thin stilettos that I bought to go with her dress. They have a mirror-like silver finish and they're doing amazing things for her legs. Hannah had argued that they were impractical and that she wouldn't be able to chase after anyone in them—but tonight we're gathering information. No running required.

"Tickets?" The beefy guy has a nose that looks like it's been on the losing side of a few fistfights and he's built like a brick wall. Is that OTT for a gallery? I'm not sure.

Hannah hands our invite over and the beefcake scans a small barcode on the back of it. "Mr. and Mrs. Essex, welcome."

Interesting. I don't remember giving our surname to Dom when we spoke in front of the barbeque, but he obviously got it somehow. I press my hand to the small of Hannah's back and we're ushered into the cloakroom area. It's chilly out tonight—rainy and damp in that typical Melbourne early spring way—

and so we offload our outerwear. I try not to stare as Hannah shrugs out of her coat, revealing her long, lean legs and a scandalous triangle of chest. The bare skin contrasting with long sleeves looks edgy and sexy. She's put on a little makeup and fluffed out her hair, so that it falls in shiny brown waves to her shoulders. I don't quite understand why she made that comment about being a little girl playing dress-up yesterday, because she looks every bit the perfect Mrs. Hannah Essex to me.

"Shall we?" I hold my hand out to her, and she takes it. There's that blush again, tinting her cheeks and neck and the tips of her ears.

"Stop looking at me like that." The words are spoken low, for my ears only.

"Like what?"

"Like you're a wolf who's gone weeks without a fresh kill." Her hand slips into mine. "And I'm a big, dumb deer who's stumbled into your path."

I pull her close to me as we weave through a large, modern archway which opens into the gallery's main room. The exhibition is…not quite what I expected. Sculptures dot the room, abstract shapes that somehow manage to look erotic—like bodies entwined—without actually resembling anything at all.

The lighting is low, except for a few strategically placed red spotlights which give the room an almost club-like atmosphere. Electronic music plays over the speakers, but not so loud that it inhibits conversation. There are waiters circling the room, wearing blood-red tuxedo jackets and carrying trays of pink-tinted sparkling wine.

Hannah cocks her head. "This is different to what I thought it would be. Although, to be fair, my experience with galleries is limited to that one time I went to NGV on a high school excursion."

"Same."

Even living in New York hadn't tempted me into the local pastime of spending hours staring at things my brain isn't creative enough to process. I'm more of a hands-on guy. This is a bit...cerebral.

"They're kind of sexy." Hannah steps closer to the sculpture nearest us. She leans forward slightly, her eyes narrowed and a cute little wrinkle in her nose. "Is that weird?"

"It's not weird at all." A woman appears beside us, her dark hair shaved on one side and reaching down to her shoulders on the other. "This collection is about capturing the feeling of oneness that two people experience in love and lust."

"This is your work?" Hannah straightens and puts on a smile.

"Yes, I'm Celina Yang." She extends her hand and Hannah accepts it.

"Hannah Essex, nice to meet you. The pieces are very...thought-provoking."

"Thank you." Celina smiles. She's a striking woman, barely more than five feet two and wearing flat shoes. She's dressed in red to match the theme of the event—a dress that looks as avant-garde as her work. Two large diamonds glitter in her ears. "I take a lot of inspiration from my own relationships."

"Looks like you have some good relationships," Hannah comments. Then she looks up, as if the comment had slipped accidentally. "I mean…the sculptures are beautiful."

That's my Hannah. Smooth as sandpaper.

Celina laughs. "Being comfortable with one's sexuality is a very pure thing, despite what society might lead you to believe. Sex is when we are at our truest and most vulnerable."

I watch Hannah inspecting the sculpture. This one is two pieces of twisted material—a shiny black that's so glossy it looks like there's a fine layer of ice over it, and a matte, velvety black.

"You can touch it," Celina says. "This is meant to be an interactive exhibit."

For some reason Hannah's eyes flick to mine as her hand comes slowly—hesitantly—down to the sculpture. At first she brushes her fingertips over the sweeping curve of the matte black material, but then—as if enjoying the feeling—she presses her palm flat over it and moves it along in one smooth but firm stroke.

This shouldn't turn me on. It's a sculpture that looks like nothing. An adult version of Play-Doh. But watching her hand move, growing bolder with Celina's encouragement, has all the blood in my body rushing south. What the hell is wrong with me?

"Try it." Hannah holds her hand out to me, tempting like the devil herself.

I step forward and allow Hannah to take my hand. The sculpture is strangely soft beneath my fingertips. As I glide my hands back and forth, it changes from smooth to rough.

"It feels so strange," Hannah says.

"It shows the dual-edge of a toxic relationship," Celina says. "The very thing that can feel good and comforting, can become painful when turned on us."

I watch as her eyes drift across the room. There's a man standing by himself, his long figure encased in a black suit. He's fair-haired and when he turns, I recognise Matt instantly.

"Some people are no good for you, even if you want them to be." Her hand toys with one of her earrings, the large clear stone looking almost pinkish from the red spotlight above. "But it looks as though you two don't have that problem at all."

"We have our ups and downs," Hannah says, winking at me. "Right now, I'd say we're up."

Who *is* this woman? The Hannah I know is prickly and has a tongue that could slice bone. But now she's soft and flirty. It's part of her act, of course—Hannah Essex rather than Hannah Anderson.

"Well, you should think about getting one of the sculptures for your bedroom. Never helps to inject the room with more sensuality." Celina smiles and her hand drops away from her earring. "If you're interested, I can help you pick one that will be a good fit."

"Thank you. We'll definitely consider it," I say.

Celina moves on to the next cluster of people.

The room is moderately full, but there's still plenty of space to move around. I notice more people interacting with the sculptures now—touching and getting close. Hannah sticks by my side as we drift on to the next piece—it's a harder and more aggressive shape made of gold and silver. The two pieces of metal bow away from each other before coming back to twist into a small spire at the top.

This time Hannah doesn't hesitate to reach out and touch it. "Do you think it's true what she said?"

"About what?"

"That sex is when we are at our truest and most vulnerable?" Her eyes don't meet mine and I wonder what game she's playing—is this about our cover... or something more?

My memory drifts back to the night she propositioned me. We'd graduated from the academy and there was a huge house party—one last hurrah before we were all scattered across the state. Many new constables work in rural areas for a period of time, finding their feet and helping communities that don't have much police coverage. Hannah had never been a big drinker, so the champagne had hit her hard. She'd been falling all over me, giggling with her cheeks and ears pink and hair mussed and eyes wild.

I'd never seen a more beautiful woman in all my life.

Don't you want to kiss me? she'd asked. *I've seen you look at me and I never knew if it meant anything but I hoped it did. I'm not supposed to like you because you're dangerous for a girl like me...but I do.*

Dangerous. The funniest thing about it was that if anyone was dangerous in that scenario, it was her. Because she was smart and beautiful and courageous and so kickass it made me want to burst. But I'd been with a girl like that before—where I'd loved as hard as my teenage heart knew how. The day I'd lost it all I'd broken into so many pieces no one knew how to put me back together.

"Owen?" Hannah cocked her head. "You didn't answer my question."

"I guess it's true." I shrug. "I'm not sure I would say it's a vulnerable thing, though."

It never was for me...not after the first time. These days, sex is blowing off steam and scratching an itch. It's fun and enjoyable, but it's never about vulnerability. In fact, being vulnerable is the thing I avoid most in life. Because getting close to someone has never worked out well for me in the past—I've lost a mother and father and a brother and a grandfather and the girl I loved.

That's a whole lot of loss for one heart to handle.

"Yeah, me either." She looks as though she's seriously considering Celina's words. "Sometimes it's just about fun, right?"

CHAPTER EIGHT

Hannah

GOD, WHAT AM I saying? This whole event has my head mixed up. I'm wearing a revealing dress, touching erotic sculptures and talking about sex with my colleague. This is *not* who I am.

I should have my eye on the prize. I should be hunting out Dom and Rowan and trying to figure out if they're part of the jewellery theft ring we're supposed to be tracking down. But it's like I've inhaled some kind of drug and my brain is in a lusty pink fog.

The way he looks at me, with those intense blue eyes, makes the rest of the room evaporate. I've wanted a lot of things in my life—to climb the ladder at work, to have the respect of my father and brothers, to one day have a family of my own. But I've never wanted another man as much as I want Owen right now. The years have grown my desire for him, making it stronger and more unwieldy.

He encircles my wrist with his fingers and tugs

me closer, as any husband in love with his wife might
do. I tilt my face up, trying to read him. But Owen's
poker face is world class. He's a master joker, a friend
to all…and known by none.

"What are you doing?" he asks.

The heat from his body melts me and I pull my
hand away from his grip and press it to his chest.
His mother's ring glimmers. "Making conversation."

I'm not, though. I'm dancing around something
I know I shouldn't be doing. A suggestion which
has occupied me with increasing strength from the
very second we were left alone in our apartment at
21 Love Street.

"It's not a smart conversation," he says.

"Because you're going to reject me again?" I don't
know why I'm setting myself up for this.

"I should."

Should. It wasn't a yes, but it wasn't a no, either.
"Because we work together?"

Owen's lips lift into a smile. "That should be the
reason *you* keep your hands to yourself. I've got no
interest in rejoining the force."

"Then why?"

"Because you don't want casual sex."

His assumption that he knows me so well—
regardless of how accurate the statement is—annoys
me. Okay, fine, so maybe I already know sex with
him wouldn't be casual even if it was a one-time only
deal. So what? I'm a grown woman and I know how
to deal with the consequences of my actions.

"That's my decision to make," I reply. "And I

haven't voiced what I want, so I'm not sure why you think it's your place to tell me."

We're close now. So close that if we swayed it would look like we were slow-dancing. The people around us might assume the intimate chatter between us is verbal foreplay—and I guess it is. I can't seem to do the sensible thing and back away, because the moment I heard about his move to New York, I thought I'd lost him forever.

Who falls for the most unattainable guy in the world and expects to survive without any bruises on her heart? I'm a fool.

But maybe a few bruises would do me good. It's been so long since I did anything that wasn't work. And yes, I want to solve this case and prove my boss made the right decision to promote me...but this could be my last chance to have the man who's always occupied my head. What happens behind the closed doors of our apartment isn't anyone's business.

This was *precisely* why I wanted us to play brother and sister...because I knew that one kiss for the sake of playing a role would be enough to unlatch the feelings I've locked up tight for far too long.

"Then tell me, Hannah. What do you want?"

Out of the corner of my eye, I spy something that gets my intuition tingling. And, as much as I desperately want to keep playing this game with Owen, the case *does* come first. "Matt and Celina are arguing."

"Huh?" Owen blinks and I entwine my fingers with his, pulling him toward the next sculpture in the exhibition. "Where?"

"Your nine o'clock." I lean over so it looks like I'm reading the little gold plaque. "They're standing by the hallway."

"Got it. She looks pissed."

I let my gaze drift casually in the direction of the argument. A few people have noticed and are moving away, so Celina and Matt head down the dark corridor together, disappearing into another part of the gallery.

"Think it's something?" I ask. I stand and lean my head against Owen's shoulder, so we can speak without anyone hearing.

"Not sure. Did you notice her earrings before?"

I nod. "Big stones. Could be fake, though."

"We should try to get a photo to compare to the list of stuff that went missing in the Collins Auction House robbery." His voice is low, gravelly. He could be reciting a shopping list and still make it sound like the sexiest thing ever. "I had a funny feeling about them."

"Me, too."

I walk forward, unhurried. Partly because I don't want to draw any attention, and partly because it's the only speed I can maintain in these damn heels. Owen is beside me, his hand still in mine. I feel as though my body is burning up. We receive curious glances from other people in the room—but nothing that gets my police officer senses tingling. My dress demands attention and Owen...well, he's always got appreciative eyes on him. The open-collar shirt and grey suit pants make him look every bit the hot Aussie millionaire he's supposed to be.

We slip past the gold sign that tells us this hallway is "for staff use only" and follow the voices.

"Then why did you invite me here?" Matt sounds irritated and in the quiet pause, I can hear sniffling. "I thought we agreed to part ways after..."

I shuffle closer to a bend in the hallway, and I can tell they're just around the corner. Celina is definitely crying.

"Can you walk away so easily?" she asks. "After everything we shared?"

"*You* were the one who said you couldn't do this anymore. I was ready to go all in."

"No, you weren't. Because you would have listened to me if you'd cared at all about my feelings."

It's a lover's spat. Nothing more. I'm about to motion for Owen to head back the way we came, when she mutters something under her breath.

"Here, take these bloody things. I'm not going to wear something you *stole*." There's a long pause and the sound of something dropping against the floor.

"Don't be ridiculous, Cel. They were a gift." Matt sighs. "Does it matter where they came from?"

My brows shoot up and Owen nods. This could be something—because I am *damn* sure she's talking about the earrings.

"Yes, it matters. It should have mattered before but I was willing to look past your...unethical activities." She huffs and the sound of shoes knocking against the floor makes my heart kick up a notch. *Shit*. They're coming this way. "You promised me you'd get out of that stuff. It's dangerous."

Owen backs up as silently as possible. The hallway isn't long but I'm moving slow and a little unsteadily in these heels...we're not going to get back out before they come around the corner. And there's nowhere else to go.

As I sense a flash of movement, Owen pushes me against the wall and his lips are hard on mine once more. It's even better this time than it was the first—because anticipation has been fuelling my every movement. My every waking moment. I open to him like a flower, my body warm and pliable in his hands. The soft groan that comes from the back of his throat is everything.

The scent of his cologne winds through me, and like a creeping vine it wraps around my heart and lungs. I'm intoxicated by him. Enraptured by the way his hands smooth over the fabric of my dress, tracing my boyish shape and making me feel every inch a desirable woman. They tell me a perfect lie and I'm in too deep not to believe it.

I slide my tongue along his, tangling my fingers in his hair and taking my fill. By the time we're done— pink-cheeked and breathing a little heavier—Celina and Matt are gone. I turn my head in time to see Matt walking out of the gallery on the other side of the room. Celina is mingling with the guests as though nothing happened.

"Did you see anything?" I pull back and right my dress, which has ridden up my thighs.

Owen shakes his head. "No. I was a little distracted."

It's a problem. These kinds of distractions lead to cases going unsolved...or worse. We've lost good men and women in the past when someone makes a mistake. When someone has their eye on the wrong thing.

Guilt surges through my veins. I've got this amazing opportunity in front of me and I'm letting my libido lead me astray. I *know* this thing with Owen won't go anywhere, but I can't let it go. Maybe sex cravings are like food cravings? If you want something sweet, the best way to dissipate that feeling is to nibble on some chocolate.

"What did you make of the whole 'unethical activities' thing?" I ask as we slip back into the main room.

"It's vague, but it cements Matt as someone to keep an eye on."

The gallery is much fuller now and it's harder to get close to the sculptures. So we tuck ourselves away in a corner, pretending to inspect one of Celina's few charcoal sketches. This one depicts a woman with her face screwed up with pleasure. The blurry figure of a man is behind her, with his hand at her throat. It's intense. Sexy and a little dangerous and it socks me in the chest.

"She's talented," I murmur, watching Celina weave through the crowd.

There's no sign of her tears now. Her face is radiant as she works the room—touching arms and leaning in close to create a sense of intimacy geared toward making people open their wallets.

"She's not wearing earrings anymore." Owen slips

a hand around my waist as we spot Rowan across the room. His face lights up in recognition and he heads over. "I think we need to make sure you get a business card for Ms. Yang. A private consultation might be a good chance to get some information."

I nod. "Maybe putting something like that in our bedroom might spice up our sex life." I say it partially for Rowan's benefit, loud enough that he'll hear us acting like a regular married couple.

But heat flares in Owen's eyes—turning the icy blue to pure flame—and his fingers flex at my hip in a way that's instinctive. It's *not* for show. I'm convinced I'm not the only one being drawn in by this carnal tide. He feels it, too. Underneath the teasing and the butting heads, there's something simmering.

But he won't pull the trigger. Why? For a long time I thought it was because he wasn't attracted to me. But the way he looks at me now, darkly engrossed and with an intensity that threatens to burn me alive, I reconsider.

The fact is, I can't keep going around and around like this. My brain is like a spinning top, and I need to focus. Tonight, I'm going to do something stupid, something that proves I'm a glutton for punishment.

I'm going to proposition Owen again.

CHAPTER NINE

Owen

I LEAVE THE gallery with Hannah close to 11:00 p.m. We stay longer than most, chatting to Rowan and Dom. Rowan told us in hushed tones that Matt and Celina had a tumultuous relationship—on again and off again. Their strange work hours and the pressures of their perfectionist tendencies had put them under a lot of strain. Before we left, Hannah got a card from Celina and promised to call for a private appointment.

Now, Hannah and I stroll along the Southbank Boulevard. I'd suggested a cab, but she wanted to walk. Processing time, she called it. I'd rather be back at 21 Love Street and straight into a cold shower, because her dress is turning my resolve to mush and her gently smudged lipstick has me thinking about what I could do to further ruin her makeup.

Sparkling lights bounce off the Yarra River as we walk, and the night air is filled with the sound of music and laughter. This part of the city is full of bars and restaurants and, despite the chill in the air, people are out in force.

"Do you think much about the academy days?" she asks me, out of nowhere.

"Sure. They're fond memories." I'd made a lot of friends back then—though many dissolved after I left. It's something I've learned over the years—when you hang out with ghosts for too long you can easily become one.

She steps up to the railing overlooking the river. "Was it hard to walk away?"

"No." Self-preservation is the easy route.

"Not even a little bit?"

"Are you mistaking me for someone with a heart?" I aim for a joking tone and miss by a long-shot. "I left my grandmother two months after my granddad passed. I was her only other family…and I left. Like a coward."

Shit. Why did I say that?

The sincerity shines out of Hannah's eyes like she's turned into a fucking Care Bear. I don't want her to look at me like that. I'm not a person to be saved. Hell, I'm not a person to be loved. I operate best in the middle ground between friend and ac-quaintance.

"Why did you go? I'm not buying the whole 'I'm chasing a whim' thing."

"You don't need to buy it because I'm not sell-ing it."

Nobody from my police force days is aware of my past, except for the people who run the psych evaluations and the superiors who looked over my file before I entered the academy. I haven't told a single person unless it was absolutely, one-hundred-percent necessary. Not even Max knows, and he's the closest friend I've ever had.

"You were missed," she says quietly, almost as if reflecting to herself. "By a lot of people."

"By you? I thought you hated my guts."

"I did...for a bit." She leans against the railing and tilts her head up at me—all lashes and big brown eyes and a sweet expression that's softer than anything I've seen from her before. "It's hard not to hate the guy who made you a laughing stock."

"You were hardly a laughing stock."

"Really?" She pushes back up to a standing position and folds her arms. "Let me see if I remember this correctly. You snuck into my room, found my diary and decided to do a dramatic reading to a bunch of my peers."

"Firstly, I didn't sneak into your room. I was visiting Vanessa and she opened the door. Secondly, it wasn't like I had to scavenge for the damn thing. It was right there on your nightstand...in a box. Under a picture frame."

Okay, fine. It had been hidden and I'd hunted it out.

Hannah rolls her eyes. "And how do you explain busting open the lock, huh? Did it fall off when you picked it up because your hands are so strong no metal can withstand your grip?"

I laugh and the feeling drives all the way through

me, loosening my muscles. Thawing the ice cage around my heart. She always had that effect on me. It's hard not to like a girl who can make you laugh from down deep.

"I may have encouraged it to open," I reply. "With a paperclip."

"You picked the lock on my diary like a ten-year-old boy!" She's blushing again and I know we're thinking about the same thing.

Hannah Anderson, who'd always seemed like this straitlaced, buttoned-up good girl, had been harbouring some dark and dirty thoughts…about me. At the time, I did *not* expect to see my name on those pages. She'd always acted like I was a bug to be swatted. Or some gum stuck to the bottom of her shoe.

When I decided—in my young, stupid brain—that it would be a good idea to read her diary, I had not planned to make it a show. But my roommate had caught me, demanded to know who it belonged to and rounded up a bunch of guys to listen in. I *never* divulged Hannah's name. Ever.

But someone obviously figured it out.

"Do you remember what it said?" she asks. She's luminous under the moonlight and street lamps, her dress glimmering through the gap between her coat lapels. That peek of bare skin is everything and nothing—the best kind of tease.

I want him. Even though I don't truly know what wanting is because I've never slept with anyone before. But I want to send everyone away for one night—just one—so I can lose everything I have to

him. I want to know what it's like to be fucked. Will
it hurt? Will he lie with me afterward? I have no idea
if I'm even on his radar. Owen could have any girl
here, but I want him to have me. *Hard.*

The words were forever imprinted on my brain.
They'd circled like vultures, preying on my sanity
and concentration. The night she'd come to me after
we graduated, with sooty eyes like blackened pits,
my fucked-up brain hadn't been able to shut out the
darkness. The second I started to feel anything about
Hannah, all I could think about was the dead girl I'd
loved more than anything else.

"You do remember," she says. "You just weren't
interested."

"Believe me, it wasn't like that. I only took the
damn diary because I wanted to know more about
you and being a dumb kid, I didn't think I could ask."
He shook his head. "I never meant for anyone else
to see the pages."

"Water under the bridge now," she said with a
shrug. "It's not like it stopped me doing anything I
wanted to do…well, not most things anyway."

I don't respond to the innuendo hanging in the air.
We shouldn't be talking like this—not when we've
got shit to do and a case to close and not when I'm
leaving the second it's all over. "Nothing will ever
stop you, Anderson. You're a force."

"Why do you say sweet things like that when I'd
rather you say something dirty?"

My head snaps toward her. "Don't tempt me."

"Why?"

"Because I can't go there. Not with you."

Her face falls and I want to explain. I want to tell her that it's nothing to do with her and everything to do with me. I want to tell her that it's because I'm not capable of treating her the way she deserves to be treated. That I can take her to bed, but that will be it, and I don't know if I can handle the look on her face when I leave after it's all done.

"It's…" Fuck. I'm *so* not good at this. I can walk away from my troubles like a boss, but staying and talking…I suck at it. "You're hot, okay? It's nothing to do with that."

She tilts her head in a way that reminds me of an adorable puppy. "So it's not because there's a lack of physical chemistry."

I laugh. "Hell no. That's not it at all."

We're still standing at the river, and a group of drunk girls totter past giggling and singing. On the water, there's a cruise boat stuffed full of partygoers. Music floats toward us and so does the sound of laughter and cheering. They're all so obliviously happy.

"I'm not asking for a ring, Owen." She nudges me with her elbow. "I already got that."

"What *are* you asking for?" I go against my better judgement with that question, but the air is burning up around us and we're standing close enough that I could capture her lips with mine.

"One night." Her chest rises and falls with a big breath. "Get it out of our systems. I'd like very much to be able to concentrate on the job and I just…can't. Not with the tension distracting me."

One night, no strings, with the girl I've crushed on ever since she walked into the first-day induction session at the Victoria Police Academy. It would be so easy to say yes.

"No." The word comes out a lot weaker than I'd hoped.

"Why?"

"Because the whole one-night thing doesn't work when you know the person. It's all fine to say we'll act like it never happened, but we both know that's bullshit."

"What if I wasn't me?" There's a darkness to her expression, a simmering heat that pulls me in. "What if I was someone else?"

"What?"

"I'm already playing a role. Hannah Essex." She wriggles her fingers and my mother's ring glints in the light. "I can simply change roles and be someone else."

She wants it that badly? My fingers twitch and my cock is aching for release—I've been in a semi-state of excitement for days and this is only making it worse. How long before I break? How long before my willpower is a billion glittering shards?

"Surely you're not intimidated by a bit of role play?" Her tongue darts out to moisten her lips and I'm about ready to fall to my knees in front of her.

"I'm not afraid of role play." I grit the words out.

"Then I'm going to be in that bar, ordering a

drink." She turns and points to a little hole-in-the-wall place with the ambient glow of low-hanging lights. "If you come find me, we'll pretend to be other people for the night."

Bloody hell. "And if I don't come find you?"

"Then I have my answer."

She turns and walks across the tree-lined boulevard, pausing at the edge of the bar to shrug out of her coat. Her dress glimmers, like stars winking at me, beckoning me closer. I catch the flash of her toned, bare legs and those shiny silver shoes before she disappears inside.

CHAPTER TEN

Hannah

MY HEART IS pounding a million miles a minute as I enter the dimly lit bar. The place is full, but not bursting. A beautiful curved bar in gold and pearl-white wraps around the back two corners of the room. Ornate pendant lights emit a warm glow, and velvet chairs dot the space, where people sit drinking and talking. Most wear suits or pretty dresses—they've probably come from seeing a show at the Arts Centre.

When a couple vacate the bar, I claim one of the empty seats.

Will Owen follow me in here? Is he outside stewing over his decision or has he already started walking home? I can't get his words out of my head.

Nothing will ever stop you, Anderson. You're a force.

When it comes to work and my career, I've worn that label with pride. I'm ambitious and I have the respect of my colleagues and superiors. But the second I shrug out of my blue uniform, I somehow shrug out of my confidence, too.

"What can I get you?" The bartender smiles.

"A French 75, please." I'm craving something fizzy.

My eyes stray to the door, where a couple walks in. They're arm in arm and so into one another that the room shoots up a hundred degrees. Is it pathetic that all I want is for someone to look at me like that? I'm an independent, intelligent woman but...

Just once I want to be *that* girl. The girl who gets the guy, the girl who stops traffic. Is it so bad to want to feel desirable? To feel sexy and coveted and beloved?

The bartender places my drink on a coaster and I pay. Bubbles race to the top of the champagne flute, where a delicate curl of lemon peel sits, curving over the edge of the glass. I stare at it for a moment, hanging in a delicious limbo between fear of rejection and the possibility that I may have something exciting in front of me.

The cocktail is tasty, dry champagne with a hint of sour lemon. As I watch the door, I twist Owen's mother's ring. I still haven't gotten used to wearing it. But for tonight it's on the wrong finger. I slip it off and transfer it to my other hand.

I turn back to my drink and run my finger over the rim, trying to make it sing like I used to when I was a little kid. I count my breaths in and out, clinging to hope.

Please come to me.

I remember how mortified I was when I found out my diary had been read aloud. I knew Owen had done his best to conceal my identity. But people talked and theorised—we all wanted to be investigators, after all.

Rumours spread. I'd denied it, of course. And then the diary had turned up back in my room seemingly of its own accord. I knew he'd put it there. And part of me had been excited that he knew how I felt. Unfortunately, nothing had come of it.

"Is anyone sitting here?"

I turn toward the deep voice and swallow back the excitement surging through my veins. Owen has a dangerous edge to him. His usually playful smile is nowhere to be found, and his vibrant blue eyes hold me captive. Will he play my game?

"No, please." I gesture toward the empty seat next to me. "It's all yours."

He eases himself onto the bar stool and signals to the bartender. 18-year-old Talisker, neat. I've never seen him drink anything but beer. He looks at me while the bartender pours, his expression smouldering and unreadable. The corner of my lips lifts into a smile, inviting him closer. He knows what I want, so now the ball is in his court.

I hold my breath…waiting.

"I'm James," he says.

My thundering heart almost trips over itself with joy. It's happening. "Annabel."

"Are you from around here, Annabel?" An American accent has crept into his voice that's doing funny things to my insides. Is he drawing on his time in New York?

My mind spins. I don't have a backstory planned— I don't know who I'm supposed to be. Hell, I have no idea how this role-play thing is supposed to work. Perhaps part of me never thought he'd say yes...

"I'm in town on business." I sip my drink. "For one night."

"Just one?" There's that cheeky twinkle.

"Yes. I'm..." Think, dammit. "A researcher."

"And what do you research, Annabel?" The way he says my fake name sounds like sex itself.

His drink arrives and he brings the heavy glass up to his mouth, tipping his head back. As he swallows, I watch the muscles working in his throat and I find my own totally devoid of moisture.

"I research the five senses and their effect on the human body." My creative mind kicks into gear and it's like slipping a costume over my head. "Such as how the other senses increase in strength to compensate when one is no longer accessible."

"That's an interesting field of research."

"It's very hands on."

Our bodies are turned toward one another, my legs crossed so that my knees sit between his open legs. Owen leans one arm on the bar and watches me closely. It's different to every other time he's looked at me.

"How do you test those things?" he asks.

"It's pretty simple. I can show you right now, if you like?"

He nods. "Sure."

"Close your eyes."

There's something deeply appealing about having this strong man under my spell. Owen is physically fitter than most men…even most cops. He's easily over six feet, broad-shouldered and has the kind of sculpted, muscular arms you'd expect of an action hero. But having him here in front of me, eyes closed, while he awaits my instruction makes me feel all kinds of powerful. I usually only get that surge of confidence at work.

But this is purely personal.

I take the lemon rind from my cocktail and slowly bring it under his nose. I see the recognition in his facial features, even though he doesn't open his eyes. "What do you smell?"

"Lemon."

"But a second ago you had no idea it was there."

I leave the peel there for a second before placing it on a napkin on the bar. Then I lean closer to him, being sure not to touch him. When my lips are right by his ear, I blow cool air onto his skin and he shudders.

"With your eyes closed, everything else feels more intense. Your sense of smell and touch compensate for your lack of sight." I place my hand on his thigh, feeling hard muscle beneath the fine fabric of his trousers. "It's something that helped our ancestors when they had nothing but the moonlight to guide them."

Where the hell is this coming from? I've fully embraced the role—Annabel, the sexpot researcher. It's helping me be less like my typical awkward self, and more like the woman I *wish* I was.

"In fact," I say, pausing to clear my throat. "I'm here recruiting test subjects."

Owen's eyes open and he looks at my hand resting on his thigh. "What are the requirements?"

"Single men between the ages of thirty and thirty-five. Must be in good health." I let my gaze roam over his body in a way I've never done before.

I dwell in the details of him—in the blond hairs dusting his arms where his sleeves are rolled back. In the way his Adam's apple protrudes at his neck. In the sharp cut of his jaw and the hard slash of his cheekbones. In his bluer-than-blue eyes and full, curved lips. He's so attractive it borders on obnoxious. *All* the female recruits had a crush on him— charming Owen, who could befriend anyone. Who was always quick with a smile and a joke.

He was a boy, then. And now he's filled out into this complex, mysterious man.

"Anything else?" he asks.

"Must be free for one night of testing," I reply. "One *whole* night because…I like to be thorough."

"Sounds like I fit the bill." He knocks back the rest of his Scotch and I'm so nervous and excited

I'm worried my heart is going to bust its way out of my rib cage. "I don't suppose you have a spot open tonight?"

"Actually, I do."

CHAPTER ELEVEN

Owen

MOST PEOPLE DON'T know this about me, but I make decisions with care and consideration. No one expects the joker to have much going on upstairs...but I do. I let my head take the lead, instead of other less reliable parts like my heart, or my dick.

Tonight, however, is a rare exception.

My head is literally screaming at me to back away from this bad decision. But all the blood in my body is currently supporting another appendage. Hannah—posing as a sexy researcher named Annabel—slides from her bar stool, her eyes never leaving mine, and I'm done for. No amount of worrying about the case—about tomorrow—is going to stop me from taking the delicacy she's dangling in front of me.

I follow her from the bar and help her into her coat the second the night air hits us. It's colder now, spitting with rain, and I tuck her close against my body. "Where does your research take place, Ms. Annabel?"

She looks up at me and I see the cogs turning. She's considering whether we should go back to the apartment. That's not a good idea. A hotel will make it easier to keep sex and the job separate.

"I've got a room we could use," I say, leaning into my role of anonymous travelling businessman. "If you don't mind working out of a hotel."

"That sounds great," she says breathlessly.

We walk along the river's edge, our heads bowed to the fine, misting rain and our hands entwined until we reach the Crown Entertainment Complex. The hotel here is swanky to the max and has a price tag to match. The only room available is a suite and the nightly rate makes Hannah's eyes bulge—but I hand over my credit card and within seconds we're whisked up to heaven. The room boasts an incredible panoramic view of Melbourne, with glistening lights and a luxurious white sectional facing the window.

I can already see how incredible she'll look laid out on it—naked, with the moonlight dancing on her skin—while I feast on her. My body is tightly coiled, like a spring. There's a pressure building inside me that's been growing for years.

"Please remove your coat," Hannah says in a formal voice. She's already hung hers on a stand by the front door. "If you could also remove your shoes and socks, that would be most helpful."

The clipped, efficient tone makes me smile. I bend

and untie my dress shoes, toeing them off and removing my socks, as instructed. She hangs my coat next to hers and when she walks back to me, she's holding a tie in her hands. It looks to be made of the same fluffy white material as a bathrobe.

"I'm going to blindfold you now, so we can begin." She waits a moment and I give her a quick nod, letting her know it's okay to proceed.

I've always known Hannah to be a take-charge kind of woman, and it thrills me to know it transfers to the bedroom. I love being in charge, too, but there's something insanely hot about a woman who wants to take pleasure into her own hands. Tonight, I am willing to be her test subject—to play this role and revel in whatever that mysterious brain of hers has planned.

She wraps the blindfold over my eyes, tying it in a secure knot behind my head. And then nothing. I can't detect her movement, because the plush carpet absorbs the sound of her stilettos.

She makes me wait.

The seconds tick by and my desire grows like a storm, swirling and building, rising until it fills me completely. When her soft touch brushes the front of my pants, I'm hard as stone and aching for her.

"Ready?" she asks, her lips brushing my ear.

"I've never been readier."

We've both waited a long time for this.

CHAPTER TWELVE

Owen

IT DOESN'T TAKE long for the blindfold to work its magic. In seconds, I feel my other senses ramping up to accommodate for my lost sight. The gentle kiss of cool air is amplified where my collar sits open, and it's so quiet I can hear the *pitter patter* of rain against the windows. I smell the rain, too—in her hair as she moves around me, mingling with whatever fruity shampoo she uses. I'm driven immediately to the edge of sensation, to the edge of wanting.

There's a tug at my shirt. She's undoing my buttons…slowly. I sense her teasing through the way she pops each one open with an agonising pace.

"You must be doing well to afford such a fancy hotel room," she says, tracing the V of skin at my chest with her fingertip. But the sensual touch does little to hide the curiosity in her voice. The question, no matter how it's posed as part of this role play, is genuine.

"I'm doing well, but money doesn't make the man."

"It certainly doesn't," she murmurs. She works her way to the last of the buttons and then pulls the hem free. "Money doesn't buy decency."

I know the opposite is more likely—money is the reason I have no family. Money is what caused them to be taken from me. "Greed brings out the worst in us."

I would have burned all my parents left me if I'd been allowed. A teenager—blinded by rage and grief—has no use for zeros in a bank account. Because whatever future they might have secured—education and houses and finery—means nothing to an orphan who only wants his parents back.

"I'm feeling a little greedy now." Her hands toy with the buckle at my waist. "Is that so bad?"

"This is totally different." And *this* greed, I can handle.

The buckle makes a metallic *chink* as she yanks the leather through the loops on my suit pants. The sound of my zipper being undone slashes through the quiet air—through my thoughts. I'm about to embark on a hot night with a woman I've wanted for a long time. I need to get my head out of the past.

As if sensing my need to retreat from this conversation, Hannah says, "I'm going to strip you completely. Then we're going to see how you respond to different stimuli."

"Like what?" The anticipation is a fist around my cock. I'm desperate for more, desperate to see what she has planned.

"I can't tell you that. I need to measure the…

strength of your response." Her voice is low and husky.

She shoves my pants down my legs, dragging my boxer briefs with them, and helps me free. I'm totally naked now, and knowing that she's fully dressed makes this even hotter. My cock bobs up against my stomach, hard as concrete and oh-so-ready for her. But after a few seconds of nothing, I realise that Hannah has disappeared.

The silence is broken by the click of her heels over tile—has she gone into the kitchenette or the bathroom? I don't know the layout well enough to tell. There's a brief rushing of water, a dull, metallic sound and then that damn clicking again. I let myself dwell in the vision of her legs in those heels. Hannah is muscular—always devoted to stamina and speed. And her daily runs haven't been interrupted by this case. She gets up at the crack of dawn every morning without fail.

I know the purpose of her runs aren't for physical appearance, but there's no denying the activity has given her shapely legs and a firm ass. Both of which have been on my mind since our kiss in the garden.

I wonder where she is now. The clicking has stopped, and the robe tie is a surprisingly effective blindfold. I need to relieve a little of the tension, and I hesitate only a moment before reaching down to wrap a fist around my cock. I don't think I've been this hard in years. Never mind the fact I lost my taste for casual sex some time ago. But this…is not that.

Not casual. Not meaningless.

I stifle a moan and I run my fist up and down, giving a little twist at my swollen head. I imagine it's her hand doing the work, pleasuring me. Exploring me. Pulling the tip of me to her willing, open lips. My balls are tight. Achy. Never mind that I rubbed one out in the shower this morning, trying to make sure I kept my desires in check.

So much for that.

"Owen, uh… James…" She loses the role play for a moment, her voice ragged-edged with need. "I need you to stop that so we can properly start testing."

I release myself, reluctantly. But it's clear she was watching me for a while before she told me to stop. I can hear it in her voice. Dirty girl.

"Anything else I should refrain from doing?" I ask, letting my words come out slow and lazy.

"Just follow my orders," she replies. "If I don't tell you to do something, then don't do it."

CHAPTER THIRTEEN

Hannah

I'M SO OUT of my depth. I can only hope my voice sounds more commanding than I feel. Because right now, I want to melt into a puddle at Owen's feet.

His body is a masterpiece. Hard sculpted muscle shapes his arms, shoulders, legs and abs. A dusting of blond hair creates a delectable trail from his bellybutton all the way down to...

God. I can't tear my eyes away. Of course he's perfect everywhere. Watching him touch himself, watching those slightly rough, strong tugs and the way the swollen head of his erection poked out the top of his fist... Let's be real, I'm already a puddle.

"We're going to start with scent," I say. I've found a bowl of fruit in the kitchenette and I've selected an orange. I press my fingernail into the flesh, piercing it. The ripe scent of the fruit's flesh comes through. "What can you smell?"

I bring the orange under his nose, trying hard

not to think about how I want to rush through this and sink straight to my knees so I can take him in my mouth.

"Hmm, fruity." His voice is roughed up, desire-laden. God, it makes my toes curl in these ridiculously high heels. If a man can have that effect with his voice, what will happen when he finally touches me? "Citrus. Orange or mandarin."

"Very good." I've collected a few items for us to use in this role play: a glass of chilled water, a fork and an individually wrapped chocolate. A condom that I'd stashed in my purse...just in case. "How about taste?"

I peel back the rind from the orange and extract a small piece of flesh. Coaxing his mouth open with my thumb, I wriggle the fruit between his lips. He readily accepts it.

"Definitely orange."

The chocolate is next. I unwrap the foil and see something flicker over his face—like he's trying to figure out what the sound is. But I don't give him any clues. Instead, I pop the chocolate into my mouth and take my time enjoying the small, decadent moment. Then I press into him, bringing my lips to his, and he responds hungrily. The taste of chocolate mixes with the orange he's just consumed.

"Tastes like a Jaffa," he says, bringing his strong arms around me. "So sweet."

"Not yet," I rasp, pulling out of his grip. I want to draw this out—because I have the power now. I'm in charge.

And the second he gets his hands on me I'm going to fold like a house of cards.

"Am I not a good test subject?"

"You're not very good at following instructions." I pick up the fork and press the spiked end into his thigh—not enough to hurt, but certainly enough to elicit a response. His erection twitches and his hands ball by his sides. "How is your sense of touch?"

"Heightened." His voice is wire-tight.

I trail the fork over his chest, letting the metal scrape lightly against his skin. I imagine the contrast feels good—a little pain, followed by something softer. I press my lips to his neck, breathing in the faded scent of cologne on his skin. Sucking so the blood rises to the surface.

The soft imprint of lipstick fills me with a sense of warm possessiveness—like I've claimed him. Marked him.

"If you want this to last more than five fucking seconds, you're going about it all wrong, Hannah." He speaks softly, the growling sound like a fine blade along my nerve endings, making my body sing. "I'm breaking character to tell you that."

"We're almost there," I purr, emboldened by the effect I'm having on him.

I'm not quite done toying with him. I step back and watch him for a moment, let my eyes have their fill. Then I bring my hands to the zipper that runs down the side of my body, keeping my dress in place. I drag it down slowly, letting the sound slice through the air. Then I shed the garment, making a show of dropping it to the ground.

"What can you hear?" I ask him.

"Are you...?" His hand twitches, as if he's going to touch himself again but I make an *uh-uh* sound. "Are you undressed?"

"Almost."

I'm in lacy underwear, heels and no bra. But I hook my fingers under my waistband and drag the black silk and lace down over my hips. I step out of the underwear and dangle it from one finger. Then I move closer to him, draping the silk over his swollen cock. I drag it up his length, wrap it around him and rub the silk over his skin.

"Hannah," he growls.

"Annabel," I correct him as I pull the underwear back and whip it across his stomach. His body jerks and his nostrils flare, but not from pain. Oh no, it's all pleasure now.

"Annabel. Is that...?"

"Yes."

He stifles a groan. "I want to touch you."

"Not yet."

I toss my underwear onto the floor and slowly sink to my knees. The water glass beckons and I take a big mouthful, relishing the slide of the cold liquid down my throat. But the water isn't intended solely for hydration.

I take another big gulp and set the glass down. I saw the tip once in Cosmo, to drink cold water or suck on ice cubes before giving head. The sensation is supposed to be amazing for the guy. It was one of those cheesy articles: *Ten Ways to Pleasure Your Man* that I used to laugh at with my girlfriends back when I thought blow jobs were all about the guy.

But right now, I want nothing more than to take Owen into my mouth and suck him until he forgets why he ever said no to me. Until he understands the giddy, lust-fuelled attraction that turns my brain to jelly.

I don't want to be the only one feeling this way.

"What are you doing?" he asks, his hands reaching forward to see if I'm there.

I brace one palm flat against his stomach and lower my mouth to the tip of his cock. It's beaded with pearly liquid, and I wrap my lips around him.

"Fucking hell." His fingers drive through my hair, flexing against my scalp in a way that mixes the sharp snap of pain with a whole lot of pleasure.

He's hot and pulsing on my tongue—tastes and smells earthy in a way that's one-hundred-percent masculine. Yeah, this isn't just for him.

"That..." He grunts. I release him for a second and look up, catching the way his head lolls back as I continue to work him with my hand. "Christ, that feels good."

I lower my head down again and relish in the power cursing through my veins. I've never felt like this during sex. Never felt like I could bring a man to his knees. But the sounds coming from his mouth tell me all I need to know—for now, for this moment, I'm in charge.

CHAPTER FOURTEEN

Owen

THE CONTRAST IS enough to undo me. Hannah's mouth is somehow hot and cold all at the same time. Her fingers form a tight ring at the base of my cock and her mouth works over me in a way that feels so good it makes my head spin.

I keep a tight grip on her hair, pumping my hips back and forth. But I want to see her now, because I'm the kind of guy who likes to feast with my eyes. I yank the blindfold off and toss it to the floor.

Holy. Freaking. Shit.

Hannah's naked, except for her glossy mirror-finish heels, which poke out behind the round curve of her ass as she balances on her knees. Her lips are swollen, wet. Her cheeks are flushed the prettiest shade of pink...the tips of her ears, too. With each bob of her head, her dark hair brushes over my stomach and thighs.

"Look at me," I command.

Hannah tilts her face ever so slightly, enough to

angle those big brown eyes up. But her mouth continues working me—her tongue circling my head, her cheeks hollowing as she applies the perfect amount of pressure. It's even hotter with the eye contact.

Sparks shoot through me, and I feel so damn alive. I haven't felt like this in…years. The whole time I've been in New York, I've been a shell. A hardworking, hard-partying shell.

"Testing time is over," I growl.

"Can't hang on?" she teases, rocking back on her feet and standing.

If I thought the heels made her legs look good before, then she's damn near goddess-level now. Her body is incredible. She's got these strong, broad shoulders which I never really thought would be a sexy feature, but they're perfection on her.

"You're so beautiful." I'm not sure this kind of talk is meant to be part of our one-night, this-isn't-really-us deal. But I can't help it, the words are gone before I can contemplate the consequences.

Her gaze drops to the floor for a second, her dark, sooty lashes shielding her expression. She doesn't know what to think and neither do I. All I know is that I want her. Desperately.

"I feel like we're not doing very well at this role-play thing," she says.

"Are you kidding me? That water trick was… Fuck." I step toward her, my hands zeroing in on her hips. Her skin is soft and silky, and she feels like heaven. "I think you blew every one of my five senses."

"Four," she corrects me. "No sight, remember."

"If you don't think I'm getting my fill of that right now, then you're dead wrong."

We're in the middle of the hotel room and Hannah's body is backlit by the cityscape outside the window. Lights sparkle and wink, and off in the distance some fireworks bloom over the Docklands. They're not close enough to hear, but I spin Hannah around so she can watch.

"Look." I point, as I guide her to the window. "What a view, right?"

"It's beautiful," she breathes. I'm behind her and she presses her palms to the glass. "Fireworks always make me happy."

The explosions of green and purple and red create silent music in the distance. I lean forward, lining her back with my front. "Keep your hands there."

I run my fingertip down the length of her spine. Then I curve my hand over her hip, pressing my palm to her stomach before driving it slowly down, and gently delving between her legs. Hannah shifts, widening her stance. Inviting me in. She's wet. So fucking wet.

I slide my fingers through her pussy, dragging the moisture toward her clit. The sensitive little bud is so swollen, she jerks against my hand with even the softest touch.

"Oh no." Her head drops back against my shoulder.

I still. "Do you want me to stop?"

"God, no. It's…" She turns her face and looks up

at me shyly. "I have a feeling it's going to be over way too quickly."

"Luckily there's no limit on what we can do tonight. I'm yours until we check out." I circle her clit with my forefinger, enjoying the way she rubs against me. My cock is nestled against the top of her ass. "All damn night."

"Good," she sighs. "Keep going."

Tremors are already running through her and my fingers are soaked. In the reflection from the glass, I see the faint outline of us. Her legs are wide, and her face is screwed up with pleasure. I, on the other hand, look like a man possessed—eyes wild and hair mussed and jaw tight.

I'm worried the second I sink my cock into that tight pussy I'm going to blow my load quicker than a teenage boy on his first fuck. But like I said, we've got all night. I want nothing more than to watch the sun come up while we're bleary-eyed and satiated and aching all over.

She gasps and rocks against my hand. "I'm going to come."

"Don't hold back, baby. Take what you need." I work her, rubbing my finger against her clit. Faster, a little more pressure, helping her to ride the wave until she's shuddering, whimpering. Until she's calling my name like I'm a goddamn deity.

Hannah slumps back against me, aftershocks causing her to tremble. I scoop her up and she loops her arms around my neck, like I'm her last tether to earth. I know, as a guy, making her come should have

me feeling high on sexual power. But it's this—that
trusting, easy, sweet way she leans her head against
my shoulder—that has the power to break me.

I get to the bedroom, stopping only to retrieve
the condom she's thoughtfully supplied, and slowly
lower her onto the plush covers. Then I slip her feet
out of her heels, dropping them to the floor one by
one. We've left a breadcrumb trail across the hotel
room—discarded clothes, abandoned items from our
"sensory testing" experiment. Now it's just us with
nothing in our way. We're in a perfect bubble, where
yesterday and tomorrow don't exist.

A thought niggles at me, telling me that it's naive
to think this won't impact tomorrow. But I'm so far
into the fantasy nothing can drag me away. The
only thing that could stop me is Hannah herself, but
her big brown eyes stare up at me—her lush mouth
parted—and she's a picture of wanton lust.

"I never thought this would happen," she says,
her voice close to a whisper. "I thought you would
always be an unfulfilled wish."

I slide my hands up her thighs, parting her. My
thumbs trace circles against her fair skin and she
shivers, propping herself up so she can watch. "You
should be spending your wishes on someone better."

I know the second the words are out of my mouth
that I've said too much.

Hannah cocks her head. "You never struck me
as the kind of guy to have an inferiority complex."

"I don't."

I simply know what I'm capable of and what I'm

not…and where I foresee it causing problems. But the easiest way to deal with questions I don't want to answer—the way I *always* deal with it—is to distract the person asking.

I kiss the inside of Hannah's knee. It's the softest of kisses, a bare graze of lips and her skin ripples with goose bumps. Oh, Hannah. She's still sensitive from the orgasm I gave her a few moments ago. Still reeling from the pleasure.

I want to draw this out—stretch the anticipation until neither one of us can take it—but I can't. For too long, I've denied myself what I wanted. What we both wanted.

I slide my hands under her ass and pull her to the edge of the bed, setting my mouth on her pussy like a man starved. She bucks against me, fingers driving through my hair and nails digging into my scalp. Her words aren't fully formed and she squirms—wanting more and less and in equal measure. She tells me to keep going when I pull back for the briefest second, blowing cool air across her swollen skin in a way that makes her back arch against the bed.

Then I'm on her again. Feasting on the honeyed taste of her, licking and sucking until she rolls her hips, grinding herself against my face. Yes, baby. Take it. Take all of it.

"Owen," she moans, the keening sound like a shot of pure adrenaline. "Yes!"

I'm wired, like a spring pulled tight. The need to drive into her is pounding in my head like a religious chant.

Take her, take her, take her.

When she comes, her fist flexes against my scalp and she clamps her thighs around my head. It feels like her orgasm goes on forever; she rocks until she's wrung every last bit of pleasure from it. Watching her flop back against the bed—one arm flung over her eyes—is a picture I'll never forget. Moonlight dances over her skin.

"You're so beautiful." I climb onto the bed, grabbing the condom, and encourage her to come with me.

Propping my back against an obscene number of pillows, I tug her closer. She straddles me, her knees digging into the soft cotton on either side of my legs. For a moment she hovers there, her eyes locked on mine. Like she's looking for something—but what, I have no idea.

Hannah leans forward, her hair brushing my cheek. I feel her lips at my ear, her warm breath sending anticipation slicing through me. "Don't be gentle."

"You want it rough, huh? You want to make sure you're not walking straight tomorrow?"

She pulls back, her pupils blacker than ink. There's a glazed look to her now, like arousal has dulled her edges. Like she's sinking into sensation. "Yes."

She plucks the condom from my hand and tears the packet open. Squeezing the tip, she places it over the head of my cock and begins to roll it down. Condoms aren't usually sexy. Necessary? Hell yeah. But part of the foreplay? Not really…until now.

"Keep talking," she says, her eyes meeting mine like smoke and fire.

She likes the dirty talk? Can. Fucking. Do.

"Spread your legs, baby. I want to make sure you're soaking wet before I stick my cock in you." I grab myself with one hand and angle toward her, dragging the tip through the slick moisture, rubbing back and forth in a way that makes her mewl. "You're so wet. So ready for me."

"I am," she breathes, her chest rising and falling with choppy breath.

I reach behind her and sink my fingers into her ass, guiding her toward me. She feels like heaven, like sin and temptation and all that's right with the world. Planting her hands on my chest, she shifts so that I'm pressing against her entrance.

"Sink down slowly," I command. "I want to feel every little bit until I'm in as far as you can take me."

"Yes." The word is a hiss.

She bears down and takes me inside her. She's so tight I have to press my head back against the pillows for a second so I don't lose it. But damn, it's like she was made for me. We fit together perfectly.

"So full," she gasps, her forehead touching mine. She presses down more, taking me inside her, stretching to accommodate me.

"That's it. Slowly." I press a kiss to her lips, my hands rubbing circles over her ass to relax her. "Don't tense up."

I feel the movement as she gives in and slides down the last little bit. It's everything—and I sit there for a moment, still and quiet. Giving her time to adjust. Hell, giving myself time to adjust.

I'm fucking Hannah Anderson.

My mind spins. The amount of times I've jerked off in the shower to this very fantasy... God. I don't even know how many times. All I know is that I never thought I'd be here. That I shouldn't be here.

But that I want it more than anything.

"I'm good," she whispers.

If only she knew that I needed that moment of stillness as much as she did. But I'll never let on.

"You trying to tell me to hurry up and fuck you?" My voice is low, gravelly. "Greedy, greedy girl."

This Hannah is different to the woman with the blindfold. She enjoys being in charge, but I think she equally enjoys letting someone else sit in the driver's seat. It's exciting, how open and curious she is. How playful.

"You want a quick and dirty one-night stand, huh? You want to be thoroughly fucked? Tomorrow you're not going to be able to take a step without remembering how good it felt to have my cock in you. I'm going to leave you satisfied and sore, so when you sit that pretty ass down you'll have to squeeze your thighs together."

"Bloody hell." She's practically panting as she wriggles against me, frustrated. Not wanting to wait.

I fill my hands with her ass, lifting her up so I can

tease her for one more minute. So I can see the plea in her face before I give her what she wants.

"Owen."

My name is like a prayer and a sentence all at once. I'm lost to her, lost to how good we feel together. Lost to the reality that I've well and truly screwed myself for the rest of this job. Because I won't be able to forget what she looks like—wild-eyed and open-mouthed. I won't be able to forget the way she looked up at me as she sucked my dick. The way she teased me, taunted me. The way she sees everything.

I'm a goner.

"You feel so good." I thrust up into her, driving hard and deep. She's so wet there's no resistance at all. "I'm going to bounce you up and down until I feel those beautiful thighs shake."

"I..." She's incoherent now. Babbling pleasure sounds that started off as words but ended up as sighs and moans and gasps.

Wrapping my arms around her, I move us to the edge of the bed so I can plant my feet against the ground for leverage. When I stand, she locks her ankles behind my back and clings to my neck. She's all muscle, but she's still light enough for me to carry. Light enough that I don't need to lean her against a wall.

"Don't drop me," she gasps.

"I've got you."

Her mouth is on mine, ravenous. Can she taste herself on my lips? Her body is soft in my hands, letting me control the pace. I slip my hands under her thighs and move her body how I want it. How it feels good.

I slide her up and down my cock, flexing with each stroke as I go deep. I start off slower, taking my time but soon I'm losing control. My balls are achy and full, and they slap up against her with each stroke, drawing me close to the edge. She smells like faded perfume and perspiration, a potent combination. And her lips are firm and smooth, her tongue driving into my mouth as I screw her senseless.

"Oh God...yes, that spot." She bows in my arms and her internal muscles start to pulse.

I've got no hope of hanging on now, as she draws me deeper. I hold her tight and thrust up, pounding into her over and over as we chase release. I'm so close, our pleasure is a pinpoint and I chase it. I shut my eyes, going back to what she did to me before, letting my other senses take over.

"Owen," she whispers into my ear, her voice hoarse. "I want to feel you come."

I'm a dead man. A slave to pleasure.

There's nothing but the smell of her, the subtle saltiness on her lips. The sound of skin slapping against skin. And the feel of her—hot, wet, tight.

"Hannah," I groan, bouncing her up and down, my movements stiff and jerky.

Then I go deep one last time and I shatter, my cock pulsing inside her as I come. Hard. It's that moment that she tips over, too, her body squeezing mine so tight I think I might faint from the intensity of it all. After a moment, I stumble back to the bed and drop down, folding us onto our sides while I'm still inside her.

The shock waves of orgasm ripple through us and she curls her hand into mine. I want to hold her forever.

CHAPTER FIFTEEN

Hannah

I WAKE COCOONED in plush, expensive sheets, like I've been sleeping on a thousand-thread-count Egyptian cotton cloud. The pillow cradles my head and sunlight streams in between a gap in the blinds, bathing the hotel room with a buttery glow. I wonder if I've been smiling all night. Every part of me aches—I'm overworked and overloaded. I'm satisfaction personified.

But when I roll over, my hand automatically reaching for him, reality jolts me. His side of the bed is cold and the sheets are pulled up neatly, which is a surprise. Normally I sleep twisted in my sheets, the endless spinning of my mind causing me to toss and turn. So either Owen screwed me so good that I slept like a log…or he tucked me in and rearranged the sheets when he got up.

Thinking about that gives me a funny feeling in my chest.

I push up and swing my legs over the edge of the

bed, my mind churning. The idea of putting on that sexy black dress this early in the morning makes me cringe, so I settle on wrapping myself in a fluffy bathrobe.

What is it going to be like between us this morning? Will he be remote and act like it never happened? Will he tell me he had a good time? I'm not sure which is worse. Because as much as I had the time of my life last night—and got *exactly* what I wanted—I'm far from getting it out of my system. In fact, I want nothing more than to search him out and drag him into the shower.

"For all you know he already left," I mutter, scrubbing a hand over my face.

A rustle on the other side of the room startles me, and Owen walks into the bedroom from the little corridor that leads to the rest of the suite. "No dice, Anderson. You can't get rid of me that easily."

"Don't high-flying businessmen usually take off at first light?"

"Well, this *is* my hotel room. So I guess you should have been the one to take off." He's wearing jeans and a fitted black hoodie, and looking every bit as delectable as he did last night in his suit pants and shirt.

Wait a minute… "How did you get changed?"

I hadn't even given a thought to what might happen this morning, and whether or not I'd need to do the "walk of shame" back to 21 Love Street. Although that term strikes me as dated—there's nothing shameful about having sex. They should really call it "the walk of blisters" because lord knows putting on those wretched heels again will be hell on my feet.

"I went back to the apartment."

That's when I notice Owen is carrying a calico bag over one shoulder. "I didn't even hear you leave."

"You were dead to the world." The corner of his lips quirks up and it's the sexiest expression I've ever seen. Not quite a smile, not as hard as a smirk. Just something crooked and imperfectly in the middle. "And I figured you probably wouldn't want to head home in that dress from last night. It's chilly out."

My heart melts. "You went all the way back there to get me a change of clothes?"

"It's not far." He shrugs, as if suddenly trying to downplay the kind gesture. "And there's coffee on the table out there."

Okay, now I *really* melt. The way to my heart is not with chocolate or flowers or any of that gooey crap—it's with a so-strong-it-punches-you-in-the-face coffee. Almost as if the fumes of caffeine are carrying me, I drift past him into the main room of the hotel suite. Two white takeaway cups sit side by side—identical except for the black Sharpie scribble. A flat white, his. And a triple-shot latte, mine.

"Come to mama." I take the cup in my hands and bring the liquid gold to my lips.

"I ran into Rowan this morning." Owen picks up his coffee and sips. I catch a glimpse of us in the mirror and we look like a couple who's been together forever—him with his hair mussed and stubble on his jaw, and me—looking equally mussed—wearing a robe. "He mentioned there's a barbeque on for building residents today. Apparently, they do it once a month."

"Seems like a very social building." The place where I live currently is nothing like that. "Might be a good way to meet some of the other residents…if you think it's time to start talking to people."

I can tell my teasing hits the right spot when Owen shoots me a look. "Very funny. But yes, I agree we should go."

"What do you know, we finally agree on something."

Owen puts his cup down and stalks forward—I see a hint of the fire from last night. A fire which has burned me so bad I'll never lose the scars. Last night was…everything. Everything I knew it would be, everything I hoped it would be. Everything I was terrified of because there's no way in hell one night will ever be enough.

"I think we agree on something else." He reaches out and traces the edge of the bathrobe, starting near my collar bone and going all the way down to where the belt is knotted at my waist.

"What's that?" My voice trembles.

"That you're crazy hot."

I'm not sure I agree on that, but I like the way I look reflected in his eyes. I'm the best version of myself—the most confident, the most desirable. I'm not ready to leave the hotel. Like a junkie, I need one more hit. Just one more…

We're entering a dangerous place, going back on the agreement we made for this to be a one-night thing—if we're breaking our own rules already, then what hope do we have of controlling the beast we've unleashed?

What hope do *I* have of protecting my heart?

Because I know Owen is worried I'll want more than he's willing to give. Truth be told, I'm worried about that, too.

He tugs on the knot, loosening the fluffy fabric and letting the robe fall open. "Fucking hell, Anderson. You've got me hooked."

"I thought you were supposed to call me Annabel," I say. I wish I could get out of my own head and go with the flow. I wish I could indulge in my desires and stop always worrying about the consequences.

If he keeps touching me, I know I'll give in. I'm powerless when it comes to him—but that doesn't mean I'm not worried about getting hurt.

"Yeah, I totally forgot about that when I woke up this morning." He rakes a hand through his hair. "You'll always be Anderson to me."

His statement makes me feel simultaneously better and worse. The role-play game was fun, but it was never going to give us a free pass to forget what happened.

Here and now it's us.

"What happens in the hotel stays in the hotel?" he says with a cheeky smirk.

Boundaries. I'm not sure they'll work but it's

enough that my rule-loving brain puts a checkmark in that box.

"What happens in the hotel stays in the hotel," I echo.

"You weren't ready to leave this morning, were you?" he asks.

I shake my head, biting down on my lip. "Not even a little bit."

His head dips to mine with a force that makes me gasp. The roughness of his jeans is heaven and hell against my bare thighs, the friction driving me wild.

The kiss is raw, possessive. His tongue claims mine and he tastes of coffee. He backs me up against the sturdy wooden table and his hips pin me in place.

"So good." The words come out muffled against my throat where his teeth scrape against my skin.

"I want to touch you." My words trail off into a groan as his lips find the hollow at the base of my throat.

"You'll touch me when I say you can touch me." His grin almost melts me on the spot. "I'm going to pay you back for making me wait last night."

Oh God. Is there anything sexier than a guy in control? Last night I had fun, but I love knowing that Owen can flip the tables on me. He keeps me guessing.

He's so hard, and the length of him digs into my belly. I'm panting and desperate, my thighs clenching to quiet the sensation that's gone from an insistent throb to a roaring. "But last night—"

"I'm not pretending to be an anonymous businessman now." He lowers himself, grasping my wrists and holding my hands in place before setting his lips on my skin. He's kissing my breasts, gently tugging on my nipples with his teeth. Each little nip makes my knees shake. "I'm me and you're you."

I nod, my voice lost. I'm me and he's him. We're us. Ourselves…no pretending. It's risky as hell. But while we're here, we're not working the case. It's a line of separation.

What happens in the hotel stays in the hotel. Or am I clutching at straws?

"Ditch the gown." Owen releases my hands and steps back.

I shrug one shoulder out of the fluffy robe, and then the other. It slips heavily to the ground. He's still as a statue, legs grounded in a stance of pure masculinity. One hand rakes through his hair.

Owen whips the hoodie over his head and takes his T-shirt with it. I automatically reach out to him but he catches my hand and spins me around. Bracing my hands against the table, I arch back to press against him.

"What did you say to me last night? Don't do anything until I explicitly tell you to." He nips at my ear lobe, his face buried against my hair. "Keep your hands on the table."

I force myself to breathe slowly. I've never had a guy make me feel like this before. He's controlling the pace, but not in a way that makes me feel inferior. I'm almost relieved. He's taking the lead, taking the pressure off my shoulders.

Suddenly, my back is cold and the sound of a zipper cuts through the air, followed by the soft thud of fabric hitting the floor. Then warm flesh presses against me from behind. Hot palms skim my thighs, the curve of my butt and my hips.

"Please," I whimper. "Oh my God, please."

"Slowly, Anderson. Don't rush it." He kisses the back of my neck while he slides his hands all over me, mapping me. Learning me. "Just enjoy."

How could I not? His hand slides up my front, cupping my breast and thumbing my nipple until I'm sagging against him. My hands curl over the edge of the table, but I'm in serious danger of dissolving onto the ground like a melted ice cube.

"Can I touch you yet?" I need to be active in our lovemaking. If this is the last time I can have him, then I don't want to be a bystander.

He doesn't respond but he guides my hands behind my back and down to his cock. The guttural moan tells me he wants it as much as I do. The soft glide of my palm over his steel-hard erection makes me throb.

"I want to look at you."

"Bossy." His amused tone makes me smile. "I thought I was in charge."

"I let you *think* you're in charge."

"You're a handful." He spins me around and I drink him in, the flushed cheeks, wild blue eyes and a body fit for a museum sculpture.

"*You're* a handful." I stroke the length of him, swallowing at the satisfying weight in my palm.

The cool air makes my nipples peak further. As if he senses my need, he drops his head to one stiff peak and draws it into his mouth. The hot wetness of his lips and gentle flicking of his tongue has me squirming against him, squeezing him and stroking him firmly in response.

"What did I say about going slowly?" he growls.

"Going slow is for wimps." I grin wickedly.

"Temptress." His eyes flash and he hoists me over his shoulder, a palm landing down on my butt with a loud crack.

"Oh!" Warmth spreads through me and I'm tingling all over.

He carries me to the bed as if I weigh nothing, and he sets me down with a gentle reverence. For a heartbeat he only looks, his eyes like blue fire and his face set into a mask of wonder as if I'm the most beautiful woman in the world. In that moment, I feel as though I am. But the spell vanishes when his face morphs into one of pure heat.

"Get on all fours," he says.

Biting back a moan at the sexy command, I comply and climb onto the bed, facing away from him and sticking my ass in the air. It's like he has the controller to my body. The rustling of a foil packet gets my attention. I'd only stashed the one in my wallet last night.

"Where did you get that?" I turn to look over my shoulder.

He breaks his confident-Owen façade for a minute and a shy smile slips over his face. "I stopped on the way back to the apartment. Just in case you wanted…"

He was thinking about it. Thinking about me. I whip my head back around so he can't see how I'm slayed. How does he do this to me? But before I can spiral, he's behind me.

"All good?" His voice is softer now, thick with desire.

I nod.

"Say it, Anderson." His lips trail down my spine. "Nice and loud."

"Yes." I swallow. "I want this."

Then he's filling me, burying himself deep. Each stroke brings me closer to the edge. He slips a hand around my waist and dips between my legs, finding my sweet spot.

"I don't even want to know how you're so good." I press back into him, receiving each long, deep thrust with pleasure.

"Build-up. Years and years of you tempting the shit out of me."

I press my face down into the bed covers and lose myself. The sounds of us fucking—skin slapping and hard breathing and hearts thundering—fill my head. It's so good I can't speak anymore. I'm melting into sensation.

So good, so good, so good…

"Fuck, Hannah."

My name is a strangled plea on his lips, and it's enough to send me over one more time. I shudder, my body spasming with pleasure. It sets off a chain reaction, and he's thrusting deep. His body covers mine, and he whispers dirty things into my ear. Telling me all the ways he's thought about having me, all the ways he wants to have me.

I know it's the sex talking, but I let myself believe for a second that it's real.

Then he pushes deep inside and follows me into oblivion. As the fireworks fade, he lowers himself onto the bed and pulls me against him.

"Good?" His hand traces designs over my thigh. Each touch is feather-light, worlds apart from where we were moments ago.

I nod, unable to form words. My brain stutters like he's short-circuited me.

"I didn't hurt you, did I?" There's a sweet note of concern in his voice, perhaps a tinge of regret.

"No, you didn't hurt me." Not physically anyway. Emotionally…I don't know yet. God, this is awkward. Why can't we stay in post-sex bliss forever? "So…uh, what now?"

For a moment he doesn't say anything. But then he gets up and heads into the bathroom to dispose of the condom. Looks like he's not sure the best way to handle things, either. Maybe it was too soon to ask…

But there's a part of me that always needs to know my next step. It's how I operate in my job and in my life. Ambiguity is the enemy.

"We get back to work." He grabs the bag with my clothes from the table. I can see he's picked up a few things, perhaps unsure what I might want to wear.

The gesture is sweet, but the magic is all gone. It's my own fault. I knew I would feel like this.

"Back to work." I nod. "Right."

It's not what my heart wants to hear, but I shake off the disappointment. If I feel bad, that's on me. Unrealistic desires and all that.

I hurry into the bathroom to change. Which seems a little useless considering he's seen me naked a lot in the last twelve hours. My body is one thing, however. My emotions are totally another.

"Are we…okay?" he asks through the door.

"Sure." I doubt it convinces either one of us.

"I told you there was a reason I kept away, Hannah."

I swallow. Damn him, when he says my name like that it always reaches inside me. Makes my heart squeeze. When I'm Anderson, he's all playful and fun. Owen the Joker. When he calls me by my rank, he's trying to get under my skin. And when he says Hannah, usually it's with a coating of sarcasm because I've told him off.

But this is different.

It's softer. More. Everything.

I can't handle that right now. I need a less vulnerable emotion to cling on to, something that doesn't make me seem like the weaker party. I choose frustration.

"What is that reason, exactly?" I ask as I tug my outfit on. "If you really want me to understand then why don't you tell me something real?"

"Messed-up childhood. What else do you need to know?"

Everything. I don't need to know it, but I want to. For some reason—and against every bit of sensibility in my usually *very* practical brain—I want to be closer to him. And it hurts to be held at an arm's length.

"Life is short," he adds. "I want my life to be as easy as possible."

"Wow. Stick that on a motivational poster and I'll hang it on my wall." I roll my eyes. The sentiment disappoints me, because it doesn't fit with the man I believe Owen to be. He does care...even if he doesn't show it. "Don't you think everyone would be happy with an easy life? But spoiler alert, life *isn't* easy."

I come out of the bathroom and spear him with a look. I'm not buying this BS.

"Is this the point where you tell me things happen for a reason?" he grunts. "I've heard that recycled bullshit a thousand times over."

"So you're going to do this case and then return to being a party boy in New York?"

I'd heard stories from Max—that Owen had a sweet bachelor pad and liked to hit the clubs on a regular basis. It seems like a complete waste to me. Owen is one of the best officers I've ever worked with—despite his inability to show up on time. He's a joker, sure. But he's got a sharp mind and a desire to do good.

"How do you know I was a party boy in New York?" He folds his arms across his chest.

"People talk."

"Fucking Max," he mutters. "What did he tell you?"

"Nothing much, just that you've been acting like you're twenty-two instead of thirty-two. Clubbing, drinking…" Probably sleeping around, although Max never actually said it and I *certainly* don't want to think about it. Especially not now. "Avoiding commitment of any kind."

"I'm committed to my job."

"The new one?" I shake my head. "You wanted to climb the ranks. You wanted to protect the people in this city, make Melbourne a safer place."

He stares at me, eyes smouldering and jaw pulled taut. But then he shakes his head like he's telling himself not to bite. "I'm going to walk back to the apartment. Clear my head."

The door swings shut behind him and I sink down onto one of the dining chairs surrounding a small glass-and-chrome table. This is the Owen I know— the one who walks away when things get real. The one who dodges tough questions and close connections.

This is your own fault. You pushed for more when he was very clear about what this meant to him.

I bring the coffee to my lips and tip my head back. Yep, it's stone cold. Ugh.

I look around the fancy hotel room, remembering how last night made me feel. How this morning made me feel. The power that surged through my veins. And the pleasure…oh, the pleasure.

That kind of connection only comes when there's more than sexual attraction between two people, but I have to accept that Owen has made his stance clear. He's not looking for anything real.

And for the sake of this job, I have to be okay with that.

Later that afternoon things are a little tense with Owen and me. We've been circling around one another all day. But the barbeque is a great way to meet some more of the residents and perhaps find out more about our prime suspect: Matt. So we have to suck it up.

The weather is chilly—but the sky is clear and bright. Lights have been strung up and outdoor heaters emanate a warm glow. The covered area has great views of the lush green garden and vegetable patch. For a moment, I forget I'm in the middle of the city and I imagine that's *exactly* what the property developers were going for. It's a slice of outdoor heaven in the middle of the big smoke.

A group of men cluster around one of the barbeques, and I immediately spot Rowan, who seems to have everyone enraptured with one of his stories. Three women sit at one of the tables, chatting and drinking wine. Several more people mill about, shaking hands and smiling.

"It's Hannah, right?" A woman with huge brown eyes and a kind smile stands and motions for me to take a seat.

I recognise Ava right away. She's the schoolteacher from level five, and she lives next to Rowan and Dom. I liked her instantly the first time we met—she's warm and welcoming. A little shy, but I imagine if she wrangles four- and five-year-old kids all day then she can probably dole out the whoop-ass when it's required.

"Good memory." I pull out a seat and get settled. Owen waves before heading toward the group of guys.

"I'm so glad you came," Ava says and I get the impression she means it. "It's a really social building to live in. Let me introduce you around. I think you met Emery already?"

I turn to the woman next to me—she's got a slight build and sharp eyes. Both times I've seen her now she's been wearing a *Game of Thrones* T-shirt. This one says You Know Nothing. "Nice to see you again."

"Likewise." Emery nods. "Always good to get some fresh blood into the building."

"And this," says Ava, "is Drew."

Drew is stunning. Long blond hair in a perfect Gwen Stefani platinum, smudgy dark eye makeup and a sleek all-black outfit. She's got the sexy goth thing down pat. "Hannah, was it? Nice to meet you. Don't get attached—I won't be around long."

"Yeah, yeah." Emery rolls her eyes and reaches for an empty wineglass. She pours me some white wine and hands it over. "Little Miss Jetset can't stay in one place."

"You travel a lot?" I ask.

Drew nods. "I'm a flight attendant and usually I'm based in London. I was in Dubai before that."

"Such a glamorous life," Ava says with a sigh.

I sip my wine. "What brought you home?"

"Wedding." She says the word like it makes her physically ill. "Hate the damn things. But my sister is signing her life away, so I gotta be there."

I blink. "Oh, that's…lovely."

Emery laughs and slaps her hand down on Drew's back. "I knew I was gonna like you."

"An old friend lives in this building," Drew says. "But she travels a lot, too, so that worked out perfectly. Staying with my parents on top of the wedding would have been too much to handle." Drew's gaze sweeps over me, taking in details. Her eyes are a pale silvery blue, almost ethereally lacking in colour. With the dark eye makeup, it's a striking combination. "That's a big hunk of stone there. You're married?"

"Yeah." I nod and give her the practised smile that should accompany my answer—serene, happy. Not showing an ounce of the confusion and frustration that's been swirling in my head ever since this morning. I point over to where Owen stands, chatting with Matt. "That's my husband."

"Cute." Drew winks. "How did you two meet?"

"University. We had some of the same classes." We're keeping our stories close to the truth, thereby reducing the chance we might slip up given it was my first time undercover. Swap police academy for university and we could use pretty much any of our old stories and make them feel authentic. "We were friends for a long time first. He didn't want to date me, actually. But I won him over."

"Look at how in love she is!" Ava sighs dramatically. "You can see it all over her face."

Heat floods my cheeks and I gulp down some of my wine. I'm not *that* good an actress, and it terrifies me that Ava can see something I don't want to show.

It's good for the cover story. And you are *a good actress, that's all this is.*

But I know that look comes from somewhere deep inside me, a part I've been hushing for years. I like Owen…a lot. Last night was more than sex to me even if it wasn't to him.

"You must be one of the lucky ones." Drew leans back in her chair and her eyes drift over to the men. There's something in her expression that's difficult to read. "To find a guy who won't promise you the moon and then vanish the second he gets what he wants."

Ava and I exchange a glance, while Emery nods empathetically. I get the impression there are two opposing views on love in this little group. I can't help letting my gaze drift to Owen. He's talking and laughing.

God, he's gorgeous. When he looks back at me, catching my gaze with his, I'm ruined. But I need to get my head in the game. I'm not going to hang my hopes on a fantasy.

"So give me the lowdown," I say. "Who's who in this building?"

That's what I'm here for. Information. A clue as to who might warrant our attention. Because, for the first time in my life, I'm struggling to keep my focus on work and I can't drop the ball now. Not when I've finally gotten to where I want to be.

"Well," Ava says with a cheeky grin. I suspect the sweet schoolteacher might enjoy a little gossip, which is good news. "Looks like your husband has already met the Lively brothers."

"Rowan is a grade-A playboy," Emery chimes in, the edge of her lip curling. "Thinks he's God's gift to women."

"He's not *that* bad." Ava rolls her eyes. "Sure, he's a little cocky but he's a nice guy."

"She's only saying that because she's had a crush on Rowan's brother, Dom, since the day she moved into her apartment." Emery shoots me a smug grin as she reaches for the wine to top herself up. "Dom is a great guy, actually. They run a gallery together, family business."

"Yes, I went to one of theirs shows," I say. "What about their friend, the chef?"

"Matt?" The two women exchange glances and eventually Ava offers a strange little shrug. "He's... intense."

"What do you mean?"

"I get the impression he's got some issues. He was dating this woman for a while and it's this on again, off again thing. We could hear them fighting sometimes when we were visiting a friend on his floor."

"Yeah, they *loved* a bit of drama." Emery taps

her chin. "But he went off the rails a bit after the last split. Quit his job and holed up in his apartment. Dom hinted that he'd fallen in with a bad crowd."

Interesting. Ava and Emery continue on with their assessment of everyone who lives in the building—from the cute young couple with the newborn twins, to the glamorous older lady who apparently was the muse of some big Australian designer back in the day—I struggle to pay attention. Matt is definitely still at the top of my suspect list.

When my gaze swings back around to the rest of the barbeque action, I find Owen looking right back at me. The intensity of his stare sends a shiver down my spine and my traitorous body reacts, priming me for what I want—more. More of last night. More of his lips on mine. More of his hands romancing my body.

But I have to keep my eye on the prize and, unfortunately for me, the prize is *not* another night of fantastic sex with Owen.

CHAPTER SIXTEEN

Owen

"WAIT, SHE WANTED *how* much?" I shake my head.

"Twenty thousand dollars," Hannah replies. "And that was for the little sculpture."

Hannah had her meeting with Celina Yang this afternoon, following up from our visit to Dom and Rowan's gallery a few days ago. Now we're having a drink and bite to eat at the pub across from 21 Love Street. The great thing about this pub is that if you sit at the bench that runs across the front window—and put up with the rock-hard stools—then you have a perfect view of the entrance to our apartment building.

It's been two nights since the barbeque. Three since Hannah and I crossed a line and did things I can't get out of my head. Just long enough since we fumbled the "morning after" that Hannah is finally opening up to me again. Frankly, it's happening sooner than I suspected.

Not that it makes me feel any less guilty about the

way I handled it. I shouldn't have ended the conversation by walking out like that. But I *always* retreat when it comes to that stuff.

"I almost choked on my coffee," she continues. "I mean, I know she's an amazing artist but geez! Who has that kind of money for something so… frivolous?"

"Lots of people would say art isn't frivolous." I'm goading her and her narrowed expression says she knows it, too.

"Twenty thousand dollars on anything that doesn't serve a functional purpose is frivolous." She's nursing her beer, bringing it to her lips every so often but not taking more than the barest of sips. Eventually the waitress will try to move us on, so they can seat customers who'll drink more. But for now, we have time to wait. And watch.

Thankfully this spot is out of the way of the other tables. It affords us some privacy to talk, while keeping an eye on the building. Apparently Matt is going out today, and we'll tail him to see if we can dig up any more information.

"So, what did you say?"

"I told her that you'd promised me something special for my birthday and I was interested, but that I would *not* be purchasing my own present." She rolled her eyes. "I sounded like such a tool."

"You stayed in character then, that's a good thing." I grab one of the corn chips sitting on a platter between us and dunk it into the guacamole. "Shitty thing about this job number four hundred and two:

most of the time we have to pretend to be awful people."

She nods. "Every morning I have to remind myself 'who' I am, you know. Like this—" she gestures to her hair, tight black jeans and low-cut silk blouse "—isn't me. The woman who expects her husband to buy her whatever she wants, no matter the price tag."

"You got something against rich people, Hannah?" It's come up a few times now, her discomfort with money.

"It's not that. I just..." She shrugs. "My dad worked his ass off for very little, always taking overtime and doing the unsociable roster to bump up his pay. My brothers and I were grateful to have him home so we could eat a meal together, never mind buying a game console or designer jeans. I guess it seems sometimes when people have a lot of money they think 'stuff' is the end goal. Status symbols, keeping up with the Joneses. To me, that's not the stuff that matters in life, you know? I want quality relationships. Not money."

For a second I'm rankled by how easily she references her desire for relationships. The way she talks about her family is a thorn under my skin. It's easy to say relationships are important when you've never had the people you love ripped from your arms.

But this conversation isn't one I want to have with her, and work is the perfect excuse to avoid it. "What about Matt? Did Celina mention that she saw us in the hallway when they were arguing?"

Hannah grabs a corn chip and scoops up some

guacamole. "I actually brought it up, pretending I was embarrassed we'd heard them arguing but reassuring her that all couples go through it."

"Good move."

She crunches down on the chip. "Apparently they had a 'passionate and turbulent' affair. She said two personalities that big are bound to clash."

"Did she say why they broke up?"

"Not exactly. Only that he got in with a bad crowd. Which is exactly what I heard at the barbeque. But that could mean anything. Drugs, maybe. Gambling. Regular deadbeats of the non-criminal variety."

"But Rowan and Dom are not 'the bad crowd' then?"

Hannah shakes her head. "I didn't get that impression. My gut tells me they're not involved, unless he's using the gallery in some way."

"I agree." Nothing about Rowan or Dom raises any red flags. They appear to be open books, decent blokes. I've met a lot of criminals in my time and I don't get that vibe from them. "I haven't turned anything up."

That was the frustrating thing; *none* of them had a criminal record. After feeding information back to Max and the team at headquarters, Rowan, Dom *and* Matt were cleaner than a freshly scrubbed shower. They didn't even have any shitty misdemeanours on them. Nothing.

"Something is staring us right in the face, but we can't see it yet." Hannah wrings a napkin in her hands.

As if on cue, a figure exits 21 Love Street. It's

Matt, wearing a dark bomber jacket, jeans and boots. His head is bowed and he's tapping away at his phone.

"See that?" Hannah asks subtly, as she leans over to grab another chip.

I love watching her slip into work mode. There's a sharpening of her attention, a laser-like focus that comes to her big brown eyes.

"Got it."

From where he's standing, Matt can see straight into the pub windows. It's a plus for our visibility, and also a minus. If we watch him too closely and he looks up at the right moment, he'll catch us. If he does, we'll wave and make out like we're calling him to join us.

"Suspect is crossing the road," she says softly. "Approaching the pub. He's entering now."

A few seconds later, the front door of the pub pushes open and Matt strides in, heading straight for the bar. There are two bartenders—a man and a woman. Matt approaches the man, who's covered in tatts—a sleeve on each arm, and one that stretches up the right side of his neck. He's got a gauge piercing in one ear and a chunky set of rings on one hand. The kind of rings that would bust up a face in a fistfight.

Hannah has lost visibility now, as her back is partially to the bar. I turn, pretending to lean into her all while giving myself a better view of the suspect. "He's talking to the bartender, but he's not sitting. Now he's taking something out of his jacket."

She raises a brow. "What is it?"

"Envelope. Possibly cash."

Matt looks behind him, but his gaze doesn't swing in our direction. There's a lot of telltale signs that someone is nervous—sweaty brow, fidgeting, difficulty maintaining eye contact. He doesn't display any of those things, but there's a frenetic energy to him. Something that seems a little…off.

It's those details—the small inconsistencies—that often unravel a criminal's plans. They're also what make some cases hard to crack, because we can't arrest someone based on a "feeling." Well, I can't arrest anyone full stop. I'm only here to gather information, to try to make a link between this case and the one I worked five years ago.

"He's going out back," I whisper. "Bartender is going with him."

Hannah turns to see where they're going. The two men disappear into a door marked *staff only.*

"We should follow them," Hannah says.

"We'll get stopped in a heartbeat. Or it will *look* like we were following them." I rake a hand through my hair and then I'm struck with an idea. "I wonder if this place backs onto an alley. We could go around."

"I've got a better idea." She slides off her stool and musses her hair so it looks a little wild. "Stay here."

"Don't even think about it." I reach out to grab her wrist, but she dodges me, giggling as if I've said something incredibly funny. Then she turns, weaving through the tables in a way that's ever-so-slightly unsteady, like she's a bit drunk.

Dammit, Hannah.

I sit on my stool, stewing for a bit. I know what she's doing and I know it wouldn't be the first time an undercover cop got intel by pretending to be drunk. Hell, it wouldn't be the *thousandth* time. But we don't know what's back there. We don't know where the exits are if she gets trapped. We don't even know what the plan is because we don't fucking have one. We were supposed to be keeping an eye on Matt by waiting until he left the building and then slipping out of the pub to follow him discreetly.

Only we'd had no idea he'd walk straight into our stakeout spot.

I do *not* like the idea of Hannah going back there alone. The female bartender doesn't even give her a second look—after all, there's nothing unusual about a tipsy girl in a pub. Hannah makes out like she's headed for the ladies' room and when she clumsily sidesteps two women coming the other way, she ducks into the same door Matt went through a few minutes ago.

Then she's gone.

Immediately my body reacts with visceral displeasure—my heartbeat kicks up a notch and my pulse pounds in my head. I don't like this at all.

She'll be fine. Hannah is a perfectly capable police officer and she knows what she's doing.

But I've already broken out into a sweat, my palms itching as I rub them down my thighs, trying to quash the sensation. No, something is wrong. I can feel it in my bones. I get off my stool and try to follow her. But my plan is foiled when I attempt to enter the staff door and a big, burly guy comes out the other way carrying two plates.

I attempt a casual laugh. "I'm sorry, my wife had a bit to drink and I think she went through here."

"I didn't see anybody."

"Is that the kitchen?"

The guy looks at me suspiciously. "Yeah. Kitchen and our loading dock. But I didn't see anyone."

The loading dock.

I head out the front of the pub and immediately curl around to the right. If there's a loading dock, then there's a way for vehicles to get in.

I race around the corner, my heart thudding like a fist pounding against my rib cage. In my mind, the worst-case scenario is already playing out. Hannah surrounded, vulnerable. But my mind is playing tricks on me and suddenly I'm seeing something old.

Photos. Blood splatter. Bullet holes. Mum. Dad. My brother. The girl I thought I'd be with forever.

"Hannah!" I call as I turn the corner.

I'm panicking. The feeling washes over me like sickly sludge, addling my brain and my ability to think. I see her. She's talking to a group of men and one of them grabs her arm. There's a smile on her face, but it's brittle like old plaster.

Fuck.

I storm up the alley, dodging the stinking garbage bins that smell like rotten food. There are three guys, one of them is Matt. If I go in too hard, we might lose any chance of being able to talk to him later. I could royally screw this up. But no amount of logic will stop me now, not when I see the guy who has Hannah's arm in his meaty grip tugging her away from the group and further down into the alley.

CHAPTER SEVENTEEN

Hannah

I'M IN CONTROL HERE. I have to tell myself that because fear charges through my veins like a shock of electricity, filling me with jittering energy. I'm in control.

Sure, beefcake number one is holding my arm so tight I'm sure he's going to leave a bruise. And okay, of *course* I would feel safer if I had a weapon handy. But I know how to handle a big guy. I know exactly where my elbows and knees need to go. And I know, beyond a shadow of a doubt, that he thinks I'm a dumb drunk girl and based on that he will underestimate me in a fight. Which I will *absolutely* use to my advantage.

"C'mon, pretty girl." He leers at me with his colourless eyes, and his puffy lips curve into a smile. "Let's go this way."

Dark hair, dark eyes. Heavy brow and bulbous nose. Tattoos on his right arm that peek out from his cuff. They're coloured tatts. Faded, though. Details rattle through my brain at lightning speed, all getting logged away so I can compare them to mugshots Max provided us at the beginning of the assignment.

"No," I say in a kind of singsong voice my roommate uses when she's had a few too many Chardonnays. "I don't want to go that way."

I glance at Matt, who doesn't even try to intervene. And he knows who I am, because I saw it on his face the second we made eye contact. Not that he mentioned it, however. He acted like he'd never seen me before. I'm pissed he's willing to let a neighbour get into trouble like this, but his inaction tells me something important. He's scared of these guys.

"I want to talk." I bat my eyelashes at beefcake number one and then a waft of rotting garbage hits me. I don't need to pretend to be grossed out by that, so I let my natural reaction play out. "Why are you hanging out in such a stinky street? Haven't you got anywhere nicer to go?"

"We're conducting business, sweetheart," beefcake number one drawls.

"Are you garbagemen?" I giggle and sway on my heels. "Is that why your business is out here?"

"Do we look like garbagemen?" Beefcake number two glares at me. He's also dark-haired and dark-eyed, but seems cleaner cut. No tatts that I can see.

"She's a stupid drunk bitch," Matt says, almost snarling at me. But the action feels a little forced, like he's trying to draw attention away from me.

Speaking of drawing attention...

I catch sight of Owen rushing up the alley toward

me, his face filled with worry. Shit. He's going to blow everything. I'd hoped to poke around a bit more, see what else came out. I can handle these guys, especially since there are a ton of security cameras focused on the loading bay. They wouldn't do anything in plain sight, so all I have to do is make sure I don't stray too far.

"What the fuck?" Beefcake number two swings his head around and jams his hands into his pockets as Owen approaches. "Can I help you, mate?"

His tone has the acid-dripping edge of someone who is definitely *not* greeting a friend. Owen catches the cue and slows, arranging his face into an expression that's more world-weary than fearful. "Just looking for my wife. She has a tendency to wander off when she's drunk."

Beefcake number one raises a brow and looks at me. "This guy's your husband?"

My mind spins. If I lie now, I might get more information out of these guys, but at what cost? Who knows what they'll do to Owen. Not to mention that Matt would be curious as hell. I can't risk it.

"Oh, hey." I make my voice syrupy sweet as I wriggle out of beefcake number one's grip. "There you are!"

"Here I am," he mutters, rolling his eyes. He looks at the three men and shakes his head. "A word of advice—don't get married."

I pout and allow him to lead me back down the alley, past the graffiti-covered brick walls and a seemingly endless collection of stinking garbage bins. Eventually, we curve around a corner and find ourselves on Love Street.

"I had that handled," I say, tugging out of his grip. My drunk act is totally gone now. "I told you to wait inside."

"While that giant monster tried to drag you into some abandoned corner? There were three of them, Hannah. You're not invincible." It's only now that I notice how absolutely and totally pissed he is. I don't think I've ever seen Owen this mad before.

But he's not the only one. "You didn't even give me a chance. How long was I out there? Barely five minutes. Not even. Three minutes."

I storm over the street, letting my resentment flow freely. It doesn't matter if people see us fighting, because we can chalk it up to me being an "angry drunk." Neither one of us says a word until we make it into our apartment. But if Owen thinks I'm going to let him off the hook, then he's about to have a rude shock.

"You impeded this investigation," I say as I dump my bag onto the couch and kick off my heels. I'm keeping my voice low, but I can tell he understands how pissed I am. Good. "I could have secured important information."

"You could have gotten yourself in a whole lot of fucking trouble." He's vibrating now. The emotion pours off him like a wave, washing over me and mixing my feelings up. Usually, when someone cuts my grass like that, it's because there's doubt over my capability. The force doesn't have as much misogyny as it used to, but it's still there.

This, however, is different. Owen seems genuinely worried about my safety. But ultimately, that doesn't matter. The job comes first.

"*I'm* the detective on this investigation." My voice is low, hard-edged. Soft enough that nobody walking past our apartment would be able to hear, but loud enough that Owen gets the message. "Not you. So that puts me in charge. *I* call the shots."

"I'm not going to sit on my hands while you act like some dumb rookie, Anderson." He rakes a hand through his hair. "Do you have any idea what could have happened? Do you have any goddamn idea what the world is like out there?"

"Do I have any idea?" I shake my head. "What do you think I do all day? Write reports and apply my lipstick?"

"Fuck." He's pacing now, moving back and forth like an agitated cat. "I know you can handle yourself. This isn't… I didn't say it because you're a woman, all right? It's got nothing to do with that."

"Then what is it, huh? Would you have busted in on Max?"

"Probably." He lets out a sharp laugh. "Once a worry gets in my head…"

"I work on the street every day dealing with the community. Dealing with bad people. I know what I'm doing." My tone is a bit softer now that he's calmed down. "I'm good at my job and I *don't* make dumb rookie moves."

When he looks up at me, I see something I've never seen before. Darkness. Owen's eyes are peering into another world—something beyond me—that's filled with pain. It's his history, the past he never speaks of.

"Look, I should have given you more warning. I'll concede to that." I touch his arm. "But you don't have to worry about me, okay? I was trained by the best."

"I can't *not* worry, Anderson. It's why I left." He stalks over to the kitchen and flicks on the coffee machine with such aggression it's like the appliance has personally offended him.

"What do you mean?"

His back is to me. The black leather jacket makes him look even bigger, tougher. Blue jeans cup his ass and thighs, shaping his muscular legs to perfection. The back of his wavy blond hair is mussed. He's run his fingers through it one too many times. God, he's beautiful. From every angle. But spending this much time with him has shown me there's a tenderness beneath the joker exterior. A damaged part he does his best to hide.

The silence is broken by the hum of the coffee machine. "Owen?"

"I left because I couldn't handle the thought that I might...lose a friend on the job." He still hasn't faced me. "And I was right, wasn't I? How long after I left did we lose Ryan in that raid? It happened within weeks."

I remember the story like it was yesterday. Ryan was a young officer on the rise—smart, action-oriented, brave. He, Max and Owen were nick-named the Three Stooges during our academy days. But Ryan was killed during a raid because he went against orders, thinking he heard a child crying in-side a drug lab. His story was a warning to recruits—don't be impulsive, *never* disobey an order. In fact, Max had taken Ryan's death so hard he'd also left his job for a period of time, following Owen to New York City. Difference was, Max returned home to give it another shot.

"Why didn't you come back for the funeral?" I ask.

"I couldn't." He turns around, his jaw tight. Eyes faraway. "I couldn't stand to be around death any-more. It follows me everywhere."

I want to run to him, because my heart is shat-tering into a million pieces. I want to fix him, put him back together. I want to do whatever I can to make him whole.

"Don't." He holds up a hand. "Don't look at me like that."

"Like what?"

"Like you think I'm a project."

"What happened to you?" I'm closer now, as though someone has my feet connected to a remote control. As though he's a magnet and I'm being drawn to him against my better judgement. "When you were young, what happened?"

"You really want to know?" His eyes are so blue it almost hurts to look at them. But they're red-rimmed now, wild and angry and sad and terrified. "You want every sordid detail, huh? Well, I should have fucking died the night my parents did. I should have been gutted and robbed like they were."

"What?" I shake my head.

"My father was working in Papua New Guinea for a big bank. We were supposed to be there for two years while he was CEO. One night we were going to a charity gala. My mother was dressed to the nines and covered in diamonds, and my father looked at her like she was the most beautiful creature in the universe." He swallows, his hands curling into fists. "My brother and I were going with them. It was the first time we were able to go, because there'd been threats against us. Kidnapping threats. It was common, we were told. Desperate people trying to make money any way they could."

My stomach swishes and I clamp my hand over my mouth. "Kidnapping?"

"And worse. The night of the gala I was sick, and my mother wanted to cancel. But she was already dressed up, and my brother was so excited. I convinced them to go, told them to have a good time because I wanted to stay home and play video games on my own without my little brother bugging me." His jaw twitches. "Since my ticket wasn't going to be used they took Lillian."

"Who's Lillian?" I search my brain for the name but come up empty.

"She was my girlfriend. Her dad was my father's chief of staff, and so when he took the job in PNG, her family came with us. She was…" He swallowed.

"She was my first everything. I was so in love with her, I'd told my father I was going to marry her the second I turned eighteen. In fact, I was the one who suggested they take her with them that night—because she had this new dress and she looked so fucking beautiful in it. I wanted the world to see how beautiful she was."

Oh no. I feel my eyes well, the path of his story laid out like a horrible, twisted road in front of me. I can see when he talks about her, that he *was* so in love. That he's still so in pain.

"Their usual driver was sick, so they had a different guy. Apparently he went off the approved route, and they were stopped by a group of men. They robbed my parents, but something went wrong. Maybe my father fought back? They ended up killing everyone in the car. My mother, my father, my brother, my girlfriend…everyone I cared about."

I can only stare for a minute while my brain catches up. It's like I'm swimming through mud, trying to understand how Owen is even standing right now. How he's even functioning. My mum ran off with another man when I was twelve and it shook me to my core. But it also shaped me—made me determined to be the best person I could be. Determined to show the world I was fine without her, and that my dad and brothers were all I needed. It made me driven, ambitious, hardworking.

But to lose one's entire family… I can't even comprehend what my life would be like. What *I* would be like.

"I don't want your sympathy," he says. I feel like I'm seeing Owen for the first time now—I'm seeing all his scars and bumps and bruises. All his pain and suffering. His outer shell is so shiny and so tough, I'd wager there are few people who ever get to see him like this. "I...I know I should have trusted you to handle yourself back there. But I'm not good at letting go when I think someone I care about might get hurt."

"You care about me?" My gut is filled with swirling, conflicting emotions. I've never felt like this before, not with anyone.

"Of course I do, we're friends." He cringes as my face drops. "Fuck. This is why I didn't want to go there with you. Why I shouldn't have touched you. I'm damaged goods."

Even in all of this, he's still worried about me. Sure, I'm pissed that he charged in and tried to act like I was a damsel in distress. But I get it. I get him more than I ever have before.

The worst part of it is, I *want* him more than ever before.

CHAPTER EIGHTEEN

Owen

I LOOK AROUND the kitchen and realise I'm standing in the kind of place I would never own. Marble countertops, gold hardware, custom cabinetry. Expensive coffee machine. There's a painting hanging in the kitchen and a small chandelier above our heads.

A fucking chandelier in the kitchen.

I loathe the idea of being rich because it's the easiest thing to blame for that night. If we'd never had money—if my mother hadn't been wearing those diamonds—I might still have my parents. My little brother, who'd annoyed the shit out of me when we were kids, I'd give anything to get him back. And Lillian…

Hannah looks at me with her big brown eyes and those long silky lashes. Compassion pours off her, because that's what she does—she cares. I don't want her to care. I don't want her to hug me and tell me everything will be okay. Because it's not okay.

It's never going to be okay.

But the second her hand comes to my chest, it's like the demons in my head go quiet for the first time in years. She holds eye contact, unblinking. So sincere I almost have to turn away.

"I want to make you feel better," she says.

"My problems can't be solved by fucking," I say. Damn, if only the people who'd called me a player and a lady-killer could hear me now.

But that's the thing, *this* is me. The person that I haven't let anybody see...except her.

"But they can't be made worse, right?" Her hands glide up my chest and she presses closer. Her hips are flush with mine, and when she rises onto her toes, her whole body rubs up against mine. I'm hard in an instant, my mind swinging like a pendulum between what I want and what I know is right. "Maybe blowing off some steam will do you good."

"What happened to one night?" I turn us around and lift her up onto the kitchen countertop. Sliding my hands up her thighs, I part her legs. She's wearing tight black jeans and a pretty silk blouse that's the inky colour of the sky at night. She's got this glossy stuff on her lips that makes it look like she's been sucking on a red icy pole and *that* makes me think of how she sucked my cock after having that cold water in her mouth.

"I wanted one night to be enough." Her eyes are hooded now, as I rub my hands up and down her legs, getting so close to the sweet spot between them. "I'd hoped that if I gave in, then I'd feel satisfied and..."

"And?"

"It's only made me want you more."

"Hannah…" I rest my forehead against hers.

"Don't feed me that bullshit about me falling in love with you. I'm in control of that and I won't let it happen." She nails me with a confident stare.

"So it's nothing to do with me being a sap and pouring my heart out?" I know she's only saying this stuff for my benefit…but it works.

"Nope. You're hot, that's all." A wicked smile curves on her lips. "I can gag you if it'll make you feel better."

"You're the one who's always yappin'. Maybe *I* should gag you." I lower my mouth down to hers and she tilts her face up, inviting me closer.

"Maybe you have to make me feel so good I can't speak."

Challenge accepted. I kiss her hard, drawing her to the edge of the kitchen counter so I can stand between her legs. I lean into her, my cock almost bursting behind the fly of my jeans. Underneath the soft material of her blouse, she's bare except for a tiny scrap of lace masquerading as one of those soft bra-things. I like it—no hooks. My palm cups her breast and I rub in slow circles, kissing down the side of her neck. There's a soft *thump* as her head lolls back against the kitchen cabinet and a delighted *hmm* as I find her hardened nipple with my thumb.

"You make the best sounds." I peel the blouse over her head and she lifts her arms without me asking. The soft bra is next, and her rosy nipples beg for my mouth. "So sexy."

"It's hard not to make sounds when you're doing that." Her fingers drive through my hair, holding my head at her breast. "Although I had a guy once tell me I was too loud."

I look up, my face screwed into an expression of disbelief. "What a dickhead."

"Right?" She laughs, her cheeks pink now as if she's embarrassed to have told me that. But I love how open she is. How vocal. "It's not like I *try* to be loud."

"What about when it's just you?" I move my head to her other breast and she arches into me.

"When it's just me?" A small, self-conscious laugh escapes her lips. "It's usually more the sound of the vibrator I have to worry about."

Holy hell. The thought of pretty little Hannah Anderson with her legs spread wide while she works herself over with a vibrator is possibly the hottest thing I've ever imagined.

"Tell me you brought one with you. I *need* to see that for myself."

There's a beat of silence, and when I look up she's even pinker than before. "Well, I didn't *mean* to bring it with me, but I got a travel one at a hen party one time and…I kind of left it in my suitcase."

I wrap my arms around her waist and pull her down from the counter. "Go. Now."

She's shaking her head and laughing, one hand covering her face like she's half mortified but half loving it. I'm *one-hundred-percent* loving it, obviously.

I follow her into the bedroom and she digs around in her suitcase. The item she retrieves looks almost like a lipstick—slim and silver. But when she twists the base, it buzzes.

"Get on the bed."

She sucks in a breath and does what I command. "What now?"

"I want you naked."

She places the mini-vibrator down and works on her jeans—popping the button and drawing the zipper down so she can shimmy out of the fabric. She takes her underwear with it. I palm my aching cock through my jeans. This is going to be one hell of a show.

With an almost shy smile, she crawls back onto the bed, grabs the vibrator and sits up against the headboard. "You want to watch me play with myself, Owen?"

"God, yes."

"Do you want to watch me come?" She's using this soft, breathy voice that's doing all kinds of crazy things to me. I'm so hard I could hammer nails, but I resist the urge to get out of my clothes. Anticipation is going to make this so much better.

"Yes."

Slowly, she parts her legs so that her knees bow to the side and rest against the bed. It gives me a perfect view of her sweet, pink pussy. Taking her time, she runs her hands up and down her inner thighs, as if warming up.

"Nervous?" I ask.

She shakes her head. "I never thought I'd be the

kind of person who wanted to put on a show...but I really do."

"You're a vision, Anderson."

"Hannah." It's not the first time she's corrected me, but her message is loud and clear. Now, in this room, we're not role-playing as husband and wife. We're not role-playing as high-flying businesspeople in town for one night only. Heck, we're not even role-playing as friends who like to wind each other up. Because we moved past that the moment I walked into that bar and took her up on her offer, and she's not going to let me forget it.

"Hannah." It sticks in my throat, almost drowned out by the thumping of my heart. "I want to watch you."

She looks up at me with smouldering eyes, and the second she twists the little silver bullet and a vibrating sound fills the room, the air around us is electrified. But she doesn't rush into it—oh no, she's a master of anticipation. First she runs her hands up and down her thighs, dragging the nails of her free hand hard enough to make faint pink marks on her porcelain skin. They disappear within an instant, but the sensation is enough to make her shiver.

I'm stock still. A statue rooted to the ground of the plush bedroom. Sucking on her lower lip, Hannah drags the vibrator lightly over her sex. She sinks back against the mountain of cloud-like pillows in varying shades of expensive white cotton and silk. Her dark hair makes a striking contrast, the slightly frizzy curls creating a halo effect around her pretty face. She's all big eyes and pink lips, all delicate fingers and softness. The silver vibrator hums as she continues to build up to what I've asked her to do—to put on a show for me.

"Ready?" she asks with a wicked glint in her eye.

If I were any *more* ready, I'd be stripping out of my clothes quicker than I could say my own name. But I am not going to waste this experience with her, so I shut my mouth and nod.

Hannah rubs the vibrator against herself, lowering it down to her entrance where she pushes it inside just a little. The sight of that shiny silver disappearing into her pussy is enough to fry my brain. She works it in a little, then back out. Repeating this motion until she's dripping. Then she uses the vibrator to drag that moisture up to her clit.

With one hand, she holds herself open, and the other works the buzzing device in slow, even circles. God, yes. Her cheeks are flushed pink, and it goes everywhere. To her ears, and down her neck. Her eyes flutter shut and her mouth falls open, and that's when I'm hit with the full force of her power. The sounds coming out of her—keening moans and panted little yeses—are everything.

I strip off my shirt and shoes and socks and jeans, dumping everything unceremoniously into a pile. Hannah hasn't even noticed; her eyes are still clamped shut and now she's sunk her teeth into her bottom lip as she works the vibrator faster. She rolls her hips, as if simulating what she wants to come next. It's glorious. Vulnerable and yet strong, and so honest.

That's the one thing I have always admired about Hannah…she is who she is. Unlike me, who's so far deep into character that I don't even know who I am anymore. Being with her is like having a light shone on the darkest, most damaged part of me.

For a moment I consider walking away and denying myself because it's the easiest option. As if she senses my swirling thoughts, her eyes slowly open and she looks at me through her lashes. "Come here."

I sink to my knees on the end of the bed, but she beckons me closer still. I crawl up beside her and run my palm over her legs—up her shin, over the curve of her knee and up her thigh.

"I want you to touch me while I do this." Her voice is soft, whispered. But her gaze holds me prisoner and I know I'd never be able to deny her. "It's better with something inside me."

I can't help but moan, and I trail my hand over the curve at her hip and dip down over the slick lips of her sex. I brush past the vibrator and down further, noticing how she angles herself to me. Encouraging me.

"Yes, there." Her eyes are shut again and I rub my fingertip against her entrance, coating myself in her. When I push my finger inside, she lets out a satisfied gasp that makes heat surge through me. "Fuck me with it."

I slide my finger in and out, slowly at first. Testing her. But her head turns and she whispers in my ear, urging me on. Her sex is hot and tight, and I'm so wound up I want nothing more than to sink my cock in her. But I want to see her come first. So I stroke her harder, faster. Following the rhythm she's set and soon she's shaking. Her thighs tremble and her muscles clench around my finger.

"Oh God, Owen." She turns, pressing her forehead to my chest as she starts to come. "Yes, yes."

She works the buzzing device over her clit until she's cresting, and I sink another finger inside her at the last second. She shatters, crying out my name so loud I *know* the neighbours must hear us. And that doesn't bother me one bit. Because the second she comes back down to earth, those big brown eyes locking on to mine, I know I haven't been this happy in years. Not for most of my life.

But I don't want to feel like that. I don't want to have those "what if this could be it?" moments. I'm terrified by the way she makes me feel. Absolutely, utterly fucking terrified.

"I turn into an animal around you." She presses her lips to my chest and I stroke her hair, taming the fluffy flyaways that frame her face. "I lose all sense of myself."

"Or maybe you lose all sense of who you think you're supposed to be." I tilt her face up to mine and kiss her long and slow. "Maybe this is *exactly* who you are."

A curious expression flitters over her face. "And this is exactly who you are, isn't it?"

"A guy who likes sex?" I try to hide myself with a cocky smile, but it's too late. I've shown too much.

"That crap won't work anymore." She presses her

hands to my chest and pushes me back against the big bed.

With lazy, languid movements she straddles me, her knees digging into the covers on either side of my hips. My worries are dulled now, smoothed over by the feel of her warm body as she grabs my hands and tugs them up to her breasts. I love this confidence in her. It's the ultimate turn-on.

And I love her breasts, obviously.

"I see you." She arches into my touch, letting out a satisfied hum as I flick my thumbs over her nipples.

"And?" I can't help but ask, even though I know it's only going to lead down the wrong path.

"I like it. I like knowing who you really are, under all the smiles and the jokes. You're a good person, Owen."

No, I'm not. I'm a broken guy with crippling survivor's guilt who abandoned his grandmother when she needed him most. The only thing I've ever been good at was my job as a police officer, and I couldn't even handle that.

I am *far* from "good."

I want to correct her, but her hands slither down her body and reach for my cock. When she touches me, I can't focus my brain on anything else. Her hands slide up and down, squeezing me. Working me over. I let my head sink back into the pillows.

"Feels good?" she asks, her voice husky and low. Her hands continue to play with my cock.

"That's a rhetorical question, right?" I'm mesmerised by her fluffy cloud of hair and the intense expression on her face—her pink-flushed cheeks and sooty lashes and her kiss-roughened mouth. "Yes, it feels insanely good."

We pause to grab a condom and she's back on top before I can miss her—rolling the rubber down my length. Dragging the tip of me back and forth through her slick folds, she teases me for a second before she finds the right spot. Then I'm entering her. Both of us groan when she hits that point—where I'm all the way in, and she's totally filled by me.

Hannah swears under her breath, moving tentatively at first. "Oh God. That feels…"

"Fucking incredible."

The gentle rocking of her hips is like sweet, sweet torture. It's too slow and too much and too everything. "Owen." My name is a sigh on her lips. "I think I'm ruined."

"Me too, Hannah."

She leans forward, lining my chest with her body and settling her lips against the curve of my neck. "Say it again."

"Hannah."

I reach down and fill my hands with her ass, coaxing her to fuck me faster. I thrust up into her, my hips bucking against hers and I lose myself in the moment. In her. In the stupid denial that we can walk away from all this, unscathed and unchanged. But it feels too good to be true. Too much like I've come home for good.

"Fuck me," she whispers in my ear. "I want to feel you for days."

So I give her what she wants. I sit up, pulling her with me so she's settled in my lap and I'm still deep, deep, deep inside her. I hold her tight ass and thrust up into her. Her breasts graze my chest and she moans—a long, low sound that will penetrate concrete and plaster. A sound I never want to stop hearing.

A sound that will haunt me.

But I'm lost now, buried inside her. Wrapped up in her. Filling my heart and lungs with her.

"That feels so good," she pants.

I'm chasing the edge of oblivion, and I reach for the silver bullet that's still sitting on the covers. With one arm around her waist for leverage, I use my free hand to guide the bullet between us, so it's hitting her most sensitive spot. She gasps, shuddering at the sudden stimulation. When she explodes, it's perfect—loud and honest and so fucking hot I can't help but follow her over the edge. I thrust up into her as deep as I can go, and come hard. My cock pulses and I abandon the vibrator, choosing instead to wrap both my arms around her and hold her as tight as I possibly can.

CHAPTER NINETEEN

Owen

HANNAH IS ASLEEP. I'm standing alone in the ensuite, staring at my face in the mirror. Staring at my shell-shocked expression.

The condom broke.

I didn't notice it when I pulled out of her, too enraptured with her hazy, smouldering gaze. Too busy falling head over heels for her. But when I came in here to clean up, I saw it. The split latex. The fact that my whole world could be turned on its head with one tiny little rip.

I never wanted to be a dad. I never wanted to have a family.

I can't be that guy.

I'm *not* that guy.

Fuck.

My heart is pounding like a drum, and the sound of blood rushing in my ears makes me want to scream. I grip the edge of the basin so hard my knuckles are snow white. What do I do?

What if she gets pregnant?

I'm being sucked down a vortex, my thoughts building on one another like an avalanche. I splash my face, but it does nothing. The universe is determined to mess with me, by taking something good and turning it into my worst nightmare.

And what about Hannah? She just made detective. This would not be a good time for her to get pregnant, I'm sure of it. But I don't know what she thinks about the whole having kids thing. She's always struck me as a family girl—the way she talks about her dad and her brothers.

Oh God. I can't do that.

I check on her for a brief moment, not daring to touch her in case she wakes. I dress silently as a ninja, holding my breath each time I take a step. My head is a war zone—and I need space to think. What I also need is to get my head back in the game.

Work always calms me. And the quicker we figure out what's going on at 21 Love Street, the sooner I can get back to my life in New York.

But what if Hannah is pregnant?

I can't think about that now. Being home has reminded me that I tend to get close to people when I shouldn't. And even though I live alone in Manhattan, I've made friends at work. Like my boss, Logan, and my colleagues, Aiden and Quinn and Rhys. I care about them all.

Maybe it's time to go someplace new. Start over again and do a better job at not getting attached. The idea of being able to pack up at any time and move

on is so freeing—I need to know that I can escape.
That I can pull the ripcord.

I'm panicking like a trapped rat.

But the thought of leaving Hannah after what
we've shared settles like a stone weight in my stomach. It's going to suck, but I *did* warn her. If there's
a baby involved… Christ. I don't know what I'll do.

I go down to level three to see if Matt is home.
Maybe talking to him will help me get out of my own
head and back onto wrapping this job up as quickly
as possible. The elevator pings and I step out in time
to see Matt entering his apartment.

"Hey!" I call out and it looks like he's trying to
scurry away from me. Coward. "Wait."

I rush him, jamming my foot between the door so
he can't close it. This bastard didn't say a word while
Hannah stood there, that ugly-faced brute grabbing
her like she was a piece of meat. And he didn't say a
damn thing when I came barging in, having to pretend to be some dickhead husband happy to degrade
his wife in order to get out of trouble.

"What do you want?" Matt growls. That's when
I get a good look at his face—he's got a black eye
and a split lip.

"What happened to you?" I plant my hand against
his front door and invite myself in. The place smells
like a dorm party—beer, pizza and BO covered up
with cheap cologne. "You should get some ice on
that."

"No shit," Matt grumbles. His good eye is blood-
shot, like he's been on something.

"Someone's done my work for me." I fold my arms and lean against his wall. Matt seems to take the hint that I'm not leaving, and lets the front door swing shut behind him. "It's not much fun giving someone a black eye when they've already got one."

Matt grabs an icepack from the freezer and wraps it in a tea towel. "This about what happened before?"

"You're a regular fucking Sherlock, aren't you?"

He eyes me warily, and I lean into my persona. Owen Essex is a spoilt rich boy who grew up without anybody crossing him.

Matt sighs. "I don't want any trouble. Your wife interrupted my business. Trust me, I did her a favor pretending I had no idea who she was."

"How do you figure that? Looked like one of your mates was feeling her up."

"They're *not* my mates." Matt winces as he presses the icepack to his eye. "Be pissed if you want, but the fact that they don't know either of your names is a good thing."

I watch Matt's movements—he's defeated. His shoulders hunch forward as he leans against the breakfast bar. He's stocky in build, like he might have been muscular at one point but now he's out of shape. I spy multiple empty Coke bottles dry and open around the couch. Two pizza boxes on the slick glass coffee table. It's a jarring sight given that the apartment has very expensive things—a Bose sound system, giant TV…and one of Celina Yang's sculptures.

"You playing with a rough crowd?" I ask, my eyes continuing to scan the room for any useful information.

"Why do you want to know?" Matt asks warily.

"I might be looking for some new friends."

"These guys don't make friends." For a second I see real fear in his eyes, and my suspicions that he's got anything to do with the jewellery theft ring are dwindling by the second. He doesn't look like he'd have the stomach for it. So I switch tactics.

"I see you've got one of Celina's pieces." I walk over to it. It's huge—almost comes up to my waist and stretches out at least three feet—and made of a white material that's so smooth I can almost see my own face in it.

"Not for long. She's going to pick it up." He comes out of the kitchen area and walks over. "Never mind the fact that I helped get her started. I funded her first show, paid for a space back when no galleries would take her. I paid for the catering and a photographer. I helped launch her."

His bitterness is toxic.

"Why did you break up?"

"Artistic differences. I wanted to settle down and have a family, and she didn't."

I think back to the conversation I overheard at the gallery, when Celina accused him of doing things that were "dangerous and wrong." "And she had a problem with you stealing shit."

Matt's eyebrows shoot up. "What's *that* supposed to mean?"

"I'm not stupid, Matt. I know you're into something with those guys and Celina didn't like it."

"Did she say something to you?"

I lift one shoulder into a shrug. "Not to me."

Matt takes the bait and shakes his head. "Fucking women. Always talking, talking, talking. Look,
it's not like that. I made some mistakes, got myself
in trouble and now I'm getting myself out. But I'm
not a criminal, no matter what she says."

"Stealing makes you a criminal, doesn't it?"

"I didn't steal those goddamn earrings." He pulls
his icepack down and his eye is swollen and puffy.
"I won them."

"You won them?"

"The guys in the alley have a high-stakes poker
game once a month. I cleaned one of them out, after
they brought me in thinking I'd be easy pickings. He
lost all his dough, so he bet the earrings and I won
them, too." Matt frowns. "I gave them to Celina because I was trying to win her back, but she figured
out I didn't buy them."

Ah, so *that* was the unethical activity. Matt had
himself a gambling problem.

"And then the guy and his goons started turning
up at the pub and hanging around at the restaurant
where I was working until they got me fired."

It wasn't the first time I'd seen this play before—
the poker game might've been a set-up. Get some
sucker in, let him win and then extort him afterward.
But that would only work if the diamonds were fake,
and my gut told me that wasn't the case. Maybe one

of the Romano crew stepped out of line. Got greedy, lost to Matt, and now the higher-ups were demanding their cut.

"Why don't you give the earrings back?" I ask.

"Serge doesn't want them back. He wants help."

"What kind of help?"

Matt shook his head. "I can't say."

Should I let him know that I have suspicions about who's working him over? That I know these people won't stop until they get what they want…and then some?

"You're in deep shit, Matt." I say it so seriously he turns to me, his face going white. "I know those guys, okay? They're not going to leave you alone."

"Wh-what do you mean?"

"They're part of a crime gang. Ever heard of the Romano family?" I watch as Matt sways. "You had no idea, did you? They're into a lot of things. Drugs, jewels, cars. Diversification, that's how they keep funds coming in. When one operation goes down, they've got the others to keep the cash flowing."

"How do you know all this?"

"I know people." I lean forward, doing my best to intimidate the poor guy. I feel bad for him, since he obviously has no idea what he's gotten himself into, but I can't let it show.

"What do you want?"

"The diamonds." I place a heavy hand on Matt's shoulder. "Go to Celina, get the earrings back and give them to me. Or you're going to have more problems. But, if you help me, then all this will go away."

"You only want the earrings?" he asks, his voice shaky.

"Just the earrings. If you help me, I'll help you."

"Here." Matt rushes over to a unit on the side of the room and yanks a drawer open. He plucks out a blue velvet box and thrusts it at me. "Take them. I wish I'd never seen these damn things."

I take the box and flip the lid open. Inside are two perfectly cut square diamonds suspended from a ring of smaller shimmering blue stones. Now I know exactly how we're going to lure the Romanos out of hiding.

CHAPTER TWENTY

Hannah

I DON'T KNOW how long I slept, exactly. But what I do know is that it was the deepest, most peaceful sleep of my entire life. I barely remember Owen leaving the bed. He sent me into a bliss coma and I've awoken more rested and more satisfied than ever before.

It's a problem. Because I'm not someone who has sex purely for pleasure's sake. I don't judge anyone who does, and I've wished in the past that I *could* be more like that. But the fact is, I'm not. I *need* a connection. And for all the teasing and taunting and the playful antagonism I've shared with Owen over the years, I *do* like him. A lot. More than I should.

Because falling for Owen is a fool's game.

He's a ghost. A guy who flits in and out of people's lives because he can't bear to get close. I understand why, now. But it doesn't change how he behaves. Only justifies it.

I head to the shower—filling the room with steam and the scent of lemon soap. I glide it over my body, over all the places he touched and with each new spot, I remember how it felt with him.

I've been dragging my heels with this case, focusing on sex more than my job. It's so unlike me, because my career is everything. But in this particular instance, career success means losing Owen. The better I do my job, the faster he'll leave.

I want to explore this thing between us—this insatiable, burning chemistry that makes my body glow. That makes my heart glow. I want to know if it will burn itself out, or if there's something special and lasting underneath the attraction.

The taps twist silently beneath my fingertips, shutting the water off without the squeak I'm used to back home. I step out of the shower and drape myself in one of the many fluffy white towels that fill the linen cupboard, using the long ends to get the excess water out of my hair.

In the mirror, my face is pink and happy. There's a crinkle to the corner of my eyes that isn't usually there when I'm working an important case. That's his influence—he lightens me, grounds me.

The sound of a door slamming on the other side of the apartment fills me with trepidation. I hear the keys hitting the glass bowl and then footsteps.

"Owen?" I don't bother to dress right away, instead wrapping myself up and heading into the living room, damp hair trailing a few scant water droplets over my shoulders and chest. "Where did you go?"

He turns when I come up behind him, his blue eyes a little wild. It takes a good ten seconds for him to drink me in, but the warmth we shared earlier is gone. There's a hardness to his handsome features now, a remoteness. This is Owen's MO: at the first signs of connection, retreat.

"I paid our friend Matt a visit." He digs his hand into his pocket and pulls out a small velvet box. Inside are the earrings I'd seen on Celina the night at the gallery. "He didn't know about the connection to the Romanos, though. He won these in a high-stakes poker game."

"Not entirely surprising." I peer at the earrings, dazzled momentarily. "Where there's organised crime, there's gambling."

"Right." Owen closes the velvet box. "Something has been bothering me since the alley. But I couldn't put my finger on it until I spoke with Matt. He mentioned the name Serge."

Oh shit. "You think it's…"

"Sergio Benedetti? Yeah. We haven't heard anything about him since he was a kid, so that's why I didn't recognise him. But he looks a hell of a lot like his dad, now that I think of it."

The Benedettis were deeply embroiled in a crime gang responsible for some of the worst drug trafficking Melbourne had ever seen in the '90s. Mostly amphetamines, but they also had a hand in protection rackets, illegal gambling and prostitution. Eventually Sergio's father was murdered by a rival when he was only five years old. The Benedetti crime family folded and Sergio was sent overseas to live with relatives in Italy.

I shake my head. "Maybe he's back trying to climb the ranks with the Romanos. That's how his father started out—joining an existing family and then getting powerful enough to branch out on his own."

"That's exactly what I was thinking," Owen said.

"We'll get that info to Max and see if we can confirm it's him."

"And then we try to draw him out."

"Do you think Sergio has been dipping into the merchandise?" I worry my bottom lip between my teeth. "Maybe he's skimming off the robberies to fund a gambling habit."

"Quite possibly."

"We have to get ourselves an invite to the next poker game." I'm excited by this new lead, and intuition tingles in my blood. We're on to something.

"*I* have to get an invite to the game," Owen says, stuffing the box back into his jacket.

"Excuse me?" I narrow my eyes at him. "Since when is this *your* assignment? I won't be left out."

Owen rakes a hand through his hair and exhales through his teeth. Something's wrong—I can feel it in my bones. When he left our bed, he was loose and relaxed. Now he walks like a tiger who's been caged, with agitation rippling through his muscles and a slight hunch to his shoulders.

"It'll be dangerous, Hannah."

The way he says my name is like a knife straight into my heart. It's tender and terrified, and not at all how I want it to sound. "This whole job is dangerous, which is why we have procedures. I *did* listen during my academy training."

"I know, I know." He walks to the big windows that overlook South Melbourne. It's a clear, cloudless evening. The sky is purple-tinged and the last streaks of sunset paint the horizon in coral and gold.

"What's wrong?" I go to him. I want to draw him close to me, but I'm confused—wanting what I shouldn't and in far too deep to avoid getting hurt. "If this is about before, I promise next time I'll communicate better. I saw the opportunity, but I should have told you what I was doing."

"It's not that. You made the right move."

"Then what? Is this because we've had sex?" I shake my head. "I know you've got this impenetrable wall about you, and I understand why. But us having sex has nothing to do with our job, and it certainly doesn't affect my ability to be a good detective."

"The condom broke."

For a moment there's nothing—no blood in my veins, no air in my lungs. No contractions of my heart. I'm a shell, unable to comprehend what's going on. "Wh-what?"

"The. Condom. Broke."

I step back, bracing one palm against the glass to steady myself. How had I not noticed? How had I not instinctively felt that crucial change? It's never happened before—not once. Not when I dated that dropkick I should've ditched after the first date, and not when I tried to convince myself to love the guy who was so right on paper, but failed to give me sparks.

I've always wanted to be a mother...but not like this. "When were you going to tell me?"

"I'm telling you right now."

My head is spinning like a top. I press my hand to my stomach, realising I'm still dressed in a towel. "Why didn't you come straight back to bed and tell me?"

"I...I don't know. I freaked out." Owen looks at me with panic in his eyes.

"I'll go to the pharmacy." I sound *way* calmer than I feel, but my dad always said I was like a duck in a crisis: calm on the outside, and moving like mad beneath the surface. Was medication one-hundred-percent guaranteed to work? What were the chances I would end up pregnant? I had no earthly idea.

"If for whatever reason it...doesn't work, I'll take care of you and the baby."

The sincerity in his voice melts my heart. A baby now would be the worst possible timing, but if I *do* end up pregnant then I'll make it work. No matter what. I have to admit that knowing Owen would be involved makes me feel a smidge better. "Thank you."

"Seriously, whatever you need. I...I haven't touched my parents' money. It's sitting in an account because I wanted nothing to do with it, so if you need a new place, baby stuff. I'll get you anything."

I blink. "You're talking about money?"

"Well, yeah. I know babies are expensive. It's probably the *only* thing I know about them." He rakes his hand through his hair again. "And you'd need your own place, too. Somewhere safe, which means well…shit, I don't know what the stats are like anymore. Maybe we can get hold of the crime report—"

"Owen." I hold up a hand, halting him. "I don't want your money."

"What?" It's like I've shaken him out of a trance. He's gone into solution mode, thinking about living arrangements and baby supplies, but all of that is second-tier stuff. "I can't let you manage that alone."

"But what about *you*? Not your bank account or your family's money. I mean you…if you were a dad." I grip the towel hard against me, feeling suddenly like I'm standing on a cliff face, with a sheer drop below. "If I end up pregnant, what are you going to do?"

"I'll be back in Manhattan. I'm leaving the second this is all over." The words come so automatically, it's like salt on an already raw wound. He didn't even hesitate for a second. All of this—being home, being with *me*—hasn't given him pause about his life.

I wasn't expecting anything different, but it still hurts. "Right."

"Fuck, I didn't…" God, this is so awkward. "I can't stay here, Hannah. You know that."

I bite the inside of my cheek, trying to keep all the words and feelings inside. He's right, I *did* know that. We argued about it the night of the gallery, where he tried to draw boundaries because he predicted I'd want more. And he was right.

He'd been right all along.

"Not even if you'd fathered a child? You're telling me you'd want nothing to do with us?"

"I'm not cut out for that life. I don't…do the family thing." How is it possible that he's so handsome, even now? Even with all that anguish on his face? "This is exactly why I tried to keep things professional."

"It takes two to tango, Owen." Sure, I encouraged things along, but he still said yes. He still walked into that bar and sat down next to me, knowing where it would lead. He still came to bed with me today. We're *both* party to this.

"I'm not blaming you. I'm setting expectations." When he looks at me, it's like being lanced through the heart. "I like you…a lot. Too much, in fact."

"That is the biggest load of bullshit I've ever heard."

"It's not. The whole reason I tried to steer clear was because I knew how risky it was. You're my kryptonite. You're like sunshine and fucking fairy floss and fireworks and I will suck that all out of you."

His voice is ragged. I know he believes himself—that he'll bring me down or be forced to relive the loss and pain he experienced as a boy, in some way. But it's a cop-out. A protection method. And I deserve more.

I deserve a man who's not afraid to commit. And even though I know there's something between us—something I want to explore more than anything—I won't put myself in a situation where I get discarded because he's too scared to try.

"You don't get to say that stuff unless you plan on acting on it." I look up at him, doing my best to hide my feelings away. I've shown him too much already. "I'm going to the pharmacy now, and you're going to figure out how to get us *both* into that poker game. Then we're going to pretend like none of this ever happened."

Owen turns back to the window, stony and silent. I don't know whether he's annoyed at me for calling him on his bullshit, or whether it's a self-reflection thing. Either way, I have to do my best not to care.

CHAPTER TWENTY-ONE

Owen
One week later...

I CAN'T EVEN count the number of screw-ups in my life. They range from stupid things, like putting my foot in my mouth when dealing with a client, to bigger things, like assuming the most important thing about a potential accidental pregnancy is the money.

It's the easiest aspect to tackle because money is black and white. It's unemotional and removed. Which is exactly why Hannah is pissed. It's not the conversation we should have been having, but every time I imagine her pregnant my brain shuts down.

I don't have it in me to be a dad or a husband. Because I'd wrap my child and my wife in bubble wrap, stifling them with my fear. I have to stop myself doing it now, as Hannah and I step out of the taxi next to an alleyway that's black as midnight. She looks like a million bucks wearing a little black dress that hugs every mouth-watering line of her body, a sparkling clutch bag, my mother's topaz ring and the earrings that Matt gave to Celina.

I didn't want her to wear them. It will be a flashing red cape to Serge. But the higher-ups are getting antsy, and they want more information. So we're taking the provocative approach.

In the past week, we've confirmed a few things. Number one: Serge is, in fact, Sergio Benedetti. He's been back in Australia for two years, mostly laying low and building his network. He runs the monthly poker game, along with the goon who'd had his hands on Hannah the day of the alley incident. But word is that he's a loose cannon and isn't playing by the Romanos' rules. So we might be able to get something out of him.

Number two: according to building records, five apartments at 21 Love Street have residents who moved in less than six months ago. We suspect the reason this building was chosen by the Romanos was due to its proximity to several "old money" suburbs. In addition, residential buildings are not only subject to higher privacy restrictions but they also attract a hell of a lot of attention when it comes to police activity.

Which is why my old team had struggled to get information prior to our undercover op.

Hannah walks into the alley without waiting to see if I'm following. The past week has been like this between us—tense, quiet. Her forging ahead while I overanalyse everything.

"Hannah." I catch up to her, encircling her wrist in my hand. "Stop for a minute."

"What?" She keeps her beautiful face neutral and looks up at me between sooty lashes. Her makeup is dark and smudgy, sexy as hell. Her lips are glossy and have tiny flecks of glitter on them. God, I want to kiss her right now. Every night when I go to bed alone, I wake reaching for her.

"We're a team. We play this together, okay?"

She nods. "I know."

"That means no flying solo."

Her eyes search my face. "Are you worried I'm going to lose all your money, dear husband?"

There are footsteps behind us. I feel like we need to get on the same page, but we're out in the open now. And at home—in our "marital" apartment— she treats me like a stranger.

"I trust you." I pull her toward me and she doesn't resist.

The footsteps get closer and I lower my head to hers, fully expecting her to turn away. But instead she opens, her lips parting and her chin tilting up, and she readily accepts my kiss. Her lips taste like vanilla and she smells like fruity heaven. Her arms wind around my neck and she rises up on her toes, brushing her incredible body against mine.

I wish we were back home, so this kiss could go somewhere. My hands find her back and the sweet, gentle curve at the nape of her neck.

The footsteps continue right past us. The second they're out of earshot, she pulls away and smooths her hands over the bottom of her dress. Her eyes look a little wild.

"Come on." She reaches for my hand and tugs me forward. "We're late."

In truth, I have no idea of the etiquette of an underground, illegal high-stakes poker game. But I can't imagine they're sticklers for punctuality.

The instructions I've been given were vague—a red door down this alley. How far down? I have no idea. But everything is in place. Matt suggested us to Serge and his crew, planting the idea that we're dumb and rich and looking for a thrill.

"Is that it?" Hannah slows as we come close to a door that looks like it could be red if it wasn't entirely hidden in shadows. "It looks deserted."

"On purpose, maybe?" The door is set slightly back, with a single step raising it from the ground. We're about twenty metres from the main road to our right, and to our left the alley continues on in semi-darkness. "Let's see what happens."

We knock once on the door—a loud, single rap that feels like a gunshot in this quiet place—as we've been instructed. I count to five and then knock again, twice this time. The door immediately swings open and we're greeted by a giant hulk of a man. He's built like a house, with tatts and a dark, thick goatee.

"Who invited you?" he asks.

"Matt, but he got Serge's approval." I meet his eye, unwavering. Cocky. "We want to make some money."

The doorman grunts, a slight smile lifting his lips. "I hope you're prepared to pay up."

"Won't need to." I give him a wink and drag Hannah through the door. "I never lose."

I catch his amused expression as he shuts the door behind us. No doubt Matt sold us well—I get the impression he's been expecting us. Now we're in what looks like the bowels of a commercial building—concrete walls and concrete floors and more concrete above. A tag in black spray-paint is the only thing that breaks up the endless grey as we walk toward a door at the other end of the hall; the only one that's not marked with a sign. Hannah's heels click and the sound bounces around us.

"You good?" I ask her as we make it to the unmarked door, and she nods. Her eyes flick to mine and stay there for a moment, but she says nothing.

Should I know, somehow, if she's carrying my child? Should there be some instinctive certainty in my gut? I have so many questions, and I've been bottling them up for the past week. But worse than the questions is the niggling feeling that I *want* to know what's going on…and not so I can manage my exit.

I like Hannah. A lot. And the more times I say it in my head, the stronger the feeling gets. Since Lillian, I haven't been with another woman who made me question the way I lived my life. Who made me reconsider what I wanted for my future.

Except her.

Hannah is a balm for my soul and at the same time, she's a prickle under my skin. I can't shake her. I don't want to shake her. But I don't know how to navigate it because the only thing I've ever been good at is running away and starting over.

"Stop looking at me like that," she says under her breath as she follows the same knocking pattern we used outside. "You're making me self-conscious."

If only she knew how far beyond sex and attraction this was.

You could tell her that...

But I can't. Not right now, when we're walking into an environment we can't control. Tonight, though, I'm going to lay things on the table. I don't have any promises to give, but I want to at least be honest. I want to do the one thing I've never wanted to do before—talk about the future.

"You're my wife, why wouldn't I look at you like you're the most beautiful woman in the world?"

"Touché," she says softly. "Sometimes it's hard to tell what's real and what's in my head."

Before I can respond, the door is pulled open. The contrast from the harsh, grey corridor to the inside of Sergio Benedetti's gambling playpen takes me aback. It isn't quite as sleazy as I'd thought—there's music and the walls are a rich red, covered in old-fashioned wallpaper with a faint print like one might imagine of a speakeasy. There's a heavy chandelier in the middle of the room and tables set up with everything from blackjack to poker to mahjong.

We're greeted by the guy who grabbed Hannah's arm the day we caught Matt and Serge together, and he wastes no time in sliding his gaze all over her

body. My fists bunch by my sides and I have to fight
the urge to crack this guy in the jaw. But Hannah
reaches down and slips her hand into mine, the gesture bringing me back to earth in less than a second.

I regret bringing her here, having her be in harm's
way.

"Welcome," the beefcake says. "Serge isn't here
yet, but he's looking forward to meeting you in more
polite circumstances."

Polite? I want to scoff.

"The feeling is mutual," Hannah replies smoothly,
squeezing my hand. "But for now I'd love to see how
the cards will treat me."

"What's your poison?" His eyes aren't quite on
her face.

"Blackjack. And champagne?" She offers him a
coy smile and he immediately signals for a guy in
all black.

We're shown to a table with three other people
already seated—a woman in a red dress and a sparkling necklace, and two dark-haired men in suits.
They appear to know one another, but the woman
is playing alone. Hannah slides into the empty seat
and I stand behind her, one hand protectively on the
back of her chair.

We'd agreed up-front that Hannah would play
most of the games. After a few practise runs, it was
clear she could hold her own *much* better than I
could. I'll survey the room. Our guess was that if
she tried to walk around, she might get approached,
but I will be able to move around less noticeably.

Given there were probably fifty-something people in the room and I could count the women on one hand, it appears our assumptions were correct.

But the thought of leaving her here, alone, fills me with an ice-cold dread. This room is a viper pit. The men running the show are standover guys, hired guns who couldn't give a shit about the lives of the people inside. All they care about is the money. About making sure the house wins.

"Welcome, Mrs. Essex," the dealer says as Hannah exchanges her money for a stack of chips. He knows our names. Interesting. "It's a pleasure to have you at my table."

Hannah nods. "Thank you."

"Please place your bets into the betting square in front of you. This table has a thousand-dollar minimum."

I immediately sense the tension in Hannah's posture. This minimum bet is much higher than we'd anticipated, and our budget from HQ won't stretch that far. So I lean down and place a hand comfortingly on her shoulder, as though whispering sweet nothings in her ear.

"You got this. I'll bankroll us if need be."

Something flickers across her eyes as she turns her head toward me. She looks at me differently now—like I'm not the person she thought I was. I regret telling her about my parents' wealth, but we might need to rely on it now. Five grand won't take us far, and I refuse to walk out before we meet with Serge.

"All minimum bets are reached." The dealer waves his hand over the table and settles it onto the top of the deck. "All players will be dealt two cards, face up, and the house will receive one card. If you receive two cards of the same denomination, you may choose to split the cards by placing a second bet, equal to your first."

The dealer places the cards out, one by one, with the fluid motion of someone who's done this action thousands of times before. Hannah receives a pair of eights. It's not great—starting with sixteen points means a sixty percent chance of losing the round.

"I'll split," she says and the dealer slides the two eights apart. Hannah counts another small stack of chips and places them into her betting square. It's risky, going hard on the first round, but it's also the move a confident gambler would make—and that's exactly how we have to come across.

I have no doubt Serge will be watching us.

The woman to the left hits twice, and busts. One of the men stays at eighteen. The other hits and brings his total up to nineteen. I hold my breath as the dealer turns back to Hannah. She hits on her first eight—takes it to twelve, sixteen and then bust. The second hit results in a score of fourteen. Hannah taps the table again and another six comes out. That's twenty.

I can almost hear her sigh of relief. "I'll stay."

The dealer has a five to start with. Then a picture card for a total of fifteen. He needs a six to beat Hannah, or anything less not to bust. His hand glides over to the deck, his deft fingers pulling another card from the neat pile.

It's a six.

"Blackjack."

Shit. A flute of champagne has appeared beside Hannah, but both of us were concentrating so hard on the game that we hadn't even noticed its arrival.

"It's just a warm-up, my love." I pretend to whisper the words, but say them just loud enough that the men beside her will hear. "I'm going to take a look around. Will you be okay?"

She nods and pretends to sip her drink, my mother's ring winking in the light. "Don't be long."

I bend down and plant a kiss against her cheek. "Let me know when you're ready for a bite to eat."

It's our code, if she needs me to pull her out. I touch her shoulder for a brief moment, and then wander through the tables as though I'm trying to figure out what to do next. Most of the men here are in custom suits, with expensive shoes and even more expensive watches. For a moment, I'm transported back in time to the parties my mother would throw for all the other overpaid expats and corporate fat cats. I remembered seeing them at the funeral, having them shake my hand. Wondering if anyone really cared or if it was all for show.

They named a boardroom after my father in the bank's Sydney headquarters. Journalists hounded my grandparents for their comments about the deaths and whether they would sue the bank. They never did.

I often wonder what my parents would think of me

now—with no ties and my affinity for fresh starts. I've done well in every job I've had. I was a great cop and a high-performing security consultant. But my careers, like my relationships, are short-lived.

I rein the memories in, pushing down the pain and channelling it into something greater. My gaze catches Hannah across the room, looking like the only flower in a field of weeds. She's the only person since Lillian who's made me wonder whether it's worth the risk to wish for more. In her arms, I could pretend I had what I'd taken for granted as a child—family, security, love.

Love? I know it exists. But what I feel for Hannah is unlike anything else I've experienced. I can't compare it to teenage love, when that feeling was so pure and untainted. What I feel for Hannah is more… complex. Complicated.

Unwanted, but nonetheless there.

"Excuse me, Mr. Essex?"

I turn to find one of the beefcakes looming over me. "Yeah?"

"Please follow me."

CHAPTER TWENTY-TWO

Hannah

I TRY NOT to think about the fact that I blew two grand in a single round of blackjack. I try not to think about how much that money could help people in our community—how many meals or school uniforms or books it could buy.

You're helping the community by bringing down organised crime.

But it doesn't ease the sting. And without Owen's calming presence behind me, I'm adrift. The dealer asks us to bet on the next round and I slide my chips forward, fighting a disgusting sickness in my stomach. This time I receive a ten and a two. When I hit, I immediately bust.

Three grand gone. I'm panicking. We've only been here fifteen minutes and I've lost over half our money. I push up from my chair and thank the dealer, almost tripping over my own feet in order to get away.

I scan the room but can't find Owen. This place

is bad, bad, bad. But so far, our poking around 21
Love Street hasn't yielded anything and we can't get
a search permission for the entire building without
something to go on. This is our best shot.

"Hannah."

I turn when I hear my name, coming almost nose
to nose with Sergio Benedetti. Tonight he's the slick
power-player in a fitted black suit, black shirt and a
blood-red tie. Devil's colours.

"What a pleasure to see you again." He reaches
for my hand and brings it to his lips. I resist the urge
to pull away.

"Thank you for the generous invite." I tilt my
head, feeling the earrings brush against my skin.

"You're a vision. I admire a woman who has good
taste in jewellery."

Unlike most men here, his eyes don't drift to my
cleavage. Oh no, Serge only has eyes for the sparkly
things in my ears.

"Where did you get those spectacular earrings?"

I smile, bringing my hand up to fiddle with the
diamonds, remembering how Owen coached me to
play it. "Oh, these old things? I've had them forever."

Serge's expression hardens for an instant. "They
suit you."

"Thank you."

"I've got a bar set up out the back for my VIPs.
I'd love for you to join me."

My senses immediately prickle at the invitation—
something isn't right. I'm not a VIP. Well, other than
the fact that I've given the house three thousand dol-

lars. But compared to the people who come here regularly, that would be nothing.

"That's very kind of you to offer—"

"I'm insisting." Serge smiles and it's like a dog baring its teeth.

"Why don't I find my husband and then—"

"He's already received the invite."

My heart stalls for a moment. They have Owen out the back already. But how? I'd only played one more round after he went for a walk. I swallow against the fear mounting in my throat. If I walk away now, Serge will know something is up.

"I would love a drink." I hold my hand out, allowing him to lead me away from the safety of the full room.

We weave through the tables, slowed by wannabes basking in the sunshine of Serge's attention. Here, he is king. The master of his domain. The criminal underworld is full of men with god complexes. It's why there's so much bloodshed. Greed, pride, fury. Retribution. They don't care about anything else.

"I was very pleased when Matthew told me about you and your husband." Serge's lips are close to my ear—and it's nothing like when Owen whispers to me. Now I'm fighting every feminine instinct that tells me to run, reasoning with myself that this job will never *not* be dangerous.

And what happens when you have a baby at home?

Hell, I don't even know if I'm pregnant. I'd promised myself I'd never let having a child frighten me away from this career—my dad didn't. My brothers didn't. Max didn't. But I can't deny there's a tiny little seed of doubt unfurling in my gut. Would I walk into this potential ambush if I had a family waiting at home?

I honestly don't know.

We reach a door at the back of the room. With each step, my head is screaming louder and louder for me to get away while I can. When I falter, Serge's grip tightens. He says nothing and neither do I. Before I know it, we're leaving the gambling room and heading into a dimly lit corridor. The heavy door swings shut behind us, cutting off the music and general din with guillotine precision. We're in a sound-proof area and soon I know why.

A keening wail comes from the other end of the corridor, behind a closed door.

"This doesn't sound like a VIP experience," I say.

God, what if that's Owen?

"Oh, but it is." Serge's grip tightens further and the pretense is dropped. "I knew the second you walked in here I'd need to deal with this."

He seems angry now, and it makes his Italian accent more pronounced. It's almost unnerving how he can switch back and forth between sounding Australian and Italian, like it adds another level of mystery about him.

"I have no idea what you're talking about." Rule number one of being undercover: never blow the cover yourself.

"If you think I'm stupid enough to fall for Matt's

suggestion that you would be an easy target, then you're very *very* wrong." The rolled *r*s sound like a motor trying to start. "I take my business seriously, Mrs. Essex, and I do *not* appreciate people trying to cut into my profits."

Okay, so he doesn't know we're cops but he thinks we're...competition?

"Excuse me?" I try to pull out of his grip but I'm rewarded with a sharp yank that I feel all the way up to my shoulder.

"Enough talking." He drags me to the room where his men are waiting. Someone is slumped over in a chair—dark hair, heavier set. Shit, it's Matt.

"What have you done?" I try to rush forward but Serge calls one of his men over and he pins my hands behind my back.

Matt lifts his head and I can see blood caked around a cut on his forehead and on the side of his mouth. His eye is almost completely swollen over. There's a man standing behind him, who grips him by the hair and pulls his head back. For a moment I'm stuck; there's a detail here I'm missing. Something that catches at the edge of my brain. A memory.

The man who's holding on to Matt looks so familiar...

Then it hits me. He's the concierge employee who helped us the day we moved in, the one who showed us up to our apartment. He joked with Owen about being married. We've seen him several times since, manning the front desk of the building.

He must be intercepting the jewels. He would

know who lived in every apartment of the building. If anyone saw something suspicious they would likely tell the front desk…and he could keep it quiet. Having someone on the building staff made perfect sense. They'd hear gossip, complaints, reports… everything.

But he wouldn't have heard about an undercover operation going on in the building. Which means Owen and I might get out of this.

I look at Serge with narrowed eyes. "Are you trying to prove a point? Fine. Consider it proven."

Serge's smile widened. "People tend to forget points unless they are made very clearly."

The concierge guy holds Matt's head back and Serge swings an open palm in his direction. The cracking sound echoes in the small office and Matt spits blood onto the floor. My heart is racing—Owen isn't here, which means Serge lied…or they're holding him somewhere else.

Please don't hurt him. Please don't hurt him. Please don't hurt him.

"Where's my husband?" I ask through gritted teeth. "If you've done anything to him…"

"What? You're going to blind me with your diamonds?" Serge sniffs. "If you want to operate in this world, you need to toughen up. Privileged little princesses don't last very long, you know. Their stupid husbands don't, either."

If something happens to Owen, I don't know what I will do. I'm still angry at him for offering me money instead of having a *real* discussion about what a pregnancy could mean. I'm frustrated that he's so unable to connect unless we're in bed.

But it's funny how fear clears the fog surrounding my feelings. I don't want Owen to go. I want him to stay...with me...forever. Baby or not.

That's only if we get out of this alive.

CHAPTER TWENTY-THREE

Owen

THE SECOND I realise what's happened, I feel sick. When I left Hannah at the blackjack table, I was cornered by a beefy suited guy who tried to convince me that Serge wanted to take me to some VIP lounge out back.

Not a good sign so early in the night. If Serge was really looking to get his money out of a couple of dumb schmucks, he'd let them play the tables for a bit. He'd show off. Make them want him.

But getting us out the back as quickly as possible means he wants to avoid us interacting with people. Aka witnesses. So I decline the invite, saying I promised Hannah a drink. Only now I see her heading through a door on the other side of the room on Serge's arm.

Fuck.

I pretend my phone is ringing and bring it up to my ear, turning my back on Serge's henchman. The second he looks away I hit the speed dial for the number Max set up for us.

"Hey, sorry we can't make it tonight. Hannah isn't feeling too well." It's the code we've instigated for the operation. I've just told the team that Hannah is in danger.

"Oh no, has she been sick long?" The female officer on the other end of the line is checking for details.

"No, it hit her very suddenly. Just a moment ago. But I haven't caught it yet."

"You should keep your distance then." She's telling me not to go after her, which goes against every fibre of my being. "Hopefully she's feeling better soon."

The cavalry is on the way. Max was informed that we were coming here tonight, so the team knows where to find us.

The thought of leaving Hannah feels wrong on every level. I know I shouldn't go after her—and before this assignment I would have been a good soldier. Followed orders. But if anything were to happen…

The memories swirl again—identifying my family's bodies. God, my little brother. Seeing them lying on those cold, silver trays almost killed me. It definitely killed something inside me. Something vital and precious. Something that would have let me live like a normal person.

If I lose Hannah…

I can't even bear the thought of it. Tonight is a preview of what our life would be like if we were together. Hannah won't stop being a cop, and I haven't got it in me to sit at home and worry.

I can't risk anything happening to her, even if it means putting myself on the line. I turn to the henchman and gesture to the door across the room. "Looks like my wife went ahead of me."

I can't live with the threat of the past repeating itself over and over. It will destroy me and, in turn, I'll destroy her. So I'm going to get her out now and then I'm done. I'll head back to New York, quit my job and figure out where to go next.

Clean start, no attachments.

"This way." The henchman leads me to the back of the room, through a doorway and down a corridor. There are voices—crying. I strain to listen. It's not Hannah.

"Doesn't sound like the kind of bar I usually go to," I say.

The henchman grunts. "This is a special bar. VIP service."

There's a sound of something hitting flesh, followed by a groan. "Very important prisoners, huh?"

He grins. He's got a gold tooth, a shaved head and the kind of cold eyes that look like there's nothing behind them. "You're funny."

He opens the door to an office. There's a map on the wall with pins and Post-it notes, half of which are dangling by one corner, their glue strips long dried up. In the middle of the room, Matt sits in a chair. There's blood on the floor and on his chin. He's taken a few punches and he's going to have another nasty shiner, but thankfully he's breathing and conscious.

Hannah stands on the other side of the room,

hands behind her back. Her face is a mask of fury, not fear. A rush of emotion overwhelms me, pride and terror and something warm and perfect and uncomfortable.

Love. It's been so long I almost didn't recognise it, but there's a pounding in my blood that tells me I would take a bullet for this woman. I would stand in between her and hellfire. And judging by the look on Serge's face...I might have to.

"What's this all about?" I take the approach of playing dumb.

"This idiot thinks we're trying to compete on his turf." Hannah rolls her eyes, cutting in before Serge has the chance to speak. She's trying to tell me not to blow our cover...he doesn't know we're cops. But he will, the second the SOG—special operations group—turns up.

"You clearly don't know my wife very well," I say. "She's not exactly built for...working."

"But you are, aren't you?" Serge comes forward and I stand strong. The henchman is behind me, blocking the exit, and something cold and hard presses into my back. "You approach *my* people and ask questions about my fucking business." He glances at Matt. Shit. I should have known he'd get scared and talk. "And your wife happens to stumble across a meeting, pretending to be drunk."

If Hannah is shocked that he knew it was an act, she doesn't show it.

"I was going to play it nice, let you off with a warning. Then you turn up tonight, showing off *my* jewels." He slams a palm against the wall and the sound vibrates in the cold concrete building. It feels miles from the plush gambling room. "I will not be disrespected in my own house."

"What do you want, huh? We came to play cards, not to get into an argument." I make myself sound as bored as possible.

"Matt told us everything. You said you could help him." Serge comes forward, his eyes black like coal. He has a frantic energy about him, an aura of insta-bility that has me on edge. "How do you intend to do that if you simply want to play cards?"

Fucking Matt. The guy had no idea what he was getting himself into—his gambling addiction made him weak, vulnerable to people like Sergio Benedetti.

"Look at him, you believe a word coming out of his mouth? A guy like that will say anything to get what he wants." I gesture to the hunched-over man, as if he means nothing.

"But you just want to play cards, right?" He reaches into his jacket and pulls out a gun. It's small calibre, easily concealable. Probably has the serial number filed off so it won't be traceable if they need to dump it. Now I have two guns on me—one in front, and one behind. I don't say a word and men-tally beg Hannah to do the same.

All I have to do is stall long enough that the SOG guys get here.

"Don't! Please." Hannah's voice is wire-tight. "It was all my idea, not his."

Serge raises a brow. "Isn't that sweet."

"Shut up, Hannah." My voice is rough.

"Seriously." She stands, both hands in the air in front of her in a gesture of surrender. "Owen wanted nothing to do with it, but I thought I could win big. I thought I could come here and show you up."

Fuck. What the hell is she doing?

Serge slowly rotates so his gun is on Hannah. "Really?"

"Yes." The way her lip trembles makes my insides twist. "Please, let him go."

Serge closes in on Hannah, his gun aimed directly at her forehead. The easy smugness is now gone, replaced by rage and something swirling and uncontrollable. He backs her up against the desk, pressing the gun right into her skin. If he pulls the trigger, there won't be anything left of her.

"She's a cop." The words come out of my mouth before I can stop them, and they suck the life from the room.

"What?" Serge looks at his henchmen and then me.

"If you kill her, you'll have the full force of the Victoria Police hunting your ass down." I suck in a breath. "But I'm not a cop. So I'm your better option."

"He's lying!" Hannah is looking at me with huge eyes.

"I think you're right." Serge stares at me. "He *is* lying."

"We're not really married." I grit the words out. "We're colleagues. I'm a security consultant who was brought on to track a jewellery theft ring at 21 Love Street. Hannah is not my wife."

"Then why put yourself on the line for her, huh? You think I'm stupid." He shakes his head. "I know what two people in love will do for one another. They'll say *anything* to protect the other person. I would know if either one of you was a cop."

I can't breathe. Panic has seized my chest and I know I have to do something, or else there's a very real chance one of us will get shot before backup arrives. I will not allow it to be Hannah.

The gun is back on me, thank God. Hannah is shaking her head at me, like I've lost the plot. I have. I left protocol in the dust the second I exited the main room.

"There's only one way for you to get out of this. Go now, before our backup gets here."

Doubt flickers across his features. He doesn't know whether to believe me. "You're bluffing."

"Nope."

"Well, then there *is* only one way out of here." He turns back to Hannah. "And the only good cop is a dead cop."

A sound outside makes everyone crank their head to the door. There's screaming and shattering glass, and chaos is coming from the gambling room. The door to the corridor must be open. Backup is here, but until I see the unit of men and women in their tactical gear, I'm not safe and neither is Hannah. I use the moment of distraction to lunge forward, grabbing Serge's gun and wrenching his arms up. It goes off, shattering the light overhead, and plunging us into semi-darkness.

There's a sound of gasping, a scuffle and another shot goes off. I hear shouting, but something doesn't feel right. There's a pain in my side. But I keep going. I'm on top of Serge, holding him down. We're struggling. I throw a fist, but I'm starting to move slower.

A second later the SOG members filter into the room.

CHAPTER TWENTY-FOUR

Hannah

My eyes feel completely raw. After exhausting myself trying not to cry in front of my colleagues, I eventually took a shower so I could do it in peace. Last night should have been a bad dream. But now, I'm curled up in a hospital chair waiting for Owen's eyes to open. I want to take him home so he can wake up somewhere that smells like life—like bread and coffee and fresh sheets.

He got shot trying to protect me. The doctors told us the bullet missed his organs, but he lost a fair bit of blood. If the special ops team hadn't arrived when they did, the outcome could have been very different. I could have watched him bleed out on the floor. I could have watched him die.

The thought brings on a fresh wave of tears. My knees are drawn up to my chest, and I wrap my arms around them. I don't know whether it should make the situation better or worse, but this morning I got my period. Yep, not pregnant. I took one of those early-signs tests just in case, but the results were clear as a bell. Over the past week I'd grown curious about the idea of having a child, enough to know with certainty it's something I want in my future.

The problem is, I also know with certainty it's something I want with Owen.

Last night, when I thought Serge was going to shoot Owen, I was beside myself with fear. It's made me understand him a little more. Nearly losing him has messed me up inside. I'm jittery and tense and I snap at anyone who comes within a metre of the room.

He lost his whole family and the girl he loved. It must be this same feeling times a thousand. Times a million. I don't know if I would be strong enough to go on with life, like he has. And now I can see why he keeps running away from people. I understand it.

A tear slides down my cheek and I swipe at it angrily with the back of my hand. I feel totally and utterly useless, and it's so foreign that I want to scream. Normally I'm the person who knows what the next step is. I'm the person with the plan and the to-do list and the solutions.

And now I have...nothing.

"Are we still man and wife?" Owen's voice is scratchy.

"Nope, just another statistic." I try to force a smile, but it's watery and weak.

"Then what are you doing here?" He cringes as he tries to sit up, so I rush to get the bed's remote. When he pats the space next to him, I sit.

"Being a good partner."

He's pale and has rings under his eyes. There's a cut on his cheek and another on his temple. He looks like an anti-hero, the broody bad boy in some Hollywood blockbuster. Hotter than hell, even after it all.

He tilts his head. "What are you staring at?"

"Just wondering how on earth you can get shot and still look better than me." I want to keep things light, but I'm feeling as if there are concrete blocks on my feet.

"Shut up, Anderson. Everybody knows you're the pretty one."

Anderson. He's playing the joker again, retreating into his shell. "I um...the SOG guys went to 21 Love Street last night before word could get to the rest of the Romano crew."

"And?"

"They found a whole lot of jewels. Drugs, too. The guy who was holding me last night worked the concierge desk, and he's intercepting the jewels. Max got him to cave and we figured out which apartment they were operating out of." I trace a rip in my jeans, watching the frayed edges of the denim move under my fingertip. "Now they've got security footage from the building to back it up. They're bringing in the staff for questioning over the next few days."

"So you did good."

"*We* did, you mean."

Owen closes his eyes for a moment as he tries to move. He's in pain and I'd be willing to do anything to make it go away. "You're the brains, Anderson. Own it."

"Max says they're confident Serge will talk. It will really help with the wider Romano case. Between that and what we got from the concierge guy, there should be enough to put a task force together now—the jewel theft, drugs, illegal gambling. It's solid evidence."

"That's great."

"Which means we're done with the assignment. The doctor said they want to keep you here for a bit, make sure you're healing up okay."

His expression says it all. Owen knows I'm stalling. "What are you dancing around?"

It's like the air has been sucked out of my lungs— I have so much to say and no idea where to begin. My thoughts are a traffic pile-up, one bumping into the next until it's nothing but a jumbled mess. "I thought we should talk about us."

He looks at me with those endless blue eyes and this time there's no sparkle. No smirk. Maybe I've picked the wrong time, but if I know Owen, he'll get himself the hell out of here the second the doctors allow it. Then…I might not ever see him again.

"I was really scared last night." Saying this is like ripping myself open. I've always been strong at work. There are unspoken rules for women, even these days. You can't admit to being frightened. You can't cry. You *have* to be strong. Always. But right now, I'm not at work. I'm not here for my job. I'm here for him, and for myself. "I thought you might die."

"I thought that, too."

"You risked your life." I curl my hands into fists.

"So did you. You tried to convince a gangster to shoot you instead of me."

"Didn't work, did it? I'm obviously not very convincing." I almost jump out of my skin when Owen's hand covers mine. "I went into that room alone, because I thought you were in there, which was a mistake. I could have ruined everything."

"And I followed you in there against orders, so I think we can call it even."

The silence between us is broken by the hustle and bustle outside the hospital room and the intermittent beeping of the machines tracking Owen's vital signs and administering his pain relief.

"I'm sorry I made the whole baby thing about the money," he says. "It was the only thing I could make sense of, to be honest. I know you wanted us to talk about the realities of having a kid, not just the finances."

"I overreacted." I shake my head. It feels like such a dumb argument now, with last night hanging over us as a reminder of what's really at stake. "I was feeling vulnerable, so I snapped because it wasn't what I'd hoped to hear."

"What did you hope to hear?"

I swallow. There's a lump in my throat that feels as big as a boulder. "That maybe you'd want to stay and see what happened. Maybe we could be more than a fling."

His jaw tightens, but I don't know if it's pain or

frustration or something else. Owen is Fort Knox with his emotions. But I need to know how he feels.

"It's going to sound like a fucking cliché to say it's not you, it's me. But it's true." He sighs. "You're perfect, Hannah. You're kind and smart and a total badass. You're the best cop I know."

"But?" It almost kills me to say the word, no matter how much I know it's coming.

"Your job puts you in danger every day and…I don't think I could take it." He shakes his head. "It's my weak spot, not yours. I'm already screwed up about relationships and loss, and knowing you've got the kind of job where you're in the literal firing line would make me crazy. Last night, I would have taken a bullet for you."

"You *did* take a bullet for me." I'm crying now and the tears won't stop. They start slow—fat drops that well and fall, until they come faster. Owen reaches up, even though I can see it pains him, to brush them away from my cheek.

"I would have taken ten bullets. Twenty." His blue eyes hold me captive and I want to promise him everything…but I can't.

"I'm not going to quit my job," I say.

"You shouldn't. Victoria Police is better with you in its ranks." His hand squeezes mine. "You're amazing and I'm broken."

"You're not broken, Owen."

"The second I thought something was going to happen to you…" The worry that streaks over his face is raw and so stark it makes my breath catch in my throat. "I have purposefully stayed away from you ever since I started at the academy, because I knew I'd fall for you."

"How could you have known that?"

"I just did. You had this spark about you, the way you told all the boys that one day they'd be reporting to you."

I laugh, in spite of the tears. I'd gone into the academy believing I needed to assert myself—I was young and plucky and more than a little obnoxious. But Owen had never made me feel like I needed to prove myself. He made me feel...respected. Equal.

"Why do you have to be so damn charming while you're rejecting me?" I swallow, trying to stem my emotions.

"I'm sorry. I want more than anything to be the kind of guy who makes you happy...but it's not me. You don't want someone who wakes up with night terrors, who feels like running away is the most natural thing in the world. You don't want someone who's going to bring you down."

"Don't tell me what I want, Owen." I pull my hand out of his grip and stand, my body filled with mixed-up, conflicting emotion. "One minute I'm perfect and the next you're pushing me away and trying to act like you know what's best for me."

"I'm saving us both a lot of pain."

"It doesn't feel like that. It feels like you're not willing to give us a chance even though we both want to be together." I look up to the stark white ceiling of the hospital room as if I might find answers there. "And I do...want to be with you."

"Is this about the...that you might be pregnant?"

Shit. It almost slipped my mind that he doesn't know—I've been too focused on what happened last night. "I'm not pregnant. And yes, I'm sure."

He looks at me as if waiting for me to elaborate.

"I don't know how I feel about it, either," I add. "I'm both relieved and also disappointed, if that's even possible."

"You want to have a family."

"I do." I shake my head. "I think this whole thing solidified it. I want to be a mother. And it's crazy but when I think about having a family, I see us. I know that's like the quickest way I could make you run, but these last few weeks...we fit together. I don't know what it is yet, but my gut tells me it's worth fighting for. We *have* something, Owen. This connection isn't something I've ever felt with anyone else."

He turns his head away, so I can't see what he's thinking. "I know exactly what this is and that's why I'm running scared. I don't want to hurt you. I don't want to hurt myself."

"So that's it? I'm in the 'too hard' basket?"

When he turns back to me his eyes are red. There's no tears on his face, but I've never seen him so close. I've never seen the weight around his neck as clearly as I do now.

"I'm not going to say something dumb and false to push you away," he says, swallowing. "But I'm telling you as honestly as I can, I can't do this with you. I'm sorry."

I'm shattering into a billion jagged pieces. The floor tilts beneath my feet as fresh tears prick the backs of my eyes. I knew this is how it would end, but it still hurts as if he's taken a shotgun to my heart.

"I understand." I stick my hand into my pocket, where I've stashed his mother's ring. The stone glints in the light, as if mocking me for even having a glimmer of hope that we might make it. "I'm really sorry this didn't work out."

"Me, too."

I place the ring on the table beside his hospital bed and turn to head out of the room. There's a nurse waiting and I have no idea how much she heard, but I duck my head and keep on walking. Inside, I'm falling apart.

No matter how illogical it is, I know exactly how I feel. I love Owen and I wanted this to work so badly it makes me crazy. But I won't pursue someone who can't take a chance on me.

I can't do that to myself.

CHAPTER TWENTY-FIVE

Owen

By the time the hospital lets me out, I'm feeling like an animal who's finally been released into the wild. A still-hurting, probably-going-to-get-feasted-on-by-a-lion animal, but I am free, nonetheless.

I'm on antibiotics and painkillers and moving at a snail's pace up the driveway to my grandmother's house. She's lived in the same house since before I was born. It's a squat place with thick canvas blinds that protect against Melbourne's dry, hot summers. The garden is small but neat, with roses and begonias and agapanthus. When I was a kid, she made me help with the weeds, teaching me all the flower names and how to care for them. It was a lost cause, since I've never owned a plant.

I knock on the security screen, rattling it against the front door. There's the sound of the television inside—a game show, judging by the cheering. A second later, the door swings open.

"I don't want whatever you're selling," she says,

her voice as husky and deep as I remember. I hadn't realised it until now, but God, I've missed it. A cheeky smile tugs at her lips. "What's the secret password?"

"Lamington." It was my favourite sweet as a kid—a fluffy square of sponge dipped in chocolate and rolled in coconut. "It hasn't changed, right?"

"No." Her smile falters a bit when she sees I'm moving slowly, and when she reaches up to hug me it's with far less vigor than I remember. I'd called her this morning to let her know I was coming by, and to warn her that I wouldn't be in great shape. "Does it hurt?"

"Yeah. But they've dosed me up on meds."

She steps back and holds the door, her small frame wrapped in a chunky sweater and wool skirt to ward off the chill. The house is toasty and smells like home. I know she's been baking all morning; the evidence lingers in the air with the scent of coconut and sugar.

She leads me through to the kitchen, which hasn't changed a bit. "It was nice to bake something knowing you were coming over. I don't do it much anymore. It's not the same when it's just for me."

I don't know whether she means because I left or because my grandfather died. Probably both. I had no illusions of not feeling like a piece of shit today, but we certainly came to that point quicker than I'd anticipated.

"You want a coffee?" She heads straight to the kettle, almost as if it were a rhetorical question.

Within minutes, I've got a steaming mug in front of me and a perfectly square lamington.

When I take a bite, I send pieces of shredded coconut skittering all over my plate. "So…"

"So." My grandmother isn't going to give me an inch.

"I'm sorry I haven't called."

Her eyes are a little cloudy these days, but she has the kind of stare that could reduce a grown man to a snivelling mess. "You should be."

"How have you been?" I feel like a dumbass, trading questions like one might with an acquaintance. "I've missed you."

Her expression softens. "I've missed you, too."

"Are you doing okay?"

"It's been hard, but I keep going. It's what your grandfather would have wanted." She bobs her head and her eyes suddenly well. "I think about him every day."

In contrast, I've actively tried to suppress my memories of the strong man who stood with his arm around my shoulders as we buried my parents and brother. He and my grandmother were the stuff of relationships goals—they'd battled hard times, struggled with money when my mother was a kid, and were so utterly and deeply in love until the day he passed away.

"Would you change any of it, knowing how it would turn out?" I sip my coffee, relishing the bitter warmth.

"Do I wish your parents hadn't left the house that

night? Of course. But wanting to change the past is a fool's game. It won't lead anywhere good." Her cup shakes slightly in her hands. She's eighty-five now. The same age as my grandfather when he died. "You don't think every single person in the world has something bad happen to them? We've suffered, but we're not alone."

I am. I'm alone because it's how I've made myself—refusing to commit, refusing to set down roots. Seeing every damn part of my life as a temporary stage before the next move. I thought it's what I wanted because it was safer. Easier.

But watching Hannah walk out of the hospital room was the hardest thing I've ever done.

"Here." I pull my mother's ring out of my pocket and set it on the table. "I'm returning this to its rightful home."

"I don't want it." She stares me down, looking like she wants to dump a cup of coffee on my head. "In fact, I was thinking about getting rid of all your mother's jewellery."

"Why would you do that?"

"I have no use for it. It's gathering dust and your mother always believed that diamonds were made for wearing."

"If it's about the money, I can—"

"Owen Graham Fletcher." Her voice is like ice and I'm still as a statue, suddenly reverted to being a kid again. "After your parents died, I ended up with enough for several lifetimes. I had to tell you not to forfeit your own inheritance by giving it to me. It's not about the money."

I'd forgotten that. I'd tried to get my grandparents to take it all, but they'd put it in a trust until I was old enough to access it.

"Then why sell the jewels?"

She sighs. "Because I'm getting older and I know you won't want to be bothered dealing with it all when I'm gone, so I figured I would take care of it now."

I reel as if she's slapped me in the face. "You're talking like you're already gone."

"And you *act* like I'm already gone."

Her words slice through me, cutting bone and flesh. And I don't have a single defence against it, because she's totally right. I haven't been there for her. At all. I've ignored her voice mails, messaging back only when I know she'll be asleep so I don't have to experience the pain of facing my own flaws.

"I understand why." She reaches across the table and places her hand over mine. She's cold, like always, and her knuckles are more arthritic than I remember. But her grip is strong, sure. "Owen, what you went through…it's a hell that no child should ever have to experience. But at some point you need to understand that the past is the past. It's okay to hurt. It's okay to be scared. But you act as though you also died that day and you didn't. You're alive, so start living."

She's almost vibrating with emotion—frustration at what she sees as time I've wasted, and anger that

I've treated her so poorly. Shame trickles through me, like icy drips along my spine. If only the people who think they know me could see me now. At the security company in New York I'm the one who makes everyone laugh, I ease tension when things get tough and I play pranks on my colleagues. My old academy friends came in droves to the hospital over the last few days, clapping hands on my shoulders for a job well done. Praising me.

But my grandmother sees through it all. She *knows* me…and so does Hannah. The fact that I even told her about my past should be a sign that I trust her more than anyone.

But what if one day I'm here—like my grandmother, grieving every day.

Aren't you already here?

"I know you boys are often raised not to show any emotion, and if I ever contributed to that I regret it," she says. "But maybe you should talk to someone. A professional."

I recoil at the idea. People over the years have suggested counselling and therapy and God knows what other hippy-dippy things. Tarot cards, or some shit. The idea of sitting in someone's office being asked to talk about my feelings makes my skin crawl.

"I don't want to talk to anyone."

"I know you don't," she says. "But it's something to think about. When is your flight home?"

I swallow. "Haven't booked it yet."

The surgeon had suggested that I stay in Melbourne a while longer, so they could check on the wound and ensure it healed correctly. But it wasn't exactly phrased as an order. I was lucky that everything went smoothly in the ER—the bullet didn't ricochet and hit anything important. The surgery to retrieve it was straightforward. It could have been a lot worse.

In reality, I could go home now.

But something happened as I lay in the hospital room, the space around me filling up with cards and teddy bears and bunches of flowers. I spoke to a lot of people about how lucky I was to be alive. The surgeon, and nurses, my old colleagues and, of course, Gary Smythe. Max came to visit, too, and he showed me pictures of Rose and the baby.

And all the while I thought about Hannah.

Hannah, the woman I could have been killed trying to protect. The woman who was there when I woke up, who sat on my bed and poured her heart out. Hannah, my undercover wife who'd lain on that fancy bed and given me more pleasure than I'd known in years. The woman who continued to break through my shell, even when I dissuaded her at every turn.

"I would have thought you'd be rushing to leave." My grandmother tilts her head.

"I did get shot, you know," I quip drily.

She shakes her head, her sharp blue eyes—my mother's eyes and my eyes—piercing through me. "I know not to take the joking answer as the truth."

"I thought about not going back to New York at all. I could pick some place new and start over again." At the time it had seemed logical, but now the words felt wrong. "But then what? I keep doing that every four or five years until I run out of places to go?"

"You tell me."

Everything feels wrong now, all my old ideals and goals. All my old avoidance tactics. But the only thing that doesn't feel wrong—staying here and trying with Hannah, rebuilding my relationship with my grandmother—is fraught with risk.

"Why do you find it so easy to work in an environment where people shoot at you, yet the thought of having a meaningful conversation has you running away like a terrified animal?" Her question isn't sugar-coated at all, because that's not how my grandmother plays.

"Because I'm not scared of death." The words pop out of my mouth before I can even consider them, and I know it's my deepest truth. "I'm scared of surviving."

"Hmm." She leans back in her chair and crosses her arms over her chest.

If a little old lady could mic drop, then that's what my grandmother just did.

I stand, slowly and painfully, curling into my injured side. This conversation has stirred up everything and I need to get away to think. If I'd really wanted to leave Australia, I would have booked my ticket on the hospital Wi-Fi. Because that's how I am.

This revelation is making me question everything, and my grandmother's words are swirling like a tornado in my head. The possibilities I've never allowed myself to consider are gathering steam. I've been changed by this experience—by living with Hannah, by getting shot. By this very conversation.

You're alive, so start living.

"It would kill your mother to see you wasting your life." My grandmother comes around the table and pulls me into a hug. "Don't do that to her."

"What if it's too late?"

"It's not." Her head barely comes up to my chest and I look down at the curly grey hairs covering her head, and the tops of her shoulders covered in a thick, fluffy wool. She's small and frail and I've almost made the mistake of wasting the years she has left. "And Owen?"

My throat is so clogged I can barely speak. "Yeah."

"I forgive you. I hope you can forgive yourself."

CHAPTER TWENTY-SIX

Hannah
One month later...

I FIND MYSELF walking along Clarendon Street in South
Melbourne, heading in the direction of Love Street.
It's my day off and I'm utterly restless. My head's been
in a fog at work, and I'm stumbling over my words in
meetings and missing basic things. It's grief over losing Owen, and I need to distract myself. Instead, I've
wound up here. I look up at 21 Love Street—at its chic,
modern design and fancy glass-and-chrome entry.

Maybe I've come here to say goodbye. Who knows.
"Hannah?"

I turn at the sound of my name and see Drew
striding toward me. She looks the same as she did
the night of the barbeque—long platinum hair that
swishes by her lower back, all-black outfit and a
wicked glint in her silvery eyes.

"Oh, hi." I struggle for what to say—how much
do the people in this building know about who I really am? Do they know my marriage was a fake?

"I haven't seen you around much." She smiles and comes up beside me, her arms folded tight against her chest over the front of a studded leather jacket. "I wondered if you and that hunky husband of yours had moved out. But then I heard about the redecorating."

"Redecorating?"

Drew looks at me a little strange. "Yeah, I bumped into Owen this morning and he was telling me about all the changes he's making."

I shake my head. How could she have bumped into Owen this morning when he was supposed to be back in New York? When he *was* back in New York a week ago…not that I was bugging Max for updates or anything.

Glutton for punishment.

"Is everything okay?" Drew touches my arm and peers at me. "You look a little pale."

"I'm just…" I don't even know what to say. Am I imagining things? Is this one of those moments where I'm about to wake up any second and realise I'm alone in my bed, with my roommate banging around in the kitchen?

"Don't you faint on me, girl." Drew wraps an arm around my shoulder and steers me toward the entrance. "Let's get you a glass of water and somewhere to sit down."

I allow myself to be propelled forward, my heart pounding and my head swimming. I've tried so damn hard not to think about Owen in the last month since

I left him in his hospital bed. So damn hard I've given myself a headache over it. Daily.

But the fact is, I've been miserable without him. Just like when we finished our training at the academy and I knew I wouldn't see him as often. Just like when I found out that he moved away to New York and that meant I had to let go of my fantasy that one day we'd bump into each other and find some spark between us.

"Here, sit." Drew pushes me down onto one of the plush velvet chairs in the foyer. "I'll get you some water."

She heads over to the front desk and talks to the concierge. I think about making a break for it. I could be up and out the door before Drew has a chance to catch me. And it's not like I'll have to see her again.

But then what? If Owen really was here, then I had to know what was going on. Why had he come home? And, more important, of all the places he could live...why here?

My stupid heart was hopeful. Too hopeful.

Because I still wanted him. Deep down and with all my heart, I want to go back to that time where I got to pretend he was mine and I was his. To that night where he walked into the bar and made all my wildest fantasies come true.

Drew is back in a flash with a bottle of water from the vending machine in the building's management office, and she presses it into my hands. "Here. Drink."

The liquid is cool against my heated throat. "I don't have my keys."

"Are you okay to walk? I'll take you upstairs. You're not...?" Her eyes drop to my stomach and I shake my head.

I'm not pregnant, but I've thought about it a lot. About the family I want to create, about the kind of mother and wife I want to be. But none of it makes sense without Owen.

Each step toward the elevator makes my pulse race. Drew chats happily as we ascend to the top floor, catching me up on the gossip of the building. Hook-ups and flirtations and how she suspects that this building puts a spell on people. 21 Love Street...the place to find a happily-ever-after. She seems lighter than when I first met her, happier.

When the elevator door chimes and I walk out into the hallway, I'm hit with memories. The taste of Owen's kisses, the feel of his hands at my waist. The way he looks first thing in morning—with hair rumpled and an easy, sexy smile.

And the way he looks when I'm seeing something more. The vulnerability he shows no one else.

The door to our old apartment is open and music plays. There's a bang and a rattle inside, and when I get closer I see the place is nearly empty. It's all white walls and plastic on the ground.

I step inside and clamp a hand over my mouth. Owen is shirtless. Faded jeans sit low on his hips, highlighting his trim waist and cut abs. And *God*, those vee muscles that point down into his waistband.

Something white—probably his T-shirt—is hanging out of the back pocket of his jeans.

Drew mutters something and laughs, nudging me with her elbow before turning and leaving me. Owen hasn't noticed me yet because he's focused on a spot on the wall where he's gently sanding. Then, almost as if he senses that crazy, electric feeling running through me, he looks up.

"How long were you going to wait to tell me you were back?" The question flies out of me. I didn't know it was possible to feel horny and hurt...but here we are.

"Long enough for me to get this place repainted, but before I started buying too much furniture." He cocks his head, looking at me curiously. "You had to go and ruin the surprise, didn't you?"

I laugh, in spite of my crazy, mixed emotions. "What surprise?"

"I wanted to do things the right way this time." He rakes a hand through his hair. It's longer now, and it curls around his ears. There's flecks of dried paint in it, and over his hands. "Set down roots. Make a home."

But for how long?

As if he sees the questions dancing on my lips he says, "I'm not running anymore. I'm going to own what happened to me and move forward, instead of continuing to look back."

"So you bought this place?" I look around. It's a shell now, without any of the furniture that was here before. "What about your job?"

"I am now happily unemployed." He looks it, too. Happy. Content.

"So this is…for now? Forever?"

Forever isn't even in Owen's vocabulary. That was always the issue—he wanted freedom to run and I'm the kind of woman who commits. I pick something and stick to it. He avoids attachments. Not exactly a match made in heaven.

"Is anything forever?" He gives me one of those Owen shrugs, but this time it feels honest. Not like an avoidance tactic. "If I could have my way and know how the future would turn out, then yeah. But I don't even know how tomorrow will turn out."

Ain't that the truth.

"All I know is that this place made me the happiest I've been since I was a kid." He jams his hands into his pockets. "Being with *you* made me the happiest I've been since I was a kid."

I don't know what to say. I'm stunned. "But our conversation in the hospital…"

"I was still processing everything. I thought I had my whole life figured out. I was going to keep running, keep avoiding. Easy peasy. Then you came along and my head got all messed up. My heart got messed up. I started wanting things I thought I didn't deserve. And when we thought you were pregnant…"

When his voice cracks it's like someone reaching into my chest and squeezing my heart.

"I was terrified, honestly. But I kept thinking about it—what it would be like to have a family. How I knew you'd be an amazing mum." His smile is charming and sexy and just a little bit shattered. "And I wondered if maybe I could be a good parent, too. If I could be a good dad and a good husband."

"Of course you could be." He has no idea how much goodness is in him. "Just because something bad happened to you doesn't mean it was your fault."

"I know. I, uh…my nan convinced me to speak to someone."

"That's really great, Owen. How was it?"

"Weird. Uncomfortable." He laughed. "I hated it, honestly. But I'll keep at it because I know it'll help in the long run."

My eyes are swimming and my heart is hopeful, because the man I see before me is a man who's turned a corner. He's got so much to work through. But now he's trying. He's moving forward.

He comes closer and I try not to stare at how incredible his body is. I'm trying to be supportive, but *damn*, it's not easy. "Eyes up here, Anderson."

"Then put a bloody T-shirt on." I fold my arms over my chest, turning away because I know my face is now the same shade as a tomato. My ears are burning, too.

He grins. "What are *you* doing here, anyway?"

"I happened to be in the neighbourhood." It comes out way more defensively than I want it to. "I bumped into Drew and she brought me up here."

"You didn't tell her we're not married anymore?"

"It didn't come up in conversation. Anyway, she said she spoke to you earlier today and it sounds like *you* didn't say anything, either."

"Didn't come up in conversation," he echoes. "Funny that."

We stare at each other for a minute, like two dogs eyeing one another up. There's a crackling tension between us—it's vibrant and exciting and I feel better than I have in weeks. Better than I have ever.

When I'm with Owen I feel powerful and excited and...I feel like I can conquer anything.

God, I want this to work. I want with all my heart to go on this crazy, magical ride with Owen and see where it takes us. Because my gut tells me this feeling I have—this fluttery, terrified, glittering feeling is special. It's love. There's a path before us that leads somewhere beautiful, if only we have the courage to walk it.

I can see myself growing old with Owen. I can see it as bright and vivid as if it were a photograph in front of me. I know him, know his quirks and his pain and his heart.

But I can't sacrifice who I am—my career or my desires for the future—because he's afraid. If we're going to do this, then it'll be with dreams intact and hand in hand as equals. Fear and all.

CHAPTER TWENTY-SEVEN

Owen

I KNOW WHAT I want but trying to put it in words is like dangling myself over the edge of a cliff. The potential consequences roar inside me. The difference now is that something else is louder—hope. Standing in this empty apartment, with Hannah's big brown eyes watching me, is surreal. I never thought I'd get to this point.

But going back to New York solidified it all. I quit my job to a hearty slap on the back from my boss, Logan, and the warmest of wishes from his wife, Addison. I gave up my rented apartment and didn't feel even an ounce of doubt. When I told my accountant I was finally going to use my inheritance to start a new life, I could practically hear my mother's voice urging me on. Encouraging me.

One day you'll understand, she'd said to me a lifetime ago. *Real loved ones stand in your firing line, and you in theirs. They see the very best and worst of you, and they love you anyway.*

Hannah *has* seen the worst of me. The ugliest parts of me. And yet here she is, standing with her hands knotted in front of her and sincerity shining out of her face.

"I don't think I'm going to be very good at this," I say. "But I'm going to try."

My hands are still in my pockets and my mother's ring is in there. It's become comforting to me, in these last few weeks, because every time I look at it I think of the two women who've made me understand what it means to be a good man. I've kept it in my pocket since the day I visited my grandmother, needing to know my family was close, even if only in spirit.

"I've taken the easy route since my parents died, thinking it was the smart thing to do. No one calls me on my shit because I'm so good at hiding all my scars most people don't even know they're there. Most people don't look very closely."

"But I did." Her words are soft.

"You did. You looked closer and kept asking, and I *knew* you'd be like that. Ever since we were in the academy, I knew you were smarter and more perceptive than most people. You *saw* me and I didn't like that." I shake my head. "But I realised after being here, in this apartment with you, that I'd been flying under the radar so long that I didn't even know who I was anymore. I wasn't a cop, because I quit that. I wasn't a grandson, because I deserted my grandmother. I certainly wasn't a son or a brother. I wasn't…anything."

"We're all *something*, Owen." Hannah steps forward, as if she wants to touch me. But her hands stay fluttering by her sides. "Even if we don't know what it is yet."

"I had to figure out what I wanted to be. Start from scratch. Pretend like I had all the options in front of me when my parents died." I pull the ring out from my pocket and her eyes glitter like the diamonds surrounding the big, beautiful smoky-coloured stone.

Unusual and pretty, like Hannah.

"And I figured that maybe I could be your partner. Maybe I could be a guy who deserves someone like you." My throat is all tight and the feeling is foreign and strange. "Maybe we could start over at 21 Love Street for real."

"I'm not going to quit my job, Owen. I know it's probably going to stress you out and make you worry, but that's who *I* am." A tear plops onto her cheek and she brushes it away before I even have the chance. That's my Hannah, independent to a fault. And damn if I don't love that about her. "But that doesn't mean I don't want this. I do, I want it so bad."

"I'm not asking you to quit your job. I won't lie and say it won't worry me sick when you're working a case, but you're doing what you're supposed to be doing in life." I swallow. "And I want to come back. To Melbourne, to you, to the force, to my grandmother. I want to give my life a second go. And I want to do it all with you by my side."

"You have no idea how happy that makes me." She comes closer still and throws her arms around my neck, pressing her lips to my skin and her body to mine. "We fit, Owen. We make each other better. When I'm with you, I feel like I can take on the world."

"I hope the world is shaking in its boots, then." I grab her hand and hold the ring, my eyes locked on to hers. "My mother would have loved you, you know."

Hannah blinks rapidly, trying to stem her tears… and failing. "If she raised someone as amazing as you, then I'm sure I would have loved her, too."

"Will you be my partner in this crazy adventure? I have no idea what I'm doing and I'm one-hundred-percent certain I'll screw something up. But I promise you I'll always listen, and I'll always put you first. Before anything."

"Owen, none of us are perfect. I'll screw up, too and that's fine. But the main thing is that we love each other as best we can…and I already know this feels right. It feels good and beautiful and perfectly imperfect. I knew how I felt about you a long time ago, and learning about your past didn't change that. It only made the feeling stronger."

"So we're doing this, for real?" Excitement fizzes in my veins at the thought of waking up here, day after day with Hannah in my arms. I've never wanted anything as much as this.

"For real," she says with a nod. "I won't even complain about having to be your wife this time."

I laugh and it's like a weight has been lifted off my shoulders. She watches as I slip the ring onto her finger.

"I can't wait to marry you, Hannah," I say.

She's taken the world and painted it with better colours. Given me hope and happiness and purpose. "I can't wait, either. I guess this means you'll have to stop calling me Anderson."

"You want to be a Fletcher?" I didn't think my heart could be any fuller.

"Of course I do, Owen." Her eyes glimmer. "There are plenty of Andersons running around in the rest of my family. I figured we could even your side up by one...or maybe two?"

A baby. It's the very thing that terrified me a month ago and now it's something I want. Sure, it's still daunting, and still something that's guaranteed to knock me on my ass. But I'm not afraid of that anymore. Not now that Hannah and I are a team. A family.

"Hell yeah, I want it all with you. I'm all in." She kisses me long and hard and I don't know how I ever got to deserve her. "I guess we've got some explaining to do to the neighbours. They're going to be mighty confused if we suddenly get married... again."

Hannah hugs me close and presses up on her tip-toes, a wicked smile curving her lips. "I don't care about what they think, since I have a *way* more pressing concern."

"What's that?"

She starts to lead me toward the bedroom, her eyes full of fire and love. "I'm hoping you've still got a bed in this place."

Damn. I'm the luckiest man alive.

* * * * *

TEMPORARY TO TEMPTED

JESSICA LEMMON

One

Prospect number seven was not going well.

Andrea Payne's eyelids drooped as Dr. Christopher Miller yammered on. At this rate hell would freeze solid and Satan would win a gold medal in figure skating before she found an appropriate plus-one for her sister's wedding.

Her sister Gwen was the second to last of the Payne women to marry, which left Andy dead last. Not that Andy had ever been anywhere near walking down a runner in a wedding gown, but this marriage would widen the gap already setting her apart from her married—and one soon-to-be married—sisters.

Years ago, when she'd moved to Seattle, Andy had set out to prove that she didn't need a boyfriend; didn't need anyone. She'd set out to prove that in business, *in life*, she could stand on her achievements and skills.

In her family, charm and poise were worth more than achievements, and for that she could blame her mother, former Miss Ohio Estelle Payne. Andy would settle for relationships with high-paying clients, thank you very much.

There was a contract between them, after all. That was sort of like marriage.

She returned her attention to her date, boredom having set in a while ago. It was a shame he wasn't going to work out. On paper, Christopher was everything she was looking for in a date for her sister's wedding. He was a doctor, well-dressed, nice-looking and comfortable talking about himself.

Really comfortable.

"Anyway, I was able to help out a patient in his time of need, which is what this job is all about." He arched his eyebrows and pressed his lips together, trying to appear humble. "He was lucky I was there."

Womp.

She'd tried her ex-boyfriends first—a whopping total of three of them—over the last month and a half before resorting to a dating app that had resulted in three other duds and "lucky number seven," Christopher here.

She gulped down the last of her chardonnay and flagged the waitress for a refill. Her date never broke stride.

"It wasn't the first time I've been tasked with removing a mole, but it's never an easy fight, and far more dangerous than anyone would imagine."

She sucked in air through her nose and plastered on what she hoped was a genial smile while surreptitiously checking out her surroundings. She'd noticed a trio at the bar earlier, and her attention returned there again. A guy and a girl who hadn't taken their eyes off each other and another guy who was there as a third wheel but didn't seem particularly bothered by it. She'd assumed he was waiting for his date while he had drinks with the couple, but then Andy noticed him flirting with the bartender. Maybe she was his girlfriend, though nothing between them hinted that they knew each other on an intimate level.

People-watching was one of Andy's favorite pastimes.

She enjoyed making up stories about strangers, testing her observation skills. She only wished there was a way she could find out if she was right about her instincts.

The single guy—a gut call—at the bar was handsome in an earthy way, his light brown hair winding into curls here and there like it was in need of a trim, his shadowed beard a far cry from Christopher's sharply shaven jawline. Where Christopher resembled a firm pillar in a Brooks Brothers suit, the guy at the bar was in an approachable button-down pale-blue-and-white checked shirt, his tie—if there'd ever been one—long since tossed, and the sleeves cuffed and pushed to his elbows. He was drinking a bottle of beer, an expensive IPA if she wasn't mistaken, and that made her like him more.

"Andy?"

She jerked her attention to Christopher, who was a dark-haired, poor man's version of Chris Hemsworth. Not bad for a girl who was desperately seeking a date, but something about the good doctor was bothering her. Particularly that he was full of crap. Brimming with it, in fact.

How would she tolerate the entirety of a four-day wedding with him?

"Lost you there." He smirked and then continued the story of his latest medical triumph, talking down to her as if she still held her first job working part-time at a perfume counter. Not that he'd know what she did for a living. He never asked. If this bozo knew who he was trying to impress, he'd shut his mouth like a sprung bear trap.

She wondered what ole Christopher would say if he knew she was *the* Andy Payne, master of marketers. Sultan of sales. The oft-sought-after, rarely duplicated expert who was essentially a puff of smoke.

Everyone thought she was a man…on paper. She'd kept her identity a secret from everyone—including the many publications who'd interviewed her.

The New York Times.

Forbes.

Fortune.

That random mention in *Entertainment Weekly*.

Andy Payne was known for whipping companies into shape, and throughout her illustrious five-year career she'd managed to garner the attention of others with a clean black-and-white website and zero personal or identifying information about herself. When she showed up at the company, they knew on sight that she was a woman, but by then they were under her spell…and they'd signed a nondisclosure agreement.

Mostly she worked with men and, as she'd experienced in her first attempt at beginning a business as Andrea Anderson (last name chosen for alliteration), complete with a mauve and silver website filled with flowery words and cursive fonts, male clients didn't want to pay her what she was worth.

Enter her new identity. Andrea was easily changed to Andy, and she used her real last name. She let her clients' assumptions that she was male work in her favor.

"…not that I need *another* house in Tahiti." Christopher offered a smug smile and leaned back in his chair. Apparently, that was her cue to swoon or something.

She'd wasted enough time. First on her exes and now on the Find Love app. The wedding was in two weeks and she didn't have time for another round of failed interviews disguised as dates.

Andy hated to admit it, but in a deep dark corner of her heart she longed to be more like her sisters. She desired praise and approval from her mother. She wanted not necessarily to "fit in" but she would love not to *stand out*. In this case that meant appearing happily coupled off and avoiding needling observations from family members like that cousin at her sister Carroll's wedding.

I wish I was brave enough to show up at a wedding alone. If I didn't have a date, I would've just stayed home.

It wasn't enough to have a cardboard stand-in by her side, no, no. Andy needed to impress. Ideally her date could thwart those sorts of comments before they started.

Sadly, as impressive as Christopher believed he was, he wouldn't cut it as a proper wedding date.

Still. He was all she had. Time to get real.

"Christopher. I selected your profile because I need a date for my sister's wedding. The gig is three nights, four days in amazing and luxurious Crown, Ohio. Your airfare will be covered and your hotel room will be separate, but also covered. You will be tasked with being my date, pretending to find everything I say amusing, and impressing my mother and father. You're skilled at bragging about how great you are but I will also need you to recognize that I'm in the room if we have any hope of pulling this off. Are you up for the mission I've presented you, or do you want to call it a night?"

He watched her carefully, an uncertain look on his face. "Are you— You're serious."

"As a heart attack. Which I hear you know a lot about."

"You want me to pretend to be your boyfriend."

"Yes."

"At a wedding."

"Yes."

He leaned forward and squinted one eye, his lips pursing as if deciding if the trip to Ohio would be worth his time, energy and effort.

Andy's palms were sweating. Not because she was excited by the doctor, but because her search might finally be over.

Then the idiot blurted, "Do we at least get to fuck?"

Yeah. They were *so* done.

"Good night, Christopher. I'll take care of the check."

"Wait, Andy—"

She tossed twenty bucks on the table to cover their drinks and marched to the ladies' room. The money would cover the single drink they'd each had and then she could go home and—

And what?

She was flat out of solutions. She had no close guy friends she could ask. Hell, she had no close girlfriends who might help her make a plan. What she had was money and prestige.

Just the thought of showing up at Gwen's wedding alone pissed her off. She refused to fail. It wasn't in her nature. Plus there was one other itty-bitty reason why showing up with a date was preferable.

One of her ex-boyfriends had been invited. She'd stooped low enough to call, which was bad enough, but then she learned that he was dating Gwen's best friend who was in the wedding. So that was gross.

Matthew Higgins had greeted her like no time had passed since they parted. *Well, well, well. If it isn't her royal highness.*

The Ice Queen. That was her.

Thank God she hadn't asked him to be her date. She'd played it off like she'd simply thought of him out of the blue and wanted to "catch up" and then ended the call before she died of humiliation.

At the double sink, she dug through her purse for her lip gloss, which evidently she'd neglected to pack in her clutch. She sighed in defeat. It'd been a long month.

A long *life*.

Around the time she'd dated Matt, she'd been sure she'd wind up marrying eventually. Until he repeatedly teased her about her lack of warmth. She wasn't enough for him, and as much as she wished she could refute that, she'd also seen evidence in her family of what she was lacking. She wasn't as bubbly as Gwen. She wasn't as bold as Kelli. She wasn't as stylish as Ness. She wasn't as athletic as Carroll. As one of five girls in the Payne family, Andy was the unofficial black sheep. She'd just as soon not draw even more attention to their differences by becoming the last single one. Yet here she was.

For all the confidence and kick-ass-ness she possessed at work, she didn't want to be singled out or excluded from couples' activities.

Plus, nothing chapped her ass more than giving up.

She peeked out of a crack in the swinging door of the ladies' restroom to watch Christopher exit the bar. *Thank God.* Also, her twenty was still on the table, which was a plus. The last guy had taken her money and left, and she'd had to pay the waitress again.

There were no good men left in this city.

In the *world.*

"I can't catch another bouquet without a date," she whispered to herself. As humiliating as it was to catch the blasted thing—that her sisters always aimed her way—nothing was more humiliating than returning to the table with the flowers in hand and no date in sight. Guests always looked on in pity, as if she was going to die alone.

Her gaze snagged on the attractive guy at the bar and her back straightened with determination. If she was right about her observations, he was single. He was also sort of flirting with the bartender which hopefully meant he was looking.

Approaching him would be a random shot, but so had approaching every other guy she'd been out with. Maybe instead of taking home the cute bartender, he'd agree to bail out the too-serious, frosty, desperate-for-a-wedding-date single woman hiding in the ladies' room.

Probably not.

But Andy wasn't a failure.

She wouldn't *allow* failure.

She stepped from the restroom and spotted him—alone. The guy with the attractive facial hair and almost boyish curls. Except everything about the sculpted jaw and rounded shoulders screamed *man*. He was alone. Which meant the couple he'd been with had gone elsewhere.

Now was her chance.

Maybe her last chance.

"Money," she muttered.

She didn't have time for a get-to-know-you chat followed by the prospect of a date followed by her warming up to mention, "Hey, so my sister is getting married in two weeks…" She had to cut through the small talk and arrow straight to the point. Cash would make that a hell of a lot easier. She opened her clutch to count her credit cards. Five. That should be enough.

She rounded the corner to the ATM at the back of the bar, a plan in mind and a glass of good chardonnay in her belly.

She would take the simple approach and ask him if she could pay him to come with her to Ohio. Enough with faux dating and weighing the odds. She needed a date, and hopefully this guy needed a couple grand.

On a mission, she slid the first of five credit cards into the machine and punched the withdrawal button.

She would find a date to Gwen's wedding.

And she would find him tonight.

Two

Gage Fleming finished off his IPA and tipped the bottle's neck at the bartender. "I'll take the check when you have a second."

Seattle had come out of a long winter and cool spring, and was now firmly entrenched in summer. The energy was different during the hot months. The skirts were shorter and the nights were longer, and for him, the workdays were longer, too. He hadn't left his desk until well after seven thirty—hadn't gotten here until well after eight thirty. Given the hellacious week he'd had at the office, it didn't surprise him that he wasn't as upbeat as usual.

"Sure thing." Shelly was petite, wearing a ball cap with her ponytail sticking out of the back. Her lashes were thick, and her lips were shiny with gloss. Cute as she was, he didn't plan on asking her out. Even though she was his type, from her shapely calves to her low-cut V-necked T-shirt with the bar's gold-and-red emblem on it. Even though she'd been offering her smiles freely and borderline flirting back with him, Gage wasn't feeling it.

His best buddy Flynn and Sabrina, his other best buddy

turned Flynn's girlfriend, had taken off a few minutes ago. Gage hung around at From Afar, finishing his beer after a long week and what felt like a longer workday.

He'd been friends with Flynn, Sabrina and Reid—who wasn't in the country at the moment—since college. Sabrina being in the mix was nothing new. Her being in love with Flynn and vice versa: totally new.

Gage had said yes to the after-work beer, not thinking it'd be any different than any other hangout they'd had before. It had been different, though, since the couple couldn't keep their hands or eyes on anything in the room but each other. But he couldn't begrudge his friends. A few months back, Flynn and Sabrina had slipped from the friend zone to the in-zone. Flynn was the happiest he'd been in a long while.

"Here you go, sweetheart." The cute blonde winked at him and moved away to greet another patron.

If he wasn't mistaken, that lifting feeling in his chest was relief at his decision not to dance the dance with her. Flirting was easy—hell, second nature—to him. Asking her out wouldn't be an issue. He had it down. He'd heard yes more times than no, and often heard "Yes!" shouted with exuberance later the same night in his bed.

Over the past few weeks, however, he'd noticed he was tired of the game. Going out on a few dates, a round or three of spectacular sex (or *okay* sex—but even okay sex was pretty damn good), and then finding his way out before things progressed to anything serious… If they got that far. Lately, he'd grown tired of the awkward parting in the middle of the night or the next morning. Tired of the walk of shame.

Thirty years old was too young to be this jaded.

You're just tired after a long week. Don't analyze it to death.

He leaned forward to pull his wallet from his back

pocket, ready to pay and take his gloomy self home, when he noticed a stunning vision striding toward him. He froze, the scene unfolding in slow motion.

Strawberry blond hair washed over slim shoulders in a waterfall of color, bright against the narrow black sheath dress draped over her slender form. Electric blue eyes flashed with determination. She was long-limbed, her walk confident, and her full pink mouth was set in a firm, un-smiling line. One eyebrow was arched and she homed in on him like he was the target and she was a missile.

With his next breath, his libido returned. Lust slammed into his solar plexus and dried out his mouth.

Which made no sense.

In those heels, in that dress and with no smile to speak of, it was obvious he was in the presence of a way-too-se-rious woman. He'd had a close call with a woman like this one in his past, and he'd since decided that cute, bubbly bartenders were more his style.

Even so. Intrigued and more than a bit curious, he shoved his wallet back into his pocket when it became clear that this striking woman was coming right for him.

This one, he'd dance with. If only to shake things up a bit.

He'd buy her a drink, turn on the Fleming charm and see what happened. It'd been a while since a woman had snagged this much of his attention. Whether it was the strawberry blonde's determination or the set of her small shoulders, he couldn't be sure, but he couldn't tear his eyes off her. How could anyone look that damned delicate and at the same time like she ate nails for breakfast?

He didn't know. But he was going to find out. Some-thing told him that she'd be worth it, no matter the cost.

"Shelly, I'll have another IPA after all," he said to the bartender, and as the strawberry blonde placed a manicured hand on the back of the bar stool next to him, he smoothly added, "and whatever she's having."

"You got it." Shelly dipped her chin at the strawberry blonde. "What'll it be?"

Strawberry yanked her gaze from Gage, her expression almost shocked that the bartender was talking to her. "Um. Chardonnay."

Shelly fetched their drinks and Gage turned to greet his guest, pulling the stool out for her to sit.

"No. Thanks," she replied coolly, almost like the "thanks" part was an afterthought.

Instinct told him that she wasn't as cool and calm as she pretended to be. If she was actually the man-eater she portrayed, she'd look him in the eye right now. Instead, she appeared to be steeling herself for some sort of proposition. Maybe she'd had a bad breakup, needed a little rebound.

That he could do.

"Can't enjoy your chardonnay without having a seat," he replied easily, patting the stool with one hand. Her eyebrows slammed down over her pert nose and she pegged him with an expression that bordered on fury.

A *zap!* hit him low in the gut. A warning drowned out by intense curiosity.

Let's tangle, honey.

A glass of chardonnay and a bottle of beer appeared in front of him, and without breaking away from her fiery blue gaze, he handed over the wine. Strawberry's nostrils flared, but she took the glass, tipped it to her lips and had sucked down a third of it by the time he'd lifted his bottle.

Yep. She was definitely here on a mission.

She set the glass down with a loud *clink*. "I'll pay you two thousand dollars to spend a weekend with me."

Gage lowered his beer without taking a sip. His mouth was poised to say the word *what* but he didn't have a chance to say anything before she was opening her purse and showing him the contents. Stacks of twenties were packed into it, facing every which way like she'd robbed a convenience store before propositioning him.

"I'm attending a destination wedding in the Midwest in two weeks. Your flight and separate room will be paid in full. I'll give you two thousand dollars to go with me."

Just as he'd settled on the notion that this beautiful creature was certifiably insane, a flicker of doubt lit her expressive eyes.

"I need you to pretend to be my boyfriend for the duration. I know Ohio doesn't sound scenic, but Crown is a beautiful, quaint town. And there will be food," she added with a touch of desperation. "Really good food."

Her throat moved as she swallowed thickly, her outer layer of surety and confidence flaking away.

Seemed he was right about her being on a mission, but damn, he'd been wrong about her not being a man-eater. She was so similar to his ex, he wouldn't be surprised if she pulled off a mask to reveal Laura herself.

He took a long slug of his beer and then swiped his tongue over his bottom lip. This woman was either crazy or desperate or both. Figured. He should've known a woman this beautiful would be nuttier than a sack of trail mix.

"Well?" Her eyebrow arched again, her too-serious expression snapping seamlessly into place. "I don't have much time, so I'd appreciate an answer."

Was she for real?

He'd never imagined she'd march over here and demand to…to…*hire him* to be her date, let alone expect him to agree without so much as a casual introduction. For all he knew, she would lure him in with promises and then steal his identity.

Or my kidneys.

The answer was an easy no, but he wouldn't let her off the hook without making her explain first. He opened the edge of her purse with his index finger so he could examine the cash inside as he pretended to consider her offer.

"How will payment work? You just hand me all the money in your purse and then I give you my phone number?"

"No. Of course not." She snatched her bag out of his reach. "Then I'd have no guarantee you'd show up. I'd give it to you at the wedding."

"Why would I clear my weekend plans and fly with you to Ohio on a promise of two thousand dollars if I don't have any of it?"

A frown muddled her pretty face. "You can have half. But I need your phone number. And your address. And your word."

Unbelievably gorgeous and absolutely crackers. It was a shame.

"But I need your answer now."

"Right now." His gaze locked on her pink mouth and he had a moment of regret for not getting to have a taste of her lips. To feel how silky that red hair was against his fingertips. He lifted his beer bottle, delaying. The kissing and fingers in her hair were an impossibility but his curiosity to watch her reaction still burned. He was trying to decide what she would do when he said no. Would she slap him or scream at him or run from the bar?

"Yes, now," she said through her teeth.

Damn. Maybe he could convince her to stick around after he shot her down.

"I can't help you out, Strawberry. I don't particularly like the Midwest. And despite what first impression I must've given you, I don't need two thousand dollars. But if you'd like to finish your wine—"

That long swath of hair flicked as she turned on her heel and tromped toward the exit. Option C it was. She left behind a plume of softly scented perfume and a fantasy that lasted the rest of the week. One about long, silky hair and a parted pink mouth. About her beneath him naked atop those bills scattered over his bed…

Whoever she was, she left an impression. The way looking at the sun left bright light burning behind his lids for a while.

Gage turned back to his beer. Even though Strawberry was a little nutty, he honestly hoped she found a date to that wedding in Ohio.

Three

"Today's the day."

Gage rubbed his hands together and then fired up the espresso machine in the executive break room.

"What day's that?" Reid, back from his recent trip home to London, asked.

"The day that Andy Payne guy comes to save Gage's rear end," Sabrina answered as she tipped the half-and-half into her mug.

"Not *my* rear. *Our* rears," Gage corrected. "This is going to help boost sales, yes, but this will also take some of the pressure off Flynn." He grinned at Sabrina. "You're welcome."

Last year Gage had come up with the perfect solution for the senior staff at Monarch Consulting, who had been giving Flynn holy hell. When Flynn's father died, leaving Flynn in charge of the company, a lot of the men and women who were used to the way Emmons had run things hadn't taken too kindly to Flynn. Gage's suggestion—*brilliant* suggestion—was to focus on sales, create a huge boom in business, which would satisfy shaky investors and give a needed boost to everyone's bonuses. It was hard to complain when extra money rolled in.

"Oh, I'm welcome, am I?" Sabrina chuckled.

"If it's gratitude you want, mate, just ask," Reid commented.

Gage didn't want gratitude, but he did want results. The company had felt as if it was teetering on a foundation of marbles last year and he hadn't liked it at all. Monarch Consulting was the workplace Gage had called home since college. He didn't want to work anywhere else. He loved what he did, loved his friends and in no way wanted to end up working at a fish hatchery like his parents. Flynn's success as president ensured all of their successes.

Flynn stepped into the room, picking up on the conversation. "Let me guess. You have your panties in a wad of excitement over the arrival of the guy made of smoke?"

The guy who was the key to stabilizing Monarch, bringing in extra money *and* a business boom?

Hell, yes.

Andy Payne was a fixer of sorts who was known for not being known. He'd been interviewed but never filmed, and his About page was devoid of a photo or any description of him as a person. Gage wasn't sure if he bought into the hero-worship BS surrounding Andy Payne's reputation, but the man's results were rock solid. Every employee had signed nondisclosure documents before Payne's arrival.

Plus, if this Andy guy was half as good in person as he was on paper, Monarch would be set and Flynn's leadership would go unchallenged. Succeeding was the only option. Gage had never taken a backwards step since he'd set foot in Monarch and he wouldn't start now. He had goals to double the company's revenue, and making his sales department shine would tuck in nicely with that goal.

It was a big goal, but Andy Payne was a big deal. With his help there wasn't anything standing in Gage's way.

* * *

Andy strolled into the Monarch building wearing her best suit. Bone-colored, with a silky black cami under the jacket, her Jimmy Choos an easy-to-navigate height. She had to work in them, after all.

She'd never understood any woman's desire to sacrifice form for comfort. She wasn't a fan of compromise.

Andy hadn't accepted her fate from the weekend, either. Yes, she'd quit the dating app that'd been a total waste of resources. And, yes, she had felt the sting of embarrassment about propositioning a handsome stranger at a bar, but that didn't mean her search was over. There was still a chance, though slim, to find a stand-in date. Maybe she would meet a nice guy on her way out of this very building. Or maybe at the resort.

Doubt pushed itself forward but she fervently ignored it. Instead she allowed herself to feel the familiar thrum of excitement as she rode the elevator up to the executive floor. First days were her *favorite*.

She'd done extensive research on Monarch, noting that the only photo of the staff was one gathered outside the front of this very building, their faces tiny and nondescript. If businesses were to entrust Monarch with their well-being, they needed to see the trustworthy faces who worked here.

Unlike most businesses, Andy had worked hard to keep her identity under wraps. She had no qualms about pulling a bait and switch on day one. By then everyone was invested and her reputation had preceded her. She never blatantly led her clients to believe Andy Payne was male, but much like the assumption that a surgeon was always a man, so, too, was one made that the wild success of her Fortune 500 business must be attributed to someone with a penis instead of a pair of breasts.

The pay gap that existed between men and women didn't exist for her, thanks to her subterfuge. Her clients paid what was asked, and it was too late to pull the plug once the contracts were signed. She wouldn't apologize for it.

She was absolutely worth it.

She was the best at what she did and she endeavored to leave every business better than she'd found it. Monarch was going to be another link in a long chain of satisfied customers.

With a flip of her hair she exited the elevator on the executive floor. Three huge offices with glass walls stood empty, a front desk staffed with a young blonde woman in front of one of them. Andy was early, so probably the executives hadn't come out of the coffee or break room yet. Muted voices and laughter came from an unseen room in the back.

One of those voices likely belonged to Gage, the senior sales executive who'd hired her.

"May I help you?" the assistant asked.

Andy addressed her by her name, advertised on the nameplate on the front of her desk. "Hello, Yasmine. Andy Payne for Gage Fleming."

"Andy Payne?"

"That's me." She grinned.

"Oh, of course, Ms. Payne. We have you set up in the conference room as you requested."

Yasmine quickly recovered from her surprise at discovering that Andy was a woman. Good for her.

In the conference room, Yasmine pointed out the projector and offered to fetch Andy an espresso.

"Americano, if you can."

The other woman dipped her chin in affirmation and left.

Andy unloaded her bag on the table—a rigorous sales plan and a dossier on Monarch minus details on the man she was meeting, since she'd learned virtually nothing about him via the website.

Done right, they could implement her suggested changes

in the week and a half she had before she would have to fly
to Ohio for Gwen's wedding.

Gag. Just the thought of that bit of unfinished business
rankled her.

But Gage Fleming had hired Andy on her merits at business, not based on whether or not she was datable. She
shoved aside all thoughts of the wedding and focused on
what she did most—what she did *best*—fixing companies.

Flynn and Sabrina left the haven of the break room,
Gage and Reid following behind. On their walk to their
offices, Gage asked Reid, "How was your trip?"

His British friend, coffee mug lifted, grinned. "Grand."

"Because of…"

"Suzie Daniels. A pretty American in a foreign land
who needed companionship from a local who was willing
to show her a good time." Reid rested his palm over his
heart. "I showed her repeatedly. Lucky lady."

Gage had to chuckle. Reid was a playboy and a half, but
he was also a nice guy. No doubt Suzie Daniels had kissed
him farewell and hadn't regretted a single minute of their
time together. Gage hadn't been as fortunate with his past
hookups. He must throw off a serious boyfriend vibe. The
women he dated always wanted more, always wanted it
too quickly and weren't happy when he declined. The last
woman he dated had told him he'd wasted her time and said
she wished she'd never met him. Ouch.

"And your weekend?" Reid asked, stopping next to
Gage's office.

"Went to From Afar with Flynn and Sabrina on Friday
night for a drink after work. After they left, the strangest
thing…" Gage fell silent when he spotted a flash of red
hair in the conference room. And when her head lifted
slightly and he caught sight of her profile, he recognized
her instantly.

She was the woman who'd attempted to buy him like a suit off a rack. The more he'd thought about that interaction the more it had bothered him. Not because he felt cheap or used, but because the beauty who'd invaded his dreams had truly believed the money was going to seal the deal with them. As if she didn't have enough confidence to strike up a conversation about what she needed, but instead felt the need to offer him cash.

"Holy hell." Gage grabbed Reid's arm and dragged him back into the hallway they'd just exited, Reid complaining since he'd sloshed coffee onto the carpet and narrowly missed his shoes. Gage had done a good job of spilling his own coffee on his shirt. Hot liquid burned through the pale blue button-down, and he swore.

"What just happened?" Reid shook coffee droplets off his fingers.

"She's stalking me." Gage scrubbed at his shirt with one hand.

"Who?"

Reid peered around the corner and Gage slunk farther into the hall. When he'd concluded that the redhead was "crackers," he'd thought he'd been half joking. Apparently, he hadn't.

"That's the woman I was just going to tell you about," Gage whispered, though there was no way she could hear him from the conference room. "She approached me at the bar Friday night and offered to pay me two grand to spend a weekend with her."

Reid's eyebrows lifted, wrinkling his brow. "And you said no." He stole another peek and regarded Gage dubiously. "Why?"

"Because she's insane?" That seemed the only reasonable explanation now.

"You're the insane one, my friend, if you didn't snap her

up and have your way with her right there on the bar top. Hell, I wouldn't have charged her at all."

"The offer wasn't for sex. It was for me to fly to Ohio and attend a wedding. She wanted me to pretend to be seeing her or something."

"Oh." Reid's disappointment was obvious. "That's not the same thing at all."

"No. It's not." Gage returned to the break room and set his mug aside. He grabbed a dish towel and scrubbed at the coffee stain low on his shirt.

Reid wasn't far behind. "What's she doing here?"

"I have no idea."

"Gage?" Yasmine stepped into the break room. "Andy Payne is here to see you."

"Perfect timing." Gage gestured at his soiled shirt. "Tell him I'll be right out. Who's the redhead?"

Yasmine blinked. "Andy Payne."

"Andy Payne is the fixer, love," Reid told her gently. "We want to know who the vixen in the cream-colored suit is."

"Andy Payne," Yasmine repeated with slow insistence and enough confidence that Reid and Gage exchanged glances.

"*She's* Andy Payne?" Gage asked, still trying to wrap his head around the idea that the woman who approached him at the bar was the "guy" he'd hired to whip his sales team into shape.

"Surprising, right? How sexist are we?" Yasmine shrugged. "I thought Andy was going to be a dude, too."

Reid smiled to beat all. "I believe I'll go with you to meet this Andy Payne, Gagey. Do bring up Friday for my benefit, yeah?"

"No," Gage growled, his head still spinning with the new information. "I'll go alone to meet...her."

As he exited the break room, he muttered, "Again."

Four

The projector was positioned, her laptop open and the PowerPoint presentation cued up.

Andy tidied the bound sales plans—one for her and one for Gage. She'd arranged herself at the head of the conference table and placed the report to her left elbow at the corner. She found it easier to coordinate a plan when they weren't facing each other from opposing sides.

Sometimes these meetings went smoothly, with the managers or CEOs who'd hired her easing into the adjustment as they learned that Andy Payne was the female currently introducing herself. Other times, they reacted angrily and accused her of pulling a fast one on them. Mostly it was the former.

They'd hired her for her expertise, and that was what she reminded them of when she arrived. She'd only had three men ever react poorly and had only ever lost one job because of it. The sexist bastard. No matter, her contract was ironclad and nonrefundable. She'd bought a weekend spa retreat with the money that particular time and had no qualms about enjoying her paid leave.

She sat on the edge of the padded chair and turned her head in time to see a man rapidly approaching the conference room. She recognized the scruffy jaw, the slight curl to the longish hair on top of his head…and the answering recognition in his caramel-brown eyes.

She stood slowly, feeling her jaw drop to the floor as he shut the conference room door behind him and looked down his nose at her. Although she wasn't that much shorter than him.

"*You're* Andy Payne," he said flatly.

Her mouth still agape, she managed a stunned nod. Warmth seeped from her cami, over her décolletage and up her neck. No doubt she was turning a stunning shade of pink while he watched her.

And he did watch her. Carefully. And unhappily.

As quickly as she could move, she slapped the lid closed on her laptop and yanked the cord free from the wall. "I'm—uh," she said as she hastily stacked the reports. "I have to…um…"

She yanked her bag off the chair but the strap caught, scattering the pages in her dossier on Monarch to the floor along with several pens, her cell phone charger and a tube of lipstick.

This was going well.

She crouched to the floor to sweep the contents of the bag back into it. "You must be Gage."

"In the flesh." He knelt next to her and picked up one of her pens that had fallen to the floor.

"I didn't know you were you when I approached you on Friday or I never would've done it," she said as she gathered her things. A lock of hair swept over her eye and she blew a puff of air from her lips to move it.

"You don't say." His eyebrows flinched slightly, but some of the anger simmered away, his expression almost bemused as his eyes roamed over her face.

He was stupidly attractive. Even more so in a suit. Even with a coffee stain on his shirt that looked fresh. That attraction was all the more reason why she couldn't stay another moment. She'd never be able to look him in the eye again after she'd… God…*offered to pay him* to be her date.

"I'll refund your money for the consultation contract." She snatched the pen from his hand and stood. He stood with her and the view of the rest of him was finer than it had appeared on Friday night. His muscular chest pressed the confines of his shirt, a dark blue tie in place and knotted just so. His slacks were navy as well, and a brown leather belt bisected his waist. His shoes matched—expensive and shiny.

"First you want to hire me, now you want to give me a refund. You offer to pay me an awful lot."

She blanched.

"And the hell you will." He folded his arms over his impressive chest. His unsmiling mouth pursed. "I hired you to do a job. You're not running out on me just because you—"

"Don't say it." Her eyes sank closed and she palmed one burning-hot cheek. Was it possible to die of humiliation? "I know what I did and I apologize." She reopened her eyes and turned them up to his. "Please tell me you didn't tell anyone about it?"

"I told my friend Reid. He works here. You'll meet him later."

"You told someone?" Her voice was edging along hysterical and she forced herself to calm down. "You could've kept that to yourself."

"Is that a joke? A gorgeous woman approaches me in a bar and I decide to stay one drink longer to get to know her and then she offers to pay me two grand for my companionship? It's a hell of a story, *Andy.*"

He thought she was…gorgeous? And he'd wanted to get to know her?

It was far and wide two of the most flattering compliments she'd heard in a while.

"I didn't know you were *the* Andy Payne when I told him. I thought you'd tracked me down at work, and that you were going to… I don't know, try and reconvince me."

That was fair.

Why would he assume she was here for any other reason? She'd been on a mission to achieve her goal on Friday and had—incorrectly—assumed that when she ran from that bar, mentally vowing never to return, she wouldn't see Gage again.

She hadn't asked him his name, either.

"I wasn't myself that night. I was angry about my date not working out and then I noticed you—" She snapped her mouth closed before she accidentally said too much, and then rerouted the conversation. "This is no fault of yours. I'll go directly to my office from here and refund your money immediately." She added the laptop and reports to her bag and pulled it over her shoulder.

"No deal." He stepped in front of the door and blocked her path.

"Step aside, Mr. Fleming."

"Not going to happen, *Ms.* Payne." His nostrils flared as he pulled in a breath. "I hired you. You agreed to do a job. I know you're the best—I did my research. You've been cited as an asset by hundreds of companies, and I'm not letting you go because you made a mistake and now you're uncomfortable. We have a contract. I was told your fee was nonrefundable."

That was true. Normally. "I'll make an exception."

A warm, gentle palm landed on her upper arm. His voice was equally gentle when he said, "I don't want an exception. I want you to stay and double or triple our numbers like you promised. This is important."

His words were sincere. And a good reminder that she

prided herself on her work ethic. She *never* let clients down. She worked tirelessly for them because their businesses mattered. Employees had families to care for, and when she made their companies more money, the companies in turn lined the pockets of those hardworking men and women. What she did wasn't about fattening up greedy CEOs. She did this work for the people. All of them.

And right now Gage looked like someone who needed her help.

"Did you find a date for the wedding yet?" he asked.

She blinked, stunned by the change of topic.

"I'll go," he said. "You stay here for the time you promised and I'll go with you to Ohio to your sister's wedding."

"But—"

"I suspect you'll insist, so I'll let you take care of the room and flight, but you can keep the two grand." He dipped his chin in a show of sincerity. "Okay?"

As much as she hated to admit it, his offer was really, *really* tempting. She had to face reality, and the reality was that she was no closer to finding a date for Gwen's wedding than she was to sprouting wings and flying there on her own steam.

A bigger part of her was tempted simply because of Gage. He was attractive, and had found her attractive, and she wouldn't mind spending more time getting to know him. Of all the dates she'd set up in an attempt to find a companion for Gwen's wedding, Gage, from his warm brown eyes to his shiny leather shoes, was the only one who'd made her heart flutter. Dr. Christopher certainly hadn't wanted to get to know her better. He hadn't even had the decency to turn the money down.

Even so, she found herself answering, "I couldn't ask you to do that."

"Too bad. You already did, on Friday night. Now I'm accepting." He lifted her bag off her shoulder, his fingers leaving behind an imprint of heat she couldn't ignore. He set the bag on the conference room table, pulling her laptop out and extracting the reports, one of which had an ugly crease on the otherwise pristine cover.

What a metaphor for Andy herself right now. She'd come in here neat and poised and now felt more than a little bent.

He opened the laptop screen and took the wrinkled report and sat in his seat. She again considered refusing his offer. Her pride told her to bolt and never look back.

There was only one problem. She needed him.

Almost as much as he needed her.

Five

Gage had to hand it to her. Andy knew what she was doing.

A week later, he sat at a conference table with Flynn and Reid and his right-hand guy on his sales team, Bruce, reviewing the numbers. The numbers were good.

Really freaking good.

"Bonuses will look great this quarter," Bruce commented, his smile wide. A thirty-nine-year-old father of seventeen-year-old twins, he could use the extra money. Both of Bruce's daughters would be graduating and going to college soon.

"Share the good news," Gage told him. "That's all I have. Flynn? Reid? Anything?"

"Not on my end," Flynn said. "Just, good job."

Reid echoed the sentiment, shook Bruce's hand, and then Bruce left the executive floor with some really good news for the sales team.

"She's as good as she claims," Flynn commented to Gage. "Andy."

"She is."

"And bloody fast," Reid commented. "I've never seen anyone swoop in and offer suggestions that work immediately."

"She's amazing," Gage admitted. She was also all business. She strode in here Monday through Friday to train, observe and then meet with Gage on her findings. He'd done some observing of his own—of her—and he couldn't escape the idea that she'd walled part of herself off.

Last week, when he'd walked into this very conference room, she hadn't been determined and all business. She'd been flustered and embarrassed. She'd been *human*. He liked witnessing that human side of her—the flush to her cheeks as her seriousness chipped away leaving her open vulnerability visible. She was able to get shit done, took no crap from anyone, and yet he'd noticed a shier, more withdrawn part of her.

"Are the two of you still on for the wedding arrangement?" Reid asked, a troublemaking twinkle in his eye.

"I agreed to help her out so she wouldn't walk. You'd have done the same thing. It's only a weekend."

Four days, technically, but he was trying to downplay it. He'd agreed so she wouldn't walk out, yes, but he'd also agreed because learning that the woman from the bar and Andy Payne were the same person had intrigued him in a way no other woman had in years. He wanted to cash in on his fantasy vision of her beneath him, sure, but he was also curious as hell why she felt the need to pay someone—him, specifically. She'd hinted that day in the conference room that there was something about him that had drawn her in. Why him? What had she seen across that bar that made her approach him?

In the time she'd spent at Monarch he still knew next to nothing about her. She was as uncrackable as a sealed safe. He still wasn't sure what he was supposed to "do" at her side at the wedding. What role was he to play other than a date who danced with her or fetched her a glass of champagne? He needed to find out, but in order to do that he had to get her out of Monarch and into an environment where she wasn't so…distant.

"She's not light and bubbly like the women you're used to seeing. Maybe a wedding will loosen her up." Reid stood.

"She's serious about her job but that's not a bad thing," Gage said in her defense. He rose from his chair and Flynn followed suit.

"It's not," Flynn agreed. "She's a hard-core professional. Does everything she says she's going to do, and follows through like a boss." The description sounded like Flynn himself.

"I was just pointing out that she's the opposite of the type of woman you gravitate toward." Reid narrowed his eyes. "Lately."

What Reid was not-so-subtly hinting at was that Andy was, at first glance, a lot like Gage's ex-fiancée.

He didn't want to talk about Laura any more than he wanted to bring up politics at a dinner party. He'd admired her strong work ethic and serious nature. In the end, he'd believed in them more than she had.

She'd broken the engagement, coldly stating that he wasn't enough like her. He had a case of the "toos." He was *too* likable, *too* fun and *too* easygoing. She'd claimed she needed someone "serious" about the future. The corrosion of that engagement was his biggest failure.

Gage hated failure.

He'd been sure that Andy was that same kind of woman—cold, calculating—until he'd witnessed her flustered. Seeing that chink in her armor had drawn him in rather than pushed him away. He hadn't completely understood it. After the hell Laura'd put him through he'd be smart not to pursue Andy at all.

But he'd never been one to back down from a challenge,

and Gage sensed there was warmth and gentleness underneath Andy's rigid exterior that had yet to surface. The more of her flaws he exposed, the more he proved that the attraction wasn't some masochistic repeat of the past with Laura, but some new, fascinating layer to Andy herself.

He liked that she had an imperfect, human side that rarely showed, that she was a mystery waiting to be uncovered. That she didn't have it together 24/7. Plus she was downright sexy. If he found an opening to show her how sexy she was, he'd happily oblige.

Not that his agreeing to be Andy's wedding date had been totally magnanimous. He'd needed her to stay on at Monarch for both appearances and results, and a few days in Ohio seemed a small price to pay.

Flynn and Sabrina had left the office around five. Now that Flynn had a girlfriend in Sabrina, he rarely worked as late as he had before. Reid had a date as well, so he'd packed up and followed them out. That left Gage alone in the executive corner of the office, waiting at his desk for Andy's daily report, which came at around 5:30 p.m.

She strolled in wearing her office attire of black pants, low shoes and a silky white shirt. Her gold jewelry was simple and understated, except for the large-faced watch, which she glanced down at before she entered.

Mouth a flat line, determination in her eyes, she stalked toward him like a hungry lioness. Much like the first time he'd seen her, he watched her approach with an even mix of intrigue and attraction.

Could he uncover the fun, flirty girl under that armor? Was there one?

"Your team is exceptional, Gage," she said, skipping over a greeting. "Which is in no small part thanks to you being a dedicated, earnest leader."

His eyebrows lifted at the compliment he wasn't expecting. But then she spoke again and made it obvious that she'd come in here with an agenda.

"I have an itinerary, your plane ticket and a few other details to cover for this weekend's wedding if you're available for a quick rundown. I know it's last-minute, but I've been busy."

All business, he thought with a smile. He'd always enjoyed a challenge but, he was realizing, lately he'd pursued challenges professionally rather than personally. He hadn't chased women who'd challenged him since Laura left. Then again, Andy had been the only one who'd tempted him to do so since.

"What are you doing right now?" he asked her.

"Now?" Her eyes widened slightly.

"Yeah. Now. Dinner?"

She shook her head like what he was saying didn't compute.

"Are you hungry?" he pressed.

"Yes."

"Are you busy right now?"

"I'm always busy."

He waited.

She shrugged and affected an *unaffected* expression. "Fine."

"Great. I'll drive."

"Where are we going?"

"Why? Are you picky? Have allergies?"

"No." She frowned.

"Then don't worry about it." He winked, enjoying throwing her off-kilter.

He needed a little more fun in his life and Andy *definitely* needed a little more fun in her life. He liked that she seemed unused to a man strong enough or willing enough to take her on. He just liked her, dammit, though he wasn't yet sure why he liked her this much.

* * *

In the immediate seconds following Gage's invitation to dinner, Andy wanted to blurt out that she needed to change first. Thankfully she resisted that very female urge. Just because Gage was playing her date at the wedding didn't mean he was one tonight. She would pretend they were an item, enjoy the reprieve from her family's judgment, and relish showing up an old ex-boyfriend who thought she'd been carved from a block of ice. But she'd keep the boundary lines very clear in her head. Gage had agreed to be her date for one reason: because he'd needed her expertise at work.

Without something to gain, he wasn't interested in her—he'd turned her down that night in the bar, after all.

Still, being around him was a rare exception she admitted she was tempted to enjoy. She was a hard sell to any man—even without the offer to pay him. A man who was both professional *and* not intimidated by her success was a rare commodity. Like finding a unicorn.

Even though her arrangement with Gage wouldn't last any longer than her sister's reception, Andy figured it'd be good to get to know him so that her family wouldn't suspect she'd bribed him to come. The only thing more humiliating than showing up at her sister's wedding with a fake date would be everyone learning that she was faking it.

But the stray thought about changing for dinner with Gage had rocked her. Why would she care what he thought of her appearance if they weren't doing this for real? She'd long ago accepted that a forever-and-ever relationship wasn't going to happen, and yet something about Gage—about his charm and kindness—made a small part of her wish this was real.

He wasn't intimidated by her. If anything, the more prickly she was, the more laid-back he seemed to become. Laid-back and yet more than a little commanding.

It was an odd mix. She didn't have him figured out yet.

Which was why she'd spent the weekend writing up the wedding itinerary and finalizing the details of their arrangement. She needed to get them on the same page, and fast, if they had any prayer of pulling this off.

At least she'd have Gage by her side when she inevitably bumped into her ex-boyfriend Matthew. The thought of him smugly pointing out that she was as frigid as she'd always been irritated her.

She wished she didn't care. Wished she didn't want to rub her ex's nose in her business success—*and* her relationship success—in spite of the label he'd given her years ago. But she did.

She was only human, after all.

Gage chose a fairly high-end restaurant downtown for dinner. With its black tablecloths and dim lighting, candles in the center of the table and à la carte menu, it was a touch more romantic than she'd counted on. Maybe she should've insisted on going home to change rather than continue in her casual work attire—if only to fit in with the well-coiffed crowd.

The host pulled her chair out for her and she sat, lifting the menu to study the options.

"Wine, Andy?" Gage asked. "Or should I call you something else in public to protect your secret identity? Bruce Wayne, maybe."

"Ha-ha." She lowered the menu to give him a slow blink. "I'll stick with sparkling water, but thank you."

When their waiter came by, Gage ordered a bottle of Cabernet alongside her sparkling water.

"We never finished the first drink we had together," he pointed out. "Tonight would feel stuffy if we didn't indulge."

She did indulge—one glass had the rigors of her workday melting off her shoulders like butter in the hot sun.

There was something about Gage that brought out her relaxed side. Maybe it was his own casual attitude. How he
could wear a suit in a fancy restaurant as well as he did and
still smile as genially as if they were lounging on his sofa
together…it was beyond her.

Andy had accepted that she simply wasn't the fun, care-
free type. Outside of this agreement with Gage, she couldn't
imagine snagging his attention. And yet being around him
felt strangely comfortable—which was probably why she
didn't hang around him at work. She didn't want to be un-
duly comfortable and slip up—she had a job to do. She
couldn't pretend to be able to live up to his fun, easy-going
standards. That simply wasn't who she was. Except that
she needed to be *really* comfortable around him at Gwen's
wedding for this charade to work.

After they'd eaten their dinners, they settled in to finish off the wine, Gage resting one masculine hand on the
rim of his glass. He lifted it the same way and gestured to
her with the stem.

"Let's hear the plan."

Was it any wonder he was fantastic at his job? He exuded
confidence and charm, and if she were a twitchy CEO in
search of a consulting firm, she'd buy an air conditioner
from Gage in the wintertime. Just to urge forth that sincere, pleased smile.

To please him in general.

That thought brought forth another, one of pleasing him
in a physical way. With her touch, with her kiss.

Alarming, since Andy had just tasked herself with keeping things between them strictly professional. Why did he
have to be so damned attractive? Why did he have to be
so damned likeable? Why did he act as if he liked her so
much in return? That was the real lure. He seemed to like
her just as she was—prickly and unapproachable, rigid and

serious. She really wished he'd have let her pay him so the lines weren't so blurry.

"I emailed you an itinerary," she told him, firmly setting the conversation back on solid ground.

"When?"

"In the car on the drive over. Do you want to cue it up so we can review it together? It covers the schedule in detail, including what time each event starts and where we'll be staying. I left your airline ticket at my apartment but I can bring it to Monarch tomorrow."

"Those aren't the kinds of details I need from you, Andy."

"No?" She wasn't sure what else there was. Unless… "I did type up a detailed family member list, but that seemed like overpreparing. If you and I were really dating, you wouldn't necessarily remember all their names."

"Those aren't the details I need, either." He shook his head, took a sip from his wine and swallowed.

When his tongue stroked his lip to catch a wayward crimson drop, she pressed her knees together under the table. His mouth might be the most distracting part about him.

"I need to know," that mouth said, lazily pronouncing each syllable, "how much physical affection you'd like from me."

Six

"Hold your hand. Put my palm on your lower back. Those are both givens. But what about kissing? How much? How often? How *deep*?"

Gage watched Andy carefully as he doled out each option as if on a menu like the one they'd ordered from tonight. He enjoyed the surprise rounding her wide blue eyes as much as the flush creeping along her fair skin. "When we're at dinner, would you like me to feed you a bite, kiss your hand, gaze longingly into your eyes?"

"Is any of that necessary?" She sounded worried that it might be.

"Not unless we're trying to make someone jealous. In which case—very necessary. But if you have a fairly reserved family, I'll keep the touching to a minimum."

Clearly befuddled, she shakily lifted her wine and polished off the glass. He smoothly refilled it, happy to ply her with enough alcohol to have her tell him the truth. He ignored the frisson of discomfort at pursuing Andy so doggedly. She'd caught his attention. She had his admiration. Why not pursue something physical with her? It wasn't as if he'd allow himself to get in as deeply as he had with Laura. That situation had been one and done, and he'd learned not to tempt fate.

He'd recommitted to the bachelor pact with Flynn and Reid for a reason: Gage would never again consider marriage.

Flynn had backed out of the pact after he and Sabrina had obliterated the just-friends boundary, but Sabrina was the ultimate exception. She was one of their own—who better to settle down with Flynn than the one woman who would never, ever betray him?

Gage's motivation was different. He'd been thoroughly blinded by his love for Laura. He'd felt like a complete jackass for overlooking her cold-hearted demeanor, and had assumed their physical attraction and professional goals were enough to sustain a life together. He'd been young, and stupid, and all along she'd been more concerned about his financial potential than a stable marriage. After they imploded, he'd set out to make ten times as much money as she'd earn in her lifetime just to prove her wrong.

Over the years his drive became less and less about proving Laura wrong. Gage had grown to love success, and was a damn good leader. His strengths had served him well and he'd helped his best friend build a company and a sales team they could all be proud of.

Gage was a different person now than he was when he'd been engaged to Laura. Just because Andy had a similar passion for achievement was no reason to ignore the ninety-foot flames between them whenever she was near. That siren's wail he'd heard in his head was nothing more than a false alarm, concocted by the former version of himself.

"Why do you need a date for the wedding?" he asked, curious. "Why not go alone?"

"I've caught three bouquets and I don't want to catch a fourth," she answered. Strangely.

"Pardon?"

"I have four sisters. Three of them are happily married and the fourth is about to be. I don't want to catch Gwen's bouquet. If I go alone and am called to the dance floor, then Gwen will inevitably aim that bouquet right for me…" She shuddered like this was the worst fate that could befall her.

"I'm guessing not because you have an aversion to flowers?"

Andy shook her head.

"You don't want the attention?"

"I don't want the attention for being single. It's a running joke in my family."

He couldn't believe she'd admitted that much. The wine must be working. He didn't dare interrupt in case she had more to say. Turned out she did.

"I have a reputation as a hard-ass. Shocking, I know." She added a self-deprecating eye roll that he'd have found adorable if he didn't believe she was sincere. "I've never had a date to one of my sister's weddings. I'm pretty sure they think I live this lonely, pathetic existence married to my work or whatever."

"Did you date much when you lived in Ohio?"

"A few serious relationships that fizzled out. They didn't last and when we split I mostly felt relieved. One of them will be there, by the way." She chucked back the last inch of wine and waved her glass for a refill.

Gage obliged her.

"His name's Matthew," she snarled. "When we broke up he told me I'd die alone. I don't want him to know he was right."

"You're far from death's door, Andy."

"I'm not interested in permanence," she stated, a flicker of challenge in her eyes. He wouldn't argue.

"On that we agree." He clinked his glass with hers. Unbeknownst to her, she'd given him an angle to work with.

"Aside from my being your arm candy—" her impish smile emerged and brought forth an answering one of his own "—you'd like to show up this Matthew guy."

"I don't need to show him up." Bright eyes pegged him, truth in their cobalt depths. "I just don't want him to know he's won."

Gage didn't like that the bastard had coldly stated that Andy would spend her life alone any more than he liked the idea of her believing that her ex was right.

"We'll play it by ear." He reached across the table and offered a hand—handshake-style since he wasn't sure how she'd react to a more intimate touch. But when she placed her palm against his, he held onto her hand gently and made a promise he knew he'd keep. "You asked the right guy to be your wedding date, Andy. I won't let you down."

Gage had admitted during the flight that he didn't know much about Ohio. He'd told her that he knew there was a lot of corn, and that it was in the Midwest. Ohio wasn't *all* corn but there was a lot of it there.

The flight was uneventful and a straight shot to Cincinnati, but they did have to drive another hour to reach Crown from the airport. It gave them a chance to learn about music preferences—the rental car had a top-of-the-line satellite radio option—and talk about the wedding as conversationally as possible.

She didn't expect him to memorize her great-aunt's name or which grandmother, maternal or paternal, had the cane, but it made sense if they'd been dating for a while that he'd at least know her parents' and sisters' names.

"Kelli is the oldest by six years—"

"Seven," she corrected as Gage turned left onto Pinegrove Road.

"Seven. And then comes Vanessa, Carroll, you, and Gwen is the baby."

"Very good," she praised.

Gage flashed her a smile that made her tummy tighten. He really was ridiculously good-looking. She was looking forward to showing him off.

"Mom Estelle, dad Abe, but he had to work so he's coming in the day before."

"And here I sit without my gold star stickers."

"A joke. Andrea Payne, we'll loosen you up yet."

She turned to watch out the window, her lips pressed together. Gage's hand landed lightly on her leg.

"Hey. I was kidding."

"Oh, I know." She gave him what felt like an uncomfortable smile. So much for hiding her true feelings. It seemed like he could read her mind.

"Good." He turned left and drove past the wooden fence surrounding the entrance to Crown Vineyard Resort. The resort had both a man-made lake about four miles wide as well as a vineyard on-site. It made for a beautiful backdrop in the hot summer sun, the vines draped over the hills like garlands and the water sparkling under an azure sky.

Andy had secured two suites at the resort, one next to the other. She figured she could tell everyone it was a mistake made by the front desk in case it drew attention. She couldn't very well ask Gage to stay in the same room as her. He'd already been so great about not accepting payment for being here and genuinely helping her out by remembering the main branches of her family tree.

At least that'd been her reasoning until they stood at the check-in desk at the resort and she learned that there'd been an *actual* mistake at the front desk. The suite she'd reserved for Gage, paid in full, had been given to someone else.

"Unacceptable," she said, ready to fight for what was rightfully hers.

"I'm sorry, Ms. Payne. The system must've kicked that reservation out since he wasn't on the guest list. Your reservation is still in here though," the woman said brightly. "On the ground floor, king-sized bed, and a pullout sofa if separate sleeping quarters were your main concern." The woman at the counter flashed a look from Andy to Gage, probably deciding it was terribly old-fashioned to insist on separate rooms.

Gage palmed her lower back, his hand warm, and touched his mouth to her temple. "Ground floor sounds nice," he murmured, sending droves of goose bumps down her arms. "We can have coffee on the patio in the morning, and I can always sleep on the sofa if you're uncomfortable with me in your bed."

She swallowed thickly, the visual of Gage Fleming in her bed an inviting one indeed. She shifted away from him slightly. Not because he made her uncomfortable to have him near, but because whenever he was this close she was tempted to nuzzle him like a needy cat. Physical attraction to him would be helpful to convince her family and friends at this event, but she hadn't expected it in the "off" time they had together. No one was watching them, save the inept woman who couldn't provide the additional room Andy had paid for, and yet Andy had responded to him as if she had the option to have him in her bed.

She wouldn't entertain that thought. No matter how tempting it was…

He ran his hand up her back and rested it on the back of her neck, tickling her nape with his fingers and sending chills down both of her arms.

"Honey?" He smiled down at her and she forced herself to relax. He was her boyfriend for the weekend. Might as well act like it.

"Yes. That's fine."

"Great." The woman behind the counter tapped the keys on her keyboard.

How Gage's affable mood hadn't waivered today was

beyond Andy's comprehension. They'd started the morning way too early at the airport and then had gone through the discomforts of traveling—checking the bags and wedging into their tiny airplane seats. She'd fought him a little when he offered to put her bag in the overhead bin, but then realized she was standing her ground on something that shouldn't matter. If they were dating, he would of course stow her bag for her.

At the rental car kiosk, he'd insisted on driving and she'd given in on that, too. And now, the room debacle was another compromise she was making. She wasn't used to being half of a whole, or considering anyone's needs or wishes other than her own, but Gage made it easier than she'd have suspected to give up her control. It still surprised her that she'd not only let him take care of her, but that it'd also been…nice.

The woman at the front desk handed over their keycards and pointed out where their room was located, but Andy was listening with half an ear. Reason being, her mother and second eldest sister were approaching, whispering to each other as they came.

"Andrea," said Vanessa, her voice lifting in surprise.

"Hey, Ness." Andy stepped away from Gage a few inches and his hand fell away. Nervously, she smoothed her skirt with sweaty palms. "Mom."

Her mother studied Gage as well, but more dubiously than Vanessa did.

"Hi, sweetheart," her mother said, her eyes still on Gage. "Who's this?"

"Gage Fleming, this is my sister Vanessa, and my mother, Estelle."

"I've heard so much about you." Gage eased into a grin and shook their hands, and Andy felt her spine stiffen. No way would they believe this laid-back, ridiculously handsome, socially comfortable man was dating the Ice Queen.

"When Andrea RSVP'd with a plus-one, we didn't know what to think." Her mom—a beautiful woman—managed a snide smile that was somehow still pretty.

"You're the first of your kind," Vanessa added unhelpfully. "Andrea usually shows up to her sisters' weddings by herself."

"Well, unless one of you opts to remarry," Gage said as he wrapped an arm around Andy and pulled her closer, "this will be the last one."

Oh, he was good.

"We should go find our room," Andy announced, dying to run away before she inadvertently blew their cover. She was having the hardest time being comfortable in Gage's hold, especially with her eagle-eyed family staring them down.

"You're staying together?" Estelle's voice rose along with her slim, plucked eyebrows. Not because Andy's mother was old-fashioned and believed they should be staying separately but because—

"Andrea's not known for her affection." Estelle narrowed her eyes at her daughter. Andy wanted to sink into the floor. "It's…interesting to see her as part of a…couple."

Nope, her mother did not buy that Gage was with Andy for one second. Andy felt sweat prickle under her arms and opened her mouth to share the story of how they'd met at the bar—minus the part where she offered to hire him, and adjusting the timeline some—when Gage leaned in, his lips to the shell of her ear.

"Relax, beautiful girl," he whispered. "Touch my chest and smile like I just said something deliciously dirty to you."

He hadn't said anything dirty to her but her cheeks warmed like he had. She followed his instructions, tickling her fingers over his T-shirt-covered chest and closing her eyes as she pulled her mouth into a smile. It wasn't hard to do with him so close, his low, sexy voice in her ear.

He finished by kissing her temple, and when Andy faced her mother and sister, they both looked away like the intimate public display had made them uncomfortable.

She liked that. *A lot.*

Vanessa mentioned "drinks in the bar" in an hour and then she and their mother wandered off in that direction.

Andy grinned at Gage, barely able to keep her excitement in check when she blurted, "That was amazing!"

But he wasn't smiling with her.

"Are they always that rude?"

"Who cares! You should've let me pay you. You're worth every penny."

His mouth flinched like he wanted to smile, which seemed to be his default expression. She pulled her hand off his chest, having forgotten she'd left it there this whole time. "Sorry about that."

He cupped her cheek and tipped her face up to his. She was lost, admiring his handsome face for one stunned moment. "Stop acting like we're acting. You have to immerse yourself in this role, Andy. We're always being watched."

She stole a look around the room, and sure enough, another group of family members was heading their way. "Oh. Right."

"Right. Do we need to say hi to them, too?"

"I don't feel like it."

"Okay, then, let's not." Gage lifted their bags as she shouldered her purse.

Her cousins approached, wearing matching shocked expressions, one of them going as far as to say, "Andrea. You have a date."

"One who's been itching to get her alone since this morning," Gage said. "Come on, beautiful. Let's test out that bed."

Leaving them gaping in her wake, Andy followed, wanting to punch the air in triumph. Damn, it felt good not to be alone for once. To have someone have her back—hired or no.

Maybe her fears and worries about pretending with Gage were truly unfounded. What was the harm in immersing herself in this role the same way he had?

He wasn't expecting more from her, and he'd already overdelivered on her expectations. She didn't see a reason not to return the affection Gage so easily offered. Especially when they both knew this attraction was pretend.

He walked down the long corridor toward their room and she bit her lip as she watched him carry her bags. He looked strong and sure hefting her luggage. Plus he had a great ass.

She watched his butt, satisfied that she could without worrying what anyone might say if they noticed.

Mostly pretend attraction, she thought to herself.

Seven

"My sister's husbands are nice guys for the most part," Andy was saying as she walked back and forth in the hotel room.

Ever since Gage had placed their bags on the floor in their suite, she'd been a flurry of activity from changing her clothes to touching up her makeup to fixing her hair.

"Kelli and Boyd are the snobby country-club type, but Alec, Kenny and Garrett are okay. I mean, I guess. I don't really know Garrett." She huffed as she tried again to latch a necklace around her neck and Gage stepped in to help.

"Which one's Garrett? Lift your hair." She did and he easily clasped the delicate chain at the back of her neck, smiling at a cute smattering of freckles at her nape.

"Garrett's the groom." She turned, her eyes on his, her high heels bringing them almost nose to nose. "Gwen's fiancé."

She looked away quickly, like maintaining eye contact was hard for her. When she backed away, he crooked a finger, beckoning her to him. She visibly squirmed but came as requested. Sort of.

"Closer, Andy."

One more tentative step brought her to the spot where she'd been standing a second ago.

He smoothed her hair off her neck. "You and I have been dating for eight months, right?" he asked, reminding her of their agreed-upon pretend history.

"Right."

"You're going to have to learn how to be near me without flinching. Am I that unattractive?"

"No. Not at all." She looked genuinely stricken. "I'm sorry if I made you feel that way."

He had to smile. This take-charge, in-charge woman who blew into a room like a frosty chill and froze everyone around her into submission wasn't as cold as she pretended to be.

"Andy."

"What?" Now she looked just plain hurt. "This isn't going to work, is it?"

"Yes. It's going to work." He trailed his fingers down her arm and grasped her hand, brushing her knuckles with his thumb and placing his other hand on her hip. She touched his chest like she had in the lobby, and he heard her breath hitch. "How can I make you more comfortable around me?"

"I'm not comfortable?" she seemed to ask herself. "I thought I was doing better."

So she'd been trying. Interesting.

"We should kiss," she said with a curt nod. "Get it over with."

Now he did chuckle. "Get it over with? It's not going to be like a dental appointment, Andy. I promise." He gestured to his mouth. "I know what I'm doing with this."

Her tongue darted out to wet her bottom lip as she stared at him almost in wonder. He felt the charge in the air—the sexual tension radiating between their bodies. He couldn't get past the idea that she was a live wire, even if she was contented to play the role of the "Ice Queen."

He knew this was pretend—they both did—but he couldn't help wanting to pull warm, responsive Andy from her recesses. He'd started out thinking she was a challenge, but he had the distinct impression that succeeding would be an even bigger win for her.

"I'm all for kissing you. I'll let you come to me, though. I want you to be ready. Once you touch your lips to mine, I'm going to give as good as you do," he promised. "I'll match you stroke for stroke."

"Okay." She rolled her shoulders, readying herself. "I can do this."

He banked his smile as she seemed to steel herself. She closed her eyes, pulled in a deep breath and blew it out. If he hadn't already worked with her for almost two weeks and knew what a goal-oriented achiever she was, he might've been insulted. Andy did whatever it took to win, and evidently winning included kissing him.

Her eyes popped open, determination brewing in their depths. She palmed the back of his neck and slanted her face. He leaned in, mirroring her movements. A fraction away from his lips, she whispered, "Are you sure you're okay with this?"

"God, yes."

As soon as he said the words, she pressed her mouth to his. It was more of a lengthy pucker than making out, but he gripped her waist to encourage her to stay close. He wanted her to take what she needed from him.

When her lips softened, he teased them open with his tongue. She slid her tongue into his mouth and that was when that live wire jolted him. She tasted like mint and smelled faintly of cinnamon. From her hair stuff or her perfume, he wasn't sure. He hadn't noticed it in the lobby, but now it infused every inch of his immediate vicinity.

He'd expected kissing Andy to affect her, and he'd expected to enjoy it. What he hadn't expected was to be towed in by her so thoroughly. The connection—the spark—that had resulted from their fusing didn't stop at their mouths.

She held onto him—her palm gripping the back of his neck, her smallish breasts against his chest—like she never wanted to let go. He tightened his hands on her hips and aligned them with his own. She was an absolutely *perfect* fit. He allowed instinct to drive him as he took the kiss deeper. What had lit between them was a hell of a lot more than he'd bargained for, but he had zero interest in stopping. Unfortunately, she did.

Andy tugged her lips from his, her delicate throat moving as she swallowed.

Gage was still leaning forward, his lips parted, completely dazed by that kiss. Here he thought he'd be the one walking her through the lesson. He'd expected to be the one guiding her. Instead, she'd taken him hostage with her mouth and her skill. He hadn't minded at all.

Take me, honey.

"So." She cleared her throat. "I guess that's not going to be a problem."

"No," he agreed with a grin. "I guess not."

"Ready to go meet the family?" She smoothed his T-shirt that she'd wrinkled in one fist while they'd kissed.

"Sure. Let's do it," he answered automatically, and then on his way down the corridor realized that the last time he'd agreed to such an invitation it'd been when Laura asked him to meet her parents.

Gage had met Andy's sisters at the bar last night—they'd been there with their husbands, who huddled together and talked like they were comfortable with each other. Rather than mingle with them, Gage had chosen to stay by Andy's side.

He was still trying to figure out the dynamic between her and her four sisters. The mother, Estelle, was stern and unfriendly, yet as gorgeous as the rest of the women. They were all tall or tallish, long-limbed and attractive, with varying shades of red or blond hair. Estelle has passed down her high cheekbones and bright blue eyes to most of her daughters.

Andy was reserved and distant, where the other sisters were mostly cozy with each other. Gage wondered if it was because she'd moved away and they'd remained in Ohio. He'd asked her as much when they returned to the room last night, but she'd only shrugged and said, "They've always been like that."

He wasn't sure if it was her sisters who'd ousted Andy or Andy who'd ousted herself. It appeared to Gage that Andy was the one keeping her distance. Although after that run-in with her mother and Ness at the front desk, who could blame her?

But Andy had come alive when Kelli asked her about work, citing her recent successes without an ounce of gravitas. Andy didn't have to overstate her accomplishments. He knew from the experience with her at Monarch—Andy was just that good.

He'd slept like crap last night since the sofa bed was about as comfortable as a pile of cotton balls and wire hangers, but he'd lied and told his pretend girlfriend that he was fine sleeping on it. She'd tried to offer him the bed and said she'd take the sofa, and then he'd had to wonder what kind of dopes she'd been dating.

Whatever ease had come as a result of the explosive kiss last night was gone by this morning. Part of him was relieved, since he'd been thrown so off-kilter by their abundant physical attraction. Andy didn't seem the type to embark on a temporary physical affair. But most of him still wanted to kiss her again and damn the consequences, if not to slake the thirst he'd developed for the confusing redhead over the last couple of weeks.

This morning's activity, according to his itinerary, was brunch with Andy's immediate family. She stalked ahead of him across the green grass, her straight spine evidence that she was back to her no-nonsense self.

The small, catered affair was for the wedding party and close family. Andy fell into both categories since she was a sister and a bridesmaid.

After a quick greeting to a few people he'd yet to meet, they lined up at the buffet packed to the edges with mini quiches, fried potatoes, fruit and every imaginable break-fast meat there was, including prosciutto-wrapped figs.

He picked up two plates and handed Andy hers.

"Thank you," she said. "I'm not accustomed to anyone fetching my plate for me."

"What caveman have you been dating, Andy? This is boyfriend 101." Gage didn't realize anyone was paying attention to them until a bulky guy on the opposite side of the buffet table spoke.

"I was one of 'em, wasn't I, Snowflake?"

Andy bristled, her back going even straighter—Gage hadn't thought it possible. She introduced him, her voice cool and robotic. "Matthew Higgins, this is my date, Gage Fleming." Her tone softened some when she turned to Gage and said, "Matthew and I dated about seven or eight years ago."

"Oh, right. You mentioned him. The one with the pro-truding brow and big head." Gage kept his smile easy.

"Very funny." Matthew really did have a caveman vibe about him. He snapped his attention back to Andy. "Nice to know we regard each other with similar admiration, *Snowflake.*"

"Don't call me that."

"Do you prefer Elsa?" To Gage he said, "*Frozen* wasn't

out when we dated, so I had to make up my own ice-queen nickname for her."

That was what Snowflake was about?

"Freeze you out, did she?" Gage set their plates aside and pulled Andy close. His lips to her ear, he whispered, "You want a repeat of that kiss from last night, now would be a good time."

Her mouth curled into a smile of uncertainty—like maybe she thought she'd heard him wrong.

"I'm game if you are," he announced, happy to have shut out her asshole ex-boyfriend and thrilled that Andy's attention was on Gage instead. Thrilled further when Andy draped one arm over his shoulder and leaned in for a demure kiss. Not a tangle like last night, but the kiss didn't last as long as Gage would've liked.

She lowered to her heels and accepted her plate from Gage, who sent Matthew a smug smile. "She's nothing but gooey with me, big guy." He enjoyed Matthew's deep frown almost as much as him leaving pissed off.

"Thanks for that," Andy muttered as she piled her plate full of fruit. She picked through the croissants while Gage put another spoonful of scrambled eggs on his plate.

"When in doubt, make out."

Her laugh was genuine and he liked it a hell of a lot. He might have first agreed to come here in exchange for her help at Monarch, but he found he also liked protecting her from the vultures circling.

"You're not intimidated by difficult people," she pointed out. "Did you learn that at work, or is your family also challenging?"

"Sorry, can't claim dysfunction. The Flemings are scarily normal. My sister, Drew, and I are close and our parents are supportive. Although they still do weird parent stuff that embarrasses the hell out of us."

"Your sister's named Drew." Andy smiled. "What's she like?"

"She has bad taste in men, a big heart and a lot of spunk."

"Sounds like me except for the big heart. It's always been assumed that mine is missing." She sent a derisive glance in Matthew's direction.

"Sounds to me," Gage said as he placed bacon strips on his plate, "like your ex is in your head."

Eight

Andy followed beside Gage as he made his way to a table with their breakfast. He set down their plates and pulled out one of the folding chairs for her.

The theme was navy and red—Gwen's favorite colors. The tables were decorated with white tablecloths and blue vases filled with dark red roses, the silverware wrapped in navy blue cloth napkins tied with red ribbon.

Like Gwen, the décor was bold and beautiful.

Portable air conditioners stood at each corner of the tent to thwart the summer heat. Andy was glad for them since it was warm already and it was only noon.

"Care to explain your last comment at the buffet?" Gage asked as he sat across from her.

She unwrapped her silverware rather than look at him. "What?"

"Don't 'what' me. You stated you're heartless as casually as you might tell me what time it is. You can't believe that." He jerked his chin over to where Matthew sat with his girlfriend, Amber, one of Gwen's friends and brides-maids. "You don't believe you're an ice princess."

"Ice *Queen*," she corrected, spearing a chunk of pineapple with her fork. "That was a long time ago."

"That isn't an answer."

"I know my limitations. It's part of being a good leader. I'm not warm. I can't help that."

"You were plenty warm when you kissed me a minute ago," he murmured in a low, sexy tone.

He had her there. She'd kissed him to show up Matthew, but the truth was that the second her lips touched Gage's, she'd forgotten her stupid ex was standing there. She'd been lost in Gage's mouth, in his scent. Matthew gaping unhappily was a nice bonus, though.

"That was pretending." She ate the pineapple.

"That was *not* pretending."

"Oh? Are you secretly an escort on the side?" she whispered.

"Maybe." His caramel eyes twinkled before he sent her a roguish wink. "I have been kissed enough to know the difference between a woman who's frigid and one who's—"

"Don't say out of practice." She didn't want to talk about how lame her sex life had been over the last two years. About how she'd tried to be those attributes that didn't come naturally: Bubbly, fun, laid-back. In the end the real her came forward. While she knew she wasn't heartless, she definitely kept a wall around her heart. She felt she had to after the way she'd been let down in the past. No one really understood her. No one had tried.

"I was going to say nervous." Gage's eyebrows lifted. "How long's it been?"

"Long enough that there are tumbleweeds blowing around." She didn't know what made her tell the truth. Although, maybe she did. If anyone could understand the real Andy Payne, it might be Gage. He didn't look at her like a problem to be solved. He saw her success, her timidity, her vulnerability. It'd been a while since a man had bothered to see past her cool exterior.

"Cute *and* funny." He laughed as he dug into his food and Andy was struck with the oddest sense of pride. Gage was cute and funny but she couldn't recall a single time she'd ever been accused of as much.

Throughout her childhood she'd been told she was stiff. Her mother had instructed her to "loosen up" more times than Andy could count. When she and Matthew dated, he'd asked her if she could at least "appear to be having fun" when they were out. She'd always hated that comment. Like she should smile to set everyone else at ease.

Now that she thought about it, all she did around Gage was smile. Not because he goaded her into it. He made her smile just by being himself. He made her feel comfortable even in stressful situations. He helped her crawl out of her head and be in the moment. And she'd really enjoyed kissing him in front of Matthew.

You enjoy kissing him just to kiss him...

"How long did you date that bozo, anyway?" Gage shoveled a bite of scrambled eggs into his mouth.

"A little over a year."

"A little over a year. You're going to let a guy you dated for *a little over a year*, seven or eight years ago, dictate what you think about yourself?"

"This sounds like a lecture," she pointed out blandly.

Andy was accustomed to being misunderstood and/or made to feel less-than. She could hold her own. Until she was with her family, and then those old hurts crept in and made her defensive. The difference here was that Gage was new. He was part of her work, not her personal life. She could compartmentalize that.

"Are you telling me you have no damage? That no one in your past has ever inflicted a wound that carried through into your adult years? That you didn't change some aspect of your behavior because of it?"

Gage was resolutely silent.

That was what she thought.

"Everyone has skeletons in their closets," she told him.

Before she popped a strawberry slice into her mouth, she noticed two of her sisters barreling toward her.

"Hey, you two," Gwen, the blushing bride-to-be, flicked a gaze at Gage and then back at Andy.

"Good morning, Gwen. Ready for the big day?" Gage asked. It was predictable banter but somehow it sounded fresh coming from his mouth. He really was skilled with people. Andy was better with plans. Numbers. Websites.

After Gwen answered that she was "so ready!" Andy's other sister Kelli spoke up.

"Ready for the couples' cruise today?" Kelli gave Andy a saucy wink. "It'll be Andy's first, so we're pretty excited about it."

"*Kelli*." Andy let her tone be her warning, but her eldest sister was not intimidated.

"Couples' cruise?" Gage flashed a smile at Andy and she felt her cheeks heat. She hadn't exactly called it a couples' cruise. She'd told him that they were going on a boat ride, which they were. It was a sizable pontoon boat, which was basically like a floating patio, and Andy was absolutely dreading it. Unfortunately—

"I'm making her come," Gwen chirped. "Andy is totes uncomfortable about it because she's Andy, but I want all of my sisters there."

And that was why Andy was allowing this ridiculous charade to go on. She loved Gwen, and this was her big weekend.

"It's just a boat ride," Andy told Gage, though he didn't look like he needed soothing.

"With champagne and kissing!" Gwen clapped.

"It's tradition in our family," Kelli explained, pressing her fingertips to her collarbone. "I started it with my pre-wedding festivities, and everyone has carried it forward."

"Because it's fun. All eyes will be on you two. You know what you have to do when it's your first CC."

Yep. Andy's face was flame red. She could feel it. Gage's inquisitive look paired with his indelible smile of his and then, to her sisters, he said as smooth as you please, "I look forward to finding out what that is."

What was it, exactly, that had Andy wanting to hide beneath the tablecloth right now?

Gage wasn't sure, but it intrigued the hell out of him. He bade Kelli, who had a conniving glimmer in her eye not unlike Estelle's, and Gwen adieu and turned back to his wedding date.

"Are they going to make you walk the plank or something?"

"Something like that" was the only answer he got.

After brunch Gage and Andy returned to the room to change into "boat clothes." Other than a ferry, Gage wasn't really a boat guy. Not that he was intimidated by a pontoon, or by her family. He wasn't intimidated by much, especially not the couples' cruise initiation that had made Andy twitchy since brunch.

"I packed a few towels from the room into this bag, along with…" He trailed off when Andy came out of the bedroom and into the suite, hair pulled back into a slick ponytail. She wore a gauzy white cover-up over her blue bathing suit. The sight of her legs glued his tongue to the roof of his mouth and stalled his brain. Long, pale, smooth legs. Andy was tall, and at first glance appeared almost too slim. But her curved calves and delicate ankles thwarted that notion immediately. They were subtle, but oh, yes, Andrea Payne had curves.

Her eyes rounded, and her eyebrows rose. "Along with…"

It took him a few seconds to realize he'd been in the middle of speaking.

"Sunscreen." He gestured to the bag. "You're fair-skinned, so I didn't want you to burn."

Very fair-skinned. Her freckles stood out in subtle contrast like her peachy-pink lips. Lips he'd tasted and was already itching to taste again.

"Okay, thanks." She bounced past him and he shook his head. He didn't know how, but was it possible Andy had no idea how gorgeous she was? "Ready to go?"

"Yep." Board shorts and T-shirt on, he pulled the tote over one shoulder and followed Andy to the car. Twenty minutes later they were standing on a dock in the hot summer sun while her sisters and their husbands—or fiancé in Garrett's case—settled onto the wide vinyl seats.

"Whose boat is this?" Gage asked Garrett as he settled in next to him.

"Rental. Biggest, newest one they had." Garrett was Gage's height, a few years younger, but not by much. Gage had talked to him at the bar that first night. The guy seemed cool. Kelli's husband, Boyd, waited by her side while she talked animatedly to her other sisters. Gage sensed a distinct taming-of-the-shrew feel from those two.

Vanessa's husband, Alec, took the captain's chair, wearing a captain's hat to go with it. Gage had pegged Ness as a mean girl the moment she and Estelle pecked at Andy, but he didn't think she did it on purpose. She seemed to like being in charge, though, and he could tell she approved of Alec manning the boat.

Carroll, Gage decided, was the quiet sister. She was amiable and polite, with no real dog in the fight over whether or not Andy would arrive single to the wedding. Her husband, Kenny, was as laid-back as she was, more so actually.

His scraggly goatee and hippie wear gave him a definite I-smoke-weed vibe. Gage had decided Carroll and Kenny were also cool.

"Let's do this!" Gwen called, earning applause. She was the shameless youngest child, happy with the attention, not because she craved it like Ness, but more because she expected it. Cute and plucky, she beamed with an infectious smile that was hard not to return.

Andy sat primly beside him, a pair of sunglasses on her nose and a tentative, nervous smile on her face. Gage lifted her hand in his and kept his gaze on her while he pressed his lips to her knuckles. Her smile shone as bright as the sun overhead...until Ness spoke.

"Aww! Look at those two!"

Everyone focused on them and Andy promptly stiffened and snatched her hand away.

"So shy! Honestly, Andy, who would believe you two have been dating for eight months?" Ness added and sat on Andy's immediate right on the L-shaped cushion.

"Not everyone is as comfortable making out in public as you are," Andy told her sister.

"That's true. And I happen to be really good at it," said Alec from the captain's chair.

Ness smiled, but her expression was as stiff as Andy's spine.

In moments like this, when Gage bore witness to Andy's chillier side, he felt like his past had walked over his grave. As sure as he was that Andy wasn't heartless, he had doubts that pursuing a physical relationship with her—even temporarily—was wise.

During those chillier moments, he was reminded of the idiot he'd been when he promised forever to Laura. She'd made him look like a bigger idiot when he was left holding the engagement ring she returned and the remnants of his broken heart.

Since then, Gage kept things on the surface with the women he dated. He liked women and loved sex, but getting in any deeper wasn't an option. What had started out with a simple agreement to keep Andy on board at Monarch had turned into meeting her complex family, and her ham-handed ex-boyfriend.

And yet he couldn't help coming to Andy's rescue and changing the subject.

"I notice Estelle didn't make the trip," he said to Ness.

"This is a sibling-only affair." Ness swept her hair off her neck and piled it on top of her head in a sloppy bun.

"Hang on to something," Alec announced as they puttered from the no-wake zone into the larger portion of the lake. Cheered on by his passengers, he pushed the speedometer to the middle, sending Andy's ponytail whipping behind her.

Gage settled back, his arm on the bench and Andy sent him what appeared to be a gracious smile. She leaned back into the curve of his arm and he rested his palm on her shoulder. Whatever cooler moments he'd witnessed from her, she was warm where it counted. Andy was completely responsive to him and he enjoyed the hell out of getting her to respond.

Enough lingering in the past. He'd rather sit here, his arm around Andy, and enjoy the cool breeze, hot sun and random splashes of water kicked up by the buoys on the sides of the boat.

Nine

Alec dropped anchor in a private cove surrounded by trees and a few villas. Kelli and Ness opened coolers and divvied out drinks into plastic flutes. Sparkling rosé for the ladies, and ales brewed and canned by a local brewery for the guys.

Andy gladly accepted her drink, letting the bubbles tickle her throat and relying on the summer sun as well as the alcohol to take her down a notch.

Or ten.

No one made her as prickly as her sisters. She wasn't like them—any of them. Sure she might have a dose of Kelli's self-assuredness, but Andy didn't have her eldest sister's confident, sexy vibe. And while Ness was a go-getter, she wasn't plagued by Andy's shyness. Carroll was genuine and sweet, whereas Andy had never been referred to as "sweet," and the bride-to-be, Gwen, was adorable and fun. Andy hadn't been accused of being either of those.

She was the black sheep among her reddish-flaxen-haired sisters, sharing their coloring but not their person-alities. Every time she was around them she felt as if there was an invisible yardstick measuring her to see if she'd blossomed into a *Payne lady* yet, and if her mother's assessment was anything to go by—Andy hadn't.

She'd settled for being the best at her job, and excelling in her field rather than competing socially. They all knew what she did for a living—that she was the mysterious Andy Payne who was often imitated, never duplicated—but praise was more often given for personality and looks—especially by her former-beauty-queen mother.

As a teen Andy had been lanky, thinner than any of her sisters. Fairer, too. By age sixteen her nose was a touch long and her feet a *not*-dainty size ten, and she'd felt firmly entrenched into the black-sheep role she'd assigned herself.

She'd moved away from Crown, Ohio, to become someone else, someone new. Someone who wouldn't be contrasted and compared to her sisters. Her nose was still a touch too long, she was as curve-free as she ever was, and her feet were still a size ten, but she'd used her frosty personality to help build an empire. And she wasn't as socially awkward as she used to be. She was open and polite, even if she didn't exude warmth.

"That went fast," Gage said, taking her empty plastic flute. "Can I refill it for you?"

"Yes."

He pushed his sunglasses on top of his head and studied her, his eyes a lighter shade of brown in the sunlight. The stubble on his chin and jaw was short and rakish, his hair windblown and curling on the ends.

"You have nice hair."

The moment the words were out of her mouth she wanted to die. What a boring compliment. Not to mention it was more the kind of thing you'd say to someone when you'd just met them, not after you'd been in a relationship for eight months. Thankfully no one was paying attention to them or she would've just given away that they'd known each other only a few weeks. Her brothers-in-law were behind them stripping off their shirts to dive in and her sisters were huddled over the ice-filled coolers at the front of the boat, chatting.

"So do you." He wrapped her long ponytail around his fist and gave it a subtle yank, smiling as easy as you please. She swallowed thickly, unsure what to do with the attention.

"H-has it always been curly?" she stammered. Gage looked at her with a combination of heat and admiration, curiosity and a bit of bemusement. Like she was a puzzle he wanted to solve. Another new feeling for her. "Sorry. Stupid question. Of course it's always been curly."

"The bane of my existence." His smile didn't budge. "I try to keep it short, but it still curls." He pushed his hand through his hair again and the wave snapped right back into place. She had to grin. And before she thought of what she was doing, her hand was in his hair, sweeping the strands. It was soft and thick, adding a boyish charm to a man who was *all* man.

"You two are positively adorable," Gwen said, sneaking up on them. Although, you couldn't really "sneak" on a twenty-four-foot boat. Andy had been completely absorbed in her pretend boyfriend. "Did you pick your movie yet?"

"Movie?" Gage asked as Andy returned her hands to her lap.

Gwen aimed her wide grin at Andy. "You didn't tell him." Back to Gage, she said, "If it's your first couples' cruise as a couple, you have to reenact a movie kiss for everyone. Extra points for authenticity."

"Boyd and I did *Gone with the Wind*," Kelli announced proudly. "Ness, *Dirty Dancing*—"

"Complete with dance moves," Vanessa called over.

"And Carroll," Gwen said, "chose *The Princess Bride*, while I went with *Twilight*." The youngest of the Payne sisters swooned. "How I love my sparkly vampires."

"Sorry I missed that one," Andy said, genuinely meaning it. She hadn't made it home for the engagement party here at the resort, which is when the *Twilight* magic must've occurred.

"It's your turn now," Carroll told Andy. "Don't screw it up."

"But first, swimming! It's too hot not to jump in." Gwen tore off her cover-up and revealed a perfect-ten body complete with a belly-button piercing she'd insisted was still "in." A tattoo graced her shoulder blade, a smattering of butterflies and flowers in full color. When her groom called down for her to jump, she did.

Kelli wrinkled her nose. "I'm not getting in that water."

Vanessa agreed and they moved to the other end of the boat farthest from Andy and Gage, while Carroll argued they were "spoilsports" and leaped in behind Gwen.

"Movie kiss, huh?" Gage asked.

"The good ones are already taken," Andy argued.

"Not true. There are lots of great movie kisses available. What about *Dumb and Dumber*, where he tries to eat her face?" At Andy's aghast expression, he chuckled. "I'm kidding."

"I was thinking more like *Lady and the Tramp*. What could we use as spaghetti?" She looked around at a few ropes and wrinkled her nose. Definitely not. But something similar—something tame and not embarrassing.

"What about *The Notebook*?" he asked. "The kiss in the rain is iconic."

It was also…intimate. Plus, Gage would have to lift her and that would be weird. It wasn't as if Andy was dainty.

"No," she told him. "It's not raining."

He narrowed his eyelids as if he knew why she'd bowed out of that suggestion. Then his face lit up. "I've got it."

"What?"

"Nah, I'm not letting you shoot this one down or reason us out of it. I'll tell you right before it happens."

"What if I haven't seen the movie?"

"Trust me. You have."

"What if I haven't?" She liked being prepared—especially for a kiss in front of her relatives.

"You have. But if you haven't, I'll walk you through it."

But that didn't make her feel any better. Her stomach jumped in anticipation, nervousness and excitement switching places in a do-si-do.

"Why me?"

She blinked at the question. "Sorry?"

"Why did you approach me in the bar that night and offer to pay me two grand?" he asked, his voice low so as to not be overheard. "Were you out of options, or was there something else?"

She studied his rakish curls, warm caramel irises and affable smile. She could lie, but she decided not to. "You looked nice."

She winced, worrying that the comment was almost a repeat of the "nice hair" one earlier, but Gage grinned.

"And? Am I?"

"Very."

There was a distinct pause where they watched each other and the pretending seemed to fall away. A moment where Andy caught a glimpse of the possibility of more if she would only open herself up to it… if only he would.

She blinked to break the intense eye contact and Gage's smile snapped seamlessly into place.

"Take this off and swim with me." He plucked the edge of her cover-up.

"That's okay."

"No. It's not. It's a hundred-and-fifty degrees out here. Let's get wet."

Something about the way his voice dropped suggestively made her consider doing more than kissing him. If her tingling innards were anything to go by, she was starting to consider a host of other possibilities.

Naughty possibilities.

"Your face is red already. See? You're hot." He tugged at her cover-up and she let him take it off, holding her arms overhead. She was hot, all right. When the white gauzy material was done obstructing her vision, she came face-to-face with an expression on Gage she'd never seen before. Playful was his typical MO, but this look was…fiery.

Heated and scintillating.

Suggestive, and not in the "pretend" way.

"Hot," he repeated, his smirk twitching his lips. "Damn, Andy." He took her hand and helped her to her feet. Then he grabbed the personalized tote that read Gwen ♥ Garrett where he'd stuffed their towels and sunscreen and produced a bottle.

Wide, warm hands on her hips, he turned her. "I'll do your back."

Gage momentarily lost the thread of whatever he was talking about when he removed Andy's cover-up.

Beneath the shapeless square material was hiding a lithe body. Her shoulders were delicate and round, freckles dotting them like they'd been misted on with a spray bottle. Her back was muscular and strong, and he noticed more freckles as he smoothed sunscreen over her shoulders. There was something intimate about slipping his fingers under the straps of her suit, especially where her bikini top tied into a bow at the middle of her back. His fingers flinched as he imagined tugging that string loose and releasing her breasts, maybe smoothing his hands around to cup them. He'd thought she was a B-cup, but now that she was mostly undressed, he guessed she bordered on a C.

Leaning close to her ear, he said, "Is this okay?"

"Hmm?" She sounded distracted, like maybe she'd been enjoying his hands on her skin as much as he was.

"Are you comfortable with my touch?" He applied the cream to her lower back and braced her sides with his hands. "This is how our kiss will happen," he murmured into her right ear. "I want to make sure I'm not weirding you out."

In a perfect reenactment of what was to come, she turned over her shoulder to look at him, blue eyes wide and curious. A high-pitched voice rang out—Gwen's.

"They're doing it! I know the movie!" she called up from the water.

Gage jerked his attention to the guys and girls in the water, and then to Kelli and Ness on the boat. Everyone was watching.

"No practicing! Do it now!" Gwen shouted with a happy laugh.

"Gage?" Andy's voice was a soft, curious pant. "What are we doing?"

He slid his hands up her waist, lifting her arms and holding them straight out to her sides. He walked her forward to the edge of the boat as their audience cheered.

"*Titanic*!" Carroll shouted.

Over her shoulder, Andy sent him a smile.

"You've seen it?" he asked.

"Of course."

"Then you know what comes next." He tugged her hair from her ponytail, releasing the silken strawberry blond strands, gripped her waist and lingered over her shoulder. As if God was helping out, a breeze kicked her hair at same moment she turned her face to his and he lowered his lips.

The kiss was soft and expected, but what was unexpected was the way her curved bottom nestled perfectly against his crotch as he used every faculty in his brain to keep from hardening against her. She raised a hand to the back of his neck in perfect movie form and held him against her, her fingernails tickling into his hair as he moved his lips over hers.

More cheering erupted from the water and on the boat and Andy eased away from him. Perfectly comfortable and confident.

He loved seeing her that way around her family. Since they'd arrived, she'd been walking on eggshells...or thumbtacks, depending on which of her family members was around. Now, though, the feisty glimmer in her eyes was one he'd seen time and time again in a business setting, where she was cocksure and definitive.

Nothing turned him on more. Especially when she reacted that way to him.

"I'm calling it, guys," Gwen shouted. "Best couples' cruise kiss. Now you two have to stay together forever. You just won first place."

Ten

Andy showered after Gage, insisting he go first so she could take her time. He agreed since his showers took all of two minutes. Now he sat on their suite's sofa, where he was watching TV. The true crime documentary wasn't keeping him from picturing her in there, water sluicing down her trim form and droplets hanging off nipples he'd seen the outline of in her bikini top but had yet to taste.

"Dammit." He adjusted a budding erection and addressed his lap. "We're faking. Understand?"

That wasn't sinking in for any part of his anatomy, including his brain. After the *Titanic* kiss, they'd swum in the lake, the water warm on the surface and bone-chillingly cold at their feet. Since it was sand-bottomed, they'd found water about four feet deep to stand in while everyone enjoyed beer or rosé and the coolness of the water in contrast to the baking-hot sun.

During that time, Gage allowed himself to touch Andy freely and she'd glided against him, her skin slippery from the combo of smooth water and creamy sunscreen, turning him on in a way he hadn't known possible.

She was his colleague, and this was an act. She'd made that clear when she'd invited him, and by footing the bill for his stay. But he couldn't escape the niggling feeling that she was enjoying herself as much as he was. That their chemistry was hot enough that her sisters kept pointing it out.

She'd thwarted her sisters' teasing by batting her lashes at Carroll and rolling her eyes at Ness, but Andy liked him. He could tell. She responded to him. If they were to go to bed together, he would blow her mind.

The only problem was that he wasn't confident he could disentangle from her as easily as he had from, say, Heather, the last woman he'd dated. What he'd experienced with Andy so far—whether working closely with her at Monarch, or hanging out with her family—was deeper than mere surface attraction. Sex wouldn't dampen the simmering attraction between them. It would *ignite* it.

That would make walking away harder and Gage would eventually have to walk away.

The bathroom door swung aside, steam billowing from the small space. Andy emerged, her cheeks rosy, her hair wet and combed straight, a white towel wrapped around her body.

Speaking of igniting...

"I'm sunburned." She pouted.

"What? How?" He moved to her, flicking the TV off as he went and tossing the remote onto the couch.

"I don't know. Maybe the sunscreen washed off."

She turned around and peeked over her shoulder, reminding him of the boat kiss and the press of her ass against his front. He swallowed a groan.

"Here." She pressed two fingers into her red shoulder and the color changed to creamy pale before quickly fading to red again.

"Does it hurt?" He repeated the move on her back where

her reddened skin resembled her shoulders. "Did the hot water of the shower hurt?"

She paused in thought. "No. Not really."

"Then you're fine." He smoothed his fingers along her back and over her shoulder, the feel of her soft skin having a drugging effect on him. Touching her sent his fears of future entanglements up in smoke. The devil on his shoulder assured him she'd be worth it, and damned if the angel on his other shoulder didn't agree.

She came closer and gazed up at him with an earnest gaze almost as naked as she was. Such vulnerability.

Those warning bells made one more attempt to stop him but he justified that Laura had never had this much vulnerability in her eyes.

Or was that longing?

Only one way to find out.

"Do you have any idea how sexy you are?" he murmured.

Her reaction wasn't a gasp of surprise or a sigh of capitulation but instead a challenging smile followed by "Ha! You must have me confused with Gwen. Or Kelli. Or… any of my sisters."

She threw a hand of dismissal that he caught in midair. He tugged her to him, and she gripped her towel with one hand to keep it from slipping.

More's the pity.

"No. I mean you." He didn't smile, making sure she knew he wasn't playing around. "You're sexier than all your sisters put together."

"Gage." She released her hand and patted his chest as if leveling with him. "Save this stuff for an audience."

He gripped her waist and pulled her against him, her towel gaping when she let it go to steady herself by grabbing his biceps.

She didn't believe him.

She had no idea how sexy she was. And that invited a fun challenge that far outweighed his concerns of getting in too deep.

"Want me to show you?" He had to ask. She was too skittish to ask him for what she needed. Plus, he respected her. If she had no desire to find out what he had in mind for her tonight, he'd go back to that horrible pullout sofa bed. He'd go there rock-hard and in need of an ice bath, but he'd survive.

"Show me what?"

He stroked his fingers over her collarbone to her shoulder. "Well. I could point out that you're delicate and strong at the same time." He gripped the towel hanging precariously on her body, holding it closed but allowing his fingers to graze her cleavage. "Then I could mention how much I'm dying to see your breasts after they teased me by bobbing in the lake in that sexy string bikini top you wore."

Her smile slid away, lust blowing out her pupils.

"My breasts…?" Her brow crimped like that phrase didn't compute.

"And those legs." He closed his eyes, flared his nostrils and grunted for effect. "They've been killing me since you started working at Monarch."

"Gage…"

"Am I making you uncomfortable?" His eyes moved to her pink mouth.

"No. I—I was going to ask you if you were serious about showing me."

Hard-on. *Achieved.* His shorts tented and he shifted to bump into her hip.

"Hell, yes, I'll show you. Over and over if you like." He grinned. Excited. Wanting that.

"No making fun of me." She pointed, her voice stern, her finger an inch away from his face. He bit it and soothed the bite by suckling and then letting go in a long, smooth motion.

She licked her lips in anticipation.

"Definitely, you're in need of a lesson, Andy. That is… if this is a yes." He had to be crystal clear she wanted this.

"Yes," she breathed.

Oh, it was *on*.

He yanked her towel aside and dropped it in a damp pile at her feet.

Cool, air-conditioned air hit her body as goose bumps rose on her arms. Gage kept his hands on her sides, but the look in his eyes was feral in the best way. He wanted *her*. He thought she was sexier than all her sisters combined.

She dismissed the possibility that he'd lied about how attractive he found her simply to get into her pants—or *towel* as it were. Andy was no dummy. She'd worked with Gage in close proximity and had been around him enough to see his guard dropped. Gage might very well be the last salesman on the planet who wasn't full of crap.

Which meant he'd been sincere about every nice thing he'd said to her.

"I want to look so bad," he said with an impish smile, and then she realized he meant down at her nude body. He'd kept those melted-caramel eyes on hers ever since he pulled her towel off. The fact that she still held his gaze was a powerful feeling indeed.

Confidence surged through her at earning his attention, at holding the cards. Her *yes* determined how far they went tonight. He'd made that abundantly clear.

Hands on his T-shirt, she gripped twin fists of the material and tugged upward. "I'll show you mine if you show me yours."

"Deal." He had the shirt off in record time and she thanked the good Lord for her sight. Gage's chest was beautiful. The strong, firm pectoral muscles and ridges of his abs. He wasn't so much thick as lean, his waist tapering to a tantalizing V that disappeared into his shorts. Shorts that were straining against a part of him that was definitely, if outer appearances were to be believed, *thick*.

She lifted her eyes to apologize for ogling, only to find his gaze on the ceiling.

"Gage," she whispered, leaning in and brushing her lips over his. There was a benefit to being almost as tall as he was, though now that she was sans heels, she had to climb to her toes a little. "You can look now."

He cocked an eyebrow and lowered his eyes, his smile fading into an expression of awe as he perused her body. He took a full step back, holding her hands out at her sides.

"Damn."

Were a headshake and a *damn* signs of disappointment? She wasn't sure...

"Not what you expected?" She tittered a nervous laugh.

"No." He didn't let her squirm away, cupping a breast and thumbing her nipple. "Better."

His other hand held her jaw and he didn't wait for her to answer before he kissed her, sliding his tongue into her mouth to tangle with hers.

They made out long and slow, his hand moving from one breast to the other as her tender buds peaked at the attention. Her wet hair dripped down her back, leaving trails of water over her backside and doing a good job of mimicking the wetness between her legs.

By the time Gage moved to her neck and was tonguing the very sensitive patch of skin behind her ear, she was wrestling with his shorts and shoving them down his thighs.

"There she is." He sent her a grin that could only be described as wicked. "I've been waiting for you to let go with me, Andy. Since you stalked over to me in that bar, I knew this was in there. All that cool control didn't fool me for a second. You take what you want, don't you, sweetheart?"

Her heart thudded like it'd punched the air in triumph.

She *did* take what she wanted.

At work. In her business life.

But in her personal life, she'd never been so bold.

It was Gage.

He provided a very big safety net for her high-wire routine. Maybe it was their arrangement, or maybe it was simply him. He was easy to be around, comfortable in his own skin, and she'd begun replicating his smooth confidence.

"Are you asking me to take you?" she asked, her smile incurable.

"No. I'm *telling* you to take me. Have at it." He held his arms to his sides as his shorts slid past his knees. Somehow, with his shorts around his ankles and his boxers distorted by the ridge of his erection, he didn't look silly. He looked *scrumptious*.

"We're doing this." She freed him and shoved his boxers down, stomping on them with her bare feet.

He stepped from the inconvenient clothing and kissed her again, moving them to the couch. "Wait, not there. I've slept on floors that are more comfortable."

He routed them through the living room to the tiny kitchenette instead, which wasn't all that far away given the diminutive size of the suite.

"Why didn't you tell me?" Concern wrinkled her forehead. "I would've let you have the bed."

"I know." He gripped her waist and plopped her onto the tiny square of countertop. He had to move the mini coffeepot aside and bodily brace her against the counter to keep her from toppling off.

"What are you doing?" she asked through a laugh.

A laugh! While she was naked, damp parts of her freshly showered body sticking to his sexy, tanned form... She'd never had sex and laughed at the same time. What was it about this guy?

"Countertop sex. I hope. We have a serious real estate problem." He looked behind them at the tiny table and chairs that might collapse under the weight of a stern glance. "Not many options around here."

"What about the bed?"

"*Definitely* the bed. I was saving that for tonight." He kissed her softly. "Assuming I impress you enough to earn a repeat."

"Hate to break it to you…" Looping her arms around his neck, she rested her forearms on his trapezoids and tilted her head. "But considering how long it's been for me, and how forgettable sex has been in my recent and not-so-recent past, that bar is pretty low."

Eleven

And she's funny.

Funny in a clever way. He found nothing funny about her admitting she'd had forgettable or bad sex in the past. He found it...exhilarating. Not to brag—what the hell, it wasn't bragging if it was true, right?—but Gage didn't leave women unsatisfied. And he was never forgettable. Which was part of the problem, since the women he slept with began nudging him toward boyfriend status pretty soon after they did the deed.

He wanted to have a release with Andy—to experience every amazing part of her lithe body—but he also wanted to show this woman how beautiful she was. It seemed like no one had taken the time or effort to show her, and that was a crime.

She didn't curl away from him or appear the least bit bashful now. If she'd been honest about the mediocre sex in her past, he'd raise the bar so fucking high no one would ever compete with him. Gage aimed for 100 percent success in all attempts and right now, with a wet and willing

Andy Payne holding onto him and smiling at him like he was her shiny new present, he'd happily blow her mind.

"Ever done it on a hotel countertop?"

"Can't say that I have." She wobbled and he steadied her by pressing against her. The move had the added effect of his hard-on rubbing against her slick folds and, *God have mercy*, did she feel warm and welcome and good.

So good.

"I have a condom in my purse," she told him, then offered a chagrined twist of her mouth. "It's really old, though."

"Mine aren't." He didn't miss the subtle flinch. He cradled her face with one palm. "I don't mean because I had sex recently. I meant because I *bought* them recently."

"When is the last time you had sex?"

"Long enough."

"I'll tell you how long it's been for me."

"Andrea."

"Yes?"

"Do you want to talk or do you want to fuck?"

He tested her with the harsh word to learn what she liked. To his delight a smile burst forth on her face. "The second one."

Then she bit her lip and his erection gave a happy jerk.

"Okay, then. Don't fall off this countertop while I grab a condom from my bag."

"Okay." She kicked her legs back and forth, knocking the cabinets with her heels and sending her breasts bouncing in a rhythm he could watch all day. He raced back to her, fumbling with the packet, and she took it from his hand.

"Gage Fleming, I think you must be excited." Package ripped open, she reached for him. "Do you mind?"

"From now on, you don't have to ask that." He held the back of her neck as she rolled the condom on. He watched her long, graceful fingers as she sheathed him, and let out a groan.

"Did you like that?" she asked.

"I like everything you do to me. Haven't you figured that out yet?" At her entrance, he nudged, his gaze drilling into hers. He notched the head, blew out a breath and closed his eyes. Nerves tingled and his arms shook. He hadn't been this excited to slide home in...*a while*. More than that, he hadn't been this intrigued by the prospect of sex since he was a hell of a lot younger.

"Gage, yes." She sighed, a breathy exhale that tore him open. He obeyed her tugging hands and slipped inside of her, slowly thrusting as her eyelids sank to half-mast and her mouth dropped open in ecstasy.

This. This was *fantastic.*

"You feel so good," she breathed, wrapping her ankles around his butt to pull him forward on the next long slide.

She raked her nails into his hair and he slammed his mouth over hers.

"So thick," she gasped when their mouths parted. "Big. No. *Huge.*"

He gave her a pleading look. "Andy. Keep that up and this will end a lot sooner than you want it to. Got it?"

She bit her lip and nodded and that sweet, chaste expression did absolutely nothing to help him pull himself together.

He'd started this physical interaction to show her how sexy she was and yet she'd turned the tables, flattering him so much he could hardly keep his head in the game.

Scooping her to him, he tilted her hips and sank into her again. She let out a squeak of delight, her nails scraping his back.

"Yesss," she hissed in his ear. She only got louder as he continued working them into a sweaty lather, especially when he found her G-spot and pulled her down on him hard. It was awkward and clumsy at first but now she clung to him, her limbs wrapped around his while she finished him off. When she shouted her release, he buried his face in her neck and let go.

Seconds, minutes or, hell, hours, he didn't know, later, he surfaced from her cinnamon-scented skin to give her a lazy smile. It was one Andy returned, her cheeks rosy, her body sated and lazily draped over his as he held them against the countertop with what little strength he had left.

"How was that?" he asked, shameless.

The sex had been incredible and he was fishing for as many compliments as she'd dole out.

Fingers finding the curls of his hair, her mouth widened in an equally shameless grin. "You've proven you know your way around a countertop. I guess we'll see what you can do tonight in bed."

The wine tasting that evening doubled as a bachelorette/bachelor party for the bride and groom. Since this was a private event, the wedding party plus guests had the run of the patio, which had been decorated with strings of twinkle lights.

Andy was impressed by how low-key Gwen had kept the weekend's festivities. Her itinerary was nothing like Kelli's or Ness's had been—which were almost military standard by their punctual schedules—though Andy was sure if she was a bride in the future, she'd be much less laid-back than Gwen or Carroll. Gwen's wedding was happening at breakneck speed, somehow fitting in brunch, boating and a wine tasting along with a bachelor/bachelorette party into a single Friday.

"This is such a beautiful venue. Were all of you married here?" Amber, Gwen's good friend and Matthew's date, asked. Andy's ex-boyfriend wasn't sitting with the girls but with the guys, who'd poured cognac instead of wine and held unlit cigars on the other side of the winery's huge patio.

"I started it," Kelli announced, her I'm-the-firstborn-and-pioneer-of-all attitude shining through. "I found the venue and Boyd agreed it'd be perfect. Vanessa followed suit."

"Only because they had the option to be married in the vineyard," Ness defended.

"It's so funny that you all married in order, too!" Amber exclaimed with a sweep of her hand. When that hand reached Andy, Amber caught her mistake. "Oh, well. Almost in order."

Andy gave the other woman a brittle smile. *Rub it in.*

"I'm sure Andy will choose a venue that is on the West Coast when she weds," Ness said. "She's always been one to do her own thing and snub tradition."

Kelli sent a smirk to Andy that wasn't hard to decode. *If she gets married.*

"I'd love to see what kind of beautiful West Coast wedding you come up with, Andy. I bet it'd be gorgeous." Carroll smiled in support and Andy appreciated her sister speaking up for her.

"How long have you and Gage been seeing each other?" This from Amber.

"Eight months," Andy answered automatically.

"So, it's serious," Amber said.

"Looked pretty serious on the boat this afternoon." Kelli trilled.

"Yeah, I thought maybe he'd come as a friend until I saw that kiss," Ness said. "Not to mention you are absolutely glowing-happy right now."

Andy blinked around. The girls were sitting in a circle on metal chairs around a firepit dotted with citronella candles. They were all nodding their agreement.

"What happened after the boat and before this wine tasting, anyway?" Carroll asked with a teasing wink as she raised her wineglass to her lips.

A rush of confidence pushed a smile to Andy's lips. "Oh, you know. We went back to the room and showered. Then...watched some TV," she said coyly.

A round of *woots* and giggles lifted on the air and she looked up in time to see Gage smiling his approval.

She wasn't used to taking her sisters' teasing in stride, but their playful pokes didn't so much as ruffle a single one of Andy's feathers. She supposed she had Gage to thank for that, too. He'd praised her for being sexy, had turned her on like a light switch and then made love to her standing up, giving her the discretion to invite him to her bed tonight.

Andy had practically floated here on a balloon filled with her own confidence. Confidence at work, she was used to. Confidence around her family was a whole other experience.

One she embraced.

"You two are seriously compatible," Gwen said, noticing Andy and Gage's eye-lock from across the patio. "I love you together. Reminds me of me and Garrett when we first met."

"Which was what, about seven minutes ago?" Ness teased, and everyone laughed.

Gwen and Garrett had been seeing each other less than two months when Gwen announced her engagement. As crazy as it'd been to receive that email from her sister, Andy had passed it off as kismet. True love had the reputation of finding people when they weren't looking for it.

Andy bit her lip in thought. True love wasn't what was between her and Gage, but there seemed to be *something* there. She wasn't willing to deny herself the experience of sex with him, but now that it'd happened she wondered what life would be like when they returned to Seattle. When she followed up with him to ask how the team was doing in the office. She'd only asked for his help for the weekend...but what if it blossomed into more?

Did she want it to?

"Gage is yummy. Am I allowed to say that?" Carroll refilled her wine and gave Andy a cute but slightly sloppy wink.

"Yes. I think we can all drink to that. If it's not too weird for Andy that we objectify her date," Ness said.

"Gage can handle it." Andy sneaked a glance to find him laughing with the guys, though when he ducked his head to take a drink from his glass, she noted him glaring at Matthew. That made her like him more.

"Those curls are to die for. He has this sort of school-boy charm," Kelli said. "But one look at his ass and it's clear he's all man."

Andy blushed, but couldn't help adding, "You should see the rest of him."

Howls of laughter erupted in their circle and Gwen gripped Andy's forearm in support. "I love you like this! So open and happy. It's awesome."

It *was* awesome. Andy shook her head, but not in disagreement—in surprise. "I guess I always felt like the black sheep. The odd one out."

Gwen abruptly sobered, her eyebrows twin slashes of concern. "We don't see you that way."

"At all," Kelli chimed in.

"If anything you're the pioneer of all of us," Carroll agreed. "Over there in the big city making a name for yourself."

"Living life on your own terms," Ness added, and Andy blinked at her in shock.

Whatever brought forth that moment of rallying, whether the wine or the weather, Andy welcomed it.

"Thanks, guys." She raised her wineglass. "Cheers to Gwen and Garrett!"

Everyone joined in on the toast and Andy, as relieved as she was to have the attention off her, also allowed a little part of her to bask in the newfound feeling of fitting in.

Twelve

Gage caught Andy peering over her wineglass at him and had to smile. Damn, but his sexy strawberry-haired vixen would be the death of him. And if that was the way he'd go, he was sure he'd die a happy man.

Nothing had turned him on more than turning her on. Watching as she surprised herself by liking him so much, by liking sex on the countertop so much. He'd enjoyed the delighted, satisfied smile on her face as much as he'd enjoyed the sex itself. Pleasing her pleased him, and the prospect of doing it with her in a bed tonight was a welcome one. Especially after she'd had a few glasses of wine and was loose and sleepy.

Whatever flashbacks of his ex-fiancée had haunted him before, he was glad to have pushed them aside in favor of indulging with Andy.

"You and Andy, huh?" Matthew Higgins, known to the rest of the guys as "Higgs," asked.

It was rhetorical, though, a way to bring up Andy and goad Gage into a fight. Gage knew Matthew's type. Mean. Stupid. The kind of guy who had to prove he was the biggest, strongest man in any gathering. Gage couldn't care less about bravado. He knew exactly what Matthew's insistence on drawing attention to himself meant. It meant that Matthew had a small dick.

"She's always been a puzzle," said Kenny, who stroked his beard in thought. "But then I saw you two together and it was like the puzzle was a whole picture."

"Uh, thanks." But Gage's smile, though slightly perplexed, was also grateful. Ness's husband, Alec, spoke next.

"Andy surprised us, is what Kenny means, I think." Kenny gave him a thumbs-up, and Alec's eyebrows jumped. "Anyway. She's been a loner for as long as I've known her. Except, well…when she dated him." He gestured to Matthew, who puffed out his chest.

Moron.

"Eh, Andy and I weren't long for this world. She doesn't mesh with me. She's brisk and curt. Professional and cold. Smart as a whip, though. I'll give her that."

Gage's blood was set to simmer. Between clenched teeth, he managed, "Must've been you."

Matthew's lips oozed into a smile. "That so? Did you thaw our little Ice Queen, Gage?"

"She's not *our* anything, prick." Gage's anger spiked and he took a step toward the larger, dumber man. Andy might not belong to Gage, either, but he'd be damned if he'd let her ex stake some sort of claim over her.

"Okay, Higgs." Alec put a hand on Gage's chest and patted a few times. "Last thing Gwen and Garrett need is a fistfight on their wedding weekend."

"If you do anything to make Gwen cry, I'll beat your ass myself," Garrett promised, his eyes on Matthew. "Including upsetting her best friend, your date."

Garrett capped off that statement with a smile, but it was a humorless one.

"Far be it from me to ruin anyone's weekend," Matthew

grunted. To Gage, he said, "If Andy's happy with you, I guess congratulations."

"Gee, thanks, Higgs," Gage grumbled.

"I like Andy," Garrett told him, trimming the end of his cigar and passing the trimmer to Gage. "She's probably like the rest of our girls in that there's another layer to her when you two are alone. Another side of her that she doesn't share with the world."

"Gwen has a side other than bubbly and cute?" Alec asked, disbelieving. "And here I thought she was a fairy princess."

The rest of the guys chatted about their wives, but Gage found his mind wandering to his own Payne royalty. Gwen was a fairy princess, and Andy believed she was the Ice Queen—no thanks to the Neanderthal "Higgs" across from him who puffed on his cigar. Matthew had set himself away from the guys as if by choice, but they'd shunned him by subtly turning their backs.

Gage peeked over at Andy, who was sitting, legs crossed, in a pair of white capri pants and a radiant red blouse. She was smiling, her wineglass aloft, her eyes light and happy. It was so good to see her comfortable around the women she'd compared herself to for years and never thought she'd measure up to.

Gage had told Andy she was sexier than all of her sisters combined and he'd meant it. He perused the Payne women, including her mother, who was just joining them, and noticed a tall, older man—Andy's father, Gage would bet—angling for the guys.

Andy stood out in stark contrast from the women surrounding her because he knew that secret side of her the guys had hinted their wives had, too. Gage knew a part of Andy few others did, and that made him want to uncover more.

"Well, well. If it isn't the man who's stealing away my

baby girl." The tall man with white hair boomed as he held out a hand to Garrett.

"Abe. Good to see you." Garrett straightened some, taking the man's hand in a solid pump.

Greetings happened all around, with newcomer Garrett visibly less comfortable around Abe Payne than the rest of the guys. Admittedly Gage also felt a pinch of discomfort when Abe settled his navy eyes on him.

"You must be Andrea's date."

"Gage Fleming." He shook Abe's wide palm, noting the way Andy's father hulked over him, and Gage wasn't a short guy.

"Hmm. Surprised she brought someone."

Gage prepared for a comment like Estelle's or Vanessa's had about Andy not being able to scrounge up a date, but Abe surprised him by saying, "She's usually too independent and discerning to bring a date. Except for this bozo." He shot a thumb over his shoulder at Matthew, who for once looked nervous.

"How are you, sir?" Matthew extended a hand. A hand Abe ignored before sending a barely tolerant headshake to Gage.

Gage grabbed a cigar from the table behind him. "Cigar?" he offered Abe, suddenly a big fan of Andy's father.

"Thank you, Gage." Abe clapped his shoulder. "I think we're going to get along just fine."

"One more, c'mon!" Gwen goaded as she tipped the bottle of chardonnay precariously over Andy's glass. It was the end of the last bottle, however many that'd been. The waitress had efficiently removed the empties, which made counting hard.

"*Fine*. But that's it," Andy acquiesced as Gwen drained the last few ounces of wine from the bottle to the glass.

The Payne women, with their Irish blood, were no strangers to *the drink*. Andy's mother, Estelle, sat rosy-cheeked and laughing, her air of superiority drowned after the first glass. Kelli and Vanessa had relaxed, too, and Carroll and Gwen were punchy and giggly…even more so than usual.

Andy was somewhere in between, as she'd always been with her sisters. She wasn't as ruthlessly serious as her older sisters, but not as laid-back as the other two. She'd often landed in the middle, and where they'd been comfortably paired off with each other, she supposed it made sense why she'd labeled herself the odd woman out.

"Oh, great, cigars. When did they light those?" Vanessa grumbled, her good mood ebbing.

"Eh, boys." Kelli threw a hand. "Boyd knows he's not getting any tonight, anyway."

"Uh-oh, what'd he do?" Carroll asked playfully. "Forget to iron your socks again?"

Andy and Gwen sat forward in their chairs and laughed heartily at the insult. Even Kelli and Vanessa couldn't keep from joining in.

It was a true rarity for Andy to have this kind of evening with her sisters. Where every one of them was loose and relaxed and no one was passing judgment. Gwen's best friend had since collected Matthew and left, so it was only the Paynes and their significant others on the patio. Andy decided to hell with sizing them up. For the remainder of the weekend, she'd just *be*.

They might've been the dominant excuse for her bringing a date in the first place, but Gage had become more than a stand-in so that she could avoid judgment from her family. She now saw that each of them had their own issues, less concerned with Andy than she'd originally imagined. Gage accepted her, liked her, for who she was. It was past time she accepted *herself*.

"Looks like Gage is abstaining," Estelle pointed out, tipping her chin toward the group of guys. Sure enough, Gage stood, arms folded, unlit cigar cradled between two fingers. He was participating in the conversation with everyone, but not smoking. Interesting.

"That must mean he and Andy have some sexy plans tonight." Gwen elbowed Andy in the arm. "Do tell, sister. How is he?"

"How *big* is he?" Carroll chimed in.

"Girls!" Estelle covered her ears. "I'm not listening to this." Vanessa pulled their mother's hands from her ears and then Estelle said, "Unless you'd like to hear details of your father's—"

"No!" all five sisters called out in unison.

Estelle grinned, pleased that her bluff had worked.

"You don't have to be graphic," Carroll stated.

"But be a *little* graphic." Vanessa leaned forward in her chair. Even Kelli looked curious.

"I'm excusing myself to the ladies' room." Estelle threw her hands into the air and hustled off to the restaurant. When she was gone, Andy's sisters raised expectant eyebrows.

"Gage is…attentive."

"Oh, I love attentive," Carroll said, nodding in support.

"Is he a slow kisser? A deep kisser?" Gwen asked, chin in her hands and elbows on her knees.

"Yes to both," Andy answered, and sighs of delight echoed around her. "I don't know what's going to come next. He goes from kissing my mouth, to my neck, to that part behind my ear."

"I *love* that part." Kelli sat up now, too, her attention on Andy.

"What about the first time you ever had sex?" Vanessa asked on a whisper. "Where was it? How long did you wait?"

"Well…it was…more recently than you might think," Andy said, her tongue loosened from the wine, and yeah, she was caught up in the attention.

"How recent? And where? How did it happen?" Carroll asked rapid-machine-gun-style.

Andy opened her mouth, unsure what would come out of it when a low male voice interjected, "Whoa, whoa, whoa… What did I walk in on?"

Every one of her sisters sat up, backs straight in their chairs as Gage rounded behind them and aimed accusatory looks at each one.

"Leave you alone for a few minutes, and you're telling all." Hands on Andy's shoulders, Gage kneaded her tight muscles. He'd done a good job of loosening her up earlier, but now that easy-breezy feeling ebbed away.

She shut her eyes, mortified that he'd overheard her. This was why she never allowed herself more than two glasses of wine! She became caught up, the wine an elixir urging the truth from her. She'd forgotten that she had a story to keep up with: a *pretend* boyfriend she was *for real* sleeping with.

How had the lines gotten so blurry?

"Gage. We were just—" she started, lamely.

"You women are worse than those guys over there," he said, but she could hear the smile in his voice, the teasing tone that was good-natured and so *Gage*. "Ready to head back, sweetheart?"

"We noticed you didn't smoke a cigar," Kelli said, crossing her legs. She'd recovered from being busted quicker than any of them. Even Ness looked a bit chagrined.

"Not tonight."

"Oh? Why's that? Plans with Andrea?" Kelli asked.

Gage took Andy's hand and helped her stand. When she faced him, he said, "Yes. I have *many* plans for Andrea tonight."

Thirteen

"That was a close one." Andy had been on the spot in front of her sisters. The jig would've well and truly been up if she'd even hinted at the fact that hers and Gage's first time had been *today*.

"I thought I'd whisk you out of there before you had to make up a story about the first time we had sex. You liked me coming to your rescue." He tossed their suite's key card on the counter where they'd had sex hours earlier, and then he gripped her hips, pulling her in front of him. "Admit it."

He'd been dying to kiss her again all evening, and while he hadn't minded leaving her sisters with something to chew on, out-and-out PDA seemed over-the-top for Andy.

"I did love it." She swept her fingers into his hair and toyed with the curled ends. "You claimed me."

His eyes sought hers, lost in the depths of those earnest blues. Andrea Payne was a woman who was smooth and detached on the outside. A woman who knew what she wanted and how to get it. A woman who, to achieve a goal, would approach a man in a bar and offer him two grand to come with her to a wedding. What she didn't know about herself, and what Gage was trying to show her, was that she was also soft and caring, giving and loving. She was sensitive and demure, and the slightest bit shy, and every one of those attributes did it for him. Especially when they came wrapped in a package of freckles and strawberry hair and blue eyes so bright he could sink into them for days.

He blinked, jerking his chin back in shock. Normally when it came to women he wasn't this…poetic. Could be the cognac. Could be the setting—love was in the air.

Or it could be that he'd been taking this pretend role of boyfriend to real extremes.

He hadn't been a boyfriend in a long, *long* time. The last time he'd escalated to fiancé and that wasn't something he was interested in repeating. When Laura left, he'd felt filleted. Like someone had stripped out his bones and left him a heap of flesh on the floor.

Yeah, no repeats on that, thanks.

"No one would've believed we waited eight months before making love on a countertop at my sister's wedding retreat." She played with his hair some more. "We didn't wait more than a few weeks before we caved."

"Two weeks too long," he admitted, his earlier reminiscing forgotten.

Right now was about *right now.*

He'd didn't typically worry about the future and he'd be damned if he ruined the weekend with it now. He moved her hair over her shoulder. "When you came at me like a lioness in that bar, I'd decided to take you home and damn the consequences."

"Is that so?" She tilted one eyebrow. "What about that cute bartender you'd been flirting with all evening? Did you swap her for me so easily?"

"You were watching me." He narrowed his eyes in accusation.

"I—" Her mouth gaped for a second. "Only between bouts of my date talking incessantly about himself."

"What did you see when you looked across the room at me, Andy?"

"You mean other than an opportunity?"

He smirked at her deflection. "How'd you know the bartender wasn't my girlfriend?"

"I didn't. I…assumed."

"And you also assumed I was a sorry sap in dire need of two thousand dollars."

She squeezed her eyes closed, her cheeks going the sweetest tinge of pink. "I didn't think you needed two thousand dollars." When her eyes reopened, she looked up at him with such raw vulnerability, his heart clutched. "I thought it'd take two thousand dollars to convince you to say yes…to me."

He gripped her chin and lifted her face just enough to keep her eyes on him while he made sure what he said next sank in.

"Honey, I was going to take you home based on one look. Based on you stalking toward me like you wanted to make a meal out of me. And trust me when I say, I have a very good reason for not liking that look on a woman."

"Sounds like a story."

"For another day," he said. "I liked your determination. You saw what you wanted and you were coming to get it. Certainty, *honesty*, is a huge turn-on for me."

"But you said no." Her eyebrows pinched.

"You offered to pay me!" He let out a chortle, his fingers threading in her hair. "Tell me if I'd have offered you the same you would've gladly accepted."

"Oh. No. Of course I wouldn't have… I'd never…" Her fingers came up to cover her lips as she pushed his arms aside. Between her hands she said, "Gage, I'm so sorry I made you feel…cheap."

"You made me feel confused, Andy. Not cheap. In no way should you have ever felt like you couldn't earn a yes from me instead of buying it." He tugged her hands from her mouth and kissed her fingers. "You're worth it."

In the distance of Gage's mind he was aware that this was how he gave women the wrong impression: by being likable. By being honest about what he liked about them. But he couldn't help being likable any more than he could help liking Andy a bit too much. A bit more than common sense suggested he should...

Her hand came to rest on his chest and she gave him a push. "You like me determined, Fleming?" she asked, her voice hard and unyielding.

His lips twitched, but he didn't dare smile. "Yes, ma'am."

At her playful shove, he walked a few steps backward toward the bedroom.

"Good. There are things I want from you," she stated.

"Oh?" He was intrigued as hell. "What things?"

"I want to taste you." Her fingers trickled down his button-down shirt. "I want to feel you hard and heavy in my mouth."

His eyes zoomed in on her plush lips as she—God help him—swiped her bottom lip with her tongue. *Slowly*. His cock gave an insistent twitch from behind his fly.

"Take off your pants," she commanded.

Gage wouldn't allow her to do all the commanding. He had things he wanted to do to her as well. Instead of obeying, he cupped her jaw with both hands and kissed her sweetly. The sweet turned to hard, the hard to long, the long to soft. When he pulled away, she whimpered her protestation at losing his mouth. He took advantage of her being dazed and unbuttoned her pants, sliding his hand into her panties to find her damp and inviting.

Against her parted lips, he whispered, "You first."

* * *

Waves of pleasure streaked up her spine as Andy came at Gage's command. He hadn't even taken her pants off yet. Instead, he'd rooted them to the spot on the floor and moved from stroking her to sliding a finger deep inside of her. When a second finger joined the first, her talented wedding date thumbed her clitoris once, twice…and the third time was a charm.

She opened her eyes, her breathing erratic, her palms resting on his shoulders. She might topple over if she didn't hold on to him. But she didn't find a pleased smile on Gage's face, no. He was all heat and seriousness when he lowered his lips to hers. His whisper was hot, his breath coasting over her lips when he said, "That was beautiful to watch."

She'd never been with anyone like him. Someone so confident and easygoing, and…well, who *liked her*, quite frankly. She'd never liked someone as much as he liked her back, so the mutual attraction was brand-new.

"Thank you," she breathed.

That brought forth his brilliant smile. "Show, don't tell, Ms. Payne."

She bit the inside of her cheek, knowing what he was referring to. She'd made him a promise. Reaching for his hard-on, she massaged him and earned a deep kiss for her efforts. In a blur of movement, Gage maneuvered them backward into the bedroom while keeping their lips sealed. She unfastened his pants as he tore at her shirt, leaving them in a pile on the floor.

When he reached the bed, she undid his shirt one button at a time, revealing his chest and smoothing her fingers over the scant hair whorling around flat male nipples, dusting his clenching abs, and finally to that trail of hair that disappeared into his black boxers.

"I've never been so excited to have someone naked before," she said, half surprised she'd said it aloud.

"Honey, have at it." He thumbed her cheek as a deep breath lifted his shoulders and broadened his bare chest. Anticipation hung heavy in the air between them. She let it linger for a few agonizing seconds and then dropped to her knees and tugged on his boxers.

"Look at me when you do it." He wound her long hair around his fist and held it away from her face.

She licked her lips and his hips surged forward. He was suddenly intense, not the same playful guy from earlier. She couldn't wait to experience his flavor, and was trying to decide if she would linger at the head or pepper the shaft with kisses.

She started with a sweet kiss to the tip. His answering groan spurred her on, bolstering her confidence and making her sit a little taller. When she opened her mouth to accommodate him, she did as he asked and turned her eyes up to his...

Gage typically held off coming by reciting the last quarter's sales numbers in silence, but with Andy's eyes zeroed in on him, he couldn't concoct a single thought that didn't involve her. On her knees, her fingers lightly tickling his balls, and those blue, blue eyes fastened to him and holding him hostage.

He locked his thigh muscles as she took him deeply into her mouth again and again. He didn't think of sales numbers or baseball stats, or any other helpful distraction that might keep his release at bay. He didn't want to miss a single second of Andy making love to him with her mouth.

She was a glorious sight. Her pink-tipped breasts bare as she knelt there in nothing but a pair of black panties. The way she gripped his shaft with nails painted the same color red as her shirt had been.

Mercy.

She'd be his undoing. He was sure of it. He wasn't sure what that meant yet, and he wasn't sure he would've changed a damn thing if he'd known before now, but she was not unlike a female praying mantis. He was willingly, gladly allowing himself to be devoured.

Thoughts of cannibal insects and his imminent doom faded away when she swirled her tongue and took him deep. His hand that had been holding her hair out of the way tightened into a fist and he let out a grunt, followed by a plea.

"Can't...believe I'm...saying this..."

She let him go before slowly taking him deep again and his brain blanked. Seriously, he had nothing in his head during the next slick slide, but his memory returned when the telltale tingle of his pending orgasm shimmied up his spine.

"Stop, sweetheart. I need to be inside you. *Now.*"

He watched as she let him go, his length slipping from her wet, parted mouth.

God.

Damn.

He blinked. Hard. Resetting his brain and hopefully gaining a modicum of restraint. He lifted her by the elbows, helping himself to exploring her plush mouth when it reached his.

"You are so hot it's ridiculous," he panted. "You could lead me around with that move, you know that?"

She offered a pleased grin as he worked her panties down her legs. "Does that mean you're my sex slave now?"

"Yes," he said without hesitation. Though he didn't like the idea of any woman leading him around by the pecker, for Andy—for this weekend—he could make an exception and forgive himself for it later.

"On your back, beautiful. Let's do this properly."

She lay down and pushed herself up the bed, gloriously naked—all that smooth skin exposed for his eyes and his twitching fingers. He slid his hand from her hip to her ribs and back up to her breasts.

"So much better." He kissed her lightly. "No complicated countertops or vertical maneuvering."

"Yeah." Her smile the slightest bit shaky. Before he could work out what that meant, she said, "Condom."

"Right." Right! Wow. Where was his head? He'd been consumed with being inside her and totally forgotten about protection. *Rookie move, Fleming.*

Again that distant alarm rang, a little louder than before. It hinted that he was in deeper than he'd intended, but that was stupid. This was a temporary arrangement between them—they were completely compatible physically. No reason not to enjoy themselves.

Repeatedly.

He retrieved a condom from his wallet and rolled it on, returning to Andy. Then he lifted her leg and lined up with her center, enjoying teasing her. Enjoying watching her hands clench the sheets into a wad, her lips parting in anticipation.

"You want me, Strawberry?" he asked.

She didn't take him to task for the nickname, only hastily nodded.

He didn't tease either of them any longer, thrusting inside of her in one mind-melting slide. She cried out, her pleasure infusing the air with a scent not unlike the cinnamon of her perfume.

He repeated the action again, again, until she locked her legs around him and cried out with wild abandon. He lost track of his voice as well, especially when he came on what would qualify in most countries as a roar and collapsed on top of her. His entire body was buzzing, his head detached, a slight layer of sweat sticky between them.

He returned to earth when Andy's fingers found his hair. A move that was already becoming familiar to him, and was unique to her.

That caused another alarm to break through the haze of his orgasm.

But he ignored that one as well.

Fourteen

Gage woke to the telltale clicking of computer keys, his head swimming through a seascape of dreams. He opened his eyelids a crack to notice two things: one, it was still dark outside, and two, Andy was sitting up in bed next to him, laptop on her lap, naked breasts highlighted in the bluish light emanating from the screen.

He stretched his hand across the bed—king-size, so he had a way to go—and brushed her thigh with an open palm. She started, jerking her head over to him before flashing him a grin. And flashing him, period, considering the movement also shifted her long hair from where it covered her breasts and out peeked a nipple.

"What are you doing?" he asked, his voice sleepy and craggy.

"Working," she whispered. "Did I wake you?"

"Yes." He sat up in bed next to her, propping a pillow behind his back. He pressed a kiss to her shoulder. *Mmm.* She smelled good. He lingered on the second kiss and she sighed, a soft sound from her throat, before giving in and turning her head for a kiss. A kiss he almost gave her.

"Hang on." He wandered out of the suite and into the bathroom, using the facilities before washing his hands, face, and finally scrubbing his teeth. He wasn't going to kiss her long and slow if he had dragon breath, that was for damn sure.

When he emerged, she was standing in the living room, bare-ass-naked. "If you're going to brush your teeth, then I have to, too." She seemed inconvenienced by this, but he was glad to see that the laptop on the bed was closed.

He climbed back into bed and glanced at the clock, doing a double take. When Andy meandered back into their shared room, teeth brushed, he pointed at the digital readout. "It's barely five a.m."

"I know."

"Does the word *vacation* mean nothing to you?" He rarely saw the other side of six o'clock in the morning. Whenever he'd tried to start his day earlier than that, he'd met it grouchy and groggy. He was still groggy, but his grouchiness had been replaced by another feeling entirely, considering Andy was crawling toward him in bed, her breasts shifting temptingly with every move she made, her hair tickling up his body.

She rested on him, chest to chest, and Gage cupped her bottom, his grogginess dissipating when she leaned in to kiss him slowly.

"I'm an early riser."

He pushed his pelvis into hers, his arousal making itself known despite what time it was. "Me, too, but never this early."

Not that he usually had a reason to wake hard and ready. Rare was the occasion a woman stayed over. And on the off chance she had, he pretended to be fast asleep until she left so they didn't have to do this dance. Many, *many* lines were being crossed with Andy, and while he knew that wasn't cause for a panic attack, he reminded himself not to get used to it.

"What time's the rehearsal?" he asked around a yawn. "Early, right?"

"Ten o'clock."

In the morning, he knew. Evidently Gwen and Garrett had opted to rehearse for the wedding the morning of the wedding, which wasn't typical. He remembered that from the quick scan of the itinerary.

"That gives us several hours," Andy purred before pressing a kiss to his shoulder. Then his neck. When she opened her mouth at the base of his throat, he slid his arms to her back and squeezed.

"I need my beauty sleep," he joked.

"Sex first, then you can sleep, princess." She nipped his bottom lip and soothed the twinge with a kiss.

"There is some serious role reversal going on here," he pointed out. "I don't like it."

"You don't like not being in charge?"

"Correct." He was all-the-way hard now, the languid, teasing kisses and verbal sparring turning him on regardless of what ungodly time of morning it was. "I have a better idea."

He reversed their positions, rolling Andy to her back and sliding down her body as he laid kisses here and there. Her eyes widened with excitement.

"What are you doing?" The question burst from her like a bottle rocket, capping with her stopping him when he began kissing a line down the center of her breasts.

"Making sure you go back to sleep when I'm through with you," he mumbled against her skin, shaking off her hands to kiss her flat belly.

"Gage." She clamped her legs together, her hands returning to his hair. He gave her his attention and that was when she shook her head. "You don't want to do that."

"Oh, but I do." He removed one of her hands from his head and kissed her palm. "You touch my hair a lot."

The panicky expression gave way to a shaky grin.

"I don't remember any woman I've been with who played with my hair the way you do."

"Sorry."

"Not a complaint. And right now a big turn-on." He put her hand back on his head. "Pull when I do something you like and I'll keep doing it until you explode." He gave her a wink, licking a line just under her belly button before moving to her thigh and kissing there, too.

Her clean scent hit him, musky and inviting. He absolutely could not wait to taste her. To make her scream his name.

"But…"

With a sigh, he raised his face from the cradle of her thighs.

"You're sure?"

"Andy, haven't you ever done this before?" A rhetorical question, because surely…

But she slowly shook her head, and in the sparse light from the digital clock he could see her cheeks darken with color. He had no idea how that was possible, or what dickweeds she'd dated who didn't take the time, energy and effort to satisfy her—but…

He knew of one, didn't he?

He kept his eyes on hers as he lowered his lips to just above her center. "Step one—" he licked her seam, thrilling when desire bloomed in her eyes and her mouth dropped open "—let me do all the work."

Shifting her so that her knees were resting on his shoulders, he opened her to him. "Step two—" he placed another reverent lick to the heart of her "—instructions are encouraged. Faster, slower, left, right, that kind of thing."

She bit her lip—to keep away a smile, he was guessing.

Her shoulders had come down from her ears, and he wondered if that was because he'd just made it clear she had no need for performance anxiety.

"Step three—" instead of one lick, he delivered several in rapid succession, loving the way she thrust upward toward his seeking tongue "—enjoy yourself. This is all for you."

Her fingers were in his hair, seeking, pulling and pushing or a combination of all three when he went to work. When she was close, she rewarded him with a high cry and he doubled down on his efforts, concentrating on that one spot in particular designed to make her lose her mind. She never gave him instructions but she never had to. Soon she was coming, clenching around his fingers, which he'd added to help her get there, and crying his name on a weak, sated shout.

Hell.

Yes.

He kissed her hip bone and then her ribs, placed a loving peck on each of her nipples and then suckled her earlobe when he reached it. Her heartbeat was erratic, her breathing labored and her eyes closed.

"Wow" was the first word she said. And Gage, who'd meant that exploration as a precursor to some really great morning sex, decided he'd let her ride this wave into oblivion.

"Sleep well, Strawberry." He gave her one last kiss and she grunted what might've been a word if he hadn't rendered her every muscle useless. Proud of himself, he rolled over, his erection protesting. He ignored it. She needed that—worse than he'd originally known, apparently—and he'd been the first to give it to her. That special sort of release when you're the center of the attention—the very attention she'd given him without hesitation last night.

In the dark, she began to lightly snore and he smiled in

wonderment at the creature who'd brought him here, bedded him and confused him constantly.

Who was this woman?

And how, in all of his years of folly and dating, had he never met another like her?

Andy showed up for the casual brunch rehearsal wearing a light floral dress rather than the navy blue bridesmaid's dress she'd purchased for Gwen's navy-and-red-themed wedding. Gwen had eschewed the traditional rehearsal *dinner* for a casual brunch rehearsal, which was being held in a tented-off area in view of the lake.

The sky was heavy with clouds, but the weather was warm. The app on Andy's phone showed the skies clearing by noon, and nothing but sun after, which was good news for Gwen and Garrett's 4:00 p.m. ceremony.

Gage accompanied Andy to the rehearsal even though she'd assured him he didn't have to come. He didn't need to rehearse for anything. He'd insisted, though, saying he'd better regain his strength and *"have something other than you for breakfast,"* which made her remember how completely he'd spoiled her this morning.

After he'd successfully tranquilized her by going down on her, she'd slipped off into the most pleasant sleep of her life before waking him an hour later in much the same fashion. The sex had been electrifying and gratifying, and yet lazy and languid, the way morning sex should be.

She'd ridden him, her hair tickling her back, and he'd held onto her hips, lifting to meet her with each languid thrust. It was the kind of sex a girl could get used to, but that thought made her melancholy, so she'd ignored it all morning. If there was one clear boundary line between her and Gage it was that they shouldn't get too used to being together.

"I'm grabbing a bite to eat that's guaranteed to be less satisfying than you," Gage whispered in her ear.

She ducked her head, suddenly shy at the copious attention. He placed a kiss on her temple before leaving her to her sister Gwen, who appeared uncharacteristically nervous.

Uh-oh.

"Hey. Everything okay?" Andy asked.

"No." Gwen's gaze flitted left, then right. "Carroll is my maid of honor, and Garrett's best friend is Kenny, so that worked out perfectly. But you're my bridesmaid and so is Amber, and Amber is dating Matthew, who is your ex."

"Right," Andy said, waiting for the other shoe to drop.

"Garrett doesn't really like Matthew."

Andy didn't really like Matthew, either.

"But he's in the wedding party. Because I love Amber and she's in love with Matthew and wanted him to be her partner. So I talked Garrett into it, which makes me feel awful…but worse than that—" Gwen winced "—I didn't warn you about Matthew being here. I'm a giant coward."

Andy tracked her eyes past Gwen over to where the wedding party was gathered near the wedding arch. Granted, she didn't like Matthew any more than Garrett did, but she wasn't going to ruin her sister's day. "I'm sure it'll be fine, Gwen. We've survived this weekend so far without incident."

Except him referring to her as Ice Queen. But Gage had been there to stand up for her.

"He said you called him and he told you he'd be here."

Andy stiffened. She'd called Matthew to ask him to be her stand-in date, in a fit of insanity, apparently, but luckily never had to ask. Matthew had interrupted and bragged about attending with another date—Gwen's best friend, Amber.

"I did... I did call him. I was curious about how he was doing. It was a random whim," Andy lied.

"I should have been the one to tell you—to warn you. It'd been so long since you two dated... I guess I didn't give it much thought." Gwen pressed her lips together before adding, "Are you sure you're not mad at me for not warning you?"

Andy palmed her youngest sister's shoulder, relieved Gwen wasn't instead suspicious over the reason that Andy had called Matthew in the first place. "No, Gwen. I'm not the least bit mad."

"Good." Gwen's shoulders sagged in relief. "You're walking with Garrett's good friend Jon, who arrived this morning. He's in the blue shirt."

Andy spotted the slender, smiling man in khakis and a golf shirt. "Okay."

"Don't be mad about this, either, but I sort of told him you were single."

"Gwen!"

"I didn't expect you to bring a date! If he hits on you, break it to him gently."

Andy sighed. Just what she needed. First, she'd barely scrounged a date for this wedding, then she'd learned Matthew would darken the wedding's doorstep, and now she was sleeping with her pretend boyfriend *and* had another suitor asking if she was available? She'd never had so many man problems in her entire life.

One more look at Gwen showed that she wasn't her normal happy-go-lucky self. This must be what the pre-wedding bridal jitters looked like on her. Kelli had had an outburst about her bouquet containing the wrong kind of roses, Ness had dissolved into tears when her flower girl refused to wear the tiara that matched her own and Carroll had done a shot of peppermint schnapps to ease her last-second nerves before she walked down the aisle.

"I'll let him down gently," Andy assured her.

"Thank you." Gwen beamed. "I'm getting married."

"You are!" Andy couldn't help smiling back at her youngest sister. She was enjoying herself so much now that she was here. Andy had Gage to thank for that. He seemed to be the common denominator in every moment she'd been at ease. "I'm so, *so* happy for you and Garrett."

Gwen embraced her in a tight squeeze that made Andy's eyes watery. "I'm so happy for you and Gage. I know Ness and Mom can be complete pains in the rear about pairing you off, but they want what's best for you deep down on the inside."

Andy hoisted a brow. "It must be buried deeper than the mines of Moria."

Gwen giggled, loving the *Lord of the Rings* reference, as Andy knew she would. "Thanks, Andy. I appreciate you being understanding."

"Sure thing." She followed Gwen to the wedding arch, toward Matthew and the stranger she'd be paired with in the wedding, and drew back her shoulders in determination.

She could do this.

And maybe it was better if she did. She'd used Gage as her security blanket for long enough. Andy could handle this part on her own.

Better get used to it, a tiny voice warned.

Soon she'd be back in Seattle and their bout of pretending would be over. But their physical connection wasn't pretend for her at all. She wondered if it was for Gage, or if, like her, he was steeling himself for the end.

Fifteen

Around noon the clouds swept aside like curtains, parting to reveal the sunshine. By the time Gage made his way to the wedding area, the grass was dry and the day warm but not too hot.

He was invited to sit with the remaining Payne sisters who weren't included in the wedding. He overheard Ness say she'd begged off, not wanting "to deal with another useless bridesmaid's dress."

Not that he'd ever accuse any woman of being an "Ice Queen" but he wasn't entirely sure how Andy had earned that moniker over Vanessa.

Gage took the seat next to Boyd on one of the white plastic folding chairs arranged in rows. He turned to smile at the tiny flower girl walking down the aisle beside Carroll, who was helping the little girl throw petals. The tot probably had no idea why she was dressed in a white confection and all eyes were on her.

Next came the bridesmaids, and Gage turned expectantly to see Andy. She'd left him in the room, her dress in a bag tossed over her arm, and promised to see him at the wedding. There'd been an awkward moment when she'd debated whether she should kiss him goodbye or not, and then she had. Just a quick peck on the side of his mouth. He'd wished her good luck.

The sight of her now stole the moisture from his mouth. She was…ethereal.

The navy blue dress was knee-length, the sleeves designed to reveal her creamy shoulders. Her hair was pulled back on one side, the strawberry blonde color a stunning accent to the blue. The photographer leaned out of an aisle to snap a photo and Andy smiled, her plush lips shining with sparkly pink gloss. When she caught sight of Gage, her smile stayed but turned demure, the joy in her blue eyes zapping him where he sat.

Then she walked past him to take her place up front, and Amber followed. By the time the music changed to introduce the bride, Gage didn't want to take his eyes from his date. And when a white-dressed Gwen strode down the aisle to take her place next to Garrett, Gage felt his forehead break into a sweat.

Could've been you.

He'd been to weddings since his engagement with Laura had imploded. He'd always had a date, so that part wasn't new. He'd never pictured himself in the role of the groom, with a bride in white coming toward him down a long aisle.

Until right now.

Gripping his hands in front of him, he forced himself to take a few long breaths. When Boyd eyed him curiously, Gage gave him a pained I'm-fine smile. Eyebrows bowed in sympathy, Boyd patted Gage's back gruffly and then turned to watch the ceremony.

What was that about? What was the back-pat and that knowing smile supposed to reinforce? Gage swiped his brow again. When it came time for the prayer he ducked his head, but his eyes and thoughts stayed on Andy.

Andrea Payne was a puzzle, like Kenny had said.

But Kenny had also said that when Gage and Andrea were together, Kenny could see the full picture. That picture spread out before Gage now, even though he didn't quite know what to make of it.

He saw Andy in his future.

That wasn't something he'd been able to say of any woman besides Laura. But he was enamored with Andy in a way he'd never been with any woman—and that *included* Laura.

In the midst of pretending to be Andy's boyfriend, Gage was feeling particularly boyfriend-like. He was going against several rules he'd set up to protect himself, including endangering the bachelor pact he and Reid were still upholding.

Gage wouldn't muster up a version of a wedding of his own—lest he throw up on his and Boyd's shoes—but he could safely state that when he and Andy returned to Seattle, he'd like to keep seeing her.

Thing was, he wasn't 100 percent sure she wanted to keep seeing him.

So.

That was new.

Typically, it was the woman he was dating who was leaning on him a little too hard. Crowding into his space and wanting the "more" he couldn't give her. Meanwhile here he was, literally a few days into this…fantasy romance, and starting to feel a whole host of things he shouldn't.

Particularly when Andy rested her hand on the arm of the groomsman she'd been paired with and they both smiled at the camera.

If Gage were to let this affair end, he imagined Andy would eventually find a man worthy of her time. They couldn't all be duds. Maybe even after she and Gage split, the nice-guy-looking groomsman would call her up.

"Hey, Andrea. You remember me? Pencil Neck from Gwen's wedding? I thought we could get together sometime for a bland dinner before I try to impress you with a few of my lame bedroom moves."

Gage felt his lip curl at the idea of another guy trying to spend time with Andy. Possessive was another trait he'd never had to contend with. But here it was, as gritty and basal as he'd ever imagined.

Whenever he looked at Andrea Payne, a bolt of certainty shocked his gut with a single word.

Mine.

He wanted her, and he'd had her.

But he hadn't had *enough* of her.

Even though previously he'd decided beyond a shadow of a doubt that he would never get married or engaged.

Was there an in-between? Was Andy the kind of woman who would settle for some but not all?

He was beginning to think he wasn't that kind of guy. That he was instead the kind of guy who'd like to get married someday. That he was the kind of guy who'd like to have a family and a wife and buy a house with a yard he had to mow.

But only if that future included Andy.

So.

Yeah.

What the hell was he supposed to do with *that*?

Thankfully the tradition of a formal wedding party dance wasn't one Gwen and Garrett kept. The happy couple finished their dance as husband and wife and then the DJ played a song about single women that would inevitably herald the bouquet toss. Andy settled in at the round table decorated with red roses in navy vases, her hand in Gage's, content not to move. Until…

"Get up there, girl," Kelli goaded.

"Me?" Andy shook her head. "I'm not single. I'm here with Gage."

"Yes, but you're not married to Gage. Or engaged to Gage." A small frown marred her sister's forehead. "Are you?"

"No." Andy shook her head and met Gage's eyes. He looked slightly green and she could imagine why. Pretending to be her boyfriend was one thing. Pretending to be her fiancé was a whole other level of OMG. "But I'm not single."

"That's not how it works." Kelli grabbed Andy's hand and dragged her to the dance floor, where Amber was already boogying to the music.

Andy stood behind Amber and the other four girls who were on the stage, arms in the air. Gwen searched the crew of available bachelorettes and Andy quickly shook her head. Gwen smirked, slapped her hand over her eyes and threw the bouquet high.

It arced toward Amber, but the toss was high and Amber was about six inches shorter than Andy. Either the gorgeous bouquet of blue roses with red ribbon hit the dance floor and exploded into a shower of petals, thereby ruining her youngest sister's day, or...

Andy held out her hands in a show of an attempt. The bouquet landed prettily in her palms like Gwen had aimed directly for her.

Cheers rang out and Andy held her prize overhead, her headshake a combination of chagrin and *that-figures*.

But when she caught sight of Gage applauding, she felt happy she'd gone along with this farce anyway. Just to have him here with her—just to be in his company. Even if it was only for the weekend.

The DJ called for the single guys as Andy stepped from the dance floor, and this time it was not Kelli but Garrett calling to the men who'd rather not stand up and catch Gwen's garter.

Garrett shoved Jon onto the dance floor as a random smattering of single guys shuffled into their spots, beers in hand. Andy tried to hold Garrett off when he angled for Gage, but Garrett only winked at her.

"Sorry, Andrea. He has to make an attempt. Especially since you have the bouquet." When Garrett slapped Gage on the back, she also heard him say, "You don't want Jon slipping a garter onto your girl's thigh, now do you?"

Gage sent a heated glance over his shoulder at Andy and flames licked along her body like he'd touched her instead.

Saucy, silly burlesque music piped from the speakers as Garrett shimmied a garter belt from high on his bride's thigh. He slid it down the remainder of Gwen's leg with his teeth, which made everyone cheer and clap except Abe Payne, who covered his eyes when he received a few elbows to the ribs.

"Okay, gentlemen!" Garrett called out. "Who's next? Hey! Hands out of your pockets." After calling out a few of his buddies, Garrett flipped the garter into the crowd like a slingshot, and Jon made a hearty reach for it. He had a few inches on Gage, but Gage made a play for it, launching himself higher by using Jon's shoulder as leverage and snatching the garter out of midair.

Andy applauded when Gage sauntered over, spinning the garter around his finger as several of the guys patted his back.

"All he needed was the right motivation," Garrett shouted as he grabbed a chair and dragged it onto the dance floor.

"Come on, beautiful." Gage offered his hand to Andy. "Let's do this."

She tucked her palm into his. His easygoing attitude had shifted slightly. He was still fun-loving Gage, but a ribbon of seriousness threaded through him as he sat her on the chair and she lifted her leg. His smile was there, his silliness as he verbally urged the crowd on while he slid the garter up her leg, but she couldn't escape the idea that something had changed within him without her knowing. Especially when he tugged her skirt down, helped her stand and asked her to dance as the fast beat slowed into the next ballad.

Couples joined them on the floor and Andy rested her arms on Gage's shoulders as they began to sway.

"Sorry about that." She forced an eye roll even though she wasn't very sorry at all. "I appreciate you defending my honor, though."

"No way was I going to allow Jon—or Matthew—to win that prize and touch even an inch of your leg with their grubby paws."

She giggled. "All my life I've never known a man to be possessive over me, Gage. I think maybe I was lowballing you with my offer of two grand. You're worth much more."

His smile fell, and again she felt as if he was more serious than before. He pushed her hair off her neck, tracing the line from her collarbone to her shoulder. "Have I told you how good you look in this dress?"

"Thank you."

He had. At the start of the reception, when they had parted ways, her bridesmaid chores complete.

"I'm glad you asked me to be your date," Gage said, sneaking a look around to make sure no one was near them. "And for allowing me to share your bed. I have a proposition for you in return."

"Oh?" She bit the inside of her lip, a parade of naughty possibilities lining up to conga through her brain. Would he suggest sex somewhere public, but hidden in shadows? Maybe he wanted to make love by moonlight on the boat. Or maybe, when they went back to the room, he would get a bucket of ice and tease a cube along her inner thighs…

"When we return to Seattle, what if we don't stop?"

She swayed in his arms, not understanding his meaning. "Don't stop what?"

"Any of it. You coming to my place. Me to yours." He turned them in a smooth circle. "I can't promise opportunities for garters or dancing, but the rest of it—the meals, the dates, the waking you up by going down on you—" he whispered, leaning in "—why stop now?"

Sixteen

Andy had been putting off thinking about life back in Seattle until after the wedding was over. But the weekend was winding down quickly, wasn't it? It was nearing the end of the time she and Gage would spend together and now that she allowed herself to think about what that meant for them...well, *not* seeing him didn't sound even a little appealing.

"You want to keep seeing me?" She was still trying to wrap her brain around that. It wasn't a typical discussion she'd had with her mediocre dates and underwhelming boyfriend prospects.

"We're good together, Andy. I didn't come here expecting...this." He raised their linked hands to gesture around them. "To be this comfortable with you. Especially in this scenario."

"Hmm. You're going to need to explain that." He'd hinted that there was a story from his past before, but he hadn't shared it. By her estimations she had him right where she wanted him.

"Wondered if I could escape explanation." He sighed heavily.

"You can," she told him, quickly changing her tune. "You don't owe me anything. But since we're planning on *not stopping*, it would be nice to know you a bit better. Beyond the biblical sense, I mean." She winked and he chuckled, settling into their dancing rhythm with ease.

"Since you've just agreed to my terms, I suppose I could indulge you with a few details of my sordid past."

"Oh, sordid. That's a good beginning to any story."

He took a deep breath before he spoke, like there was still a part of him that was resisting. "I was engaged when I was a junior in college."

"Young."

"Quite." He lifted a sardonic eyebrow. "Laura and I... ended our engagement."

"Code for she dumped you."

"Precisely. After that engagement ended, I decided this—" he jerked his chin to indicate the wedding guests, tent and the bride and groom themselves "—wasn't for me. By then there was a pact issued by my buddies that we'd agree never to marry."

"Which buddies?" But she had a guess.

"Reid and Flynn."

"Ha! But aren't Flynn and Sabrina...?"

"Yeah, they are. He broke the contract, but after seeing them together it made sense. You've seen them. It's undeniable how they feel about each other."

"It's pretty obvious," she agreed.

"Anyway, he's been married before, and once the divorce was underway, he was the one to reinstate the pact. He was upset, as well as he should've been since his now ex-wife cheated on him with his brother."

Andy sucked air through her teeth. "Yowch. Tell me

there was nothing that ugly behind the ending of your engagement with Laura."

"No, nothing like that," he said easily enough that she believed him. "We were young. It wouldn't have lasted."

The music faded into another slow song, and they kept on swaying.

"So what is your modus operandi with dating now? Or do you exclusively bail out women in need of wedding dates so long as they pay your room and travel?"

"Believe it or not, you are my first. Typically, I just… date. I don't have any weird rules or anything, but I don't ask for more. And if she does…" He shook his head.

"So you sleep with these women and then leave a trail of broken hearts when they start wanting more?"

"First of all, there aren't that many of them and few leave brokenhearted, so stop making me sound like a lothario." He tugged her so that they were dancing cheek to cheek and lowered his lips to her ear. "Secondly, you didn't ask for more. I did."

He pulled away and pegged her with a look that said, *There you go.*

Andy digested that information, feeling like it was substantial in a way that it wasn't before.

"You haven't wanted more with the women you've dated since college, but now, after only a weekend with me, you know you do?"

"I know I'm not ready to stop talking to you. Or kissing you. Or sharing a bed with you. So I guess my answer is yes. After this weekend, I *know* I'm not through with you."

There it was. Out loud.

Right about now he should be shaking and nervous the way he'd been when he was watching the wedding procession and eyeing Andy like she might be the cause of his pending breakdown.

But he didn't feel that way. He felt like pulling her closer and inhaling her cinnamon scent.

So he did.

He clasped her back and held her to his chest and let his lips hover just over hers. Her fingers wrapped around his neck, and when she slid them into his hair, he had to smile.

"I'm not sure what to say about any of this except the truth." Vulnerability danced in her eyes but she didn't look away. His brave girl.

"Hit me. I can handle it."

"I've never had a relationship like this with anyone."

"You mean fake for the sake of your family?" he teased.

"No." But she smiled like he'd intended. "I trust you, Gage. Maybe more than I should, but I'm acting on instinct whenever I'm with you. Which is probably why I haven't denied myself much where you're concerned."

"That makes me sound like an indulgence and I really, *really* like that."

"You are an indulgence. And I never indulge."

He'd bet. Every lean curve on her not only reflected good genes but also suggested a rigid workout regimen and being mindful of every calorie she ate.

"Especially in the bedroom," she whispered before covering his lips with a soft kiss.

"Check, please," he muttered, only half kidding.

"I'm going to visit the ladies' room." The song ended and the couples on the dance floor moved away. Perfect timing.

"I'm going to the bar, where I'll grab a water and dump it over my head." When she laughed, he added, "And down my pants."

"I'll meet you over there."

But when they parted, he didn't want to let her go, holding her hand until the last possible moment when her fingers slipped from his.

"Sap," he muttered to himself, quelling the panicky feeling in his belly before it bloomed in his chest.

So, he'd asked to keep seeing her. So what? He didn't promise her forever. He could be with Andy and not end up like Flynn and Sabrina.

Gage wasn't done with her yet, and that was enough for him. They were in a safe space to continue riding the middle until it made sense not to be together any more. There was no reason to believe what they had would doom him to forever.

And there was no way to deny that her agreement to keep doing what they were doing made him damn glad he'd brought it up.

Andy walked from the frigid air-conditioned building into the warm, welcome summer breeze of the tent.

She moved to her table to grab her purse and found her sister Vanessa cradling a half-full glass of white wine and looking unhappy, which seemed to be her normal expression. Ness had always been a serious sort. Andy had that in common with her sister, but she wasn't pessimistic, as evidenced by the conversation she'd just had with Gage.

He wanted more. She wanted more. It wasn't a bad way to strike a bargain, either—he'd held her on the dance floor while telling her he'd suffered an ill-fated engagement. And that pact. She'd have made a similar deal with her girlfriends if she'd come that close to matrimony and then had her heart broken.

Andy took a swig from her water glass, lingering next to Ness for a moment.

"Everything all right?" She probably shouldn't ask, but she loved Vanessa, grumpy or no.

"It's always like that in the beginning," her sister responded darkly. Ness gestured with her wineglass to Gwen and Garrett, who were all smiles while dancing to a swing song. "The infatuation and love…and *blindness*. Then a few years go by and what's left is disillusionment and disappointment."

Andy followed Ness's gaze to where Alec stood chatting at the bar with Kenny and Gage, the three of them looking chummy. Andy lowered into the white folding chair next to her sister and leaned in. "Are you and Alec okay?"

Ness's mouth hardened into a flat line. For a moment she looked as if she might cry, but she blinked and jerked her face around, her expression flat but still pretty.

"I don't mean this in an unkind way, Andrea," Ness said, and Andy felt her back stiffen with dread. "But what you have with Gage is fleeting. So enjoy him. Enjoy the sex. The rapt excitement whenever you two lock eyes. But don't become entrenched. Don't put yourself in the position of being in a relationship you can't escape. And whatever you do, don't involve paperwork."

"We're…not planning to" was all that Andy could muster as a response.

"Save yourself." Ness finished the remaining wine in her glass and stood. "I'm getting a refill. Want one?"

Andy shook her head, shocked by…well, pretty much everything her sister had just said.

She'd thought Ness and Alec were doing fine. Thought they were happy, even. Granted, Andy hadn't seen them together much this weekend.

A niggle of doubt crept forward. Ness wasn't wrong. Even if one does make it to the altar, the ultimate step in any relationship, everything could still fall apart. And if that was the case, what could any of them count on? She stole a glance at Garrett and Gwen. How long would they be happy?

How long will Gage and I be happy?

Another peek over at Alec proved there was more under the surface than Andy had previously noticed. His smile fell when he met his wife's glare across the tent, his shoulders lifting as if bracing for bad news. Ness approached the bartender to order and Alec curtly smiled at Gage and Kenny, excusing himself before walking off in the opposite direction.

"Oh, Vanessa." Andy sagged in her seat, sad for both her sister and brother-in-law.

They'd been married, what, five years? Six? Wasn't that the point when you could relax in a relationship? Weren't things supposed to get better and better? A closer look at Kelli and Boyd showed they were having no qualms about their own marriage, slow-dancing despite a fast song playing. Even Carroll, who was shimmying with Amber, paused to blow Kenny a kiss that he pretended to catch in his fist. And obviously, Gwen and Garrett were at the peak of happiness today.

Gage parted from Kenny with a wave and walked toward Andy, his sights set on her. He held a glass of whiskey—or some kind of brown liquid—with a single, large ice cube floating in it.

"Danced out?" he asked as he sat next to her.

"Just...resting." She didn't want to air Ness's dirty laundry. It wasn't her story to tell.

"You sure?" He swept her hair aside and kissed her bare shoulder.

She wasn't sure. Not really. But at the same time she wasn't willing to mire herself in her siblings' problems. What would come of Andy and Gage remained to be seen.

They weren't five or six years into a relationship potentially circling the drain. Hell, they hadn't even put a timeframe on what they had. Continuing to see each other back in Seattle might not last a month.

She wasn't willing to stop kissing him or sleeping with him or enjoying him just because the clock struck midnight on Gwen and Garrett's wedding. No matter what the future brought.

"I'm positive," she said instead of sharing her tumultuous thoughts.

She stole a kiss from Gage, letting her lips linger over his, palming his scruffy jaw and then slipping her fingers into the open placket of his shirt.

There was one surefire way to dissolve the worry Ness had planted in the back of Andy's mind, and that was to do what she and Gage were best at doing.

By the time she ended the kiss, he was on the literal edge of his seat, his breaths hectic and erratic.

"Want to get out of here for a few minutes, have some fun, and then sneak back in and eat some cake?" she asked in her best sex-kitten voice.

"Hell, yeah, I do." He stood and pulled her with him, thrusting her purse into her arms. "Lead the way."

Seventeen

Gage pressed a kiss to the left of Andy's spine, then to the right of it, continuing the line of kisses as he drew the zipper on her dress up, up, up until she was dressed.

She sighed, contented, and admittedly sort of lost. Not literally. They might've stolen off to the woods for a quickie disguised as a nature walk, but they weren't far from the festivities. She could see the lights twinkling from the tent and hear the faint sounds of the band playing.

"That was a first," she said when Gage kissed her shoulder.

"Outdoor sex?" He scooted closer to where she sat in the grass and wrapped his arm around her waist. "I like hearing that."

"What about you?" She shifted to face him, her legs damp from the dew. Now that night had fallen and the sun was down, the humidity sitting in the air had fallen to the ground. She recognized her error in asking when a firm line found his lips. "Oh. I guess... Never mind."

"Not what you think, Strawberry." He tucked her hair behind one ear.

She'd worn a clip holding that side up earlier but had no idea where it'd disappeared to since her and Gage's...*dalliance*. Having sex outside should've felt needy and shallow, but it had been deeper to her.

"The truth is I'm experiencing a few first times with you, too," he said. "You're different."

She opened her mouth to give him a snarky "I know," but he cut her off with a finger to her lips.

"Ah-ah. Your differences are all good ones. When I'm with you, it's not about the setting or the act." He tipped her chin. "It's about what it feels like to be with you. Like I can't get enough."

Nervous at his admission, she swallowed. "Don't go endangering your pact now." The mention of him never being serious with a woman was supposed to ease her nerves and his, too.

"The pact? You think you're in danger of being proposed to?" He canted one eyebrow and gave her an easy smile.

"God, no. What was the catalyst for Flynn reinstating it, anyway?"

"Veronica. He proposed to his first wife pretty quickly. They'd only known each other a month before tying the knot. Flynn believes if he hadn't married her, they would've imploded naturally, and way before an ugly divorce, or her cheating on him with his brother. A lot of pain could've been avoided."

"Garrett and Gwen had a quick engagement." Andy cast a worried glance in the direction of the tent. "Did Flynn and Veronica start out as happy as Garrett and Gwen?"

"No." That made her feel marginally better for her youngest sister. "Veronica and Flynn were never compatible where it counted."

"He and Sabrina seem to be on the same page."

"Those two." Gage emitted an amused sniff. "They've been best friends since college. Sabrina predated Reid and me by a few weeks. Somehow Sabrina and Flynn had circled each other for years. Too distracted by dating people other than each other, I guess."

"That's sweet." And it made sense. A relationship built over years and years had a strong foundation. "They seem solid. I can see why he didn't stick to his pact… But you did."

"Yes, the Brit and I carry that torch." A self-deprecating smile decorated Gage's handsome face. "For me it was about not being engaged again. For Reid, well, who the hell knows? He was in no matter what. He's never been one to get too attached."

"I know what that's like." When she found Gage regarding her with a curious head tilt, she explained. "It's hard to get attached and then be left behind. If you're not careful, your identity can become wrapped up in someone else."

"You're the independent sort."

"As are you."

He seesawed his head like he was turning over the thought. "Not exactly. I'm a team player. I like having someone. I like dating but I rarely turn and burn them like Reid."

"You're a serial monogamist."

"I don't know about that. But I can definitely feel when I'm getting in too deep, or when she's getting in too deep, and that's when I button things up."

"Sounds sort of awful."

"You mean I sound awful now that you know how shallow I am?"

"No. I mean it sounds like an awful way to live. Like you're too afraid to keep going when there's potential for a real connection."

He watched her in silence for so long that a breeze swelled and she became aware of the music again. It also made her aware of the party they were missing.

The truth was she was afraid to pursue more with Gage, too. She'd never pursued deep connections in the past, even with her sisters. She'd gradually accepted that those sorts of relationships were for other people—people other than the Ice Queen, though that nickname had lost some of its sting.

She was changing, little by little, and the man next to her in the damp grass was a big reason why. She didn't know what that meant for them, but she did know that she wasn't giving him up just yet.

Outside of the "wedding bubble," and when they stopped pretending, did they have a prayer of making it last?

She wasn't sure that was the right question, considering Gage had made a pact never to marry anyone. She wasn't in the market for a husband, either, but she'd be lying if she said she'd never imagined what marriage might look like for her. How could she hang any hopes on what she and Gage had together, knowing that he'd walk away with hardly a second glance?

Since those thoughts were too big for her, and much too big for the end of a wedding reception, she shut them down.

"Come on." She stood and extended a palm to Gage, who was still sitting, his back to a particularly stout linden tree. "I need one more glass of champagne."

One more glass of champagne, one more dance and at least one more evening in Gage's arms before she lost her glass slipper at midnight.

Then it'd be airport, home, work and...whatever else followed. She hoped he still fancied her as much as he did in this moment.

Only time would tell.

Gregg and Lee Fleming had been residents of Leavenworth, Washington, for every year that Gage had been alive. The town was rich in Bavarian/German ancestry and boasted a festival every year to celebrate.

Gage's parents had been coworkers at the Leavenworth fish hatchery until recently, when his mother retired to start her own online business crafting quilts and pillows. His father still worked there and loved every moment of it, even though Gage had paid their mortgage off last year so that his father could retire. Stubborn old man.

Leavenworth was a shortish two-hour jaunt from Seattle, so Gage saw his parents often enough for his tastes.

His sister, Drew, admitted she'd like to see them a little *less* often, but Gage had goaded her into hosting the family visit this time around.

Drew's apartment was in a nice, newish building in Seattle teeming with millennials and career-driven singles. She'd ended up as career-driven as Gage as it turned out, the worry of ending up at the hatchery a worst-case scenario for her as well.

"Mom is driving me crazy," Drew said in a harsh whisper as she pulled the lid off a pineapple upside-down cake their mother had brought for dessert.

Dinner had already been consumed—fish tacos, of course. Gage's father insisted on bringing his hard work to the table even though Gage had eaten enough fish to sustain him for a lifetime.

"I told her *three* times that Devin couldn't come to dinner because his schedule is too demanding and still she accuses me of 'hiding' him. I don't know why they want to meet him so badly anyway. He's a chef, not a celebrity."

Gage bit his lip. To Drew, chefs *were* celebrities. She was a public relations manager for various restaurants under the corporate umbrella of Fig & Truffle. She managed soft openings mostly and was a self-proclaimed foodie. She poked at the pineapple upside-down cake and frowned.

"I should've had Devin make crème brûlée."

"Don't be a snob."

She stuck her tongue out at him and he smiled. She left

the room with a confidence that didn't used to be there. He admired the hell out of her for it—his sister hadn't always been so sure of herself.

She'd always been petite, though, which had been her downfall when she was younger. Her curvy figure had been named a "weight problem" by their less-than-eloquent mother, and Drew had referred to herself as "chubby" which showed even less eloquence.

Gage might have noticed his sister looked different at age sixteen versus age twenty, but it wasn't as if the fifty or so pounds she'd lost had made an iota of difference in how much he loved her.

He was glad she went after what she wanted. She'd always contended that good food was her number one passion, and she wouldn't sacrifice a pat of real butter for margarine no matter what health magazines suggested. She'd balanced her fitness goals and her passion, never indulging in too much of either one. Gage couldn't be prouder of his only sister.

He turned to resume making his and Drew's drinks, not the least bit intimidated by the fancy espresso maker in her apartment—they had one like it in the executive break room at Monarch. It made him laugh that while her dining room table was a scarred hand-me-down from their parents, her espresso maker was top-of-the-line and probably cost close to what it would take to replace that entire dining set twice over. Drew had her priorities straight, Gage thought with a smile.

Their parents had retired to the living room, which was connected to the kitchen. Drew came from that direction now to grab dessert plates as he finished their espressos.

He handed Drew one of the petite cups and she sagged against the countertop. "Why aren't they giving you a hard time about meeting who you're dating?"

"Because I never tell them I'm dating."

The TV was blaring so loudly that he was confident neither Mom nor Dad could overhear the discussion in the kitchen. Fine by him. The less they knew about his love life, the better.

"You would've been smart to keep Devin to yourself. Or Ronnie, for that matter," he said of her last bad breakup. Devin didn't have much more potential than Ronnie in that arena. Gage had met Devin once and, culinary degree aside, had determined he was a self-indulgent butthead, and that was putting it kindly.

"I *like* talking about my feelings." She sipped her espresso and her eyebrows jumped. "Mmm! This is delicious. So, big bro, do tell. Are you seeing anyone?"

He debated his answer for one sip, then two, from his espresso cup. Finally, he opted to level with Drew, since they'd been nothing but honest with each other for most of their lives. "Her name is Andy. I met her at work and she asked me to attend her sister's Ohio wedding with her last weekend as a favor."

As he spoke, his sister's eyebrows climbed her forehead until they were lost in her mahogany, previously mouse-brown hair. He hadn't gotten used to the darker hue yet.

"You went to a wedding in Ohio?"

"Yes."

"And then what?" She smiled like a loon.

"And then we came back to Seattle."

"Do you like her?"

"It'd be weird to attend a wedding with someone I didn't like, wouldn't it?"

"So coy. Where is she?"

"She's working."

"Monarch isn't open on Sunday."

"She works for herself. She was freelancing at Monarch." He and Drew had a mini standoff. "It's too soon to bring her in to meet the fam." *If ever.*

"I can't remember the last time you brought a girl around to 'meet the fam.'"

She was right. It hadn't been something he'd even considered. He couldn't say that he was considering it now, but when he'd mentioned to Andy he had a family thing today, he'd briefly entertained the idea of inviting her. He didn't, of course, because that would've been insane.

"What girl?" Their mother, Lee, strode into the kitchen.

Enter: the reason he hadn't invited Andy. His very loving, oft-prying mother.

"I want to hear all about her. Can you Face-Call her so we can meet her?"

"It's called FaceTime, Mom," Drew said.

"Face-Call, FaceTime. Whatever. Pull her up on your mobile phone so we can say hello."

Gage opened his mouth to say "hell, no," but their mother interrupted with "Do you have any real coffee, Drew darling? I don't like expresso."

Drew ignored their mother's mispronunciation of *espresso* and pulled a "real" coffee maker out of a lower cabinet. As she set up the drip pot, she smiled over her shoulder. "I don't think Gage is ready to introduce us to his girlfriend."

"She's not my girlfriend," he grumbled, sounding like a less mature version of himself.

"Well, why on earth not?" their mother asked. "The same reason you won't introduce us to Devin? Are we that embarrassing?"

Gage grinned at his sister, content to have the topic swivel to her. "Yeah, Drew. Where *is* Devin tonight?"

"Working," she said between her teeth.

"Well, so is Andy."

"Oh! Her name is Andy! Isn't that darling?" Lee clapped her hands. "Tell me about her while Drew makes some real coffee."

Lee wrapped her arms around Gage's arm and dragged him out of the kitchen, peppering him with questions the whole way.

He couldn't be sure but he could swear he heard his sister's tinkling laughter follow him from the room.

Eighteen

The door to Flynn Parker's top-floor penthouse opened and Andy thought for a second she'd walked into a tomb. Gray walls, black floors and dark cabinetry greeted her from the kitchen, the room closest to the door. A few flickering jar candles on the surface further reinforced the "tomb" decor.

The feeling inside was nothing like a tomb, however, and neither were the people. Andy didn't typically hang out with a group of friends. She was a loner by nature, maybe in part due to her upbringing, and rarely spent this much time with anyone when the hours weren't being billed. Conversely, Gage had a strong network of friends, which was no surprise given his abundant charm.

She'd been working like a madwoman since they'd returned to Washington, but she'd made sure to allow time for Gage and his friends. She'd even sent a nice bottle of bourbon to him at the office. She was simply happy. And "simply" anything in a relationship had been an elusive beast until now.

"Andy!" Sabrina, dressed beautifully in a bright red knee-length dress, wore a smile that was both wide and infectious. "I'm so glad you could come. I wasn't sure if you would."

Honest as ever. Andy gave a demure smile, aware of Gage's palm warming her back. They'd been home for a little over a week now and things were surprisingly...good.

They'd been back to work, back to their own beds. Andy had seen Gage twice last week. Once for a late dinner that, thanks to a troublesome new client, had happened at 8:45 p.m., and once when she went to his apartment for what was supposed to be pizza and a movie and had ended up being pizza, half a movie and sex on the sofa.

"Well, you did corner her, love," Reid said, stepping into view to pour a glass of white wine, then turning to hand it to a blonde woman standing at his left elbow. "Kylie, this is Andrea Payne. Andy, Kylie Marker."

The blonde gave Andy a limp handshake and accepted her wine. "I like your...pants."

The compliment was forced, and so was Andy's smile. She'd worn simple black slacks and a pale blue silk shirt for work and hadn't had time to change. Kylie, on the other hand, looked like she'd been poured into her little black dress, her curvy form testing the seams. She was exactly the kind of woman Andy would expect to see Reid with, but somehow not... Reid's shrewd sense of humor and elegant wit seemed better suited for a woman who could match him blow for blow. Then again, according to Gage, Reid wasn't in the market for a challenge.

Anyway.

Andy had been near Monarch today, so she'd stopped by under the guise of "checking on the sales team" but in reality had wanted to see Gage. She'd been busy since she'd been home and was trying to fit him in when she could.

Missing someone was a new concept. She normally had her work to keep her warm at night. When Sabrina had poked her head into his office to invite him over to Flynn's penthouse for "Hump Day drinks," she'd swept her hand to include Andy in the invitation. Andy had automatically refused but Sabrina had instructed Gage to bring her with him.

Andy liked Sabrina. Liked all of them, truthfully. She hadn't expected to pull a lover out of offering to hire Gage as her fake boyfriend much less three new friends, but somehow she had.

"Red or white?" Gage asked her, helping himself to the line of wine bottles sitting on the countertop.

"White, please."

"That's what I have!" Kylie exclaimed with a grin. Reid arched one eyebrow like maybe he'd just now realized he'd settled for less than his equal.

"How about champagne?" Sabrina sent a saucy wink to Flynn, who was already moving for the fridge. She bounced over to the cabinet and began pulling out flutes to line up on the countertop.

"What's this, then?" Reid asked.

"An announcement of some sort, apparently." Gage relinquished the wineglasses and stepped back, waiting while Flynn popped the cork off not one, but two bottles of Dom Pérignon.

"We're getting married!" Sabrina said as Flynn started pouring. She reached into her pocket and pulled out a shining diamond ring.

Whoa.

Andy suddenly felt out of place for an announcement this big.

The moment Sabrina slid the ring onto her finger, Kylie was on her like white on rice.

"It's beautiful." Kylie hugged Sabrina around the neck and Reid gently removed his date, who was now dabbing her eyes. "Sorry. I'm so moved when people get engaged. Or pregnant. Are you pregnant?"

"Um. No. But thanks for asking," Sabrina said with a wince.

Kylie shot a loving look up at Reid, and he turned the color of his sage-green tie. Yes, he'd recognized his short-sightedness when it came to Kylie. She was hearts and wedding bells and Reid wasn't looking for anything more than a good time.

"Congratulations, Sabrina. You two are good together and I'm happy for you." Andy accepted a champagne flute from Flynn. "Tell us how you asked."

Always a popular conversation starter in this situation.

"She was painting," Flynn said, his low baritone not hinting at what a softie he was on the inside. Andy had seen him around Sabrina at work. He virtually melted whenever she was near.

"He brought me a little paper sack from my favorite art store and when I pulled out the new paintbrush—" Sabrina couldn't finish, her throat clogging as tears came forth as easily as her smile.

"The ring was on the paintbrush. I said some stuff. The end." Flynn wrapped an arm around his fiancée and kissed her forehead while Sabrina swiped at her eyes.

Seriously. How sweet were they?

"Congrats, man," Gage said. Reid chimed in, too, lifting his flute and toasting their friends.

"Well, that was a surprise." Gage corralled Andy to one side, his hand on her back. Whenever he touched her, the stresses of the day vanished.

"A surprise? Even I could've guessed that was coming."

"I *suspected*. I wasn't sure."

"I like your friends. You're all sort of puzzling."

"Meaning?"

"Sabrina," Andy said, lowering her voice as they stepped farther into the apartment, "is so quirky you'd expect her to wear a peasant dress and flowers in her hair, but she favors fancy dresses. Flynn is gruff but it's for show, although this penthouse does make me question if he has a soul...or if he stores it in a trick wall somewhere in the penthouse."

Gage chuckled. "Sab's working on that. He inherited this place from his father. Emmons wasn't the warmest of men."

The painting over the mantel featured a pair of chickadees sitting side by side on a Japanese maple tree. The warm golds, blues and pinks were adorable and light and completely out of place in this house.

"I'm guessing that artistry was Sabrina's doing?"

"Definitely. Wait'll she moves in here. Her apartment is the equivalent of a peasant dress. Come on. I know you've got more to say." He made a give-it-to-me gesture.

"Okay. Reid is British class and pomp, the textbook playboy, but there's something about him that makes me wonder if he's acting. Though I'm not sure *he's* aware that he's acting."

"That's what every woman says about him. They've all tried to crack the Reid Code." They both looked at Kylie. "She's going to be disappointed when she doesn't succeed."

"Terribly. I can tell already she's not the one. Reid needs a woman who challenges him."

"To duels?"

"Challenges what he knows about himself." She gave Gage a playful shove.

"And what about me puzzles you, Andy?" He paired the question with his hands on her hips as he moved behind her to study the Seattle skyline out the window. In the background, his friends' laughter and banter continued.

"You were engaged before and made an unbreakable pact never to be married," she told Gage's reflection, "and yet you volunteered to come with me to a wedding and then didn't break things off after." She shrugged. "*Puzzling.*"

"I needed your expertise."

"Is that why I'm here right now?" Was she a version

of Kylie? A temporary placeholder before he moved on to someone else?

"Andy."

"You like me more than anyone ever has, Gage." She spun in his arms and even though there was a time she would've died before doing something as casual as drape her arms on a man's shoulders within sight of a crowd, she did it anyway.

"Good." He placed a gentle kiss on her lips.

"Don't tell me you two are next," Reid said with a groan.

"Aw, but they're so cute!" Kylie chimed in.

Andy and Gage separated and she studied the floor for a beat. He had a way of making her forget where she was—who she was. Was she becoming one half of a whole? The idea of her being with anyone intrinsically was foreign, and after talking with Ness, frankly a little frightening.

"I know about the pact. He's safe," Andy said with a soft smile.

"Pact?" Kylie asked, her brow denting with a frown.

Ruh-roh.

Reid's nostrils flared. He sent Andy a withering glare and she mouthed the word *sorry.*

"Kylie, let's you and I step outside for a moment." Reid took a long look at the balcony and seemed to reconsider. "Actually, let's go out into the hallway. You'll catch a chill."

"In July?" Kylie asked as Reid hustled her out of the penthouse.

"I don't think he was comfortable telling Kylie about the pact with the prospect of a balcony and a long drop to the street," Gage said.

"Right." Andy's smile faded. "It's a strange pact for the three of you, considering your goals are so different."

"You didn't see Flynn when he was married." Gage shook his head.

"I didn't see you engaged to what's-her-face, either."

"She was a lot like you." This from Flynn, who strolled into his living room, his fiancée, and her million-watt smile, by his side. "Driven. Ambitious."

"But *not* like you," Sabrina offered, "in that she was about as warm as..."

"This penthouse?" Andy supplied.

"Exactly." Sabrina's smile was approving, her eyes narrow as she studied Gage. When her gaze snapped to Andy, it said *we'll talk later.*

Andy nodded. She was looking forward to learning more of Gage's secrets.

"Give it to me." Andy refilled Sabrina's flute in the kitchen.

Reid had returned from the hallway without Kylie. He told everyone that she'd left because she had an early morning tomorrow. No one believed him, but no one asked him to explain. Now the guys had vanished to parts unknown in the five-thousand-square-foot penthouse to shoot pool, while Sabrina and Andy lingered around the drinks and snacks.

"Give what to you?" Sabrina dragged a cucumber slice through the hummus and offered it. "This?"

"The way you were looking at Gage earlier, I could swear you came to some sort of conclusion."

Sabrina covered her smile by eating the cucumber slice, and then took a sip of her champagne before speaking.

"Gage and I have been friends for a long time. Almost as long as I've known Flynn. I've seen him date, and I remember Laura, although that was a long time ago. I know that he's charming, relaxed, a great date."

"He is all of those things," Andy said carefully.

"And yet with you—" Sabrina tilted her head "—he's serious, too. I can tell by the way he looks at you that he's not as light in his approach."

Uncomfortable and almost sorry she'd asked, Andy squirmed. "I'm fairly serious myself. I can see why he'd react accordingly."

Sabrina donned her best Mona Lisa smile before humming to herself.

"You're falling for him."

Andy coughed on her next sip of champagne. "What?" she croaked, trying to recover from inhaling her Dom.

Sabrina's knowing expression didn't change as she dragged a carrot through the hummus. "I can tell by the way you act around him. The way you look at him. Not in the same way Kylie looked at Reid, which was...*needy*."

Agreed.

"But like you're seeing a future without an end date."

"I'm in no danger of being proposed to by Gage," Andy sputtered. She was thrown by Sabrina's suggestion that she was "falling" for him. Thrown because she wasn't that well-versed in relationships. She was enjoying herself, that was all. But falling for him? Hmm...

"That dumb pact." Sabrina rolled her eyes. "They act like it's carved in stone. Then the right girl comes along and they learn it's more like chalk on a blackboard."

That made sense for Sabrina and Flynn. They'd been friends since college—best friends. For Gage and Andy it was different. They'd known each other for what, a handful of weeks?

"You never know," was all Sabrina said.

But the lingering glance to her shining engagement ring told Andy everything she needed to know about what was going on in the brunette's mind.

Sabrina had changed Flynn's mind about the pact. If Andy and Gage were serious about having a future, could she change his mind, too?

Nineteen

"Where's Andrea tonight?" Reid lifted his beer and pegged Gage with a meaningful look. They sat side by side at the bar they usually haunted, though it was fairly dead for a Thursday night.

"Working."

Andy worked a lot. He'd had no idea how much he wouldn't see her when they returned to Seattle. But she was never too far away, either texting or visiting in between busy nights.

"Shouldn't you two be celebrating your three-week anniversary tonight?" Reid smirked.

"Very funny." Gage frowned.

"Refill?" Shelly, the bartender, gestured to Reid, whose glass was empty. The bar's overhead lights glinted off the ring on her finger, practically throwing sparks.

"That's new, love." Reid took her hand and turned the ring this way and that. "Are you spoken for?"

"I've *been* spoken for, but I suppose this makes it official. Bryan proposed this weekend." She beamed, her eyes sparkling like her new diamond ring.

That was a giant coincidence. Flynn had asked Sabrina this week. Love was in the air, Gage thought, shifting uncomfortably in his seat. He'd been flirting with Shelly the night he met Andy and he had no idea at the time that Shelly was someone else's.

Reid ordered two more beers and Gage tipped his draft back to drain the contents of his glass. Might as well have another.

"Soon I'll be the only keeper of the pact," Reid said with a melodramatic sigh.

"What's that supposed to mean?" Gage asked as Shelly delivered their beers and cleared away their empty mugs.

"Andy sent you an expensive bottle of liquor. To the office."

"It was a bottle of bourbon. Don't sound so foreboding."

"It means she was thinking about you. And then she unexpectedly dropped by before coming along with you to Flynn's." Reid's tone was conspiracy-theory low. "She's getting comfortable, mate. *Girlfriendy.*"

"What are you talking about?" Gage laughed to dismiss the whole "girlfriendy" thing, but he had to admit she sort of was and it wasn't bothering him as much as it should.

"With anyone else you'd be letting her down gently. But you haven't yet, have you?"

"Not yet." The words settled into the pit of Gage's stomach. He wasn't sure why. He'd been the one to suggest they keep seeing each other after Andy's sister's wedding. He'd been the one to insist on her coming to Flynn's that night. *Where another engagement was announced*, he thought nervously as he caught the glint off Shelly's ring.

"Keeper of the pact," Reid announced, lifting his beer again.

Reid was being ridiculous. Gage was no closer to proposing to Andy than he was to climbing on top of this bar and stripping.

And yet…

Something had been welling up inside him. An uncom-fortable…what was the word? *Rightness.*

He felt *right* with Andy and he hadn't had that feeling in a long, long time. And never this soon. Even with Laura, he'd been acting more on expectations than emotion.

Why was that?

"It's in the air," Reid said, echoing Gage's earlier thought. He sneered. "Love. You've not caught it, have you?"

"Love?" Gage laughed. "No. Definitely not."

If love was like an airborne virus, he could write off that weird pit-of-his-gut feeling to proximity. He'd been at a weekend wedding with Andy where every event dripped with romance. And now two of his closest friends were en-gaged to be married. Romance tended to be like glitter. It stuck to you, undetected unless the light hit it just right, and almost impossible to get rid of once you noticed it.

Was Andy like glitter?

Yes. And no.

She wasn't annoying or clingy. She wasn't staying at his place or leaving her stuff there. She was good on her own and didn't need his reassurance. But she was different than she'd been when they first met. She was independent but including him in her life.

Like he'd asked. Because he'd caught the airborne glit-ter virus and was infected. He swiped at his sweaty brow.

Possibly he was freaking out.

"It's not too late," his British friend warned, his tone scarily serious. "You've been down this road with plenty of women. If it's time to insert some distance, you know how to do it. Is it time?"

Gage let out a choking sound. "You make it sound like there's a lot of them. I date less than you do."

Deflection was the best tactic whenever backed into a corner.

"I date because I'm great at it. You date because you like being part of a couple."

Gage blinked at his friend. He liked having company, yes, but the "part of a couple" accusation wasn't true.

Was it?

Andy had accused him of being a serial monogamist. He wasn't like Reid, showing up with a new girl at every event, but neither was he Flynn and Sabrina, attached at the hip. Gage was somewhere in the middle. A "gray area" when it came to women in general and relationships at large.

"You're quite good at having girlfriends. Women like you so bloody much."

"They're not girlfriends." Aware he sounded like a twelve-year-old, Gage stopped slumping and sat straighter on his stool.

Reid smirked. "Well, they're different from hookups, which is what I'm best at."

"You're bragging about being forgettable, Reid."

"Not forgettable. Just...*unkeepable*." He nodded, happy with his own conclusion.

Gage had sworn to uphold the pact in part for Flynn, but also for himself. After his engagement imploded and Laura left, Gage never wanted to feel that unmoored again.

Success was important to him in all things. In school, he'd graduated with a 4.0 GPA—even though it meant working harder to lift his suffering grades. When he dated Laura and determined she was as ambitious as he was, it was a perfect match. He'd *known* she was The One.

Until he didn't.

Laura had come at him with a whopper of an announcement just one month after announcing their engagement. He wasn't good enough for her. Wasn't as successful as she wanted him to be. Worse, she said he never would be. *"You don't want to be in a partnership where your wife is earning more than you, Gage."*

It rankled him that she thought he'd care about how much money she earned, and how it compared to his salary. That he'd be that shallow. And then it rankled him all over again that she'd basically hobbled him, telling him he couldn't be as successful as her, when she knew damn well that success and Gage went hand in hand.

Nothing he'd said to that effect had changed Laura's mind. Her mind was made up when she'd invited him to that diner for lunch. She'd set the stage for a public breakup, and had pulled out an actual bullet-pointed list. She'd read from the notebook, never stopping to look at him.

On the surface they'd seemed like a good match, but Laura found him too "casual" and not serious enough for her taste. "We're too different," she'd told him. He'd learned that day that she was right about that. Gage was a human being with real feelings and a heart, while Laura was a cyborg with faulty programming.

It was the biggest failure of his life, that relationship—the engagement that never produced a wedding. He'd been certain of a future with Laura. One that stood the test of time like his parents' marriage. Being that wrong had thrown him. It wasn't any wonder he'd leaped into the pact the way he did...twice.

Failure in business happened, of course. He wasn't so delusional he thought himself impervious to stepping in it now and again. But failing with relationships was trickier to pull out of. His grades had temporarily dipped when Laura and he split. His social life exploded, and he'd chosen to go to parties instead of study. Hookups were a tack he tried and failed at. He didn't like meaningless flings. And yet he didn't want to be roped in again by a woman who promised forever and backed out before giving him a chance to be a success.

Laura thought they were too different? Fine. He'd date fun-loving women who valued him for who he was. He'd back out before it became too much for either of them. It was hard at first, learning how to let them down easy and walk away whole, but he'd been successful at that, too.

Then came Andy.

Independent, driven, successful Andy.

Vulnerable, open, *fascinating* Andy.

The idea of them splitting sent his mind reeling. Made his stomach toss. He'd suggested they not end things and she trusted him. He cared about her and didn't want her hurt. Would she carry his rejection with her like a wound? Or would she harness her driven, independent side and soar without him?

Option B was the *only* option. He couldn't even think about leaving a scar as deep as Matthew Higgins and his "Ice Queen" comments. Andy was better than that.

But she was also better than sticking around with a guy who wouldn't give her what she ultimately deserved.

Forever.

He'd seen the way she looked at her sister, Gwen, at the wedding. Andy might not be able to admit it to herself yet, but Gage could tell she was a woman who wanted to be married someday. And he couldn't—*wouldn't*—allow himself to take those vows.

A sigh came from the depths. He knew what he had to do. He couldn't let Andy settle for less than she deserved any more than he could string her along. Their relationship would end eventually. And maybe if he ended it sooner it'd save them both a lot of heartache.

His chest seized at the thought of not seeing her or holding her again. Of not kissing her ever again. He'd miss her like hell. He already felt like part of him was tangled up in part of her. He couldn't let his unreliable heart call the shots, though, arguably, he'd already let it call a few.

No part of this was going to be easy. He already cared

about Andy ten times, hell, *one hundred times*, more than he'd cared about Laura. And he'd been *in love* with Laura.

Or so he'd thought.

It was possible, even probable, that he'd been fooled into thinking what he was feeling for Andy was deep, unfathomed and long-lasting. As if he'd been glamoured by the couples-in-love around him and had acted on what he thought was instinct but was more…conditioning.

And if he didn't proceed very carefully, Andy could fall into the same trap.

At his elbow, Gage's phone buzzed with a text message from her.

I have dinner for us. It's Thai. Your place or mine?

Gage's chest tightened when he thought of Andy's bright eyes and strawberry-blond hair. When he thought of what he had to do he knew he had to do it before either or both of them said or did things that were unable to be taken back.

He realized now that he'd made a mistake not ending this after the wedding. He wasn't too big of a man to admit he was wrong, even if he had let things go on for far too long. Andy deserved that same respect.

My place, he texted back.

His home turf would be better. Then she could storm out like he guessed she would. Drive to a girlfriend's house and curse his name a thousand times over. There was no time like the present to recover from the misstep—before she expected more than he'd be able to give. Before she got in any deeper, or he gave her any *wronger* of an impression about himself.

He pulled money out of his wallet to pay and Reid's eyebrows rose. "Duty calls? Or should I say booty calls?"

Gage was so miserable he couldn't crack even the smallest of smiles. "You're not in the pact alone, Reid."

"No?"

"No." Gage shoved his untouched beer in front of Reid and nodded. "I know what I need to do."

He'd been pretending, which was fun at first, but now it'd gone too far. It was time to wrap up this farce with Andy.

Past time.

Twenty

Andy had never been so cheery. Happy, sure. Contented, absolutely. But joyful, humming a tune as she strolled into the high-rise holding Gage's posh apartment? She couldn't remember ever feeling this buoyant.

She hadn't been very good at balancing her time at work and her time with Gage. Tonight she was going to make it up to him. She was ambitious and she was driven and, frankly, didn't have a lot of experience including another person in her plans.

Andy wanted to include Gage for one simple reason: she loved him.

She was certain of it.

She'd been ordering shrimp pad thai and basil fried rice and it hit her as she paid for their dinner.

For the first time in a long time, she was half of a whole.

As unexpected as it was, and in such a short period of time, she'd fallen in love with Gage Fleming. She hadn't seen it coming but now that it was here, she welcomed it. As much as she contended that she didn't need anyone, she needed him. And what's more was that she didn't mind needing him. It didn't make her feel weaker or less independent. She felt stronger for it.

Love.

She finally was beginning to understand what all the fuss was about.

Excited about her newfound discovery, she'd grinned at the cashier and said, "My boyfriend and I are having dinner together."

The cashier smiled quizzically but wished her well, having no idea the monumental shift that had occurred in the ten minutes Andy sat in the restaurant and waited for her takeout.

Falling in love *was* monumental. And even though it was after nine o'clock, and even though the food was greasy Thai instead of a five-star meal, Andy was certain of her feelings for Gage.

She couldn't wait another second to tell him how he'd changed her. There'd even been a stray thought about how they could tell their grandkids one day about how they'd met. The bar story. It would kill!

Humming and happy, she pushed the number eighteen button in the elevator and rode to Gage's floor. She'd tell him tonight. He deserved to feel as great and whole and happy as she did.

She stepped out and admired her surroundings. The building Gage lived in was historical, with charming woodwork and brass handles on the doors. The lighting fixtures appeared original to the building, though Andy guessed they'd been rewired. Everything functioned and felt modern while at the same time throwing her back several decades. It was remarkable the way history worked. She was making some for Gage and herself tonight.

His apartment door was cracked, the soothing notes of jazz coming from inside. Andy knocked lightly before letting herself in. The entryway opened to a wide living room with a wall of windows letting in the moonlight. The couch was navy with deep red pillows, which had reminded her of Gwen's wedding colors the first time Andy had been here.

It was a sign. She never would've thought that before tonight, but being in love had given her new vision. Who knew what a superpower that could be?

Gage stood in the kitchen beyond the living room, pouring wine into two glasses. Red.

The color of love.

Andy was so excited she was about to burst.

"Your dinner, sir." She set down the paper sack and sidled over to kiss him. He delivered a kiss but his lips were firm and pursed, his brow a furrowed thundercloud.

"You okay?" she asked.

She lifted her wineglass and took a sip, wondering what it was that had turned Gage's mood sour. Work, most likely.

"You go first," she told him. "I had a not-so-great day at the office, too. I'll commiserate with you."

Her smile faded as a look of hurt crossed his features.

"Andy." The way he said her name was ominous. A premonition of something horrible.

The food that had once smelled tantalizing and tempting now caused her stomach to flop like a dying fish.

"I've never lied to you before and I have no intention of starting now."

"Oh?" Her hand shook, and her wineglass with it.

He pulled in a deep breath, paused to drink down half the contents of his glass and then faced her. He put the glass down. Then warm hands braced her biceps and a million alarms rang out in her head.

In a panic, she blurted, "I love you. I realized when I was picking up your shrimp pad thai that we belong together. What we have, this isn't impermanent. This is the real thing. I know it's fast and I know you have that pact, but Flynn ditched the pact for Sabrina. Do you know why?"

Gage's expression teetered on mortified, but for Andy her dam had broken. She couldn't stop talking now that she'd started.

"Flynn realized that being in love with Sabrina was more important than some silly pact," she continued. "Sabrina was someone worth making new decisions for. Flynn wanted to move forward with her because he'd seen a part of her he'd never seen before. *Gage.* That's you and me." She didn't dare slow down until she said the rest. "You were the one who excavated that part of me. I didn't know how to be half of a couple. I didn't know how to be in love. You were the one who opened those doors—who taught me how to love you."

Her voice broke. She swallowed thickly and waited. She'd said what she'd come here to say, and as naively as a virgin bride on her wedding night, she expected him to have come to the same realization as she had. She hadn't even considered that he didn't feel the same way. How could he not?

She saw now that she'd been dead wrong. The evidence was written all over his stricken face.

"Say something." Her voice was a broken whisper, her heart threatening to break right alongside it.

"We went to a wedding together," he said. Bizarrely.

"Yes." She let loose a shaky smile.

"And then Flynn and Sabrina announced their engagement. Shelly's engaged, too, by the way."

"Who?"

"Bartender at From Afar."

"Oh." She wasn't following.

"I was engaged, Andy. And Laura ended that engagement because she didn't believe in us. She was cold and calculated and completely dismissive of who we could've become."

"I'm not." Andy gripped his hands, trying to head off

another argument before it brewed. "I'm forever material. I'm a single Payne sister—the last of my kind. You opened my eyes to the fact that I'm valued and worth it. You opened my eyes to a life outside of my business. You opened my eyes to love."

"I can't love you, Andy. I can't let this go on any longer." His voice was hard and tight, like the words were fighting being spoken. "It's irresponsible."

"You...*can't*?"

"No."

Such a final word. She dropped his hands and he backed away from her a step.

Backed.

Away.

"You weren't supposed to fall in love with me, Andy. Hell, I'm not sure you are in love with me. You were caught up in your sister's romantic getaway, and I'm sure Sabrina said something last night that made you think you were—and that's not your fault. She's in love. Completely smitten. She thinks everyone can have what she and Flynn have."

For as gobsmacked as she felt, Gage might as well have reached out and slapped her.

"You think I don't know if I'm in love with you?" Gage was *deep* in the danger zone and hopefully her tone was conveying that fact. "You think I was swept up in wedding bells and engagement rings rather than coming to the conclusion about my feelings on my own?"

"Yes—" his voice rose incrementally "—I do. So was I. Too caught up to recognize we were both flirting with disaster. I'm not too big a man to admit I'm sorry."

"You're *sorry*?" she snapped.

"I never should've asked for more when I knew damn well I couldn't be the guy to give you more. Staying together is setting us up for a huge fall. A huge *failure*. I won't keep you from your future husband and waste any more of your time. What we had at Gwen's wedding was a perfect weekend. I should've left it at that."

Her hand twitched at her side. She'd never wanted to slap someone before. She did now. Just so he could feel the way she felt—like her stable footing had crumbled beneath her and she was in a free fall toward the cold, hard ground.

She settled for lifting her glass and throwing her remaining wine at him. Unaccustomed to being physically reactive, she sort of chickened out at the end and the splash fell short of his chest, landing on one side of his crisp white button-down shirt. Right about where the coffee stain was the day he'd talked her into letting him be her pretend boyfriend.

God. She'd never been so stupid.

"Bastard." Tears threatened but she swallowed down her rioting emotions.

"I'm sorry."

"The sorriest," she agreed. "Enjoy your meal."

She stomped out of his apartment without looking back, rode the elevator to the ground floor and marched to her car parked on the curb. She'd congratulated herself when she'd parked there, thinking how "lucky" she'd been to find the coveted space.

Lucky and in love.

"I'm *so* stupid," she reiterated aloud as she turned the key in the ignition. She'd known in her heart of hearts that forever wasn't for her. She'd let that doubt go, trusting Gage so implicitly that she'd agreed when he suggested they keep seeing each other. She'd allowed herself to believe the future was an open expanse with wildflowers blooming and horses galloping…

A fantasy.

One she wouldn't let herself wallow in no matter what her stupid heart thought. She could be in love with him all she wanted, but it didn't mean she couldn't move on. Gage might've put the final nail in the "them" coffin, but she had the power not to allow him in ever again.

Maybe someday she'd find it in her heart to be grateful to him for teaching her how to open up and trust and love someone.

Today was not that day.

She drove home without a backward glance, lecturing her tear ducts most of the way. The moment she twisted the lock on her front door and she was safely ensconced inside her own dark apartment, those tears came anyway, and showed no signs of stopping.

Gage stuffed his soiled shirt into the trash can hidden beneath the sink and washed Andy's wineglass, standing it on end in the dish drainer.

Then he moved to the kitchen counter, palmed the back of his neck and eyed the untouched bag of food with the receipt stapled to the paper bag.

He'd done the right thing.

But he still felt awful about it.

He finished his wine, surmising that Andy might never forgive him, but she could be free now. That he could continue working and upholding the pact because he believed wholeheartedly that engagement and marriage weren't for him. That his "feelings" couldn't be trusted because everyone in his vicinity was drunk on love.

It sounded like bullshit, even to him, so he couldn't imagine how badly it'd sounded when Andy was standing in his kitchen dumping her heart out.

What he'd done was the equivalent of stabbing her in the center of that heart with a dull knife.

"She'll get over it."

She'd have to. *He'd* have to. Viruses had to run their course, and the one he'd caught from her was a doozy. The "L" virus. He couldn't so much as think the four-letter word that hovered in the room like the scent of Thai food. His stomach gave an insistent rumble.

"Screw it." He tore open the bag, pulled out his shrimp pad thai and stowed the other container in the fridge for later.

Things didn't work out, that's all. And if the only carnage left behind from their breakup was a bag of Thai food, well, then they'd escaped relatively unscathed.

But as he dug his fork into his dinner and chewed forlornly, he questioned if he'd escaped unscathed after all.

The flavor should've burst—the shrimp was utter perfection, and the seasoning on point. Instead it was as if he was navigating a mouthful of foam packing peanuts.

"Virus," he said around another big bite. Viruses changed the flavor of food and altered a person's physical being. Which also explained that ache in the center of his shirtless chest.

He didn't hear any loud, blaring alarms like he had early on with Andy. There was only a low hum after the fallout. The sense that the worst wasn't coming, but had already come and gone. The sense that he'd made a giant mistake— one he could never take back.

He carried his dinner and wine to the couch where his heavy limbs dragged him down. Then he turned on the television and zoned out.

This, too, would pass.

Twenty-One

Gage looked up from his keyboard. Yasmine was typing away on her own laptop, and behind her Flynn's office was dark. Sabrina's, too. Flynn and Sabrina had left earlier. Something about meeting with a wedding planner and the only time the woman had available was three o'clock today.

When Gage glanced in the direction of Reid's office, he found his British friend wasn't in his chair, but heading Gage's way, whistling.

What the hell is he so happy about?

"Gagey, Gagey, Gagey." Reid said as he entered Gage's office.

"What?"

"Let's bugger off and grab drinks at Afar. It's dead in here. Everyone else has gone." He gestured to the empty-save-for-Yasmine floor.

"Pass." Gage returned his attention to the computer screen, where literally nothing was happening. He'd opened a blank document to type up a progress report for Flynn… that wasn't due for another month. He'd been spending a lot of hours in the office since he had nothing better to do than pass the time alone in his apartment.

The past nine and a half days had been absolute torture.

The feelings he'd convinced himself were fleeting and temporary hadn't gone anywhere. He'd given himself a week to recover from breaking things off with Andy, even though his instincts were bucking like a wild bronco. Everything about her leaving his apartment had felt wrong. Three days, five days—hell, nine and a half days later, it still felt wrong.

"You need to talk to someone and I'm offering my ear. But I'd rather do it over a beer." Reid unbuttoned his suit jacket and sat in the stuffed chair next to a plant.

"You and I talked already."

"I'm your best friend."

"You *were*."

Reid ignored the jab, pulling a hand over his face and muttering a swear word into his palm. "I tried to tell you."

Since Gage held Reid mostly responsible for leading him to think he needed to end things with Andy, that arrogant "I tried to tell you" comment sent his anger through the roof. He spun the chair to face his "friend."

"What, exactly, did you try to tell me, Reid?"

"That you had a girlfriend. That you liked being part of a couple. That I, alone, would hold true to the pact." He put a fist to his heart like a knight taking an oath.

"I seem to remember you telling me that it was past time to let her down gently."

"I never said that. I said I expected you to have let her down gently by then."

Gage's frown intensified; he could literally feel an ache forming between his eyebrows. "You planted a seed of doubt."

"You've got a whole garden of doubt in there on your own. Don't pin this on me. I don't want to see you hurt any more than you do, but I'm under no delusions when it comes to who I am and what I want. You, on the other hand…"

Reid shrugged and Gage wanted to hit his friend's perfectly square jaw. Or hit *someone*. At the moment hitting *himself* was justified.

"That night we went to From Afar," Gage started. "I broke up with Andy under your advice." When Reid opened his mouth to argue, Gage added, "Encouragement. Whatever. You weren't rooting for us, so don't pretend you were."

Reid's turn to frown. Good. Gage liked watching his friend's smug face slip into an expression that was borderline apologetic.

"I love her, Reid." Gage said it like he was announcing that he had only days to live. That was what that epiphany felt like.

He loved Andrea Payne and she hated him.

"Does she love you?"

Gage's heart suffered another fissure, but he barely felt it. He'd been in so much pain over the last week-plus he'd gotten used to it. "She loved me nine and a half days ago."

"Love." Reid's tone was as grave as Gage's. "It is soon."

"I don't need your commentary. You've helped enough already."

He stood and Reid did, too, stepping in front of Gage to block the path to the door.

Reid put his hand on Gage's chest to keep him from walking out. "You can't blame me for this. I was being myself. Doing what I've always done. Which is bust your bollocks. It was your job to tell me to shove it. To stand up for what you and Andy had if it was so bloody important."

Gage's shoulders sagged. "You're right."

His buddy was right.

Andy had been right.

"Andy mentioned that Flynn had thrown aside the pact because Sabrina was worth it. He was able to see it. We all were. But that was Sab." Someone who'd been in Flynn's life for a long time, not a brand-new relationship with a vulnerable, gorgeous, cautious redhead.

"First," Reid started. "Sab is a unicorn. When it came to him tossing aside the pact, we never would've stood for it had it been the wrong woman. Second, you're wrong about Flynn being the white knight. He had his head up his arse until you and I dragged him to the conclusion that he'd always belonged to Sabrina."

Gage blinked. Damn. He'd forgotten that day in Flynn's office, where Reid and Gage had to have a "come to Jesus" talk with their third musketeer.

"Points to you for realizing you're in love with Andy before Flynn and I had to come in here and pull it out of you as well." Reid patted Gage's chest and dropped his arm to his side.

"Doesn't matter. I'm too late."

Reid's mouth pressed into a line.

"Andy vanished. She's back to being the unreachable Andy Payne. She's a puff of smoke. I tried her assistant after Andy ignored a few of my calls." Gage shook his head. "Nothing."

"Did you text her?"

Gage nodded. He couldn't lay his love for her out in writing and watch it be ignored, so he'd settled for one We need to talk and a follow-up At least let me apologize.

Unsurprisingly, she hadn't responded.

He understood her caution. She'd come to him, her bright blue eyes shining with happiness, and told him to his face that she was in love with him. She deserved the same from him and he'd been too chickenshit to admit as much. Then he'd broken up with her, telling her he was sorry. *Sorry.* Like an apology would undo the hurt.

He'd never regret anything like he regretted letting her walk out of his apartment that night.

"Not like you don't know where she lives," Reid offered.

"I don't, actually. We always met at restaurants, or the airport, or she'd come to my place after she was done with work. She's impossible to track down."

"Nothing's impossible." Reid's eyes twinkled knowingly.

But it was too late. Andy had moved on. And really, wasn't it fair to *let her* move on? To let her go and heal when he'd wadded up her love for him and thrown it in her face?

"This came for you." Yasmine interrupted them before Gage could share his thoughts. She handed him an envelope and he blinked at it stupidly. "I'm done for the day, unless either of you need me?"

"Take care, Yasmine. We're heading out soon ourselves," Reid told her.

She grabbed her purse and left while Gage stood frozen in the doorway of his own office.

"What is it, then?" Reid asked.

Gage showed Reid the envelope. The printed return address in professional block lettering read *Andy Payne, LLC* followed by a PO Box number.

Monarch had paid the invoice for her services upon her arrival, so what was it? Gage half expected it to be a letter saying, "You're a dick," or maybe another invoice with a line item for "breaking my heart" with a dollar amount next to it. Two thousand dollars, maybe.

He tore open the envelope and pulled out the single item within. A check.

His guess wasn't far off. But instead of being billed, he was being paid.

His eyes locked onto the words *Pay to the order of* and then snapped to the dollar amount—$2,000.00.

She'd written him a check for two thousand dollars.

On the memo line it read *Payment in full for business trip*.

There was nothing else in the envelope. No note. No

"Fuck you." It was no less than he deserved—a final middle finger for what had happened in his apartment nearly ten days ago.

Reid let out a long, low whistle. "Harsh."

Then Gage arrived at a conclusion that hit him as hard and fast as a shot. "Except it's not."

"No?"

"No." If Andy was mad at him, she *never* would've sent him this check. What better retaliation was there than freezing him out and never speaking to him again? Instead she'd *reached out*. She might even be as brokenhearted as he was, which could mean she still loved him. Receiving this check meant she cared. About him. About *them*.

She wasn't an Ice Queen.

They both knew it.

Gage's smile found his face without him trying. "She loves me. Still."

"You're insane. That's a cold move."

"I know what it looks like, but trust me when I tell you that this—" he waved the check "—means she's not over us yet." He knew it in his heart. A heart that he'd have to serve up on a platter if he had a prayer of earning her back. "I have to tell her that I love her, too. Right now. And in person. Can you find her?"

Reid's mouth flinched into a grimace briefly—likely at the prognosis of his friend falling in love. Couldn't be helped. Gage loved Andy, and distance and time hadn't done anything to dampen that love. In fact, his feelings for her had only intensified.

"Please."

With a sigh, Reid announced, "I'm a computer-hacker-turned-IT-wizard. Of course I can find her." He tilted his head toward his office, where no fewer than three large computer screens decorated his desk. "Tell me everything you know about the mysterious Andy Payne."

Twenty-Two

Andy reread the email to her webmaster for the third time, a zing of excitement and nervousness comingling in her belly. It was past time she came out of hiding and let the world, or at least the world wide web, see her for who she truly was.

Mike, attached you'll find my headshot. Please update the website to include my photo and an About page. My bio is below. If you have any questions, let me know.

She'd never had the confidence before to stand on her own merits. She'd made many, many excuses about why she needed to keep her identity a secret from her clients, but since the breakup with Gage she'd taken a long, hard look at her life. She was done hiding. Done trying to live up to the tough-as-nails woman she'd created as a persona. She'd thought it would protect her, but instead she only felt like a coward for hiding behind that persona. It was time to step into her power. A power, ironically, that she wouldn't have if it wasn't for Gage.

He'd undone her completely. He'd peeled back layer after layer and had seen her in her most vulnerable state. He'd wooed her from her shell and defended her honor and made her realize that above all else, she was enough.

Exactly as she was.

She closed her eyes and willed back the torrent of emotions that had plagued her since the night they broke up. She couldn't change what had happened any more than she could keep from still loving him.

He'd texted. He'd called. She'd ignored both, knowing she couldn't face him with her tender underbelly showing. She had been desperately trying to rebuild her armor, to rebrick the wall that she'd been hidden safely behind that evening at the bar, when she'd offered Gage two grand in exchange for his accompaniment to Gwen's wedding.

Hiding had proved impossible.

Gage hadn't only lured her out from behind that wall, but he'd also demolished the way she'd seen the world prior to him.

Andy knew she was desirable and, unlike Gage, she wasn't afraid to face her future.

That didn't mean her heart didn't ache, or that she didn't soak her pillow every night with fresh tears, but it did mean that she wasn't the Ice Queen Matthew had accused her of being. She was a feeling, sensitive, vulnerable woman. Beautifully vulnerable.

Being vulnerable sucked.

She sent the email and shut her laptop, mind on the bottle of white wine chilling in the door of the fridge. It was ten thirty and her eyes were heavy, drooping from the fatigue of both work and personal matters.

Wine would help.

Before she'd taken her first sip of crisp, light pinot grigio, her cell phone rang. The jingle made her heart leap to her throat even though she'd silenced Gage's phone number days ago. She couldn't bring herself to delete his phone number yet. Soon, though, she'd have to close the door on what they had.

The screen showed Vanessa's photo, and Andy took a steeling breath. Rare was the occasion Ness called her, and the news was rarely good.

"Ness, hi."

"Is it too late to call?"

"No. Just wrapped up work, actually. I poured a glass of wine and was about to have my first sip."

"I'll join you. I have a bottle open." There was the sound of a cabinet opening and closing, liquid pouring. "Cheers, sis."

Andy joined her in a cross-country sip and waited for Ness to say why she'd called. She didn't have to wait long.

"Alec and I are separating. Separated. Past tense. He moved out this afternoon."

"Ness." Andy's heart, which was already crushed, hurt for her sister. "I'm so sorry."

"I wanted to tell you personally. A divorce is probably on the horizon, but we're trying living apart to see how things go."

Andy guessed that could go one of two ways. Either absence would make the heart grow fonder, or that other adage—out of sight, out of mind—would make them forget why they'd ever liked each other.

For Andy, it was option A. She wanted to believe that Gage reaching out meant that he felt the same way, but there was no way to be sure unless she contacted him. She hadn't been brave enough to do that—and quite possibly never would be brave enough.

"How's life?" Ness asked. Caught off guard by her sister's conversational tone, Andy surprised herself by answering honestly.

"Horrible. Gage and I…" She swallowed down a lump of sadness. "We broke up."

Ness let out a cynical laugh. "You should consider yourself lucky you didn't invest years in him before things went downhill. What I'm going through isn't for the faint of heart."

An insensitive comment was completely expected from her sister, but Andy didn't clam up like she used to. The new Andrea Payne didn't make herself smaller to avoid hurt feelings. She stood up for herself.

"You know you're not the only one with problems, Vanessa," Andy snapped. "Your pain doesn't eclipse mine or make what I'm going through any less upsetting. I'm a human being with feelings, not the Ice Queen whose heart is frozen into a solid block. I was in love with him. *Am* in love with him."

"Andy—"

"I told him," Andy continued, her voice watery. "I told him I loved him, because while I might not be the Ice Queen, I am very, very stupid. I laid everything on the line even though he told me from the beginning he didn't want to be married. Why didn't I listen?"

Her mini rant ended with tears slipping down her cheeks. She went to the couch, wineglass forgotten. It wouldn't help her to drink it.

Nothing would help her but time.

"Sweetheart." Ness sounded almost motherly, definitely sisterly. The hard edge from her voice was gone. "You are not stupid. You're the smartest of all of us. If there was a mistake made, it wasn't you falling in love, it was that Gage was too blind to see what he had. He really missed out on an incredible life with you."

The tears dried on Andy's cheeks as she held the phone gently against her ear. "Thanks."

"What a jackwagon."

Andy surprised herself by laughing at her sister's choice of name-calling. Even Ness let out a little chuckle.

"I have a way of letting my own misery overflow onto others," Ness said. "I'm bossy and rude. I want what's best for you, but somehow it comes out like I'm judgmental. No wonder Alec is leaving me."

"Stop talking about my sister that way."

Ness let out another laugh.

"Are you and Alec going to counseling?"

"He asked me if I would." A pause. "I told him I'd think about it."

"Ness, don't let your pride ruin what you and Alec have. I can't pretend to know what it's like to be married as long as you have, but I've seen you two together. You're good for each other. You were at some point, anyway. Is it unfixable?"

"I want to believe it's fixable but I'm afraid to try." Ness's voice trembled. "I don't ever want to feel this way again. I wonder if it'd be easier to make a rule to never get this close to someone rather than to try again and fail."

A rule...or a pact.

Andy thought of Gage and wondered for the first time since he dumped her if she wasn't the braver of the two of them. She was the one who faced her fears and won—he'd faced them and retreated.

"Don't make a rule," Andy told her sister. "Don't rob yourself of something great—whether it's Alec or a man in your future you overlook because you were hurt once before. Don't let the pain you're feeling now keep away the joy you could have later."

"See?" Vanessa sniffled, but there was a smile in her voice. "I told you that you were the smartest one."

They chatted for another twenty minutes, until Andy's eyes grew heavy and Ness begged off. She promised to call Alec and schedule the counselor, and thanked Andy for her help.

They exchanged I-love-yous, another rarity between them, and Andy curled up on the couch and closed her eyes, contented at least in part that she'd helped Ness through a rough evening.

Andy woke up to the insistent buzz-buzz-buzz of her phone. She cracked open one eye and checked the screen. It was her apartment's front desk, and typically they called only when there was a visitor or a delivery.

She blinked, her bleary eyes fighting to focus on the clock on the wall. Midnight wasn't prime visiting or delivery hours.

"Hello?" Her voice was groggy and sleepy, her mind not doing a very good job of understanding what the woman who called was saying to her.

But Andy made out two pertinent bits of information.

Gage Fleming was in the lobby.

And he wanted to come up and see her.

"He said it's urgent, Ms. Payne."

She had no idea how Gage had found her address. She hadn't purposely kept it from him—it'd been easier to meet him on her way home from work or at the airport when they'd flown to Ohio—but she was grateful he didn't know where to find her when her wounds were so fresh.

That he'd found her at all meant one of two things. A) He was angry about the check she'd sent and wanted to throw it in her face; or B) He wanted to explain himself since he hadn't shown an iota of tact when he'd broken up with her a week and a half ago.

Not that there was any great way to tell someone you didn't love them.

"Send him up." She'd hear what he had to say. She was brave. Strong. And unafraid.

How much more could he hurt her after he'd tossed her heart into the dirt?

After a quick check in the mirror by the front door to make sure her mascara wasn't on her cheeks—it wasn't—Andy opened the door and waited in the doorway with her arms folded.

She unfolded her arms and straightened, unsure if she wanted him to see her in a defensive position. Then folded them again anyway.

Dammit.

She was nervous.

Even though she wanted with all her heart not to be.

But you don't have all of your heart, do you?

No. The man currently riding the elevator up to her apartment had at least 30 percent of it.

Maybe forty.

She refused to give him more. Not without him reciprocating.

From her front door she had a vantage point of the elevator, so she watched when Gage stepped from it. He was still in his office clothes, a pale blue pinstriped shirt and trousers, a navy tie knotted at his neck. In one hand was an envelope.

She froze when he spotted her. His mouth was unsmiling and his gait long and strong. As he strode toward her she had no idea if he'd chosen A or B. His first words to her didn't clear it up, either.

"You're not an Ice Queen." He stopped in front of her and held up the envelope, torn open unevenly. A good representation for how she'd felt over the last week. "This proves it."

She didn't follow his meaning, so she said something neutral. "Paynes always repay their debts."

"You're not in debt to me. I'm in debt to you. You gave me the best gift of all." His mouth curved, reminding her of the taste of his smile. "It didn't cost you a thing but it was far more valuable than anything you could've bought."

The dangerous emotions she'd packed down into a tight ball at the bottom of her heart threatened to unravel. She crossed her arms tighter to keep it there.

"You showed me *you*. The real you. The unsure, vulnerable, shy you. And when it came time for me to man up and show you that part of me—" he shook his head "—I failed you."

That tight ball unraveled like a spring.

"This—" he held up the check inside the envelope "—is proof that you still love me."

She felt her cheeks go white as the blood drained from them to her toes. She shook her head. Not because it wasn't true but because he wasn't supposed to know that part. That check was intended to be proof that she *didn't* love him. She needed to learn how to be whole without him. She needed space and giving him the money he'd never wanted was supposed to guarantee that space. To allow her to close the door on what they had for good.

"You never would've sent me this if you didn't still love me. If you hated me, you wouldn't have given me another thought," he told her. "Like I said, you're not the Ice Queen. In fact, everything about you is fire. From your red hair to your flaming honesty to the way you heat me up with your vulnerability. I thought I'd walk away and save us both further pain but the truth is… I'm scorched, Andy. *Ruined.* I will never again be whole. Not without you."

She closed her eyes and sensed Gage stepping close to her. She'd never imagined this scenario—not in all her multiple-choice options. He'd given a speech that absolutely owned her in the threshold of her apartment.

And he wasn't through yet.

"I was trying to rebuild my own walls and failing miserably. I fell in love with you, and because I'm so hopelessly out of practice at responding to that much love, I blew it. I had a chance to claim your heart and defend your honor and I didn't."

"The pact…" were the only words she could utter. She couldn't address the "fell in love" part or the fact that she'd "scorched" him and "ruined" him for all others. That was too big.

"Fuck the pact."

She took him in—those boyish curls and caramel-brown eyes. The way being near him felt so, so right.

"If I promise to love you forever, will you forgive me?"

"I…" But more words wouldn't come.

"If I promise to be brave from now on out, can you let me in?"

A shaky nod was the most she could give him before she covered her mouth to stifle the cry. Then she was in Gage's arms, being held and shushed, the words *I'm sorry* and *I love you* on a loop on his tongue.

When he let her go, he held the envelope between them. "An Ice Queen would've kept the money as the ultimate screw-you. You, Andrea Payne, are no Ice Queen."

He tore the envelope in half and then in half again and dropped the pieces at their feet. His eyes flicked to her lips and just like before their first kiss, he said, "I'll let you come to me."

She gripped the back of his neck. "But you'll give as good as you get?"

"You bet your perfect breasts I will."

They met in the middle, their mouths crashing and their bodies fusing together—as close as they could get without being naked. But they were naked in another way—their souls had been bared.

Walls had come down.

Hearts could heal.

Pacts, like the envelope at her feet, could be torn into pieces.

"I missed you," she whispered, the tear sliding down her cheek a happy one.

He thumbed it away and smiled warmly. "You'll never have to miss me again."

Epilogue

It was a gorgeous, sunshiny, perfect day to be on the water.

The pontoon swayed gently in the cove where they'd anchored, Andy's four sisters holding out their flutes while Gage filled each to the brim with sparkling rosé.

It was a beautiful summer day in Crown, Ohio.

"Carrying forth the tradition of the couples' cruise was never not an option," Andy explained as she pulled out a plastic flute for herself. Gage winked as he uncorked a second bottle and filled Andy's glass as well as his own. "This time around, we have a new couple who will reenact a movie kiss and attempt to steal first place from Gage and me."

"A tough act to follow," Gwen offered. "Good luck, Ness."

All heads swiveled to Vanessa and her date, Mitchell. Mitch was forty years old, had two daughters who were ten and eight, though they hadn't come to the Payne-Fleming wedding, and he had a nice smile and a smooth-as-butter Southern accent.

Andy liked Mitch.

Vanessa and Alec had gone to counseling, and although it didn't result in a reunion, Ness was much happier with her new beau. Andy could see it in the loose way she draped over him on the boat's seat. Sometimes things had to break to be fixed, like Andy and Gage, but other times the break was too final and new parts were needed.

"We're a hard act to follow," Gage said. "Andy and I nailed *Titanic*."

A round of teasing "ohhs" lifted on the air.

"You say that like we didn't prepare." Ness arched one eyebrow in challenge.

"I know better." Andy playfully rolled her eyes. Vanessa and Alec had rehearsed for their *Dirty Dancing* kiss for weeks.

"Get ready to be dazzled. But not yet. We have to practice. Into the water with all of you." Ness shooed them off the boat.

"Not a hard sell today." Gage polished off his bubbly and stripped his shirt over his head. The late July afternoon was a stifling ninety-eight degrees and the humidity was set to "stun."

Within minutes of Gage cannonballing off the side of the boat, everyone save Ness and Mitch was in the water.

Arm around her waist, Gage tugged Andy to him and she wrapped her legs around him.

"God, they're as bad as we were," Gwen told Garrett.

"Worse," her husband concluded.

"Do you think they're really going to beat our couples' cruise kiss?" Gage asked Andy, ignoring the ribbing of her family to nuzzle her nose.

She held onto her gorgeous fiancé, squinting against the blindingly bright sun. "Possibly. Ness hates to lose."

"Sounds like she has a lot to learn." His eyebrows jumped in self-deprecating humor. At one point he'd been the one who was so afraid to fail he hadn't given them a chance.

He'd come a long way. Especially when he proposed at Monarch Consulting. He'd lured her to the building under the guise of meeting for lunch and then was on his knees before her, proclaiming his love for her in front of his friends.

Andy pulled her hand out of the water to admire the engagement ring. A teardrop-shaped diamond with smaller stones on the band. Gage had told her he liked to think that it was shaped like a flame.

She liked that, too.

"We're ready! Although you're going to get the PG version." Ness came out from behind the beach towel Mitch had used to shield her and stood on one of the boat's seats. She was wearing a short pink skirt, an argyle-patterned neckerchief and knee socks in the same jaunty design. Her hair was pulled back at the sides but distinctly ruffled to make her look like she'd had a few too many.

Once the song started playing, Gwen gasped. "I know this one! I know it!"

Andy watched the scene unfold, from Ness leading Mitch across the boat to her falling on a seat and letting out a loud laugh. By the time she tossed aside the kerchief and they vanished from sight, Kelli and Gwen were cheering.

Carroll was grinning, too. The husbands, including Andy's husband-to-be, looked as clueless as she felt.

Vanessa popped back into view, Mitch with her. "Sorry the kiss happened out of sight. We got a little carried away. Any guesses?"

"*The Wedding Date*, and bravo," Kelli answered.

"Yes!" Vanessa shot her fists into the air as everyone clapped.

"What movie?" Andy had to ask.

Gwen looked affronted. "Debra Messing. Dermot Mulroney. The boat scene."

"The movie where she pays the guy to be her date for her sister's wedding. Total fiction, right?" Vanessa added with a wink.

Next to her Gage laughed. "That was a good one."

"The best!" Ness corrected, and then awarded herself first place.

"Close," Gage murmured as he pulled Andy into his arms. Then he whispered so that only she could hear, "But not the best."

* * * * *

MILLS & BOON MODERN IS
HAVING A MAKEOVER!

The same great stories you love,
a stylish new look!

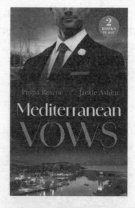

Look out for our brand new look
COMING JUNE 2024

MILLS & BOON

afterglow BOOKS

Afterglow Books are trend-led, trope-filled books with diverse, authentic and relatable characters and a wide array of voices and representations.

Experience real world trials and tribulations, all the tropes you could possibly want (think small-town settings, fake relationships, grumpy vs sunshine, enemies to lovers).

All with a generous dose of spice in every story!

OUT NOW

Two stories published every month.
To discover more visit:
Afterglowbooks.co.uk

MILLS & BOON

THE HEART OF ROMANCE

A ROMANCE FOR EVERY READER

MODERN — Prepare to be swept off your feet by sophisticated, sexy and seductive heroes, in some of the world's most glamourous and romantic locations, where power and passion collide.

HISTORICAL — Escape with historical heroes from time gone by. Whether your passion is for wicked Regency Rakes, muscled Vikings or rugged Highlanders, awaken the romance of the past.

MEDICAL — Set your pulse racing with dedicated, delectable doctors in the high-pressure world of medicine, where emotions run high and passion, comfort and love are the best medicine.

True Love — Celebrate true love with tender stories of heartfelt romance, from the rush of falling in love to the joy a new baby can bring, and a focus on the emotional heart of a relationship.

HEROES — The excitement of a gripping thriller, with intense romance at its heart. Resourceful, true-to-life women and strong, fearless men face danger and desire - a killer combination!

 — From showing up to glowing up, these characters are on the path to leading their best lives and finding romance along the way – with plenty of sizzling spice!

To see which titles are coming soon, please visit

millsandboon.co.uk/nextmonth